Praise for . . . author . . .

"Smart, sexy and scary as hell. Beverly Barton just keeps getting better and better."
—*New York Times* bestselling author Lisa Jackson on *The Fifth Victim*

"Get ready for spectacular adventure and great romance from the pen of Beverly Barton....Thrilling reading."
—*Romantic Times BOOKreviews* on *Gabriel Hawke's Lady* [The Protectors]

"With its sultry Southern setting and well-drawn characters, this richly textured tale ranks among the best the genre has to offer."
—*Publishers Weekly* on *What She Doesn't Know*

"Pure reading pleasure...sexy and clever."
—*New York Times* bestselling author Linda Howard on *After Dark*

"Ms. Barton masterfully delivers excitement, adventure and romance....Sheer delight."
—*Romantic Times BOOKreviews* on *In the Arms of a Hero*

"A riveting page turner!"
—*The Best Reviews* on *On Her Guard*

Dear Reader,

This book is part romance, part adventure, part gritty
reality, part paranormal—and all THE PROTECTORS.
Think *Stargate* meets *Brigadoon* meets *Lost Horizon,* with
a steamy love story front and center. Besides the romantic
love between my botanist heroine, Dr. Gwen Arnell, and
rugged Dundee agent, Will Pierce, the book also deals with
a daughter's need for her father's love. Experts often say
that a woman's first love is her father and that she judges
all men in her life by that relationship. Abandoned by her
father as a child, Gwen expects every man in her life to let
her down. But Will Pierce is nothing like Professor Arnell, a
man who has spent his entire life obsessed with discovering
a mythical island no one believes exists.

Thrown together in a manic search through the Caribbean,
odd couple Gwen and Will become unwilling partners. In
a race to save Gwen's father and Will's client's daughter,
these two rush headlong into an unlikely mix of mystery
and fantasy, soon learning that opposites *do* attract.
Before either realizes what's happening, my brainy, plain
Jane heroine becomes my macho, tough guy hero's only
obsession.

I hope you enjoy reading this unique love story as much as
I enjoyed writing it.

Warmest regards,

Beverly Barton

BEVERLY BARTON

His Only Obsession

Silhouette®
Romantic
SUSPENSE

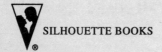 SILHOUETTE BOOKS

ISBN-13: 978-0-373-27525-0
ISBN-10: 0-373-27525-0

HIS ONLY OBSESSION

Copyright © 2007 by Beverly Beaver

Printed in U.S.A.

Books by Beverly Barton

BEVERLY BARTON

has been in love with romance since her grandfather gave her an illustrated book of *Beauty and the Beast*. An avid reader since childhood, Beverly wrote her first book at the age of nine. After marriage to her own "hero" and the births of her daughter and son, Beverly chose to be a full-time homemaker, a.k.a. wife, mother, friend and volunteer. The author of over fifty books, Beverly is a member of Romance Writers of America and helped found the Heart of Dixie chapter in Alabama. She has won numerous awards and has made the Waldenbooks and *USA TODAY* bestseller lists.

To the members of my Alabama RWA chapter,
Heart of Dixie, past and present.
Thank you for all the good times
we have shared during the past twenty years.

Prologue

My dearest daughter,

I have asked your mother to give you this letter on your eighteenth birthday. It is my hope that after reading this, you will understand why I have been an absentee father all these years, why I have let you and your mother down, why I feel that I have no choice but to leave both of you in order to continue pursuing a dream that will consume me to my dying day.

Let me try to explain. It all began for me many years ago, long before I met your mother.

There is an ancient legend that tells of a mystical island located somewhere between what is known today as Bermuda and the West Indies. The story has been handed down, from father to son, for generations since before the time of Christopher Columbus. The tales of this island and the unique people who inhabit it vary. Some say the natives of this island share the same ancestry as the Mayans and the Incas, others claim they were the first Europeans to arrive in the New World, before Columbus. A few even claim that these unique people originally came from ancient Egypt.

Most people believe the legend is nothing more than a tale told by dotty old men to awed young children and gullible adventurers. But a precious few swear the island exists—out there somewhere, perhaps in the Devil's Triangle. Some say it has streets paved with gold, while others claim it is a tropical paradise with crystal-clear waterfalls and lush vegetation. Although the stories themselves vary in many aspects, there is one detail on which all agree. The people of this mysterious, un-charted island—an island with no name—possess an enviable quality, one the outside world would kill to obtain: the average lifespan is two hundred years.

The first time I went to the Indies and sailed the Ca-ribbean Sea with my parents and brother, I was a young man of twenty. I had already chosen my college major— botany. Nothing fascinated me more than the world of plants. During our family trip, I collected specimens on every island, from the Bahamas, Cuba, Jamaica, Barba-dos, Puerto Rico and even as far north as Bermuda. My father, a banker, a conservative thinker and a strict disci-plinarian, did not understand me, and I think, perhaps, did not approve of the profession I had chosen. But my mother, sweet, doe-eyed Gwendolyn, who loved Eliza-beth Barrett Browning's poetry and adored taking my brother, Elliott, and me to the movies at least twice a week, thought I could do no wrong. So, I suppose that my father and mother balanced each other out.

I shall never forget that special summer…the last summer the four of us were together. Even then, I was amazed that my father actually took an entire month away from his successful, highly demanding job to give his family a once-in-a-lifetime vacation. Looking back, I can see all three of them in my mind's eye. Daddy with his sunburned face and thick, dark mustache. Mama with her straw hat and sunglasses. And Elliott, who had just turned fifteen, with his golden, tanned skin and sun-streaked brown hair.

We heard the legends of the mystic island at every port, each version slightly different, but each equally captivating. Being a realist, with both feet planted firmly on the ground, Daddy said it was superstitious native nonsense. Mama, on the other hand, ever the romantic dreamer, commented on how marvelous it would be to find the island and gain the Fountain of Youth secret.

I was then and am now my mother's son.

Late in June that summer, with less than a week left on our month-long vacation, we boarded the small rental yacht and sailed off from Bermuda, heading south, our destination the Bahamas. It was a warm, balmy day, with only a few fluffy white clouds in the sky. My father had checked weather conditions before leaving port and we expected only blue skies and sunshine for the entire trip. But less than two hours out to sea, we encountered sudden high winds, followed by dark, swirling clouds and an unexpected storm that tossed our yacht about with frightening force. My mother huddled with us belowdecks and prayed without ceasing for what seemed like hours. And then it happened. The yacht caught fire as if repeatedly struck by lightning. My father lowered the single lifeboat and my mother insisted that her two boys go first, which we did with great reluctance.

Everything happened so quickly that to this day, I'm not sure of the details. All I know is that once Elliott and I were in the lifeboat, our parents didn't join us, and the burning yacht sank with unbelievable speed. The choppy waters made it impossible for us to do any good with rowing, so we had little choice but to hunker down and allow the water and wind to take us where it would.

I don't know how long we drifted, how many endless days we went without food or water, but long enough for both of us to become delusional. Eventually we did little but sleep, both of us certain that death was imminent.

And then, on the very day salvation came, I awoke from a deathlike sleep to discover my brother missing. Sometime while I had slept, he had either fallen overboard or deliberately jumped into the ocean.

There I was alone, mourning the deaths of my parents and my only sibling and anticipating my own demise at any moment, when I saw the island. At first, gazing at it through the mist that surrounded it, I thought I had imagined seeing land, that it couldn't be real. I had no idea where I was or if I had possibly drifted south, southeast or southwest; or maybe simply east, out into the vastness of the Atlantic Ocean. Barely able to do more than sit up, I somehow managed to row the small lifeboat toward the island, and with each beat of my heart, I prayed that it was no cruel illusion. Could this be the Bahamas? I wondered. Or had I somehow bypassed the easternmost islands and was now approaching Trinidad? What did it matter? I saw land. I wasn't going to die.

What happened next, in the days and weeks that followed, no one would ever believe. But I ask you, my dear little Gwen, to suspend your disbelief, to open up your heart and mind to the possibility that there are indeed more things on earth than we have ever dreamed possible. There are miracles and magic and wonders to behold. I know these things exist for I have seen the mystical land of legends, met the men and women who live to be two hundred years old, who never suffer the cruelty of illness or deal with the ravages of time. You see, my child, I found the island. I was rescued by its people. And I discovered the secret of their illness-free lives and longevity.

Even then, as a youth of twenty, I longed to bring that miracle back to the rest of the world, but I was denied the privilege. These people do not welcome outsiders and would never willingly have contact with us. And they will kill to protect their secret.

They *have* killed to protect it.

After only three weeks on the island, I was forced to leave. They gave me food and water, then set me out to sea in my little lifeboat. I couldn't understand why they would save my life only to send me back to certain death. But oddly enough, the very next day I was picked up by a fishing vessel off the coast of Cuba. When I told others what had happened to me, about my weeks on the island and how I wanted to head an expedition and return to the island as soon as possible, people laughed in my face. Even the kindest and most caring thought that the legendary island where I'd stayed had been nothing more than a mirage, a figment of my feverish imagination. But I swear to you, it was real. It does exist!

This happened over twenty-five years ago and I have

spent most of those years on a quest to rediscover this uncharted island that lies somewhere between Bermuda and the West Indies. I have spent a great deal of my salary as a botany professor and most of my inheritance from my parents in pursuit of this dream…some may even say obsession. But hear me, daughter, on this island, there is a plant that exists nowhere else on earth that can give us mortals prolonged youth and protect us from illness.

When you read this, I pray you understand and forgive me for abandoning you. I love you and your mother very much, but your mother does not understand me, cannot accept my desperate need to bring this great gift to the world. She, like so many others, has decided that I am mentally unbalanced. Do not believe them.

My hope is that I will have found the island again and brought long life and health to the world's people before you turn eighteen and read this letter. But if not, then I pray that you will believe me and come to me to join me on my quest.

Your loving father,
Emery

Gwen Arnell read the letter, then folded it neatly and returned it to the yellowed envelope. Her father had written this letter eight years ago, shortly after her mother divorced him. Gwen had been ten, and despite the fact that her father had spent most of his time at work or in the Caribbean, she had adored him and treasured those infrequent but precious moments she spent with him. After the divorce, she hadn't seen him again for nearly two years. Sometimes he remembered to send her a birthday present, but often as not he would forget her birthday and Christmas. Every so often, sometimes after a year or longer, he would call for a brief conversation. She had seen him a total of three times since the divorce.

"You seem all right," her mother said. "The letter didn't upset you?"

"No."

"I had no idea what he wrote and wasn't sure how the letter would affect you. But I swore to him that I would give it to you when you turned eighteen."

"Weren't you ever tempted to open it and read it?"

Jean Arnell nodded. "I will admit that the thought crossed my mind, but it wouldn't have been right. It's the only thing your father has ever given you, the only thing he will probably ever give you, so I thought of it as your legacy from him."

Gwen sighed. "Do you truly believe he's crazy, the way all his colleagues believe he is? I realize everyone who knows Daddy thinks he's a fool."

Jean didn't respond immediately, then said quietly, solemnly, "Your father isn't certifiably insane."

"That's not what I asked."

"A tragic incident in his youth affected your father mentally and emotionally. Losing his entire family the way he did…" Jean reached out and took Gwen's hands in hers. "Emery loved me. He loved you. He still loves you, but he can never be the father you want him to be, and I really don't think he can help himself. He has allowed his obsession with finding that nonexistent island and that miraculous eternal-youth plant to consume his entire life."

"But what if the island is real? What if there really is such a plant? It is possible, isn't it?" Gwen wanted to believe in her father's dream, wanted to share it with him.

"I don't think so. There are no known islands anywhere on earth where your father claims this island was. And if it did exist, why has no one else found it in all these years? Why is it nothing more than a legend?"

"I don't know. Maybe Daddy is special, that it was meant for him to be the one to rediscover this place, to—"

Jean grasped Gwen's shoulders and gave her a gentle shake. "No. Do you hear me—no. The island does not exist. The plant doesn't exist."

Gwen looked her mother directly in the eyes. "I want to get in touch with Daddy and ask him if I can go to the West Indies with him this summer and help him in his search."

"Oh, Gwen, sweetie, no. Please, don't allow your father to suck you into his delusional world."

"Don't worry, Mother, the only obsession I have is to get to know my father. He's practically a stranger to me. Sharing a summer with him on his quest could be good for him and for me. Please, try to understand."

Jean squeezed Gwen's shoulders, then released her and said sadly, "You do what you must, but I'm afraid that in the end, he'll break your heart. Do not for one minute believe that you can ever be more important to him than his great obsession."

Chapter 1

Fifteen years later...

As Gwen unlocked her back door, she replayed the message left on her cell phone. "I'm in Puerto Nuevo. You must come here at once. I want you to be with me when I rediscover my island." Her father's voice had vibrated with excitement, the same elated tone she'd heard so many times over the years. "I have people who are interested in backing this expedition, people who believe in me, in my island."

Gwen sighed heavily as she entered her home in Madison, a short drive from the Botanical Gardens in Huntsville, Alabama, where she worked as CEO. Exhausted from trying to put a day and a half's work into one day while worrying about her father, she dropped her keys, shoulder bag, cell phone and briefcase down on the kitchen counter and headed straight to the refrigerator. Whenever a crisis confronted her, she turned to food, especially something sweet. She had spent a lifetime—all of her thirty-three years—fighting to keep her body in shape.

Of course, eating a salad would be the wise choice, but the leftover piece of cake from a recent retirement dinner for a colleague looked mighty tempting. Chocolate. Her favorite.

Grabbing the cellophane-wrapped concoction, Gwen tried to dismiss thoughts of her father's recent phone message from her mind. She seldom heard from him, but when she did, their conversations wreaked havoc on her life for weeks afterward. If only she could accept the fact that her father would never change, that he would forever chase a phantom island and be considered a lunatic by his fellow scientists. A brilliant lunatic, but a lunatic all the same. Gwen had learned years ago, after joining her father on two quests in the West Indies, that she could no more change her father than she could stop the sun from rising in the east.

Before her death ten years ago, her mother, Jean, had exacted a promise from Gwen to keep her distance from Dr. Emery Arnell and his insanity. Gwen had kept that promise, seeing her father rarely and never again joining him on one of his fruitless expeditions. But every year or so he'd call, breathless with anticipation, begging her to be a part of his great discovery, to share in the glory that was soon to be his.

Gwen removed the plastic wrap from the cake, retrieved a fork from a kitchen drawer and headed to the table. Before sitting, she kicked off her two-inch heels and wiggled her toes. Until she'd taken over as CEO of the botanical gardens, she'd worn jeans and walking shoes to work, but now she had to dress more appropriately, something suitable for her position.

Just as she finished the last bite of cake, the phone rang. Bone weary, she decided to let the answering machine take the call. It might be a solicitor. And if it was something about work, she could easily return the call later, after she'd taken a shower and put on her pj's.

The answering machine picked up. "This is Dr. Gwen Arnell. Please leave your name, number and a brief message at the sound of the beep and I will return your call as soon as possible."

"Gwen, darling girl, if you're there, please pick up the phone," Emery said, his voice quivering with emotion. "Everything is coming together for this expedition. My backers are eager for us to begin the journey. I want you with me, daughter, when I sail into the history books as the man who discovered the Fountain of Youth."

Oh, Daddy. Poor Daddy.

"Gwen…please."

She left the crumb-dotted plate on the table, shoved back her chair and stood.

"We'll set sail soon, very soon."

When Gwen reached the phone on the kitchen counter, her hand hesitated, hovering over the base.

"I…I've cashed in my life insurance policy to use as part of the investment, to subsidize this final expedition," Emery said. "But once I bring back the plant and offer it to the world, we will be rich beyond our wildest dreams."

Gwen grabbed the phone. "Daddy, I'm here."

"Gwen, how soon can you get to Puerto Nuevo? My backers are eager to set sail, as are Jordan and I."

"Who is Jordan?"

"Surely you know… Well, perhaps you don't. Jordan Elders is my research assistant. He was one of my students, a very bright boy. He has great faith in me and my plans to find the island. You see, we've come up with a theory as to why I've been unable to rediscover my island all these years."

"Oh, Daddy…"

"No, listen to this. Jordan and I believe that the island isn't visible all the time, only at specific intervals. Perhaps only certain months or even certain years. Maybe only once a year."

"Daddy, I can't come to Puerto Nuevo. I'm sorry, but my job is here in Huntsville. My life is here."

"Are you upset with me for cashing in my life insurance policy? You were my beneficiary, you know."

Gwen groaned silently, her mind reeling off a few well-chosen curse words. "No, Daddy, I'm not upset about that." But she was concerned that her father was practically penniless, that as a retired botany professor his income was enough to live on but not enough to fund repeated trips off into the vast unknown, searching for his Utopia.

"You have vacation time, I'm sure," he said. "Take two weeks. That's all I'm asking. Two weeks."

"Daddy—"

"Gwendolyn Arnell, I swear to you that this trip is the last trip, that this time I will not fail."

"I wish you all the luck in the world. I hope and pray you find your island and fulfill all your dreams, but… I can't—"

"Don't say you can't. Say you'll think about it."

Hesitantly, she agreed. "All right. I'll think about it."

"You've become your mother's daughter, haven't you?" Emery told her, sadness in his voice. "Come to Puerto Nuevo and join me, and open yourself up to possibilities beyond your wildest imagination."

"Where are you staying?" she asked, sighing in frustration. "Say if I were to join you, where would I meet you?"

"We're staying at the Pasada El Paso. It's in downtown Puerto Nuevo. Nothing fancy, but clean and safe. I'll reserve a room for you and—"

"No, don't do that. I'll make reservations, *if* I decide to join you."

"I love you, daughter."

"And I love you, Daddy."

The dial tone sounded. Apparently her father believed he had convinced her to join him. Damn him! How dare he assume she would rearrange her life to suit his needs? When had he ever done that for her? She couldn't remember sharing one birthday with him and not one Christmas since her parents had divorced.

The crazy old fool had cashed in his life insurance policy to help fund this one final folly. What would he do when this adventure turned into yet another failure? And what about these new backers he mentioned? Who in his right mind would invest money in the hare-brained scheme of a seventy-year-old botany professor notorious for having become a laughingstock to his colleagues?

What if these backers were unscrupulous people intent upon taking advantage of her father? What if they intended to rob him of his insurance money and leave him to fend for himself?

Damn it! Why couldn't her father be normal? And why, after the way he had neglected her all her life, did she feel obligated to look after him, to take care of him?

Because he's your father, she reminded herself. And he has no one else.

Gwen spent the next hour getting airline tickets to

Puerto Nuevo, making arrangements to take a week's vacation and packing her suitcase. First thing in the morning, she'd be on a flight to Mexico City, then change planes and fly directly into Puerto Nuevo.

She had no intention of joining her father on yet another quest for glory, fame and riches, but she had to do what she could to protect him from himself and anyone who might harm him.

Will Pierce arrived at Dundee headquarters on the sixth floor of the downtown Atlanta office building at precisely seven-thirty in the morning. The office manager, Daisy Holbrook, had telephoned him an hour ago while he was drinking his first cup of coffee.

"Sawyer wants you in his office immediately," Daisy had said. "He has two new cases and he wants to get agents out into the field ASAP."

When Will exited the elevator, he noted the peculiar quiet and vast emptiness on the floor. He remembered Daisy didn't arrive until eight, and the other office staff didn't usually come in until nine. As he approached Sawyer's office, the sound of voices shattered the early morning silence. He couldn't quite make out the conversation, but he paused at the closed door. Just as he lifted his hand to knock, he heard a loud crash.

"Damn it, Lucie, that was Waterford crystal," Sawyer McNamara said. "That paperweight was a gift."

"So dock my paycheck," Lucie Evans said. "For the paperweight and the glass shelves. I don't care. I'm sick and tired of you foisting off every cheesy assignment on me."

"If you don't like working at Dundee's, then—"

"I'm not quitting," she told him in no uncertain terms.

"You couldn't run me off with a stick. Not even a stick of dynamite."

"Then don't complain, accept your assignment and stop throwing temper tantrums. I'd thought that by now you would have learned to control that hair-trigger temper of yours."

"And I thought that by now you would have stopped punishing me for something that wasn't my fault."

Silence.

Strong, unnerving silence.

The door flew open. Sawyer stood in the doorway, obviously inviting Lucie to leave. When he saw Will, his gaze hardened for a split second.

"You made it here sooner than I'd expected," Sawyer said.

"If you two need more time, I can wait outside." Will wasn't sure what he'd walked in on and didn't want to know. During the year he'd worked at Dundee's, he had learned there was some sort of personal feud between the Dundee CEO and one of his agents, Lucie Evans. Why he didn't fire her or she didn't resign, no one knew. And even more puzzling was why the two seemed to despise each other so vehemently. Taken separately, each was a nice, normal person. Lucie was warm and friendly. If she had one flaw, it was that she allowed her emotions to rule her. On the other hand, Sawyer was aloof, an introvert who didn't socialize with his employees. He often seemed to have no emotions, his actions dictated only by cold logic.

"I was just leaving." Lucie zoomed past Sawyer, not bothering to even give him one of her infamous withering glares. "I'm on my way to Wyoming to investigate cattle rustling."

"Huh?" Had Will heard her correctly?

As if casually dismissing Lucie and the fact that she'd

smashed his Waterford paperweight into the glass shelves along the wall, Sawyer motioned for Will to enter.

"I'm going to need for you to go home, pack a bag and take the Dundee jet straight to Puerto Nuevo this morning." Sawyer tapped the slim file folder lying on his desk. "I just have the basic info right now, but as soon as Daisy comes in this morning, I'll have her compile a more comprehensive file on the case and e-mail it to you."

"Okay. What can you tell me now?"

"Sit."

Will took the chair in front of Sawyer's desk. Sawyer leaned against the edge of the desk and crossed his arms over his chest. Not for the first time, Will thought his boss resembled a model from the pages of *GQ*. One of the older, more sophisticated men who fell just short of being a pretty boy.

"Archer Kress contacted me at six this morning," Sawyer said. "You know who Archer Kress is, don't you?"

"CEO and major stockholder in Kress Petroleum."

Sawyer nodded. "Mr. Kress has a twenty-year-old daughter who went on vacation with some college friends to Puerto Nuevo. The Kress family has a villa there."

"Does he need a bodyguard for his daughter?"

"No, not now." Sawyer grunted. "It seems his daughter, Cheryl, and her friend—" Sawyer paused and opened the folder, glancing at the top file "—Tori Boyd are missing."

"How long have they been missing?"

"Since last night. The girls went out to a local bar yesterday evening and didn't return home this morning. Neither girl is answering her cell phone and Cheryl's car is still parked near the pier where the bar is located."

"Does the family suspect kidnapping?"

"No, not at this point," Sawyer replied. "If they did, Mr. Kress would have contacted the FBI, not Dundee's."

"Does his daughter make a habit of staying out all night? If so—"

"I have no idea what's going on in Mr. Kress's head. All I know is that he's paying Dundee's a small fortune to find his daughter and her friend ASAP. That's all we need to know, so if you fly to Mexico and discover Cheryl and her friend spent the night with a couple of local guys, then that's what I'll report to her father. But if foul play is involved, we don't want to be accused of downplaying any danger to Miss Kress."

"I understand."

"Good. So go home, get packed, pull out your passport and by the time you get to the airport, the Dundee jet will be fueled and ready for takeoff."

Will shook hands with Sawyer, picked up the file folder and headed for the elevator. Just as he punched the down button, the elevator doors opened and Daisy Holbrook emerged.

Daisy was pretty and plump and everyone who worked at Dundee's adored her. Her nickname was Ms. Efficiency.

"Good morning," Daisy said. "I hear you're off to Puerto Nuevo."

"If only I was heading down there for a vacation."

"Mmm…" When Daisy smiled, deep dimples formed in her cheeks. "I'll e-mail you all the info I can dig up on your case. You should have everything by the time you land."

"Hold the fort down while I'm gone."

"I'll try." She moved closer to Will and lowered her voice. "I met Lucie downstairs in the lobby. I hear there's a cleanup needed in Sawyer's office."

Will grinned. "Could be."

"Did you get here in time to see the fireworks?"

"I came in right as they went off."

"One of these days, those two are going to kill each other."

"Oil and water," Will said.

"More like dynamite and a lit match."

Will arrived at the Kress villa by midafternoon, armed with a healthy dossier on the Kress family and Cheryl in particular, as well as info on her friend, Tori Boyd. No matter what people said, the rich were different from everybody else. The villa was located in an exclusive area overlooking the water, an area lined with multimillion-dollar homes owned by wealthy foreigners. Mexico's Yucatán Peninsula had long been a favorite with tourists, even now when some areas were just beginning to recover from the devastation of recent hurricanes. But who could resist white sands and aqua water? Puerto Nuevo was a tropical paradise.

A maid met him at the door, asked his name and business, then escorted him into a massive living room with a twelve-foot ceiling and a wall of glass doors opening up to the terrace overlooking the Caribbean Sea.

"Señor Pierce, from the Dundee Agency," the maid announced.

Two bikini-clad young women, whom he surmised to be in their late teens or early twenties, stared at him with curiosity.

"Wow, you're the private investigator," the willowy blonde said. "Did anyone ever tell you that you look like Matthew McConaughey?"

"Can't say that they have." Will put on his serious I'm-in-charge face. "Cheryl's father is concerned about her. He believes that since she didn't come home last night, she and her friend Tori are missing."

"If he hadn't called to check up on her, he wouldn't have known." The brunette sauntered over to Will and smiled at him. "I'm Courtney and she's Kerry." She indicated the other girl with a nod in her direction. "And you're Will, huh?"

Obviously being rich didn't make you smart, Will thought.

"Yeah, right," he replied. "So, do you two think Mr. Kress overreacted? Don't you think Cheryl and Tori are missing?"

Kerry spread out on the sofa, lounging there as if she was preparing for a photo shoot. Will knew when a woman was trying to get his attention.

"Tori could have hooked up with that guy she's so hot about," Courtney said.

"What guy?"

"Oh, some geek with glasses and an Einstein IQ or something. Tori likes the brainy types."

"Were she and Cheryl meeting up with this guy last night?" Will asked.

"We don't know for sure," Kerry told him. "Courtney and I had dates last night. So Cheryl and Tori headed into town to a local bar where this guy Tori likes hangs out."

"What's the name?"

"Of the bar or the guy?" Courtney asked.

"Both."

"It's actually a bar and a restaurant," Courtney told him. "It's the Fiesta. We don't know what the guy's last name is, but his first name is Jordan and he works for some nutty old man he calls The Professor."

Will finished questioning the two young women as quickly as he could. The longer he was with them, the more he felt like a piece of meat they were thinking about devouring.

"I assume neither of you plans on leaving Puerto Nuevo anytime soon," Will said.

Courtney shook her head. Kerry responded, "We came here for a month-long vacation. We're staying. Anyway, I figure Cheryl and Tori will show up by tomorrow."

By the time Gwen arrived outside the Pasada El Paso in downtown Puerto Nuevo, she was hot and tired and longed for a shower and a soft bed. She'd flown out of Huntsville at six o'clock that morning, made a connection in Atlanta for Mexico City, had a two-hour layover there and finally boarded a plane south. It was now a little after five, local time.

Hoisting the straps of her purse higher on her shoulder and gripping the handle on her small suitcase, Gwen took a deep breath and reminded herself that she would not confront her father first thing. She'd take him out for dinner, and during dessert she'd explain that she wanted to meet his investors. If they turned out to be legitimate, possibly a couple of rich loony-tunes, then she'd return home and let her father have his new adventure. But if she felt the least bit suspicious, she'd put a stop to things immediately, even threaten the would-be investors with the police, if necessary.

The first thing she noticed when she entered the lobby was that it was air-conditioned. Thank goodness. Now, if only the rooms were.

The second thing she noticed was that the lobby was empty. Not a single soul in sight, except the man behind the registration counter. This hotel probably wasn't a tourist favorite.

She walked over to the lone man, smiled and said, "Do

you speak English?" She knew a few words and phrases in Spanish, but didn't know enough to carry on a decent conversation.

"*Sí,* señorita, I speak English," the man replied, his accent heavy.

"I'm Dr. Emery Arnell's daughter. I'm here to join my father. Would you please telephone his room and tell him that I've arrived."

The man smiled. "It will do no good to telephone his room."

"And why is that?" Gwen asked.

"He will not answer the telephone."

"He won't? Why not?"

"Because he is not here. Dr. Arnell left this afternoon."

"He left? Are you saying he checked out of the hotel?"

"*Sí,* señorita. Dr. Arnell and Mr. Elders are gone."

"Where did they go?"

The man shrugged. "I do not know."

"Does anyone here at the hotel have any idea where my father and his assistant went?"

"Perhaps, but I am the only one here now. Ria may know, but she works in the mornings, cleaning the rooms. I saw her speaking to Mr. Elders several times. Very friendly."

Knowing temporary defeat when it slapped her in the face, Gwen nodded, then asked, "Do you have a room available for tonight?"

"*Sí, sí.* You may have your father's room. It is nice and clean and faces the street and not the alley."

"I'll take it," Gwen said. "By the way, is there a restaurant nearby?"

"*Sí.* The Fiesta, down the street." He pointed in the direction. "They serve good *pescado frito* and cold beer. Very cheap."

Gwen thanked him, signed the register and took the key he offered. After dinner she would get some rest, then tomorrow she'd question the day staff and begin searching for her father. God only knew where he'd gone or what kind of trouble he would get into before she found him.

Chapter 2

The Fiesta turned out to be a bar and grill located a block from the hotel and on the opposite side of the street. Loud laughter and the roar of conversation almost drowned out the live band. Although seemingly clean, the place reeked of smoke from cigarettes and cigars. Apparently there wasn't a hostess, so Gwen found a small empty table in the middle of the room, feeling rather conspicuous as a lone American woman among so many locals. But within minutes the waitress who handed her a menu put her at ease.

"Our speciality is *pescado frito,* but I recommend the *empanadas* and a cold beer." The middle-aged redhead spoke with a definite Yankee accent.

"You're an American." The comment popped out of Gwen's mouth.

The waitress grinned. "Sure am. Born and raised in New York. Outside Buffalo to be exact. What about you?"

"I'm from Alabama."

"A Southern belle, huh?"

"Southern, yes. A belle, no."

"You know, you look familiar." The waitress studied Gwen, giving her a once-over, from head to toe. "Have you been in here before tonight? I swear I've seen you somewhere. I never forget a face."

"This is my first night here at the Fiesta and my first trip to Puerto Nuevo."

The waitress grimaced. "It'll come to me. I'll figure out how I know you." She glanced at the menu she'd handed Gwen. "So, what will it be?"

"Oh, the *empanadas* and a cold beer sounds fine."

"Coming right up."

By the time the waitress returned with her meal, Gwen had already declined two invitations, one from a gentleman who wanted her to join him at the bar and the other from a man who had asked if he could join her.

"Here you go." The waitress placed the dish in front of Gwen. "Need a refill on that beer?"

"No, thanks."

"I noticed you've had to deal with a few of our local Romeos. If you wind up with one you can't handle, just let me know."

"Thank you, Ms....?"

"Tammy Peloso, but just call me Tam."

Gwen held out her hand. "It's nice to meet you, Tam, I'm Gwen. Gwen Arnell."

Tam shook her hand, then stepped back, stared at her and laughed as she clicked her fingers together. "Damn, no wonder you looked familiar. You're The Professor's daughter, little Gwendolyn."

"You know my father?"

"Well, can't say that I know him all that well, but he's eaten lunch and dinner here every night for a week now. And he showed me a picture of his little girl once. His precious Gwendolyn." Tam studied Gwen's face. "It was an old picture. You couldn't have been more than sixteen. You were at a pier somewhere. There was a boat in the background."

"Oh, yes, I remember the photograph. It was taken when I was eighteen and went on an expedition with my father."

"Have you come to Puerto Nuevo to join your dad on his search for the lost island?" Tam asked, a hint of humor in her voice.

Gwen sighed. "I've come to find out who his backers are and if they're on the up and up."

"Taking care of the old man, huh? Good for you. He seems like a nice enough old guy, if a little odd. Sorry, but that's the truth."

"No apologies necessary. My father is a bit odd."

"Why didn't he come to dinner with you tonight?"

"I don't know where he is," Gwen admitted. "When I arrived at his hotel, he'd already checked out, and I have no idea where to start looking for him."

"Hmm…" Tam frowned. "Have you checked out the Yellow Parrot? I know The Professor's girlfriend especially likes that place."

Girlfriend? What girlfriend? "What's the Yellow Parrot, another bar and grill?"

Tam chuckled. "It's a bar all right, but they don't serve any food. Just loud music, liquor, street whores and your choice of drugs."

"This woman you refer to as my father's girlfriend—"

"He didn't tell you about her, did he? Can't say I blame

him. She's a lot younger than he is, and my guess is that she's after your old man for his money."

Her father's money? That was a laugh. "Do you think someone at this Yellow Parrot might know where my father is?"

"They might, but if you go there, be careful. It's no place for a lady."

Will checked into his hotel, a local Day's Inn, then set up his computer and contacted Sawyer McNamara with an update.

"There's a possibility the Kress girl and her friend aren't missing," Will said. "It seems the Boyd girl has been chasing after some young guy, and it could be the girls hooked up with him. If that's the case, then it's just a matter of tracking them down."

"I don't think I'll tell Mr. Kress that his daughter might be part of a *ménage à trois* and just lost track of time."

Will chuckled. "Cheryl Kress's friends staying at the villa don't seem concerned. They think her father overreacted when he found out she wasn't there and they let it slip that she'd been gone all night."

"Kress is a wealthy man. His first thought was probably that someone kidnapped his only child, but when he didn't get a ransom note or call, he came up with other equally frightening scenarios."

"Kidnapping, rape or murder aren't necessarily illogical thoughts," Will said. "Look, Cheryl's friends told me that this guy hangs out at a place called the Fiesta Bar and Grill. I'm heading over there after I freshen up. Maybe someone saw Cheryl and Tori last night and can give me an idea where to find them."

Fifteen minutes later, after shaving, combing his hair and scrubbing his hands, Will headed out of the hotel. He asked the desk clerk for directions to the Fiesta Bar and Grill, which turned out to be less than a five-minute drive from where he was staying.

The exterior of the old building was painted brick red and the front door a bright turquoise. He could hear blaring music and loud voices coming from inside. He went in and headed straight for the bar. If anybody in a place like this knew something useful, it would be the bartender. After ordering a beer, Will flashed a hundred-dollar bill and recent photographs of Cheryl and Tori.

"Have you seen either of these girls recently? Like last night?"

The bartender snatched the hundred bucks from Will's hand, then turned and filled up a tankard of beer and set it on the bar in front of him. "Pretty American girls. The blonde was laughing and talking to a young guy last night and later both girls left with him."

"What time?"

"I do not know."

"Before or after midnight?"

"Before."

"Do you have any idea where they went when they left here?"

The bartender hesitated. Will took a fifty from his pocket. The bartender eyed the bill greedily. When he reached for it, Will jerked it back and shook his head.

"Information first," Will told him.

"I heard the guy say he needed to meet up with somebody at the Yellow Parrot."

"And where can I find this Yellow Parrot?"

"Four blocks from here, closer to the wharves, on the corner of Poc Na and Kukulcan."

Will handed the bartender the fifty, then took a hefty swig from the tankard and walked out of the bar and grill. If luck was on his side, he might have the case of the missing heiress wrapped up by the end of the night.

Gwen took a taxi to the Yellow Parrot. With each passing block, she grew more tense. It didn't take a rocket scientist to figure out that this dive was in the worst part of town. But living alone and occasionally working late hours, Gwen had learned to take care of herself. She'd attended several self-defense classes, but luckily had never faced a situation where she had needed to put any of the moves she'd learned into practice.

The minute she entered the bar, she realized that a smart woman would have brought a gun with her. The interior was hot, smelly and dirty. If that wasn't bad enough, the air was so smoky that it looked as if a pea soup fog had settled inside the building. In comparison, the Fiesta Bar and Grill was upscale. Before she had gone three feet, an old drunk came up to her and asked for money. Sidestepping him, she searched for someone who looked as if he or she might actually work here, someone other than the prostitutes who were trolling for customers.

After fending off a couple of grasping young men and ignoring several vulgar propositions—all spoken in an odd mixture of Spanish and English—Gwen found the bar. She ordered a beer from the burly, bearded bartender. When he set the beer in front of her, she took the opportunity to speak to him.

"I'm looking for a man. An older American man, in his

seventies. He was probably with a younger woman. This man is my father and—"

"*Yo no hablo Ingles.*"

"Oh." He didn't speak English and she didn't speak Spanish. Now what?

While she was considering her options, Gwen noticed a young man in skin-tight black pants and a black shirt open all the way down the front, easing closer and closer to her as he made his way past the other patrons at the bar.

Great! This was all she needed, some horny young guy mistaking her for a prostitute. Although she had dark hair and eyes, she certainly didn't look like one of the native girls, not with her distinct Anglo-Saxon facial features.

"Señorita." His voice was softly accented and slightly slurred. His breath smelled of liquor. "You are all alone, *sí?*"

"Please, go away," Gwen said. "I'm not interested."

He laughed as if he found her attitude amusing. "Then it is for me to make you interested. I am Marco. And you are…?"

"Leaving," Gwen said.

She realized it had been a mistake to come here alone tonight. She'd do better to come back tomorrow and try to speak to the owner. But when Gwen tried to move past her ardent young suitor, he reached out and grabbed her arm. She went rigid.

Looking him right in the eyes, she told him, "Let go of me. Right now."

"But you cannot leave." He got right up in her face. "The night is young."

Gwen tugged on her arm, trying to break free. He tight-ened his hold, his fingers biting into her flesh. With her heart beating rapidly as her basic fight or flight instinct kicked in, she glared at the man.

"I'm going to ask you one more time to let me go."

Grinning smugly, he grabbed her other arm, holding her in place.

Suddenly, seemingly from out of nowhere a big hand clamped down on Marco's shoulder, jerked him back and spun him around, freeing Gwen. She staggered slightly, but managed to hold her balance as the tall, lanky man in jeans and cowboy boots shoved her would-be suitor up against the bar.

"I believe the lady asked you real nice to let her go," the man said in a deep Texas drawl. "Where I come from, a gentleman respects a lady's wishes."

Marco grumbled something unintelligible in Spanish. Probably cursing, Gwen thought. Or maybe praying. If she were Marco, she'd be praying that the big, rugged American wouldn't beat her to a pulp.

When the Texan released Marco, the young man made a poor decision. He came at the other man, intending to fight him. Gwen's rescuer took Marco out with two swift punches, sending the younger man to the floor. Gwen glanced down at where Marco lay sprawled flat on his back.

Her hero turned to her. "Ma'am, are you all right?"

She nodded. This man was about six-two, with a sun-burned tan, sun-streaked brown hair and azure-blue eyes.

"What's a lady like you doing in a place like this?" he asked.

"Um…searching for my father," she managed to say.

"Come on, I'd better get you out of here. Our friend—" he hitched his thumb downward at Marco "—might have some buddies itching for a fight."

"Actually, I was just leaving. I just need to call a taxi."

When a rumble arose from several men nearby, her rescuer grasped Gwen's arm and led her through the filthy, smoky bar and out onto the sidewalk. Once in the fresh air, Gwen took a deep breath.

"My name is Will Pierce," he said. "I'm a private investigator for Dundee's in Atlanta, Georgia." He pulled out his wallet and showed her his driver's license and an ID card. "If you'll allow me, I'd be glad to take you back to your hotel."

"Thank you. I…I'd appreciate that." Gwen knew she was taking a chance by trusting this man, but instinct told her she was safe with him. "I'm Gwen Arnell." Only in business situations did she introduce herself as Dr. Arnell.

"Look, Gwen, would you mind waiting in my rental car?" he asked. "I'll give you the keys and you can lock yourself in. I really need to go back inside and speak to the bartender."

"He doesn't speak English."

"That's okay. I speak enough Spanish to get by."

"You said you're an investigator. Are you here in Puerto Nuevo on a case?"

"Yeah, it seems some rich man's spoiled daughter didn't come home to her papa's villa last night and he's worried about her. More than likely she spent the night with a guy, but I got a tip that they were headed here last night. I need to check it out."

Without conscious thought of what she was doing, Gwen grabbed Will's arm. "When you ask him about this girl and her boyfriend, would you also ask him if he's seen an elderly American man, around seventy, with a younger woman. The old man would have been talking about a great adventure he was going on."

"The old man, I assume he's your father?"

"Yes." Gwen nodded.

"By any chance do people refer to him as The Professor?"

Gwen gasped. "Yes, but how did you—"

"Your father has a young research assistant named Jordan?"

"Yes, Jordan Elders. He is one of my father's former students. My father was a botany professor before he retired a few years ago."

"Ms. Arnell, it would seem that your search and mine overlap," Will said. "The young man who my client's daughter might be with is your father's assistant, Jordan Elders."

Realizing she was holding fiercely to this stranger's arm, Gwen released him and leaned her body away from his. "I was told my father checked out of his hotel this afternoon, before I arrived, but I have no idea where he's gone."

"I'd say when we find Jordan Elders, I'll find my client's daughter and your father."

Thank you, God! Gwen said a hurried, silent prayer. Just when she thought it might be impossible to find her father and help him, a higher power had sent Will Pierce to her, an honest-to-goodness private detective.

"Where's your car?" she asked, suddenly feeling more confident. "I'll wait for you while you go inside and speak to the bartender."

Will grinned. Gwen's stomach flip-flopped. Not a good sign. She seldom reacted to a man's sexual charm. Burned once. Twice shy. A brief marriage that had ended in a heart-breaking divorce when she was twenty-two had taught her to steer clear of sexual entanglements. When she dated, which wasn't that often these days, she chose stable, reliable, boring men.

"It's the blue hatchback." He pointed to the small car parked on the street about forty yards from where they stood, then he tossed her the keys. "Lock yourself in. Put the keys in the ignition. I'll be back in a few minutes."

A few minutes turned into half an hour. After fifteen minutes she'd lowered the car's windows several inches to let in cooler air. After twenty minutes she started to worry. What was taking him so long? Was he all right?

Finally, just as she reached for the door handle intending to get out of the car and go back inside the Yellow Parrot to search for Will, he came out of the bar and straight to the car. She leaned across the driver's seat and unlocked the door. He got in, slid under the steering wheel and shut the door. Without saying a word, he started the engine.

"Are you okay?" she asked. "I was beginning to worry."

He turned to face her. She gasped. He had a cut on his cheek, a bloody mouth and bruised eye.

"What happened to you?"

"After I spoke to the bartender, I got in a little altercation with a couple of your buddy Marco's pals."

"Oh, I'm so sorry." Gwen lifted her hand, but stopped herself short of touching his face. "You fought off two men all by yourself?"

Will chuckled, then grunted. He wiped his bloody mouth with the back of his hand, then shifted gears and pulled the rental car out into the street. Gwen rummaged in her purse until she found her minibox of tissues. She pulled one out, reached over and wiped the blood from Will's mouth and then his hand. He tensed at her touch, but didn't withdraw.

"Do you need a doctor?" she asked.

"Nope."

"I'm so sorry about—"

"You've already said that once. Stop apologizing. It's not your fault."

Gwen sat quietly for a few minutes, then realized that he wasn't taking her back to her hotel. Oh, my God, she hadn't even told him where she was staying.

"I'm staying at the Pasada El Paso," Gwen told him.

"And I'm staying at the Puerto Nuevo Day's Inn. If you don't mind, we need to go by my hotel first so I can make some phone calls, send out a couple of e-mails and clean my cuts and bruises."

Gwen sat there silent and uncertain.

"Look, I'm not trying to pull anything," he said. "Before Marco's pals wanted to play rough, the bartender identified my client's daughter and her girlfriend from photos I showed him. They were there at the Yellow Parrot last night, with this Jordan Elders guy, or at least I'm pretty sure that's who he was. The bartender said that the young guy and the two girls kept calling this old guy The Professor."

"Then my father was there last night?"

"Yeah, and he was with a younger woman. The bartender said he knew her, that she'd been here in Puerto Nuevo for about six months and was a regular. Her name's Molly Esteban. It seems he thinks the woman's bad news."

"Poor Daddy. He's such a damn fool."

"The bartender overheard the young guy—Jordan—saying something about their heading out tomorrow, which is now today, leaving the island."

"Where were they going?"

"The bartender didn't know, didn't hear them mention where."

"Well, if it helps any, sooner or later, my father will have to charter a boat to take him where he wants to go. If he didn't charter a boat here, then—"

"When we get to my hotel, I'll call Dundee's and have them get us the info on all flights out of Puerto Nuevo today, plus any boat or yacht rentals today."

"Your agency can get all that information for us tonight?"

"They can probably get me the info on plane reservations tonight, but it could take a bit longer to check out all the boat and yacht rentals, because my guess is that there are a few dozen rental places."

"Mr. Pierce…Will?"

"Huh?"

"I know you're already assigned to a case, and I probably can't afford to hire you, but I was wondering if there might be some way I could persuade you to help me find my father and save him from himself. After all, there is a chance that your client's daughter went off with Jordan, and Jordan is with my father, and…well, what do you think?"

Will zoomed the rental car along, darting in and out of nighttime traffic, never taking his eyes off the road. "As far as I'm concerned, brown eyes, you and I are in this together all the way."

Chapter 3

Expect the unexpected. Be prepared for anything. Never take a person or a situation at face value. Trust no one. During his years as a CIA operative, Will had learned some valuable lessons. Some of them the hard way and others by observation.

After brewing a small pot of coffee for him and his guest, he settled her in a chair in the corner of his hotel room, then he went back into the bathroom, closed the door and washed the blood off his face. He checked his bruised eye and the cut on his cheek. Minor wounds. No big deal. He swiped the washcloth over his cheek, removing the dried blood, and tossed the cloth into the nearby shower stall.

Keeping the water running in the sink to mask his voice, he used his cell phone to call Sawyer's private number. With a few well-chosen words, he explained what was going on and asked that Dundee's run a quick check on a woman named Gwen Arnell.

"From her accent, I'd say she's from the South," Will said. "Deep South. Alabama, Georgia, Mississippi."

"She claims this man known as The Professor is her father and he's in some kind of trouble?" Sawyer asked. "And our client's daughter could be with this man's assistant, right?"

"Yeah, and my gut instinct says she's telling the truth, that she's on the up and up, but run a check on her and get me as much information on her as quickly as you can."

"Give me a physical description and an approximate age. We'll probably run across more than one Gwen Arnell when we start checking."

"Late twenties, early thirties," Will said. "About five-five, medium build, maybe a little on the plump side. Fairly nondescript. Dark brown hair and brown eyes." Not beautiful, but she has good features, Will thought, but kept that to himself. There was nothing fancy about Gwen Arnell, no jewelry other than a wristwatch, and she didn't appear to be wearing much makeup, just the bare minimum. The black slacks and gray linen jacket she wore were practical clothing for travel, nothing fashionable or trendy.

"I should have something for you in a couple of hours, on your Ms. Arnell and on the plane flights out of Puerto Nuevo today," Sawyer said. "Checking the boat and yacht rentals could take longer, maybe sometime tomorrow."

"One more thing…"

"What?"

"Ms. Arnell wants me to help her find her father. I think her search and ours could well turn out to be one and the same, so do you have any objections to—"

"Do whatever you need to do to find Cheryl Kress."

"Okay."

End of conversation. Will flipped his cell phone closed and hooked it to his belt.

When he emerged from the bathroom, Gwen rose to her feet and faced him. Neither smiling nor frowning, she met his gaze head-on, a combination of hope and fear in her coffee-brown eyes. The woman had the most expressive eyes he'd ever seen. She didn't need to speak for him to understand that she was, perhaps subconsciously, pleading with him for help.

Her long dark hair, pulled away from her face and twisted into a knot at the nape of her neck, looked disheveled, and her makeup-bare face showed signs of weariness. For the first time in a long time, Will felt a twinge of protectiveness stir to life inside him. It wasn't that he thought she was some weak, helpless female. On the contrary, it was the fact that she was putting herself at risk to find her father and that she hadn't cried or tried to use feminine wiles to persuade him to help her. He figured Gwen had never asked a man for help, that it went against her nature to think she might not be able to do the job—whatever that job might be—by herself.

"I spoke to my boss," Will said. "He should have some information for us in an hour or so."

Gwen nodded. "Thank you."

"Did you have dinner tonight? If you didn't, I can run out and get you—"

"I ate at the Fiesta, but thank you."

"I take it that you were following up a lead when you went to the Fiesta."

"Yes, how did you—"

"Me, too," he told her. When she eyed him inquiringly, he explained, "Our common denominator, Jordan Elders."

"Ah, yes, Jordan."

"What do you know about him?"

"Not much, just that he's one of Daddy's former students, that he's in his late twenties and he shares my father's belief in a mysterious, uncharted island that possesses a miraculous Fountain of Youth serum derived from a plant that grows nowhere else on earth."

"What?"

Gwen rubbed her hands together nervously. "It sounds preposterous, doesn't it? I know only too well just how outlandish my father's theory is. His insistence that he once visited this island when he was twenty and knows it exists made him a laughingstock among his colleagues. He's obsessed with finding this island again and in giving to the world this incredible plant that keeps people healthy and gives them a two-hundred-year lifespan."

"Are you telling me that your father actually believes this crap?"

When Gwen's cheeks flushed, he realized he'd hit a nerve.

"Yes, he believes it, with his whole heart and soul."

"It must have been tough growing up with a father everybody thought was nuts." Damn, Pierce. Open mouth, insert foot. "Sorry it came out that way. But you know what I mean."

"Yes, I do. But I didn't actually grow up with my father. He and my mother divorced when I was ten. He couldn't be bothered with a wife and a child, not when he had to fulfill his destiny and bring good health and longevity to the world."

"So, if he deserted you and your mom, why are you here now, trying to find him, wanting to help him?"

"Because he is my father, and he has no one else who really cares if he lives or dies."

Will shook his head. Not many adult kids would give a damn about a father who had deserted them, let alone go in search of that parent, hoping to save him from himself.

"You're a better person than I am," Will told her. "My old man was no prize, but he was there, working hard to support his wife and three sons. We didn't get along, didn't see eye to eye on a lot of things, but I respected him. If he had deserted us, I wouldn't have cared if he'd rotted in hell."

Gwen stared at Will, her eyes round with speculation. It was then that he realized he'd revealed a personal part of himself that he seldom shared with others. Seldom? Hell, make that never.

Will cleared his throat. "So, where does your father think this island is located?"

"Somewhere north of the Caribbean Sea, out in the Atlantic between Puerto Rico and Bermuda."

"In the Bermuda Triangle?" Will chuckled under his breath. "Get real. Every kook in the world believes some sort of supernatural nonsense about that area of the Atlantic Ocean."

"I know it sounds preposterous, but my father swears that when he was twenty, he lived for several weeks on this island. And he's spent the past fifty years searching for it."

"Damn!"

"He's an old man, seventy his last birthday, and he's spent every dime he has on this quest." Gwen sighed lightly, her expression one of sadness and concern. "He told me that he'd cashed in his life-insurance policy to help fund this latest expedition."

"Would he pay for everything by credit card or cash?" Will asked.

"Huh?"

"If he uses a credit card, we can trace—"

"I see. But I have no idea if he'd pay cash or use a credit card. I'm afraid I know very little about my father's personal life, other than his big dream, which seems to have consumed him completely."

"Why don't you sit down and relax?" Will said, indicating the single chair in the room. "I need to check my e-mail and send off a few while we wait."

She nodded and returned to the seat. Will went over to the desk and unzipped his carrying case. As he opened his laptop, he glanced over his shoulder at Gwen. She sat with her hands folded together in her lap, her head against the chair back and her eyes closed.

Why the hell did he feel so protective toward her? It wasn't that he was particularly attracted to her. She really wasn't his type, was she? A little too plain, a little on the plump side and his guess was that her IQ was higher than his. Plain, plump and brainy. Definitely not his type. Besides, he needed to stay focused on the job.

Gwen hadn't realized she had dozed off for over an hour until Will's cell phone rang. Startled awake by the distinct ring, she came to with a jolt. Searching the room for Will, she found him standing near the window, his back to her, his voice low as he mumbled yes and no and then hung up.

"Was that your boss?" she asked.

"Yeah, it was." Will turned to face her. "Sorry the call woke you. I should have put the thing on *vibrate* instead of *ring*."

"No, no, it's all right. I shouldn't have fallen asleep. It was rude of me."

"Hey, you're tired. No big deal."

"May I ask what information—"

His gaze locked with hers. "Look, you should know that I asked for Dundee's to run a check on you."

Her eyes widened and her mouth rounded in surprise.

"I don't take anyone or anything at face value," he said matter-of-factly.

"I see."

"If we're going to work together, Dr. Arnell, we need to be honest with each other. Agreed?"

She nodded. "Agreed." Why did she suspect that while he demanded honesty from her, he wouldn't necessarily always be totally honest with her?

"So you're the CEO of the Huntsville Botanical Gardens in Alabama, huh? You're a botanist, just like your father, the other Dr. Arnell."

"My father specialized in education, exploration and history," she said. "Whereas my interests are horticulture and breeding."

"Breeding?"

"Breeding involves the development of better types of plants. It also involves selecting and crossing plants with desirable traits, such as disease resistance."

"Interesting."

Gwen smiled, knowing full well that Will found the subject as dull as dishwater. "What else did you find out about me?"

"Just the basics. Date of birth, job, address, phone number, education background. Mother deceased. Father a genius crackpot. No siblings. And I know you were married at twenty-one, divorced at twenty-two and don't presently have a significant other. No children. No pets."

"If we're going to be partners, don't you think I should know the same things about you?" It seemed unfair that he knew the basic facts about her life when he remained a stranger to her.

Will sat down on the edge of the bed, across from the chair where she sat. "Just the basics, right? Okay, fair enough. I'm thirty-nine. Married and divorced in my late twenties. No children. My father's been dead five years. My mother remarried last year and moved to Louisiana with her new husband. My older brother still lives on the ranch where we grew up and my younger brother is a doctor in Ft. Worth. I have three nephews, ages two, five and eight."

"Hmm…all right, now we're on an equal footing. So, what about our investigation?"

"Our investigation?" Will chuckled. "Well, no one using the names Emery Arnell, Jordan Elders, Cheryl Kress or Tori Boyd were booked on flights out of Puerto Nuevo today and none are booked for tomorrow."

"Then they're either still here on the island or they left here by boat."

"So it would seem."

"When will you have a report about the boat and yacht rental companies?"

"Probably not until tomorrow sometime, hopefully by midmorning."

"Then I guess I should head back to my hotel." Gwen checked her watch. "Wow, it's past midnight."

"You're welcome to stay here." Will indicated one of the two single beds in the room.

"No, thank you." This offer was probably on the up-and-up, but she wasn't about to take any chances. "I left my suitcase back at the other hotel, and I want to speak to the day staff there and see if my father mentioned his travel plans to anyone."

"Okay. I'll drive you back to your hotel, then I'll come by in the morning and pick you up for breakfast."

"Thank you."

"No problem. Like I said, we're in this together. Right?"

Feelings of security and relief welled up inside Gwen. At an early age, she had learned to depend on no one, to take care of herself, so being grateful for having some big, strong man at her side in her search for her father was a new experience for her.

Just don't allow yourself to become too dependent on Will Pierce, said an inner voice. *He's a temporary fixture in your life. A means to an end.*

Will picked Gwen up at the Pasada El Paso at nine the next morning. She wore brown slacks and an oversize tan shirt, had pulled her hair up into a loose ponytail and had applied lipstick and a hint of blush. Apparently the woman didn't own anything colorful. He'd bet her underwear was plain white cotton.

"The desk clerk at my hotel recommended Pepe's for breakfast," Will told her once she was seated in his rental car.

"Anyplace you choose is fine with me."

He grunted, started the car and eased into downtown morning traffic.

"I spoke to the day staff at the hotel," Gwen told him. "And unfortunately none of them had any idea where my father intended to go when he left Puerto Nuevo. Ria, one of the maids, did say my father's lady friend said something about going to Jamaica."

"Do you know of any reason your father would go to Jamaica? Why not charter a boat here and sail up toward the Bahamas?"

"I have no idea." She shuffled in her seat. "I assume you haven't had any word from your boss about the rental—"

"Not yet, but anytime now, I'm sure."

"What will we do if they didn't rent a boat?"

"We'll assume they either traveled with someone who had a boat or that they're still here on the island."

An hour later, just as they were topping off their big breakfast with cups of a local speciality, *café de ola*, Will's cell phone rang.

"Will, we have confirmation that a Dr. Emery Arnell rented a 422 Sport Sedan cruiser, captained by a man named Mick McGuire. And before you ask, I'm running a check on McGuire as we speak," Daisy Holbrook said on the other end. "Arnell paid cash. And according to what I was able to find out, he rented the cruiser for a month."

"Any idea if the cruiser has left port?"

"I don't have that information, yet. But the cruiser either is or was docked at the Puerto Nuevo Marina."

"Hang on a minute," he said to Daisy, then spoke to Gwen. "Your father rented a cruiser, but we don't know whether or not he's left the country yet." Talking again to Daisy, Will asked, "Any info on Jordan Elders?"

"Not much more than you already know. He's twenty-eight. Was a student of Dr. Arnell's and later his assistant. He has no criminal record. As a matter of fact, he's squeaky clean."

"Hmm…"

"By the way, the cruiser the professor rented, the *Sun Dancer,* is equipped with upgraded cat diesel engines, with 435 horsepower each. That means speed. Why would he need a cruiser with that much horsepower?" Daisy asked. "What's the first thing that comes to mind?"

"Drug running."

"Bingo. And that fits right in with what I've found out about Molly Esteban. It seems the lady's got a record a mile long."

Will grunted. When his gaze met Gwen's, he forced a faltering smile. "Thanks, Daisy. Stay in touch with any updates."

"Will do."

He put away his phone and turned to Gwen. "Let me take care of the bill, then we should head off to the marina."

When Will stood, she stood, then reached over and grabbed his arm. "I heard you mention something about drug running."

Will hesitated, then told her, "The cruiser your father rented has a lot of horsepower, and fast boats are often associated with illegal activities. But that's not necessarily—"

"We're going to be honest with each other, remember? What aren't you telling me?"

Damn, why had he made a pact with her? "Your father's lady friend, Molly Esteban, has a criminal record. It's possible she's using your father and his quest to find his mythical island as a front."

"Oh, God!" Gwen rubbed her head and mumbled a few choice curse words that surprised Will, she being such a soft-spoken Southern lady. "Daddy, Daddy…what have you gotten yourself into this time?"

"Come on." Will motioned for them to get going. "If we're lucky, they haven't left yet."

"The *Sun Dancer* left late yesterday sometime," the charter office employee, a Mr. Calvino, told Will. "Dr. Arnell seemed eager to leave."

"Do you know where he was going?" Gwen asked, praying he knew the answer.

"Kingston, Jamaica," Calvino replied.

"Which means they're probably already there," Will said.

"More than likely. I believe Señora Esteban was eager to meet some friends there."

"What do you know about Mick McGuire?" Will asked. "I assume he works for your company."

"Actually, Dr. Arnell said he didn't need us to recommend anyone to captain the *Sun Dancer*. He said that he'd already hired Mr. McGuire."

Will groaned. "Anything else you can tell us? Ms. Arnell is quite concerned about her father. Uh, his health isn't good and she's afraid he's not up to making this journey."

Calvino shook his head. "I'm sorry, but that's all I know."

"One final question," Will said. "Other than McGuire and Señora Esteban, who else was with Dr. Arnell?"

"Just his assistant, a young man. I don't recall his name."

"You didn't see two young women with them? Girls about twenty?"

"No, no young girls."

Will shook hands with Calvino and thanked him, then led Gwen out of the office and down the wharf toward the parking area.

Assuming her partnership with Will had come to an end since the girls weren't with her father, Gwen said, "I'll get a reservation on the next flight to Kingston."

"You aren't going to Kingston alone. We're in this together, remember."

"What about your assignment? Mr. Calvino said there were no young women with my father and Jordan."

"Just because he didn't see them doesn't mean they

didn't board the cruiser and head off to Jamaica with Jordan Elders."

"Are you sure you aren't saying that just to reassure me that you're not abandoning your assignment to help me find my father?"

Will looked at her intensely. "Why would I do that?"

"I don't know. Maybe you feel sorry for me. If that's the case—"

He grabbed her shoulders, startling her enough that she gasped. "I do not feel sorry for you. Got that? And if I didn't think there's a damn good chance Cheryl and Tori are with Jordan Elders, I wouldn't fly to Jamaica with you. And if you think I'm going with you because I've got ideas about you and me, think again. I like you well enough, brown eyes, but you're hardly the stuff a wet-dream fantasy is made of."

Guess he put you in your place, an angry and hurt inner voice told Gwen. She blew out a huffing breath. "That's good to know, since you're not exactly my idea of Prince Charming."

"Are you looking for Prince Charming?"

"As a matter of fact, I'm not. I'm not interested in putting up with a man, any man, not even Prince Charming," Gwen told him, her voice quavering. "My father and my ex-husband proved to me that most men are incapable of putting the needs of the woman they profess to love above their own."

Will grinned. "Good. I'm glad we got that settled." He grasped her elbow and herded her along with him toward his rental car.

She kept up with his long-legged gait, but just barely. When they reached the car, Will released his hold on her and unlocked the passenger-side door. Just as she slid into the seat, his cell phone rang. Gwen held her breath until he answered.

"Pierce here."

She watched his facial expressions change rapidly, going from curiosity to dismay. "Look, you two stay put. I'm on my way."

Will didn't say anything to Gwen until he went around the car and got in on the driver's side. He slammed his big hands down against the steering wheel several times and cursed loudly.

"What is it? What's wrong?"

"The phone call was from a girl named Courtney Downey. She and another girl are staying at the Kress villa. They're friends of Cheryl and Tori. The Puerto Nuevo police just left the villa. It seems the body of a young blond woman was found on the beach not far from here early this morning. She had a set of keys in her pocket with a key ring that had a photo of the Kress villa on it. The police want the girls to come down to the morgue and see if they can identify the body."

"Is Cheryl Kress a blonde?" Gwen asked.

"No, but Tori Boyd is."

Chapter 4

Will and Gwen had accompanied Courtney and Kerry to the morgue. Gwen had insisted on being with him when the nervous girls viewed the body of the young blonde found on the beach. He sympathized with what the girls had to face, and was damn grateful there was an older woman around to oversee the emotional young females, a job he didn't like, didn't want and avoided at all costs. Not much scared Will, but women's emotions unnerved him in a way little else did.

"Oh, God, it's Tori!" Kerry had cried, then turned around and fallen into Will's arms. Crying her eyes out, she'd clung to him.

Courtney had taken one look at the corpse, went white as a sheet and threw up. Gwen had put her arm around the girl and led her to the nearest restroom.

After their visit to the morgue, Gwen waited in the car

with the girls, playing mother hen, which apparently came naturally to her. Will went inside the police station alone and spoke to the officer in charge of the case.

"Now that the girl has been identified, we will contact her family in the United States," a middle-aged, slightly balding Detective Sanchez said.

"Tori Boyd was last seen with her friend, Cheryl Kress. I'm a P.I., working for Cheryl's father. I'd appreciate any information you can give me about Ms. Boyd's death. That info might somehow help me find Ms. Kress."

"We can't say for sure until an autopsy has been performed, but we believe the girl was strangled, so we are treating this case as a homicide."

"Any suspects?" Will asked.

"No, none at this time."

Will handed Sanchez his business card. "I'm leaving later today for Jamaica to follow a lead on Ms. Kress's whereabouts. I'd appreciate your contacting me if you get a break in this case." The only real lead Will had was knowing Cheryl had last been seen with Jordan Elders. If the girl was still alive, there was a good possibility she was with this guy.

Sanchez nodded, then asked, "Does Señorita Kress's family wish to report their daughter as missing?"

"No, not yet. They prefer for my agency to handle the search for the time being."

Will finished his conversation with Sanchez as quickly as possible, knowing he had two badly shaken and frightened young women waiting in his car. Thank goodness for Gwen. Although he'd noticed her discomfort while they'd been at the morgue, she had been a rock for Courtney and Kerry, saving him from having to deal with them.

Comfort and understanding weren't his strong suits. As his old man had often said, "That's women stuff. Leave it to them."

When he returned to his rental car, he found Gwen in the backseat between the two girls. Courtney rested her head on Gwen's shoulder, while Kerry, her eyes glazed, held tightly to Gwen's hand.

The minute Will got in the car, Gwen said, "We're taking the girls back to the villa to pack, and then we're personally putting them on the first available flight back home."

"We are?" He locked gazes with Gwen. Obstinate determination glinted in her dark eyes. "Okay, we are."

Two hours later, with Kerry and Courtney safely aboard a flight back to the United States and Gwen checked out of her hotel, Will drove the two of them back to his hotel. While they had waited at the airport with the girls, Will had contacted Sawyer and filled him in on the situation.

Will unlocked the door to his room, motioned for Gwen to enter first, then suggested she take a seat.

"I need to contact my boss and see if he's spoken to Mr. Kress before I get my stuff together," Will said. "It could be that with this new development, he'll want the police involved in his daughter's disappearance and Sawyer will pull me in off the case."

"If that happens, then you'll go back to Atlanta today, won't you?" Gwen looked at him, a silent plea in her big brown eyes.

"If I'm called off this case, I'll get you to Jamaica today and help you try to find your father before I fly back to Atlanta."

Gwen released a deep sigh. "Thank you. You don't have to, you know. You aren't obligated to—"

"All I'm promising is to take you to Kingston and make some inquires." He held up his hand in a "stop" gesture when she started to speak. "If your father's not there or already gone by the time we arrive, then you're on your own. Understand?"

"I understand."

Will sat on the edge of the bed and called Dundee headquarters. Daisy put him through to Sawyer immediately.

"I just got off the phone with Mr. Kress," Sawyer said. "For the second time today. Since learning about Tori Boyd's death, that she was possibly murdered, he's understandably upset. He's concerned about his daughter's safety, so he's flying to Puerto Nuevo later today, with Tori Boyd's parents, and they plan to speak personally to the local authorities."

"Then I'm off the case?"

"No, not at all. Mr. Kress wants you to follow any and all leads. He wants Dundee's on the case until his daughter is found."

"Okay, that means taking the Dundee jet to Jamaica today. And it's possible I may need to rent a cruiser."

"Buy or rent whatever you need. Money is no object to Mr. Kress. He wants his daughter found."

"Okay. I'll check in later, if and when I know something."

His conversation finished, Will glanced over his shoulder at Gwen. "I'm still on the case, and I've been given a blank check for expenses. Is there anything you need to do in Puerto Nuevo before we go?"

She shook her head.

"Then come on. I'll call the pilot and tell him to have the jet ready for us when we arrive at the private airstrip. We're going to Jamaica."

* * *

Gwen had never flown in a private jet before and had to admit she was more than a little impressed. She sat on the large sofa in the luxurious lounge and tried to relax. Since she hadn't gotten much sleep last night, it would easy for her to fall asleep. Maybe she should take a nap while Will was in the cockpit with the pilot. Leaning back, letting her head rest comfortably on the cushioned leather, she closed her eyes and concentrated on erasing everything from her mind.

Gwen realized blocking out the events of the past two days was impossible. Here she was flying from Puerto Nuevo to Jamaica on a private jet with a man she'd met only last night. A man she instinctively knew had seen more than his share of trouble. He had shown her his credentials. He was a licensed private investigator. The problem wasn't that she didn't trust him, at least on some level. No, the problem was that she found him attractive, and not just his rugged good looks, but the way he seemed comfortable taking charge, making decisions, helping both her and the young women who had been forced to identify the body of their murdered friend. Will was one of those guys people depended on because he got the job done.

Gwen tried to shake off the feelings that Will stirred to life inside her. He was the opposite of her father in so many ways and definitely nothing like her ex-husband. She had chosen Jeremy Charles because she'd thought they had a great deal in common. He had been a botany major at Auburn, where they'd attended college together, and he'd been the most logical-thinking, down-to-earth young man she'd ever met. After being deserted by a father who kept his head in the clouds, she had wanted a husband who had both feet firmly planted on the ground.

"Gwen?"

She opened her eyes and stared up at Will, who was smiling down at her.

"You weren't asleep, were you?" he asked.

"No, just relaxing a little," she lied.

"I was wondering if you're hungry. We have a fully stocked galley."

"I'm not very hungry."

"Come on, you need to eat something. I'm going to make myself a big, thick sandwich and eat half a bag of chips and maybe some chocolate ice cream, too. What do you say?"

Chocolate ice cream? Was he kidding? She could eat chocolate ice cream every day and never tire of it. It was one of her comfort foods. "I'll take a sandwich, no chips and just a little ice cream."

"Give me five minutes."

When he turned and headed toward the galley, she called to him. "I'd be glad to help."

"You stay put, kick off your shoes and relax again. I can put together a couple of sandwiches."

Half an hour later, with their meal eaten, Gwen curled up on the sofa, her shoes on the floor, while Will sat across from her in one of the swivel lounge chairs.

"What do we do when we arrive in Kingston?" Gwen asked. "I suppose we should check with all the marinas and—"

"That's being done," he said.

"It's being done? How's that possible?" Then realization dawned on her. "Oh, right. I forgot that you work for some high-powered investigation agency. I suppose they're running a check right now."

"They're going through the usual channels to get what

information they can. But Dundee's has contacts in various places around the world, so when we need certain information, we use locals whenever possible."

"Are you telling me that Dundee's has a contact in Kingston?"

"Yes, we do. And at this very moment, he's doing some of the leg work, saving us time when we land." Will checked his wristwatch. "In about twenty minutes."

"That soon?" Gwen sat up straight, lifted her foot and extended it enough to grab one shoe with her toe.

"It's a short flight, less than two hours."

"So, what do we do when we land, meet the Dundee contact?"

"That's the second thing we'll do. The first thing we'll do is talk to a member of the JCM, a Lieutenant Seabert."

"The JCM?" Gwen asked.

"Jamaica Constabulary Force."

"Oh. So, why are we going to the police?"

"Dundee's has notified the Kingston authorities that we're investigating a missing person's case and gave them the names of the people who might be involved."

"Including my father's name." Had her father's misadventures led to this—to him somehow being involved with one girl's murder and another's disappearance? *Please, God, don't let Daddy have had anything to do with what happened to Tori Boyd.*

"Yes, including your father's name."

"You don't know for sure that Cheryl Kress is with Jordan Elders and my father."

"You're right, I don't know it for a fact. But both Cheryl and Tori were last seen with Jordan. And Jordan left Puerto Nuevo with your father, a woman named Molly Esteban, who we know has a criminal record, and a guy named Mick McGuire, who's captaining the cruiser your father rented."

"I'm surprised Dundee's hasn't come up with information about this Captain McGuire." She noted the odd expression on Will's face. "Oh, they have, haven't they?"

"McGuire's an alias. One of many this guy has used, if he's the same Mick McGuire. He's been in the Caribbean area for years, in and out of trouble. He's been suspected of smuggling, gunrunning and drug trafficking. He's served time in prison, but mostly for petty stuff, just like Molly."

"Wonderful. Just wonderful. This McGuire man and the Esteban woman are the investors my father was so excited about. And they're criminals. Somehow, in my gut, I sensed something wasn't right about people with enough money to help my father finance his latest expedition. Not unless they were as crazy as he is."

"If we're lucky, we'll catch up with them in Kingston."

"And if we're not that lucky?"

"Then we'll find out where they went and catch them at the next port."

"That might not be possible, not if they head out to sea, straight toward Bermuda, directly into the Devil's Triangle."

Lieutenant Seabert had done nothing to allay Gwen's fears that her father had gotten himself involved with a couple of dangerous criminals. Instead, Will realized grimly, the lieutenant had only frightened her more when he told them that Mick McGuire, alias Michael Smith, Mike Willis, Micah Muir, was suspected of murder. Several murders to be exact.

If Will thought it would do any good, he'd suggest that she let him handle things with their contact, while she

waited like a good little girl in the car. But being a realist
Will knew that wasn't about to happen. Gwen was the kind
of woman who would resent a man trying to keep her
safely in the background. And that's the reason he included
her in his meeting with their Dundee contact, a wiry,
brown-skinned Jamaican named Webster. Webster was a
good operative. Dundee's had used his expertise in the
past. So had the CIA.

"Where are we meeting him?" Gwen asked, as Will
drove the rental car they'd picked up at the airport straight
toward their destination.

"The Caribbean Marina," Will replied.

"Do you think that's where my father's rental boat is
docked?"

"Webster didn't say."

"Well, what exactly did he say?"

"He said to meet him at the marina, that he had information for us."

"Why didn't you—"

"Gwen, stop asking me so many questions. You'll know
what I know when Webster tells me. Got it?"

"Yes, I've got it!" she snapped at him, obviously aggravated.

He could explain that Webster didn't deliver messages
over the phone, that he was a look-you-in-the-eye kind of
guy. But he damn well didn't feel like explaining every
move he made to her. After all, he was doing her a favor
by letting her tag along. She should be grateful and just
keep her mouth shut. But since she was a woman, that
might prove impossible.

Ten minutes later they arrived at the marina. The piers
were lined with docked sea craft, everything from huge

yachts to small fishing boats. If the *Sun Dancer* was here, Webster would know and could take them directly to it.

"He said he'd meet us at the entrance," Will told Gwen as he opened the passenger door for her.

She got out of the car but didn't say a word, just followed along beside him as he headed for the entrance. Webster, wearing white slacks, sandals and a colorful floral shirt, emerged from where he'd been waiting just inside the stone pillar entrance.

"Who is she?" Webster asked, appraising Gwen as if she were a priceless jewel he wanted to purchase.

"She's mine," Will replied, not giving any thought to his answer.

Webster lifted his eyebrows. "Not your usual, is she, mon? This one, she is a lady."

"Thank you, Mr. Webster." Gwen smiled at the Dundee contact.

"Just Webster, pretty lady."

"Back to business," Will said.

"They are not here." Webster looked directly at Will.

"They're not here at this marina or they're not here in Kingston?" Will asked.

"They were in Kingston. Molly Esteban delivered a package. They were gone, back to sea, in three hours' time."

"Gone where?" Gwen asked.

"What about the package?" Will wanted to know.

Webster glanced at Gwen. "Gone to the next drop-off. San Juan, Puerto Rico." He looked back at Will. "We think the package contained cocaine. Molly and Mick are not major players, but they wish to be."

"Have the San Juan authorities been contacted?" Will asked.

"No, mon. The time is not right."

"What do you mean—" Gwen said.

"Now, don't you worry about things that are none of your business, honey." Will hurriedly draped his arm around her shoulders and dragged her up against his side.

Webster chuckled. Gwen bristled, but thankfully kept her mouth shut.

"Who's our contact in San Juan?" Will asked.

"Jose. He's new in the business, but you can trust him."

Five minutes later Will and Gwen were back in the rental car heading for the airport. Gwen hadn't spoken to him since they left the marina. He knew she was as mad as hell.

"Okay, let me have it." He hazarded a glance at her stern face.

"Is all this cloak-and-dagger nonsense really necessary?" she asked. "And what was that 'she's mine' business all about, anyway?"

"Look, if you don't like the way I do things, then when we get back to the airport, we can go our separate ways. But I can be in San Juan in less than two hours and have a good chance of catching up with Jordan Elders. Don't forget that my only interest is finding Cheryl Kress."

Gwen fumed. Will could almost see smoke coming out her ears.

She didn't say another word all the way to the airport.

The Dundee contact in San Juan met them at the airport. Jose was short, stocky and remarkably good looking, with curly black hair and huge black eyes. He was pleasant to Gwen but for the most part ignored her.

He spoke rapidly in Spanish as he zipped along in late-evening traffic. Gwen, who was squeezed between the two men, kept her hands in her lap and listened, hoping that sooner or later, Will would translate at least part of the conversation.

He didn't. Jerk.

Glancing out the windshield, she watched the scenery flash by as they sped along. Gwen thought that under different circumstances she would enjoy doing some sightseeing. She'd never been to Puerto Rico before. Usually on vacation trips she visited botanical gardens, explored nature trails and loved collecting information about the local flora.

It was almost twilight when they pulled up in the parking area of a small marina. Jose parked the car, got out and disappeared. Gwen crossed her arms over her chest and looked straight ahead, determined not to be the first one who spoke.

"Jose is checking to see if our cruiser is ready," Will said.

Snapping around to face him, Gwen stared at him, puzzled and speechless.

"The *Sun Dancer* is one step ahead of us," Will told her. "They left here about three hours ago, after Molly made a delivery."

"Why are we renting a cruiser instead of flying to the next destination?"

"Because the next destination is the Atlantic Ocean, somewhere between here and Bermuda."

"Crap! They're actually letting Daddy go on his adventure, aren't they? But if they're smuggling drugs, why would they?"

"Your father's mad adventure is a good front for Molly and Mick. They could be headed anywhere, maybe the Bahamas, maybe Bermuda. What harm would it do to let your father think they were helping him search for his mythical island?"

"You and Jose were doing a great deal of talking. Is that all he told you?"

"No, that wasn't all. It seems five people were seen aboard the *Sun Dancer* as it headed out to sea."

"Five people?"

"Mick and Molly, an old man fitting your father's description, a young man, whom we assume was Jordan Elders and a young redhead."

"Cheryl Kress?"

"That's my guess."

"You think she didn't go with Jordan willingly, don't you?"

"I don't know and I'm not making any assumptions about why she might be with your father and his assistant."

"And with two dangerous criminals."

"Remember that it's highly unlikely your father and Jordan know Molly and Mick are criminals."

"But if they killed Tori Boyd, then surely—"

"If Mick killed Tori, he would hardly have done it in front of witnesses," Will said.

"Then my father and Jordan really might not know the kind of people they've hooked up with."

"Let's hope they don't. As long as they believe Mick and Molly are investors, people who've simply bought into your father's crazy dream, then your father, Jordan and Cheryl should be safe."

"And if they learn the truth?"

"Let's hope we find them before that happens."

Chapter 5

"What do you mean we'll have to stay the night aboard the yacht and not leave until morning?" With her hands planted on her hips, Gwen glowered at Will.

"No vessels are being allowed to leave tonight," Will explained. "There's a storm just north of Puerto Rico, one that any sane sailor would try to avoid."

"What about Daddy and the others aboard the *Sun Dancer*? They set sail a few hours ago. Why were they allowed to leave?"

"Three hours ago the storm warning had not been issued." Will paused in their trek down the pier to where their rental boat, which Will referred to as a yacht, was anchored. With his vinyl bag hooked over one shoulder and carrying her small suitcase, Will turned and faced Gwen, then he laid his free hand on her shoulder. "This Mick fellow isn't going to risk his life. Once he learned of the storm warning, he probably dropped anchor at the nearest port, probably the Dominican Republic or possibly one of the Turks and Caicos islands."

"Then why can't we take the jet and—"

"And go where? We don't know for sure where they might have docked."

The wind whipped around them, a warm, moist tropical wind, a precursor of the approaching storm. The pressure of Will's strong hand on her shoulder felt reassuring, and yet the simple contact slightly unnerved her.

"How will we ever find them, chasing after them in a boat, when we have no idea where they are?"

"Look, I'll fill you in on details later." He looked skyward. "The bottom's going to drop out any minute now, and I'd prefer not to get drenched." He grabbed her arm. "Let's get on board the *Footloose* and I promise I'll do my best to answer all your questions."

They stood there on the pier for a locked-horns moment. Gwen was growing more and more frustrated with Will's reluctance to share important information about their search for her father and his shipmates. A flash of lightning lit up the evening sky. When a loud rumble of thunder followed the light show, Gwen quickly nodded in agreement and raced alongside Will, hoping to stay one step ahead of the approaching rain.

"There she is," Will said. "She's a Sea Ray 580 Super Sport. This little yacht is a compact beauty, with two staterooms."

Gwen stopped just long enough to size up the *Footloose,* and knowing very little about seacraft of any kind, her appraisal consisted of noting it was white, clean and apparently quite new.

"It must be expensive to rent," she said.

"Yeah, probably is. But that's not our concern. Dundee's is picking up the tab."

"Of course."

"The fold-out steps are hidden in the coaming," Will told her as he tossed their bags aboard and revealed the steps within the frame around a hatchway in the deck.

After boarding, Will helped her onto the yacht. Another streak of lightning lit up the twilight sky. Gwen barely had time to notice that the aft-deck layout included a large U-shaped seating area, high-low tables and what she thought was a wet bar before Will shoved her bag into her arms.

Hoisting his own bag over his shoulder, Will led Gwen to an acrylic door and hatch, flipped a switch to turn on an overhead light, then led her down the companionway. The first thing she noticed was the abundance of lacquered wood. Beautiful. Simply beautiful. Sleek and modern in design, the galley boasted abundant storage and molded black granite countertops. A large curved leather settee was nestled against the wall opposite the galley in the neat and compact salon.

"The galley's fully equipped," Will said. "I believe the master stateroom and bath are aft, and the guest stateroom and bath are forward. You can take your pick."

"I'll take the guest room," she told him. "As long as there's a bed and bathroom with a shower, I'll be fine."

"Why don't you go check it out, and if you don't like it, we can swap. If you'd like to take a shower and change clothes, go ahead and I'll whip up some supper for us. We're supposed to have enough supplies for a couple of weeks."

"I'll put my bag in the stateroom and be right back." She

looked directly at him. "But before either of us does anything else, I want us to have the discussion you promised me."

Will grunted. "What happened to the good old days when women just did what men told them to do?"

"Remind me just what century that was."

"Okay, okay. You made your point," Will told her. "I'm going to get a beer. Want one?"

"No, thank you."

"Suit yourself."

Aggravating, macho, bossy… Gwen silently grumbled to herself as she opened the door to the forward state-room; at least, she believed it was forward. She felt along the wall for a light switch and found one. The room was tiny, the bed taking up almost all the space. But like the rest of the small yacht, the room was clean and neat. She laid her bag at the foot of the bed, then opened the door and checked out the bathroom. Will would probably refer to it as the head. Wasn't that what bathrooms on ships were called? The head was finished in Fiberglass and what she thought was Corian. White and dark blue. Nautical-print blue towels hung on the bar across the front edge of the sink.

When she returned to the lounge area, she found Will sprawled out on the large settee, one leg crossed over the other and a bottle of beer in his hand. Her stomach did a stupid flip-flop as she stared at him. It was totally illogical, not to mention stupid, of her to be attracted to him. First of all, he didn't seem the least bit attracted to her. And second, he was just a little too "me Tarzan, you Jane" to suit Gwen.

"It's raining," he said. "If the winds get rough, we'll probably be rocking most of the night."

Completely ignoring his comment, Gwen asked, "How can you be certain we'll be able to follow the *Sun Dancer*'s path?"

"Straight to the point." He saluted her with the bottle, then downed a hefty swig, emptying half the contents.

"It's not that I'm ungrateful for your help, it's just that I feel as if we're on a wild-goose chase and are accomplishing nothing."

"If any of our operatives had gotten lucky enough to find the *Sun Dancer* while it was still in port, they might have been able to put a tracking device on board." Will paused. "No questions?"

She shook her head. "Go on."

"It's possible that might still happen."

She nodded.

"You're wondering how come if an operative could board the *Sun Dancer,* why wouldn't one of our guys simply detain the ship and all aboard." He waited for her comment, but when she said nothing, he continued. "My contacts—Dundee's contacts—are independent operatives. They work outside the law, and neither they nor I have any authority in these various countries, so our guys have to be careful not to get caught doing something blatantly illegal."

"Are you telling me that you—that the Dundee Agency has contacts everywhere, on every little island in the Caribbean?"

"No, I'm not saying that. We have contacts on several major islands, but our contacts have contacts who have contacts everywhere on earth."

A tight knot formed in the pit of Gwen's stomach. "When you said your contacts, you meant just that, didn't

you? These contacts, these operatives aren't all Dundee's."
She knew before she posed the question to him, but she had
to ask, needed to hear him say it. "What did you do before
you became a private investigator for the Dundee Agency?"

Will finished off his beer. "I worked for the government."

"Doing what?"

"I worked in the field," he said vaguely.

"Like the CIA or something?"

"There's another reason none of our contacts would try
to detain the *Sun Dancer*," Will said as if she hadn't asked
about his former line of work. "We don't know what Mick
McGuire and Molly Esteban might do. They could easily
fight back, and one of the other passengers could get hurt.
Or they could take the others hostage. It's better for your
father, Jordan Elders and Cheryl Kress if we can separate
them from Mick and Molly before taking any kind of action."

"How do we know that my father and Jordan and Cheryl
aren't already hostages?"

"We don't."

"In any case, their lives are in danger."

"Yeah, I'm afraid so."

The door lock clicked. Cheryl Kress backed up against
the headboard of the bed in her small stateroom, a room in
which she was kept confined whenever the yacht came
into port. Only when the *Sun Dancer* was out at sea was
she allowed any freedom.

"I've brought your dinner." Jordan Elders entered the
room, a cloth-covered tray in his hands.

"I'm not hungry." She glared at him, hating him almost
as much as she hated Tori for getting her into this situation. Here she was trapped aboard this boat with a crazy

old coot, his assistant and his sleazy investors, while Tori was back in Puerto Nuevo safe and sound. Tori should be the one here, because it was Tori who had a thing for Jordan Elders, Tori who had planned to stow away on the boat and surprise Jordan.

"Come on, Cheryl, don't pout. You have to eat something."

"I'm not pouting. I'm pissed. I'm angry. I'm outraged."

Jordan placed the tray at the foot of the bed. "Look, I'm sorry we can't put you ashore so you can go home, but it's like Captain McGuire pointed out, we can't take any chance that you'll involve the police, maybe even claim we kidnapped you. If that happened, it would put an end to our voyage to find The Professor's island."

"I've sworn a thousand times over that I won't tell a soul, that I won't go to the police. Besides, who would believe me? I think you're all as crazy as that nut-job you call The Professor. Whoever heard of such nonsense as an island where people live to be two hundred and are never sick?" Cheryl laughed sarcastically.

"If you knew Dr. Arnell the way I know him, you'd believe," Jordan said. "He's seen this island. He's been there. When he was twenty, he spent three weeks with these people."

"Yeah, sure he did. And when I was a baby, my parents put me in a rocket ship and sent me to earth before our home planet exploded." Cheryl lifted her arms and wiggled her fingers at Jordan. "That's why I have supernatural powers."

"Laugh all you want, but when we rediscover The Professor's island and are able to bring back a miracle plant to the world, you'll understand why this trip is so important, far more important than any personal concerns you might have."

Cheryl screamed. "I'm on a boat to Hell with a bunch of psychos! Get out and leave me alone." Swinging her right hand across the foot of the bed, she knocked the tray onto the floor. Food splattered across the carpet as the plate overturned, and the open can of cola sprayed over the hem of the bedspread.

"Damn it, Cheryl, look what you've done." Jordan stared at the mess she'd made. "Why can't you look at this trip as a great adventure, one you can tell your children and grandchildren about? You realize that we could be famous, right along with The Professor, once we give the world—"

"Oh, shut up. You're an idiot, you know that, don't you?"

Cheryl eased off the side of the bed and stepped around the toppled tray and scattered food. Jordan Elders glared at her as if she were a disobedient child and he her stern parent. She marched right up to him and stared him in the face. What Tori ever saw in this geek was beyond her. He was tall, thin and gangly, with a mop of curly brown hair and a pair of— she studied him more closely—a pair of green eyes hidden behind his nerdy glasses. He wasn't exactly heartthrob material, but then, Tori always did go for the brainy types. Her last boyfriend had been majoring in chemical engineering.

"If you want to get rich, you don't have to try to find some nonexistent youth-serum plant," Cheryl said. "Get me off this boat and back to Puerto Nuevo or the States and my dad will give you any amount of money you want. A million dollars!"

He stared at her as she'd been speaking a language foreign to him. "You think I'm interested in getting rich? I want to make history, to be part of a group that will give the entire world this marvelous gift—a long, healthy life for every man, woman and child."

Frowning, uncertain if she could believe he was on the up-and-up, Cheryl shook her head and grunted. "Good grief. Are you for real?"

"Look, I'll help you clean up this mess." He knelt on the floor. "Then I'll bring you a sandwich later. But you have to promise you'll behave yourself. You can't keep causing so much trouble. I don't have time to babysit you."

Gritting her teeth, Cheryl balled her hands into fists and groaned. "You don't have to babysit me. Just let me go."

He turned the tray upright, set the plate on the tray and took the napkin and wiped the food from the carpet. "If you hadn't sneaked aboard the *Sun Dancer* before we left Puerto Nuevo, you wouldn't be here now. So you have no one to blame but yourself."

"Oh, I have someone to blame all right—Tori and you."

"How am I to blame? It's not my fault that Tori misunderstood our relationship and thought I was serious about her. You should have talked her out of following us to the marina and trying to stow away."

"No, what I should have done was let her follow you by herself, instead of tagging along and trying to keep her out of trouble." Cheryl went into the bathroom, got a towel and then dropped down on her knees to mop up the spilled cola. Her gaze connected with Jordan's. "If I'd gone back to the villa and let her chase after you all by herself, then she'd be the one stuck here with you now and not me."

Jordan lifted the tray as he stood. Cheryl got up, dumped the damp hand towel on the tray and huffed.

"Do you still not remember what happened after you and Tori boarded the *Sun Dancer?*" Jordan asked.

Cheryl shook her head. "We followed you and The Professor to the marina and saw you two go aboard the *Sun*

Dancer. We boarded the yacht so that Tori could ask you to take her with you. I knew you'd say no, and that's why I was with her, to be there when you broke her heart."

"You told me that you remembered hearing voices and Tori telling you to hide. Do you remember anything else?"

"I remember hiding in a large storage compartment on the cockpit and waiting and waiting. I'm not sure if I fell asleep or passed out. The next thing I remember was that the yacht was leaving the marina. When I came out of the storage bin, Captain McGuire saw me and dragged me to my feet. Then I screamed, and the next thing I knew, you and The Professor and Molly were all there and I fainted dead away."

"Why do you think Tori went back to shore and left you?"

"I don't know, but when I see her again, we're going to have it out."

A long, drawn-out moment of silence vibrated between them as Cheryl and Jordan gazed at each other. She didn't think she'd ever seen such green eyes, a blue green, almost turquoise.

Snap out of it, she told herself. This guy is not only a nerd, but he's crazy. Don't start thinking of him as a nice guy, as someone you could actually like. But she could pretend to like him, couldn't she? There weren't many guys she couldn't wrap around her little finger and make them do whatever she wanted. Why should Jordan be any different? She could play nice, and maybe, just maybe, he'd help her get off this damn boat and back to civilization.

"I'll bring you a sandwich later." Jordan opened the door and walked into the salon.

"Jordan?"

He glanced over his shoulder. "Yes?"

"I'm sorry I've been such a brat. And if you bring me a sandwich later, I promise I'll eat it."

When he smiled, he was almost cute.

After she'd eaten a bite of supper, Gwen excused herself and went into the small guest stateroom. She took a shower and donned her cotton sleep shirt with Huntsville Botanical Gardens imprinted across the front and a screen-printed photo of the rose garden on the back. Then she settled into the surprisingly comfortable bed and meditated for a good ten minutes until she felt relaxed and drowsy. She had begun meditating years ago, learning the technique from a friend who, like she, had difficulty winding down at the end of the day.

The wind moaned, almost like a woman weeping, as it bombarded the yacht, rocking it none too gently. Think of yourself in a big cradle, being rocked to sleep.

Just then, lightning danced in the sky outside the porthole and booming thunder announced the storm had hit. Rain poured down, the sound blending with the wind, becoming an unnerving roar.

Gwen shot up in bed. There was no way she could sleep. She could go into the salon and fix herself a drink, just as Will had after dinner. Maybe that would help her sleep.

After easing open her stateroom door, she crept into the salon, tiptoeing on bare feet across the carpet. The room lay in semidarkness, lit only by the light from her stateroom and the dim light Will had left on over the sink. As she made her way across the salon, she thought she heard a noise.

"Can't sleep?" Will asked, his voice coming from the curved settee on the opposite side of the salon.

Gwen gasped and jumped. "You scared me half to death."

"Sorry."

"What are you doing sitting in here in the dark? I thought you went to bed."

"I did, but I couldn't sleep."

"All that wind and rain and thunder are pretty noisy," Gwen said.

"Hmm... Why don't you come over here and sit down. We can pass the time by swapping old war stories."

Gwen turned on more lights. Will grunted.

"Turn those off," he told her.

She looked at him and noticed he was sitting there bare-chested and barefoot, wearing only his jeans. His chest was as richly tanned as his face and arms, and quite muscular. He hadn't shaved since they'd left Puerto Nuevo, so a light-brown beard stubble gave him a rough, rakish quality that unsettled her.

She turned off the lights and walked across the salon. When she stood over him, he patted the large leather settee. She sat beside him but made sure there was several feet between them.

"When I was a kid, I used to sit on our back porch at night, after everybody else was asleep," he said. "I liked the dark, the solitude. I had to share a room with my brothers, so there was never any privacy and hardly ever any quiet. If Mama wasn't fussing at us for fighting and roughhousing all the time, the old man was issuing orders and reprimanding us for not being tough enough."

"I had my own room," Gwen said. "And my mother was a very quiet, easygoing person. We were very close. And being an only child living with a single parent, there were times when I longed for a brother or a sister."

"I guess it's only human to want what you don't have."

"My father lost his entire family the summer he was twenty. His parents and younger brother. They had rented a yacht and were sailing the Caribbean when a freak storm came up. Everyone was lost, except Daddy."

"Was that when he discovered his mythical island?"

"Yes. My mother always said that losing his family that way did something to him, sort of warped him, so he invented this outrageous tale of an island where people live to be two hundred and are never sick."

"Did you ever think there might be some truth to his tale?" Will turned sideways and faced her in the semidarkness.

"Sure. When I was a little girl, I believed everything my father told me. And then when I was older, I actually went with him on two of his quests to rediscover his island. I was eighteen the first time and nineteen the second time. Even though I didn't believe in his island, I wanted to. It was during those summer voyages with him that I learned how truly obsessed he was with finding this island. My mother had tried to warn me that nothing and no one meant more to him than his totally irrational dream of finding the island and bringing the Fountain of Youth plant to the world."

Will stretched out his arm behind her head and leaned toward her. Gwen's breath caught in her throat. He was too close. She could feel the heat coming off his partially naked body.

"Is that why you hide behind your brains and your baggy clothes and your clean-scrubbed face and—" he lifted a thick strand of hair from her shoulder and slipped his fingers through it as he let it drift back into place "—frumpy hairdo? Because you don't ever want to get involved with a man and have him disappoint you the way your father disappointed your mother and you?"

Gwen felt trapped by the gentle touch of his hand on her shoulder. "I'm not hiding behind anything. I'm just not the frilly, girly type whose main objective in life is to attract men."

Will ran his hand down her arm, over her waist and settled on her hip. She sucked in a deep, concerned breath.

"I got a glimpse of your nightshirt," he told her. "Don't you own anything the least bit sexy and feminine?"

"I dress for comfort, especially what I sleep in."

"I made a bet with myself not long after we met that you probably wear white cotton panties and bras. Am I right?"

Gwen's heartbeat accelerated alarmingly. He had no right to ask her something so personal, so private. But the very thought of him being curious about her underwear sent quivers through her body.

"That's none of your business," she finally managed to tell him.

He inched her nightshirt up her leg enough so that he could slip his hand beneath and caress her hip. She should protest, but somehow she couldn't move, couldn't speak, could barely breathe.

"I don't know what color they are," Will said, rubbing his hand from her hip to her belly. "But they're definitely cotton."

When he chuckled, she lifted her hand, intending to slap him. She had never slapped a man, not even her ex-husband, and he had broken her young and foolish heart. But she wanted to hurt Will Pierce, wanted to make him stop laughing at her. He caught her by the wrist just as her hand neared his cheek.

Before she realized what was happening, he yanked her

forward until she toppled onto his lap. Startled and gasping for air, she didn't expect what happened next. He kissed her. A long, slow, tongue-thrusting kiss that ignited a fire in her belly. He didn't touch her while he ravaged her mouth, except for his hand, manacled tightly around her wrist. Unable to stop herself, she responded, kissing him back with equal passion.

Finally, when they came up for air, Will released his hold on her wrist and gazed deeply into her eyes.

"You kiss pretty damn good for a brainy, frumpy, no-frills gal," Will said.

She eased away from him and stood. "I do a lot of things pretty damn good."

Will chuckled. "Anything else you'd care to demonstrate."

"Not for you, Mr. Pierce, now or ever."

When she tromped across the salon and into her state-room, she heard his low, rumbling chuckle. Arrogant bastard!

Chapter 6

Gwen lay on the silk sheets, which were smooth and cool to the touch. As if captured inside a transparent bubble, Will and she touched and kissed and explored each other until every nerve in her body screamed for release. Will lifted himself up and over her, then took her with gentle force. Whimpering with pure pleasure, she grasped hold of his shoulders and gave herself over to the uncontrollable hunger she could not deny.

She climaxed with earth-shattering intensity.

Still quivering with the aftershocks of her release, Gwen opened her eyes and realized that she was alone in the round-edged bunk bed nestled inside the belly of the *Foot-loose*. Not fully awake, she ran her hand over the cotton sheets and felt terribly alone.

Will had not shared her bed. He hadn't made love to her. It had all been a dream. A sensual dream. An erotic dream.

Dear Lord, she'd never dreamed about making love with a man, any man. And she'd certainly never had an orgasm while she was dreaming.

This was bad, really bad. She kicked back the covers, hopped out of bed and went straight into the tiny bathroom. She couldn't allow herself to get hung up on Will Pierce. The very idea was totally ridiculous. She didn't like his type—swaggering macho he-man. Even though she understood that gentle, intellectual dreamers like her father, and sweet, nonthreatening types like her ex-husband, were not necessarily loyal, caring and steadfast, she would never sink so low as to jump in the sack with the first horny Neanderthal who asked her what kind of underwear she was wearing.

He hadn't just asked. He'd found out for himself. Remembering the feel of Will's big hand caressing her hip and belly sent shivers through Gwen.

No. Absolutely, positively no! She was not going to have sex with Will. She didn't have brief, meaningless flings. It wasn't her style—not in her nature.

By the time she finished showering and had dressed for the day, Gwen felt much better, confident that she could handle her silly attraction to Will. *For heaven's sake, I don't even like him!*

When she emerged from her stateroom, she found the salon empty. Was Will still asleep? Suddenly she realized the cruiser was moving. Had she been so preoccupied with her sex dream that she'd missed that all-important fact?

She climbed the steps leading up to the deck and emerged into bright sunlight and the smell of the salty ocean. Will sat on the bench seat at the helm, shaded by

the arched hardtop. She sat down beside him. He glanced
at her, smiled and nodded.

"Good morning, sleepyhead."

"How long have you been up?" she asked grumpily.
"And how long have we been out at sea?" Looking all
around her, she saw nothing but the turquoise blue of the
sea and the azure of the sky, the two meeting and melding
on the horizon.

"I've been up a couple of hours and we set sail about
thirty minutes ago."

"Why didn't you wake me?"

"I thought you needed your beauty sleep," he said in a
teasing voice.

"Ha-ha. Very funny."

"Ah, come on, brown eyes, don't you have a sense of
humor?"

"Maybe women who wear white cotton bras and panties
don't have senses of humor. Ever think of that?"

"Nah, can't say that I have, but then, I don't know many
of those women. The gals I know usually wear the black-
and-red and hot-pink silky stuff. Either that or they don't
bother with underwear at all."

"I walked right into that one, didn't I?" Gwen looked
pointedly ahead, determined not to make eye contact with
Will. "Exactly where are we going?"

"St. Mallon." He nodded toward his covered metal mug
perched in the cup holder. "If you want to do something to
help, how about making a fresh pot of coffee and refilling
that for me."

"Why are we going to St. Mallon?" she asked, ignoring
his request.

"I was in radio contact with Dundee's this morning. An

operative on St. Mallon said that the *Sun Dancer* dropped anchor there late yesterday."

"They'll be gone by the time we get there."

"Probably, but my contact said he'll try to find out where they're headed. It'll help if we know whether they're heading straight for Bermuda or if they have another stop or two on the way. If we hear something before we get to St. Mallon, we can keep going to their next destination and possibly catch up with them."

Gwen removed his mug from the cup holder and stood. "I'll make fresh coffee." As she crossed the cockpit, she paused and asked, "Any other womanly duties you'd like for me to do? Cook breakfast maybe?"

"Are you offering to cook something for me?"

"I'm hungry. You're hungry. I don't see why not."

"Thanks."

"You're welcome." *Okay,* Gwen told herself, *maybe if you're pleasant to Will, he'll be pleasant to you. There's no need to argue. We can be friendly without being friends. Or lovers.*

An hour later, after sharing a breakfast of coffee, scrambled eggs and banana muffins, they docked at St. Mallon. Will's contact, whom she suspected was a freelance operative he'd known during his years as a government agent, met them at the marina.

"Molly Esteban made a drop this morning, then they headed out." The man—whose name, she suspected, even Will didn't know—spoke with a British accent. "They're probably going to Baccara next."

"Why Baccara?" Gwen asked.

Will gave her a withering glare, silently reminding her that he'd told her to keep quiet, to let him do all the talking.

Ignoring Gwen's question, Will asked, "Did you see anyone on board, other than the Esteban woman and Captain McGuire?"

"An old man with snowy white hair and a curly-haired boy."

"You didn't see a young redheaded woman?"

"No. The only woman I saw was Molly Esteban."

"Thanks."

As soon as Will's contact left them, Will grabbed Gwen's arm, turned her around forcefully and marched her toward the *Footloose*.

"Why hasn't someone arrested Molly Esteban?" Gwen asked, keeping in step with Will as she tugged to free her manacled arm. "Or at the very least, why haven't the authorities detained her?"

Will released his tenacious hold on her but didn't slow his pace as he responded in an aggravated tone. "The contacts that Dundee's uses often work on both sides of the law. They're not in a position to report crimes, even if they're eyewitnesses to them."

"Then why doesn't Dundee's—"

Will groaned. "You ask too many damn questions."

"So Dundee's uses unscrupulous people for undercover work when it's necessary. I might not approve, but I do understand. And as for asking questions, if I don't ask, how can I learn?"

When Will didn't respond, she kept quiet until they were halfway to the boat, then asked, "How do you know you can trust that man? How can you be sure the *Sun Dancer* is really headed to Baccara? He wouldn't even tell us why they'd go there."

"I trust him as much as I trust any Dundee contact. As

for him lying to us—he'd have no reason to lie. And Baccara is the last island north of here before you hit the wide expanse of the Atlantic on the way to Bermuda. If Molly and Mick are delivering drugs, they'd hit Baccara for sure."

"Oh, I see. So, I take it that we're off on our wild-goose chase again."

"Yeah, and the *Sun Dancer* has less than an hour's head start," Will said. "It sure would help if we knew exactly where they planned to dock."

"You mean your contact couldn't find out that small detail for you?"

"Stop being a pain in the ass, will you?" He urged her into motion.

She kept pace beside him, all the while wondering why on earth she didn't just give up on finding her father and go back to her safe, contented life in Huntsville.

Because her father's life was in danger and the old fool hasn't got sense enough to know it!

But definitely not because she wanted to stay near Will Pierce.

Molly Esteban looked at herself in the mirror. *Face it, you've got ten good years left, at most.* She needed to be socking away some money now, while she was still young enough to get by on her looks. God knew, she didn't have much else going for her. And she wasn't exactly getting rich hooking up with losers like Mick McGuire. But for now he'd have to do. Why couldn't The Professor have been a rich old codger instead of a certifiable kook? The guy was crazy about her. She'd seen to that. Lucky for her, he could still get it up. At least occasionally. If there was one thing Molly knew how to do, it was make a man happy in the sack.

If Emery was wealthy, she'd marry him. After all, at seventy, how long could he live, especially with her around to give his heart a workout on a regular basis?

"You look good enough to eat." Mick came up behind her, nuzzled her neck and groped her boobs.

Shrugging him off, she scolded, "You can't be doing stuff like that. Not now. What if Emery or Jordan came down here and saw you?"

"They're all on deck," Mick said, grinning suggestively. "How about a quickie, baby doll?"

"No! And I wish you'd stop asking. We've got a strictly business arrangement for now. I'm The Professor's girl-friend until we dump him and the other two in Bermuda." She straightened her low-cut, sleeveless shirt where Mick had messed it up, then ran her fingers through her short black hair and headed for the steps leading up to the deck.

Mick caught her halfway up, whirled her around and gave her a hungry once-over with his heated gaze. "After screwing around with that old goat, you'll be hot as a fire-cracker when you're finally with a real man."

"That old goat rented this boat for us," she reminded Mick. "And having him along as a front for us is working out just fine, isn't it?"

"So far, but what happens when we finish our deliveries? If it was just The Professor and his assistant, there wouldn't be a problem, but what about the little redhead?"

"I don't know, damn it, but you are not going to kill her—" Molly lowered her voice to a whisper "—not the way you killed that other girl."

"If I'd known there was another one hiding out on this boat, I'd have gotten rid of them both at the same time," Mick said.

"As long as she believes we're Emery's friends, just investors in his hare-brained scheme, she won't be a problem. We can just unload her in Bermuda with Emery and Jordan."

"Are you really that stupid?"

She glared at him. "Yeah, maybe I am, so why don't you explain it to me."

"Baby doll, the old man, the kid and the redhead—we're going to have to dump them overboard some night before we reach Bermuda."

Baccara was the capital city of the tiny island nation of Latille, a tropical paradise with a rotting underbelly of crime and corruption. Will had been here once before, nearly five years ago. Even before he and Gwen stepped ashore at the marina, his gut tightened. He possessed a sixth sense when it came to trouble. That's why he'd slipped the 9 mm Ruger under his lightweight jacket.

"Are we meeting someone here?" Gwen asked.

"Not here. I have to go into town to meet our guy."

"You mean *we* have to go into town."

"You're staying here at the marina. There's a halfway decent restaurant where you can eat lunch and—"

"I'm not staying here. I'm going with you."

He took her shoulders gently. "It's too dangerous for you to go with me. The part of town where I'm meeting my contact isn't safe, especially not for—"

"This guy is going to take you to where the *Sun Dancer* is anchored. If you go without me, what excuse will you use when you approach Mick McGuire? If I'm with you, I can tell him the truth, that I'm The Professor's daughter and tracked him down to make sure he's all right."

"I shouldn't have told you that the *Sun Dancer* is here." Dropping his hands from her shoulders, Will huffed. "There's a good chance McGuire killed Tori Boyd and that she wasn't the first person he's killed. The guy's dangerous. I know how to deal with dangerous people, but if you're there, you'll be in the way. I'll have to take care of you."

"I can take care of myself."

"You *think* you can."

"If you try to leave me, I'll follow you."

"Yeah, yeah."

He could easily give Gwen the slip, but then she'd be wandering Baccara alone. Because, no doubt, she'd try to find the *Sun Dancer* on her own.

"Okay, you're going with me," he said, knowing a no-win situation when it slapped him in the face. "But you will do what I tell you to do without question. Understand?"

"No, I don't understand, but I'll do it. I'll do whatever you tell me to do."

He eyed her skeptically.

"Cross my heart," she told him.

"Stay at my side, keep your mouth shut and don't do anything unless I tell you to. Can you handle that this time?"

She stared daggers at him but kept silent. He took that as a yes.

"Why did Mick say we were stopping again?" Jordan Elders asked The Professor.

"He and Molly need to transfer some funds," Dr. Arnell replied as he sipped leisurely on his rum and cola.

"I don't understand why they didn't take care of everything before we left Puerto Nuevo. We're wasting a lot of time—"

"Actually, if my calculations are correct, we're right on time. These little delays have been no problem, because if we headed due north earlier, we would have been too soon. As of tomorrow, we should be able to find the island. It was precisely fifty years ago tomorrow that I washed ashore there."

"Professor, I know your theory about the island being hidden by some sort of cloaking device is as plausible as the belief in the plant that can produce longevity and good health to the people of the island, but it's totally illogical."

"I've spent the better part of the past forty-five years searching for the island," Dr. Arnell said. "I've borrowed money, acquired grants under false pretenses and used up all my own resources to fund expeditions into the vast unknown between the West Indies and Bermuda. If the island is visible at all times, then why haven't I been able to find it? Why has no one else been able to find it?"

Because the island doesn't exist. Jordan wanted to believe in the island, in the miracle plant that grew there, because he longed to be a part of the discovery that could help mankind. And because he not only respected Dr. Arnell, but he genuinely loved the old man. The Professor had taken him under his wing when he'd been his student, had become like a father to him. Without Dr. Arnell's help, he would never have gotten the scholarships to finish his studies and go on to graduate school. If nothing else, he owed the old man his loyalty on what could be his last great adventure.

"You aren't beginning to doubt me, are you, Jordan?"

"No, sir. I want you to find your island and I want to be at your side when that happens."

The Professor lifted his wrinkled hand and clasped Jordan's shoulder. "As soon as Molly and Mick return from their little errand, we will go back to sea, due north. I re-

member my father setting a course straight for Bermuda.
If we retrace the journey I took with my parents and brother
all those years ago, I'm certain we'll find my island again.
Fifty years to the day."

*Fifty years to the day. The Professor now believed that
the mythical island was visible only a few weeks every fifty
years. What nonsense!*

Or was it?

Gwen had never ridden a motorcycle and she wasn't
finding this experience something she'd ever want to
repeat. Will had explained that they needed fast, reliable
transportation to whip down back alleys, up on sidewalks
and down dirt paths. Knowing absolutely nothing about
motorcycles, she had no idea what make or model she was
at present sitting astride behind Will, but her guess was
that the monstrosity was far from new. It smelled awful,
sounded awful and resembled a rebuilt piece of junk.

Downtown Baccara looked a great deal like most Caribbean cities, and once again, she was missing everything of
any interest because they were continuing their frantic wild-
goose chase. Only this time, if luck was on their side, they'd
make it to the *Sun Dancer* before she set sail again. They
whizzed by groves of banana trees and fields of sugar cane.

When the scenery changed dramatically from what
she'd seen at their other ports of call, a sense of foreboding
crept up her spine. Shacks and dilapidated shanties
dotted the roadside.

Gwen hung on tightly around Will's waist, her heartbeat
accelerating as Will slowed the cycle, exited the street and
crept up a back alley. She felt open and exposed, knowing
there was no protection between them and the sinister

ugliness around them. They weren't even wearing helmets.
A mixture of odors assaulted her when Will stopped and
parked the cycle behind a ramshackle house. Rotting gar-
bage. Stagnant water. Human waste.

God, she was going to be sick.

"Wish you'd stayed back at the marina?" Will got off
the motorcycle, then turned and helped her dismount.

She couldn't speak, afraid that if she opened her mouth
she'd vomit on the spot.

"You look green around the gills," Will said. "If you're
going to throw up, do it now and get it over with."

Unsympathetic bastard! At that precise moment, Gwen
hated him for being so smugly superior, for not being nau-
seated himself and for not giving a damn that she was.

*Okay, Gwen, stop feeling sorry for yourself. You're a big
girl. Deal with it. You can't blame Will. He did advise you
to stay at the marina.*

Being here in this godforsaken, rancid alleyway was her
own damn fault. And the fact that she was on the verge of
upchucking was something Will could do nothing about
one way or the other.

"I'll be fine," she said, before covering her nose and
mouth to shield them from the stench.

"Shh…" he cautioned her.

A slender, ragged figure appeared as if from out of
nowhere. He spoke English with a hint of an accent, his
voice low and gruff.

"You got the money?" he asked, his gaze darting in
every direction.

Will pulled a couple of hundred dollar bills from his
pants pocket and offered it to the man. He grabbed the cash,
inspected it and stuffed it into his shirt pocket.

"I'll show you where the *Sun Dancer* is docked. That's all your money buys you."

Will nodded. "That's good enough."

Gwen's heartbeat quickened, and uneasiness shivered through her. The man, the place, the tension radiating from Will combined to issue her a warning. She was in the middle of something she knew nothing about, something dangerous.

The dirty little man eyed Gwen. "You should not bring your woman with you. For another hundred dollars, I can take her back to town and guard her for you."

"My woman goes where I go," Will said in a voice that allowed no argument.

They followed their Baccara contact, the first one that had to be paid in cash, as he turned the corner and led them along a back street. Will rolled the motorcycle along with them as they left the alley, until their guide mounted a black Moped. When Will got on the cycle, Gwen positioned herself behind him and wrapped her arms around his waist. Will's two-hundred-dollar contact led them along a dirt path, through a weed-infested area of high grass and down to the backwaters from the nearby lagoon. The guy made a U-turn, pointed northeast and zoomed back in the direction from which they had come, leaving Will and Gwen alone. Will parked the motorcycle behind a stand of tall trees, then helped her off.

"Where are we going?" she whispered.

"Northeast," Will told her in an equally low voice. "My guess is that there's a small harbor nearby, probably one used by smugglers and other unsavory characters."

Gwen groaned silently, wondering if, in her own way, she wasn't as crazy as her father. After all, here she was, in way over her head, and all because she was trying to save her father from his own madness. What was she doing here, with someone who seemed perfectly at home playing spy games in the wilds of a lawless little island?

When they had gone about a quarter of a mile, Will stopped abruptly, shoved her behind him and listened intently. Voices! But she couldn't understand the conversation, was unable to distinguish what language the men were speaking.

Following Will's lead, she crept alongside a chainlink fence that separated the wooded area they'd just come through from what appeared to be a small marina. In the distance she could see four docked boats. As they made their way closer, she caught a glimpse of two burly men deep in conversation.

Will turned to her, put his finger to his lips warning her to be silent, then reached inside his jacket and drew a gun from the back waistband of his jeans. Gwen gasped. He glared at her.

"Hold up there," a deep, threatening voice called to them.

Will whipped around, one hand holding his weapon, the other nudging her behind him, and faced the two approaching strangers. Gwen thought her heart would beat right out of her chest. Cold sweat popped out on her face and moistened her hands.

"What do you want?" one of the men asked.

"I'm looking for a fellow named McGuire," Will said.

"What do you want with him?"

"Personal business," Will said.

"This is a private marina," the taller of the two dark-haired, bronze-skinned men told him in English with no accent. "How did you get here? Who brought you?" Both men eyed the gun in Will's hand.

"I don't want any trouble. If McGuire's here, I want to talk to him. That's all."

"You going to shoot one of us?" the shorter man asked. "Bad idea. You shoot one of us, the other will kill you and take your woman."

Both men came toward them. Gwen clung to Will's arm, shivering, trying to think what she could do to help get them out of this situation. But before she had a glimmer of an idea, all hell broke loose. Will shot one man in the head. He dropped instantly. Gwen's mouth flew open, but she stopped herself just short of screaming. The other man lunged forward, barreling into Will. The two struggled, rolling around on the ground, fighting for the weapon.

While Gwen stood by, feeling helpless, not knowing what to do to help Will, the gun positioned between the two fighters went off.

Oh, God. Will. Will!

Chapter 7

Gwen held her breath for a split second, then rushed forward to where Will lay beneath the burly guard. She needed to find something to use to knock this guy in the head. If he'd shot Will—

Suddenly, only seconds after the first shot, another exploded between the two prone men. Gwen hollered, an involuntary reaction. Before she had a chance to search for a weapon of some kind, the man on top of Will lurched upward, then fell sideways and rolled over onto his back. She stared down at Will, at his bloody hand clutching his gun. Huge red spots covered his tan shirt, from belly to shoulder. Splatters of crimson dotted his jeans, his arms and his face.

Grunting, Will lifted himself into a sitting position. The men they had heard talking when they first arrived began shouting.

Gwen leaned down over Will. "Are you hurt?" Had he

been shot? Or did all that blood belong to the dead man lying beside Will?

Will came to his feet, wincing as he tensed his left shoulder. Then he grabbed her arm and said, "We have to get out of here, now!"

As they backtracked their steps, Gwen could barely keep up with Will. Twice he had to slow down until she caught up. When they reached the parked motorcycle, Gwen jumped on behind him as he revved the motor. Holding on for dear life, she glanced over her shoulder as they sped through the underbrush. She caught glimpses of two men chasing them on foot, but by the time the cycle hit the dirt path, she could no longer see anyone behind them.

"We've lost them," she shouted over the roar of the cycle's noisy engine.

"Not hardly," Will shouted back at her.

That's when she heard a vehicle bearing down on them. When she looked back, she saw a tattered old Jeep tear through the woods and onto the dirt road.

"Hang on," Will told her.

She clung to him, all the while praying like she'd never prayed in her life. Their pursuers fired at them, bullets sailing all around them, one hitting the cycle's back bumper. Will zig-zagged the motorcycle back and forth, then suddenly formed the figure eight by back tracking, swirling around, crisscrossing, and then, when the Jeep finally turned and headed toward them, he went in the opposite direction. By the time the Jeep caught up with them, they had reached the main paved road into Baccara.

Although their hunters ceased firing when they reached civilization, the Jeep continued following them, all the way into downtown Baccara. Once among the traffic and the congested streets, Will managed to maneuver them in and out, around and about, until Gwen had no idea in which direction they were headed. But she didn't care because she hadn't caught even a glimpse of the Jeep for the past few blocks.

Will pulled into an alley behind a hotel, parked the cycle and got off. Gwen didn't wait for his assistance. By the time he held out his hand, she was already on her feet.

"I need you to go into the hotel and ask them to call a taxi for you," Will told her. "I'll wait outside until the taxi arrives, then I'll get into the backseat right after you."

"You want me to get a taxi?" Her voice quivered.

He grasped her chin with his thumb and forefinger. "Take a deep breath."

She did.

"Listen carefully," he told her. "We're safe for now. I lost those guys. But we need to leave Baccara as soon as possible. If anyone sees me looking like this—" he glanced at his bloody clothes and skin "—they might call the local police. We don't want that happening."

"Because you…you killed two men."

"Yeah, because I killed two men."

Gwen nodded. "I'll get us a taxi."

He squeezed her chin, then released her. "Good girl."

Breathing in and out slowly, taking deep, calming breaths, Gwen walked out of the alley and onto the street in front of the hotel. Fixing her loosened ponytail, she straightened her shoulders, walked into the hotel lobby and went directly toward the desk clerk.

What language did they speak in Baccara? Spanish? French? English. Think, Gwen, think…. English. They speak English.

She marched up to the desk clerk, forced a cautious smile and said, "I need a taxi, please."

"Yes, ma'am," the clerk replied and made a quick phone call before informing her that the taxi would arrive shortly.

Barely keeping her smile in place, she nodded, said thank-you and walked outside where she waited in front of the hotel until the taxi arrived, approximately five minutes later. While she waited, she glanced toward the alley once, but didn't see Will.

He's there, she told herself. *He's just staying out of sight.*

When the cabby got out, he stared at Gwen, then asked, "You do not have luggage?"

"No. No luggage."

He opened the taxi door for her. She paused, glanced over her shoulder, didn't see Will and hesitated.

"Is something wrong?" the driver asked.

"No, I'm fine."

She slid into the backseat. The driver rounded the trunk. By the time he slid into the front seat, the back door flew open and Will scooted into the seat beside Gwen.

The driver swiveled around, stared at Will and asked, "Is this man with you?"

"Yes." Gwen barely managed to gulp out the word.

Will issued the driver orders, telling him where to take them—back to the marina where the *Footloose* was docked.

Gwen reached over and grabbed Will's hand. He squeezed her hand tightly.

The driver started the taxi and moved into afternoon traffic. On the drive to the marina, he kept glancing in his rearview mirror, no doubt wondering why Will's clothes were soaked in blood.

When they reached the marina, Will got out and all but

yanked Gwen from the taxi. While she waited, he pulled out several bills that she suspected were hundreds and handed them to the driver.

"You haven't seen us," Will said to the driver.

"No, sir, I have not seen an American woman with a man covered in blood."

Will gave the man a another bill. The driver grinned, then got in his taxi and drove off down the road.

Will clutched Gwen's elbow. "We need to leave Baccara as quickly as possible."

"And go where?"

"Out to sea. We'll drop anchor once we're out far enough, and then I'll plot our course for tomorrow."

"What about the *Sun Dancer?*"

"My guess is they'll head for Bermuda first thing in the morning."

"What were all those gunshots about?" Jordan asked Mick McGuire the minute he and Molly returned from their trip ashore.

"Nothing for us to worry about," Mick said. "It seems they caught a couple of people trying to rob one of the boats anchored here."

"They caught them and called the police," Molly added, a wide smile deepening the wrinkles around her eyes.

"See, Jordan, I told you it was nothing that concerned us." Dr. Arnell patted Jordan on the back, then opened his arms to welcome Molly.

Hugging The Professor, she stood on tiptoe and kissed his wrinkled cheek. "Did you miss me, darling?"

"I always miss you when you're away from me, but I know you and Mick had business to attend to." He glanced at Mick. "Are we all set now? Do we have everything we need for our trip?"

"We're all set." Mick winked at Jordan. "Are you ready to head into the Triangle and rediscover The Professor's island?"

Jordan didn't especially like Mick and sometimes got the feeling the guy was making fun of him and The Professor, but Mick was a seasoned captain and seemed perfectly willing to take them into the Devil's Triangle, in search of the mythical island. Besides that, Mick and Molly had put up part of the capital to fund this expedition.

As giddy as a child on Christmas morning, The Professor beamed with happiness. "If we leave in the morning, then tomorrow we can sail directly into the Triangle, straight to my island."

Mick grinned. "That's what we're hoping for, but it's a big ocean out there and there are no guarantees. We could wind up with no choice but to go on to Bermuda."

"No, no, that won't happen." Dr. Arnell slipped his arm around Molly's slender shoulders. "You're going to be so proud of me, my darling, when I rediscover the island and am able to bring long life and good health to the entire world."

"Emery, you must know that I hope we find your island," Molly said. "I can't bear the thought of your being disappointed."

"I won't be disappointed. Tomorrow we will find my island, exactly fifty years to the day of my first arrival there."

"You seem so certain." Molly gazed lovingly into The Professor's eyes.

Jordan wondered if the woman actually cared about Dr. Arnell or if she was simply infatuated with the thought of being married to man who might soon be famous and possibly rich.

"I have never been more certain of anything in my life," The Professor said. "The island will be visible tomorrow. It's out there…waiting for me." He looked from Molly to Mick and then to Jordan. "It's waiting for all of us."

When they boarded the *Footloose,* Will went below to change out of his bloody clothes, asking Gwen to stay topside until he returned.

Curious as to why he'd made that request, she waited a few minutes, then rushed headlong down the stairs to the salon. The door to the master stateroom stood wide open, but she didn't see Will. Walking quietly, barely breathing, she entered the stateroom and found it empty. She gazed at the partially closed bathroom door.

What is he doing? she asked herself. He probably just wants a little privacy to strip out of his soiled clothes, take a shower and put on a clean shirt and pants.

Suddenly Will came out of the bathroom and stopped dead when he saw Gwen. Gasping, unable to remove her gaze from his totally nude body, she stammered, "I'm sorry. I didn't…I'll leave."

With heat warming her face, she forced her gaze from his impressive sex and up to his muscular chest. As she inspected his broad shoulders, she noticed blood trickling from a shallow wound and realized that all the stains on Will's shirt were not from the other man's blood.

"You were shot!" Without thinking, she moved toward him.

"Don't go all female on me, brown eyes," Will told her. "The bullet just grazed my shoulder. A little alcohol and a bandage and I'll be fine."

"How much blood have you lost? Are you feeling faint?

What can I do to help you? Oh, God, Will, why didn't you tell me you'd been shot?"

"I didn't tell you for this very reason. I didn't want you to get hysterical."

"I am not hysterical."

"Do you want to help me?"

"Yes, of course I do." She gazed into his gorgeous blue eyes, and all she could think about was how much she wanted to take care of this man. Well, that and the fact he was naked and absolutely drop-dead gorgeous.

"Get me some briefs, a shirt, a pair of jeans and socks out of my duffel bag over there—" he indicated the counter space built into the wall "—while I take a shower."

"Of course." She shooed him back into the bathroom. "I'll lay everything out on the bed."

"Thanks."

As he walked into the bathroom, she couldn't stop herself from looking and was rewarded with the sight of his firm round buttocks. *What a body!*

Oh, Gwen, get your mind out of the gutter.

She picked up his vinyl bag, set it on the bed and rummaged through his possessions until she found the items he had requested. She laid out a pair of plain white briefs, a faded pair of jeans, blue cotton socks and a light-blue cotton pullover shirt.

"Hey, Gwen," Will called.

"Yes?"

"I hate to ask, but would you mind giving me a hand?"

"What?"

"Toss me my briefs and then come in here. My shoulder's gotten pretty stiff and I'm probably going to need a little help cleaning this wound and dressing it."

"Okay." She carried the briefs with her, cracked open the door and tossed the underwear to Will.

A minute later he said, "You can come in now."

She opened the door and found him sitting on the commode. There was just enough room in the tight area for her to stand directly in front of him.

"There's a first-aid kit under the sink," he said.

She nodded, turned around and bent over to retrieve the kit, but before she could open the cabinet under the sink, her backside hit Will's knees. She jumped.

He laughed, then slapped her on the butt.

"Stop that!" she told him.

"Sorry. I couldn't resist. You've got a nice ass, Dr. Arnell."

So do you. "You must be delirious."

He chuckled again.

She bent back over, being careful not to rub against his knees, opened the cabinet door and pulled out the first-aid kit. When she turned around, she discovered that Will had stood and they were now face-to-face. Actually, they would have been face-to-face if they were the same height. As it was, with him barefoot and her in tennis shoes, her head hit him at chin level.

"Maybe we should go into the bedroom to do this," Gwen suggested.

"Whatever you say."

He followed her into the stateroom, sat at the foot of the bed and waited for her to doctor him. She flipped open the kit, removed a small bottle of rubbing alcohol and searched for some cotton balls.

"Just pour it on the wound."

"It'll burn."

"I've endured worse."

A lot worse. Although unspoken, she heard those words inside her head. She unscrewed the lid on the bottle, lifted a piece of cotton gauze to catch the overflow and poured the alcohol directly over the gaping wound on his shoulder. He winced slightly. She blew on his shoulder. She laid the wet gauze aside and retrieved another piece, then placed it over his wound. Holding the dressing by the top edge, she used her other hand to pick up the roll of tape. Luckily, the tape tore easily, so she managed to rip off four strips and secure the bandage in place.

"I think you need stitches in that shoulder," she said.

"Probably."

"Otherwise, it's going to leave a nasty scar."

"It won't be my first scar, or hadn't you noticed?"

She really hadn't noticed, but now that he mentioned it, she ran her gaze over his chest and saw two separate scars, both faded to a creamy white. One slashed across his abdomen. A knife wound? The other was smaller and almost round, located on his right side. A bullet wound?

He turned sideways so she could see his back. Another scar. Ragged and pink. A more recent wound?

"Compared to the others, this is just a scratch," he told her.

She stepped back, away from him, and their gazes met. "Do you need me to help you get dressed?"

He shook his head. "I think I can manage."

"It's been years since I was on a boat, but if you gave me some pointers, I might be able to—"

"I can handle things. And we'll leave just as soon as I get dressed. Why don't you rustle us up something to eat and bring it topside?"

"All right. I'll see what I can dig up in the kitchen. I mean the galley."

When she turned to leave, he said, "Gwen, everything's going to be all right. If we don't encounter the *Sun Dancer* out at sea, we'll catch up with them in Bermuda."

"I hope you're right, but after what happened on Baccara—"

"I won't tell you not to worry about your father. He's gotten hooked up with a couple of really bad characters. But as long as he's useful to them…"

"And when my father's no longer useful to them, they'll kill him, won't they? Daddy and Jordan and the Kress girl, if they haven't already killed her."

"I'm not going to lie to you— Yes, there's a good chance they'll kill them."

"Before they reach Bermuda?"

"I don't know. Possibly not, unless Bermuda is their final destination."

Gwen stood frozen to the spot, feeling as if she might burst into tears at any moment and knowing she'd hate herself if she shed one single tear. At least, not in front of Will. She figured he was the type who not only wasn't affected by a woman's tears, but would consider her weak and foolish to waste energy crying.

She turned and walked out, choking back unshed tears.

Will sat in the cockpit, drinking a beer and staring up at the night sky encrusted with countless glittering stars. Gwen sat beside him, her legs against her chest, her arms draped around her knees. The balmy, tropical breeze blew softly through her long dark hair, which fell loose about her shoulders.

Figuring the *Sun Dancer* wouldn't head out to sea before morning, Will felt safe dropping anchor for the

night. At first light he would take the *Footloose* directly into
the Bermuda Triangle, and hope for a miracle—that they
would encounter the *Sun Dancer* at sea. His job was to
rescue Cheryl Kress. His last report from Daisy had been
that Cheryl's parents were probably worried out of their
minds because she was still missing. He knew if his
daughter was in the situation Cheryl was... *His daughter?*
Yeah, like he would ever have children. He was the kind of
man who thought kids should be born to a married mother
and father, so the odds were against his ever having a
family of his own. After all, he was nearly forty, and since
his first marriage had ended—a mutual decision that they
were wrong for each other—Will hadn't loved another
woman. There had been a couple of long-term relationships, if you can call eight or nine months long-term, and
he'd dated dozens of women, some dates ending in bed,
others ending with a kiss good-night.

"You're awfully quiet," Gwen said. "Penny for your
thoughts."

"You wouldn't believe what I was thinking about if I
told you."

"Try me."

"I was thinking about how worried I'd be if I had a
daughter in Cheryl's situation."

"Why did you think I wouldn't believe you?"

Will shrugged. "I figured you didn't see me as the
family-man type."

Gwen lowered her legs and turned sideways so she could
look at Will. "Do you want to get married and have a family?"

"What woman would want a beat-up old warhorse like
me?"

Gwen laughed. "You're kidding me, right? Will Pierce,

I've seen you stark naked and I'm here to tell you that you may be slightly beaten-up and scarred, but you're not old by a long shot. And only about half the women in the world would be interested in taking on the job of taming you."

"Taming me?" Will grinned. "Do you think I'm such a wild beast that I need taming?"

"Most definitely. Taming you wouldn't be a job for the faint-hearted. You won't succumb without putting up a fight."

"Do you think I'd be worth the effort?"

"That depends."

"On what?"

"On how much she loves you." Gwen's voice became whisper soft. "And how much she knew you loved her."

As naturally as taking his next breath, Will slid his right arm around Gwen's waist and drew her close, until they were eye to eye, a hair's breadth between them. "Dr. Arnell, I believe you're a romantic."

"The only reason you're flirting with me is because you're the kind of man who can't help hitting on an available female."

"Are you available?" His breath mingled with hers, their lips almost touching.

"I'm not your type, remember. I'm plain and plump and frumpy."

He lifted his head, putting a couple of feet between them. "I didn't say you were plump." He ran his hand down over her hip. "A little hippy, maybe, but not plump."

Realizing he was kidding her, she socked him playfully on the chest. "I've had my heart broken twice. I'm not looking to make it three times."

"What makes you think I'd break your heart? Wouldn't

you have to care about me for me to have that kind of power over you?"

"I'm not a one-night stand type of woman," she told him truthfully. "If we had sex, I'd probably rationalize things by telling myself I was in love with you. And neither of us wants that, right?"

She had him there. Gwen *wasn't* his type. Under different circumstances, he doubted he'd give her a second glance. In the past he'd gone for flashier women, usually tall, leggy blondes, with an occasional voluptuous brunette thrown into the mix.

Gwen wasn't tall and leggy, wasn't voluptuous and definitely wasn't flashy.

So why was he sitting here with his arm around her, thinking about how much he'd like to make love to her?

"No, neither of us wants that," he said firmly.

Chapter 8

What was the matter with her? It wasn't as if she'd never been propositioned before or felt the stirring of sexual attraction. She hadn't become a born-again virgin after her divorce, although there hadn't been many men in her life, and she certainly didn't think of herself as some rare gift for one lucky man. So, why was she fighting her desire to jump into bed with Will Pierce? She might not be his type or he hers, but there was an undeniable chemistry between them.

She had to be honest with herself. She wanted Will. But what if they had sex and it was great? What if after sleeping with him, she realized she'd fallen hard and fast for the big lug? That's what frightened her and what had made her put on the brakes before Will drove them both over an emotional cliff.

"So, if we aren't going to fool around, do you have any suggestions for whiling away the next couple of hours?"

Will asked, easing his arm from around her waist and sitting back on the U-shaped lounger.

"We could indulge in a dying art form," she told him.

He eyed her questioningly.

She smiled. "I'm referring to the art of conversation. You know, idle chit-chat. Or meaningful discussion. I'll tell you about mine, you'll tell me about yours."

"That last part about yours and mine sounds promising." Will scooted closer and draped his arm across the lounge's backrest, directly behind Gwen.

She looked at him pointedly. "The 'yours and mine' I was referring to is your life and my life. Remember trading war stories?"

Will sighed dramatically. "Yeah, I was afraid of that."

"So?"

"So?" he shot the one-word question back at her.

"So, why don't we spend a little time becoming better acquainted?"

"What is it with you women? Why do you want to know what a man is thinking, what he's feeling, about the previous women in his life? Men are simple creatures. I'm usually wondering how I can persuade the woman to have sex with me. And as for feeling things—I think I'd feel good if I had sex. And as for the women in my past—that's where they are, in the past, even if that past is only a week or two ago."

"Okay, so we won't talk about what you're thinking or feeling," Gwen said. "And I couldn't care less about the women in your past, even if that past was only a few days ago." She leaned her head back and rested it against his shoulder. Staring up the beautiful night sky, she thought how perfect this moment would be if she weren't concerned about her father and if Will and she were truly romantically involved. "Did you have a dog when you were a kid?"

"Huh?"

"Did you?"

"Yeah, I had a dog, my brothers and I. An old mix-breed hound. I hadn't thought about Sooner in ages. He was a damn good hunting dog."

"Sooner?" She giggled. "You're kidding?"

"Nope. The old man named him."

"You said you went hunting as a kid, right?"

"Honey, I was born and raised in Texas. I was toting a rifle when I was in diapers." He chuckled. She nudged him in the ribs. "Okay, that's a slight exaggeration, but not much. My old man loved to hunt, and he made sure my brothers and I learned how to use a rifle at a young age. By the time I was twelve, I'd made my first kill. I don't think Dad was ever as proud of me as he was then."

"I don't understand the pleasure in hunting, in stalking an animal and killing it."

"And I don't understand the pleasure somebody gets out of having a flower garden." Will leaned his head against hers.

"How did you know I have a flower garden?" Pivoting her head slightly, she glanced up at him.

"It was just a guess. It wasn't a giant leap from frumpy botanist to flower garden." He grunted when she jabbed him in the ribs again. "You don't happen to have a cat, too, do you?"

"No, I don't, but I did. Periwinkle died last year, and I haven't had the heart to get another cat to replace her."

"Periwinkle?" Will kissed Gwen's temple. "Brown eyes, you amuse me. You really do. I've never met a woman like you."

And I've never met a man like you, all macho cocky swagger and yet kind and understanding and...

"I'm not all that unique," she told him.

He ran his fingers along her shoulder in a caressing tap. "Yeah, I think maybe you are." He squeezed her shoulder. "Hey, you do know I was kidding about the frumpy part, don't you?"

"Were you kidding?"

He maneuvered her so that he could see her face. She looked right at him.

"You deliberately downplay your physical assets, don't you? You wear your hair in a bun or a ponytail, don't use much if any makeup, wear loose, colorless clothes and white cotton underwear." The corners of his mouth lifted into an amused smile. "It's almost as if you're saying don't look at me, don't notice me."

"Life is easier if you don't expect too much, if you don't long to be noticed, if you don't need someone's undivided attention, if you—" Realizing she had already revealed too much of her private self, she stopped talking.

Silence. Soft, gentle silence. The hum of the ocean, the beating of two hearts, their rhythmic breathing. Will slipped his hand between them and took her hand in his, then entwined their fingers.

"How old did you say you were you when your parents divorced?" he asked.

"Ten."

"That's a very impressionable age."

"Don't try to psychoanalyze me, okay?"

He lifted her hand to his lips and kissed it. "How much did your husband remind you of your father?"

"That's a very personal question."

"Yeah, it is."

Gwen turned her head and closed her eyes. "Jeremy Charles was a botanist, like my father. He was brilliant, just as Daddy is. Physically they resembled each other a bit. Tall, slender, distinguished. But Jeremy wasn't a dreamer. He had both feet firmly planted on the ground. He was steady and reliable, and I thought he was loyal and trustworthy."

"You married a guy you thought was an improved version of your dad," Will said. "So what happened? Did Mr. Loyal and Trustworthy cheat on you with some hot little blonde?"

"As a matter of fact, Ryan was a hot little blonde."

"Ryan?"

"Uh-huh. You see Jeremy wasn't quite the man I had thought he was."

"Damn!"

"I was shocked at first, then as time passed I realized I should have figured it out sooner. Poor Jeremy."

"Poor Jeremy, my ass!"

"No, really. We had an amicable divorce and we've remained friends," Gwen said. "He and Ryan still live in Huntsville. They're very happy together and I'm happy for them."

Will slid his arm down and around her waist, pulled her close to him and kissed her. A gentle, nonthreatening kiss. A sweet kiss.

"I've never had my heart broken," Will admitted in a quiet voice.

"Never? Not even by your ex-wife?"

"Marla and I loved each other, but it was no grand passion or anything. After a couple of years together, we realized getting married had been a mistake. Once the red-hot sex fizzled out, we didn't have anything left."

"You both needed more."

"Yeah, I guess we did. Unless I find that something more, I don't plan to get married again."

"I want something I can never have." Gwen wasn't sure why she was actually considering admitting her deepest desire to him. After all, why should he care what she wanted?

"What's that, this something you think you can never have?"

"I want a man to love me the way my father loves his dream of that damn mythical island and the miracle plant. I want to be someone's obsession, the only thing that matters to him, above all else."

"Whew, honey, you don't want much, do you?"

"I said it was something I know I can never have. It's just a silly, romantic notion."

"I don't know. I think you deserve to get what you want. Maybe someday—"

Gwen pressed her index finger against Will's lips. "I think all this fresh sea air has drugged me. I don't usually open up and confess my heart's desire to…to just anybody."

She pulled out of his arms and stood.

"Gwen?"

"I'm going below deck. We'll want to start out early in the morning, so maybe we'd both better try to get some sleep."

She escaped as quickly as she could, all the while calling herself a fool. What had possessed her to tell Will that she longed for a man to love her to the point of obsession? He probably thought she wasn't the type of woman that could inspire that kind of passion in any man. Let alone him.

Jordan Elders had unlocked the door to Cheryl's tiny stateroom and escorted her into the galley an hour ago, while the cruiser was leaving port. Now, she was sitting topside with Jordan, drinking a diet cola and finally breathing in some fresh sea air. They had kept her locked up most of yesterday and all night last night. Apparently, the others had appointed Jordan as her caretaker because he was the one who brought her food and checked on her.

"So where are we going now?" Cheryl asked, gazing to the east, at the rising sun. "North somewhere, I guess."

"Into the North Atlantic, directly into the Bermuda Triangle, in search of The Professor's island," Jordan replied.

"Does he really think he'll be able to find one little island out here in the Atlantic Ocean? Doesn't the Triangle cover thousands of miles?"

"The Bermuda Triangle, also known as the Devil's Triangle, covers over four hundred thousand square miles, and since 1854 more than fifty ships and aircraft have vanished inside the Triangle."

"Well, that's reassuring," she said sarcastically.

"The Professor found the island once or, rather, it found him. He believes the island will come to him again."

"You sound as crazy as he does." Cheryl finished off her canned cola, crushed the can and threw it overboard.

"Did anyone ever tell you that you're a whiny pain in the butt?"

"Did anyone ever tell you that kidnapping is illegal?"

"No one kidnapped you." He glowered at her, as if he had a right to be critical and condemning. "You sneaked aboard the *Sun Dancer* and hid. You were trespassing."

"I was trying to protect a friend, to be there when she got her heart broken. Tori was determined to follow you, and that's the only reason I boarded this damn boat."

"Tori had sense enough to leave before she got caught.

You stowed away, so don't even think about accusing anyone of kidnapping you."

"Maybe I wasn't kidnapped in the beginning, but I'm being held here against my will."

"Yap, yap, yap. How many times do I have to tell you that once we complete our expedition, you'll be free to go home to your rich daddy."

"You may believe that, but I don't. If your noble professor's cohorts find out who my father is, do you honestly think they won't at least consider demanding a ransom for my safe return?"

"No one else knows who your father is. Only I know, and I have no reason to share that information with anyone else. And besides, The Professor trusts Captain McGuire, and he's asked Molly to marry him. He has promised them a percentage of any material gain from the sale of the miracle plant we find on the island."

Cheryl rolled her eyes heavenward. "Are you really as naive and gullible as The Professor?"

"What do you mean by that?"

"Take a look up there at Captain McGuire." She surveyed the middle-aged man sitting at the helm. Overly long salt-and-pepper hair. A scruffy dark beard. Leathery tanned skin. A cigarette dangled from his lips. "Doesn't your gut instincts tell you the guy is a sleaze?"

"I don't judge a man by the way he looks."

"What about judging a woman by the way she looks?" Cheryl nodded upward toward the flying bridge where Dr. Arnell and Molly stood looking out at the vast ocean, searching for sight of the nonexistent island. "Does Molly look like the type of woman who'd be interested in a dotty old professor?"

"She admires and respects Dr. Arnell, just as I do," Jordan said. "Any woman should be honored to have him interested in her."

"Get your head out of your ass, will you? There is no mythical island, no miracle plant. Captain McGuire is a sleaze and probably a crook. And Molly is a whore if I ever saw one. She's probably bedded half the men in the Caribbean."

"What made you so cynical?" Jordan asked.

"What made you so stupid?" she countered.

Grunting disgustedly, Jordan grasped her upper arm. "Look, Cheryl, you got yourself in this situation and you're doing nothing to make it easier on yourself. I get it that you want to go home. I understand you're upset and frustrated, but you're stuck here with us until we either find Dr. Arnell's island or we land in Bermuda. So, grow up, will you, and stop acting like a spoiled brat!"

She jerked away from him, so angry she could spit nails. "If I ever do get home, I'm going to have my daddy make sure you're all put in jail for the rest of your lives!"

She whirled around and ran down the steps to the salon below deck. Not only would she make sure everyone aboard the *Sun Dancer* went to jail, she had a score to settle with someone else. Once she got her hands on Tori, she was going to wring her best friend's neck for getting her into this mess!

Gwen sat at the helm with Will as they headed farther out to sea on a rather bright, sunny, balmy morning. They'd been up since daylight, both of them anxious to set sail. The odds of their finding the *Sun Dancer* in the vastness of the Bermuda Triangle were probably nil, but Gwen knew they had to try. Both the *Sun Dancer* and the *Footloose* had left Baccara and were headed into the Triangle, with Bermuda as the final destination. Will had pointed out that logic dictated a northeasterly route.

"I think we should try to make radio contact with the *Sun Dancer* on and off all day today." Will took a sip from the mug of fresh coffee Gwen had brought him.

"What?" She whipped around and glared at him.

"I said—"

"I heard what you said, but I don't understand. Do you mean we could have made radio contact with them before now and didn't?"

"I did try," he admitted, a sheepish expression on his face. "More than once."

"And?" Gwen held her breath.

"I didn't get a response. My guess is that Mick McGuire has ordered radio silence. He doesn't want anyone aboard giving away their location or—"

"When I first woke this morning, I thought I heard you talking to someone and you said you were just getting a weather report. Are you lying to me? Did you speak to someone aboard the *Sun Dancer?*"

Will placed his mug in the cup holder, clamped his hands around the wheel and stared straight ahead. "I did get a weather report."

"But that's not all, is it?"

"I tried to contact your father's ship," Will told her. "But I didn't get a response. After that, I contacted several other vessels that are traveling into the Triangle today, to ask them to be on the lookout for the *Sun Dancer*. My boss, Sawyer McNamara, was able to get me the information about the other ships in the area."

"So, we do have a chance, no matter how slim, of actually finding the *Sun Dancer?*"

"Yeah, we have a chance."

She picked up on something in his voice, but couldn't quite put her finger on it. "If we don't catch up with them at sea, we'll catch up with them in Bermuda, right? That's what you said."

"Yeah, honey, that's what I said."

Suddenly she knew why she'd heard just a hint of desperation in his voice. "You're pretty sure that Mick and Molly are going to kill my father and Jordan and Cheryl Kress before they reach Bermuda, aren't you?"

Will didn't respond.

Gwen sat beside him, not saying anything else, just breathing, listening to the cruiser's motors and the steady ocean rhythm. They remained silent for quite a while, then a call on the ship's radio shattered the silence with earsplitting intensity.

The call came from a fishing vessel, the *Sea Hunt*. They had spotted the *Sun Dancer*, due east of them. While Will repeated the coordinates, Gwen memorized them.

"They're approximately an hour ahead of us," Will told her. "But I think we can catch up with them in a few hours, as long as they don't change course. There will be no reason for them to increase their speed since they have no idea that we're following them or that we know their coordinates."

Overcome with relief, Gwen threw her arms around Will's neck and kissed him.

"I like seeing you happy," he told her. "But don't get your hopes too high. We haven't caught up with them yet and when we do, there could be trouble."

An hour ago they had entered the waters known worldwide as the Bermuda Triangle. Jordan kept watch with The

Professor and Molly atop the cruiser on the flying bridge. The farther they sailed into the ocean, the more tense Dr. Arnell became, his eyes glued to the horizon, searching, silently praying that this time would be The Time.

Mile after mile of endless sea stretched before them, lay behind them and surrounded them. Although a part of Jordan wanted desperately to believe they would find this mysterious vanishing island, with each passing minute, he grew more uncertain and wondered if Dr. Arnell could endure another failure.

"Tell me again about your island," Molly said, clinging to The Professor's arm.

"You must be weary of listening to my old tales," Dr. Arnell said.

"Don't be silly, darling, I never tire of hearing you talk about something that means so much to you."

"I wish my wife had felt as you do, my dear Molly. She thought me a fool."

"She should have believed in you, and so should your daughter."

"Sweet little Gwendolyn. She did believe in me once. She even went on two expeditions with me, but as she grew older, she became cynical."

"She'll change her tune once you rediscover your island." Molly patted The Professor's hand.

Jordan watched the display of affection between Molly and Dr. Arnell and hoped that the woman's feelings were genuine, that she was on the up-and-up. But ever since Cheryl had put doubts in his mind—about Captain McGuire and Molly—he hadn't been able to shake the uneasy feeling that something was wrong, that they were in trouble. Big trouble.

"Look at those dark clouds." Molly pointed due north. "I thought the weather was supposed to be perfect today."

Jordan looked to the north. The gray clouds swirled and thickened, rapidly growing darker. Suddenly the wind picked up, and within minutes whipped around them with amazing speed.

"We'd better go below," Jordan said.

He and Molly assisted Dr. Arnell, whose arthritic knees hindered him going up and down steps easily. By the time they reached the salon, the dark clouds surrounded them on all sides and streaks of lightning broke through like giant spears of fire. The winds grew in intensity, churning the ocean, sending huge waves up, over, and onto the deck. The choppy waters tumbled the *Sun Dancer* about as if it were a toy ship.

Jordan went to Cheryl's room and unlocked it.

"What's going on? I swear I'm getting seasick," Cheryl said, jumping off her bed.

"We've run into a storm," Jordan told her. "Put on your life jacket and stay in the salon with the others. I'm going back up to find out from McGuire what the hell is going on."

When Jordan returned topside, the wind almost knocked him down and giant waves washed over him, drenching him to the skin. He tried to make his way to the helm, but barely made it on deck before he realized that this was no ordinary storm. It was as if the ocean beneath the *Sun Dancer* was whirling around and around, forming a watery vortex, and the force of the downward current would soon rip the cruiser apart and take it to the bottom of the sea.

Chapter 9

The rough winds and high waves pounded the *Sun Dancer,* tossing the cruiser about with damaging force. Captain McGuire came below, wearing a life jacket and aiming a gun at Jordan and the others who were huddled in the cabin.

"Molly, you're coming with me. We can use the life raft and provisions and have a chance to survive," McGuire shouted at her.

"We can't leave the others!" Molly screamed.

"Come with me or stay here and die with them."

Jordan wasn't sure what The Professor was thinking when he suddenly rushed McGuire, who aimed his weapon and fired. Molly put herself in front of Dr. Arnell and took the bullet meant for him.

McGuire cursed, then raced up the companionway. Jordan followed, knowing if McGuire took the lifeboat, they were all goners. Without warning, a wave crashed over the boat, sweeping McGuire overboard.

Knowing he mustn't waste time, Jordan yelled for the others to come up. Then he helped The Professor, Cheryl and an injured Molly climb into the life raft.

Once aboard, Jordan noted that Cheryl seemed to be in a state of shock. There wasn't much he could do for her right now as they rocked violently in the treacherous waters. He had other things to concern him.

"We need to make sure there's nothing on us or in the raft that could puncture it," Jordan told The Professor.

"What?" Dr. Arnell asked, his gaze focused on Molly. "We have to do something for her. Mick shot her. Why did he shoot her?"

"To hell with Mick McGuire!" Jordan shouted, totally frustrated and scared half out of his mind.

"I've managed to stop the bleeding, but…" The Professor mumbled. "She needs a doctor."

Jordan grabbed The Professor by the shoulders and shook him. "Snap out of it. If you don't help me, we're all in trouble."

"Yes, yes, my boy. What must I do?"

"Help!" a man's voice echoed through the torrent of wind, rain and roaring sea.

"Did you hear that?" Dr. Arnell asked.

Jordan scanned the area around the raft, searching for the source of the voice. He knew, even before he caught sight of him, that the voice belonged to Captain McGuire.

"Let him drown," Molly told them, her trembling hand grasping hold of Dr. Arnell's arm. "Let the son of a bitch drown."

"My dear, we can't do that. Despite what he did, he is a human being," Dr. Arnell told her.

Within minutes, Mick McGuire swam up to the lifeboat and hoisted himself aboard. Short of knocking him back into the water, Jordan had little choice but to allow him to join them on the raft.

Gwen sat beside Will at the helm as they sailed along in search of the *Sun Dancer*. The balmy wind and smooth waters added to the perfection of the warm, sunny day, barely a cloud in the clear blue sky. Despite the odds against them, Gwen felt moderately confident that they would somehow be able to rescue her father, Jordan and Cheryl Kress. That confidence came from knowing that if anyone could accomplish the impossible, it was Will.

"Did you put on more sunscreen?" he asked her.

"Not yet." She extended her arms, flipped them over and back, looking at her skin. "I'm not even pink. That SPF 50 sun blocker I brought with me really works."

Will reached over and tapped her on the head. "Keep that cap on. It'll partially shade your face."

She studied him for a few minutes. "For a blond, you sure do tan easily."

"Blond? Who me?" Will chuckled.

"Sandy brown, maybe. But I bet you were a cotton top as a kid."

"Yeah, me and both of my brothers. Our hair was so light, it was almost white. Our mother was a blue-eyed blonde. The old man had Indian blood in him. Cherokee I think. His folks were from Oklahoma. My dad stayed brown as gingerbread from working out in the sun."

"Would you believe that I was bald when I was born and now I have this thick mop?" Moving her head back and forth, Gwen flipped her loose ponytail. "My mother said

I looked like a beautiful little boy with my big brown eyes, round little face and no hair."

"I can't imagine you ever looking like a boy."

When he glanced at her, Gwen smiled and they exchanged a meaningful look.

"By the time I was one, I had wispy brown curls and was an absolute doll. Mama dressed me in the frilliest little outfits, ruffled panties and—"

"No white cotton underwear for little Gwen, huh?"

She groaned, then laughed. "You'll never let me forget about my plain, prim underwear, will you?"

"I tell you what, brown eyes, once we get back to civilization, you go buy yourself some red-hot silk undies, show them to me, and I'll never bring up the subject of your white unmentionables ever again."

"You've got a deal."

When he offered her his hand, they shook on the deal. Gwen's heart fluttered and her stomach quivered. Did he realize he had implied that they would be seeing each other again after this wild adventure ended?

He doesn't mean it. He's just making conversation, passing the time, joking around. She shouldn't make too much of their little flirtation. After all, Will was a man who liked women, and she just happened to be the only available female. Once he had his pick of women, he'd forget she even existed.

"You got awfully quiet," Will said. "Are you thinking about that red silk underwear?"

"Why red? Why not some other color?" she asked.

He kept his gaze focused straight ahead. "I think you'd look great in red. I can just imagine how red would look on you, with your dark hair and eyes and peaches-and-cream complexion. You'd be a knockout."

"Oh, I didn't know our deal included your seeing me in the red underwear. I thought I just had to buy it and show it to you."

"No way. You have to model it for me or the deal is off."

Gwen laughed. "You're crazy, you know that, don't you? Once you've found Cheryl Kress and taken her home to her father, you'll go back to Atlanta and forget you ever met me."

He turned and looked at her, a sly grin curving his lips and a twinkle in his eye. "Something tells me that you're not going to be so easy to forget."

His comment rendered her speechless.

"What, no comeback?" he asked.

"It must have taken years of practice to become so adept at telling a woman what she wants to hear." What woman didn't want to be unforgettable?

"I can be Mr. Smooth when the occasion and the woman call for some sweet-talking, but in your case…"

"In my case, what? And don't you dare think I'd believe you if you told me I'm unforgettable. I'm not that naive."

Will shrugged. "You really don't know your own potential as a femme fatale, do you?"

Before she had a chance to react, Will cursed under his breath, then said, "Look up ahead. It's the damnedest thing I've ever seen."

"What?" She followed his line of vision, toward the vast blue sky-meets-the-sea horizon. "Oh, my God!"

"Something's not right here. I need to get another weather update right now."

Gwen couldn't manage to look away, as if the mesmerizing occurrence miles in front of them had hypnotized her. The swirling dark clouds appeared to be rising from the water, from inside the spinning ocean waves. Silent bolts of lightning danced about, shooting not from the heavens to earth, but from the sea into the sky.

Will tried to radio for a weather update, then muttered a few choice obscenities.

"What's wrong?" Gwen asked.

"Our radio is dead."

When Mick McGuire scrambled toward Molly, The Professor blocked his move.

"Stay away from her. Don't you think you've caused her enough harm?"

"I didn't mean to shoot her," Mick said. "If the stupid bitch hadn't been trying to save your sorry ass—"

"Shut up and sit back," Jordan told Mick, his tone deadly serious.

Chuckling, Mick glanced over his shoulder and looked at Jordan. "What makes you think you're giving the orders?"

"You're one man," Jordan told him. "Dr. Arnell and I make it two against one."

"Make that three against one," Cheryl said, her voice unnaturally calm.

All eyes turned to her. Jordan noted how pale she was, but her dazed expression was gone, replaced with a look of anger and determination.

"You're not so brave without your gun are you, Captain McGuire?" Cheryl made her way around Mick and went directly to where Molly lay huddled semiconscious in The Professor's lap. Cheryl looked at him and asked, "What can I do to help her?"

"I'm not sure there is anything we can do," Dr. Arnell said. "I grabbed the first-aid kit before we abandoned ship, but I'm afraid I lost it when I climbed into the raft." He caressed Molly's cheek. "She's lost quite a bit of blood. Unfortunately, the bullet lodged in her side. It needs to be removed, but without the proper equipment…" Tears welled up in The Professor's dark eyes.

Cheryl turned on Mick. "This is your fault. All of it. You shot her. You were the captain and you took us right into the middle of a storm."

Mick snarled. "I'm not going to listen to your bellyaching, you little—"

Cheryl reached out and slapped Mick. Reacting instinctively, he grabbed her wrist and yanked her toward him. Screeching, she hit and kicked him repeatedly.

The raft undulated, tossing about on the waves as if it might go under at any moment. Jordan grabbed Cheryl away from Mick and pulled her against him, her back to his chest, then held her down, all the while talking quietly to her.

"Calm down. You're rocking the raft. If you keep kicking, you could capsize us. You don't want to do that, do you?"

With each passing second, Cheryl's frantic movements slowed, her screeching died away, and finally she went limp in Jordan's arms.

Holding her, he spoke to everyone on the raft. "We all need to sit low and distribute our weight. No one should sit on the sides and we can't be moving about or try to stand up."

"What difference does it make?" McGuire glared at Jordan. "We're all going to die, either now or later. We'll wind up as fish food."

Jordan knew the odds were against them. The vicious storm had taken them completely by surprise. Only by sheer luck had he managed to get everyone into the raft.

He hadn't had time to bring water or food on board. Unless by some miracle they were rescued in the next twenty-four hours, Mick's prediction of them becoming fish food would probably come true.

"The radio is dead," Will repeated, as if he couldn't believe his own words. "I don't understand. It was working perfectly."

"What can we do?" Gwen asked. "We can't sail into that storm."

"I'm going to try to outrun it. We'll turn around and head toward Nassau. It should be the closest landmass."

While Will maneuvered the cruiser, Gwen stared at the approaching storm, puzzled by the unusual clouds and lightning, both seeming to come from the water, as if the ocean and the sky somehow had switched places. Streaks of broad white light shot up from below the ocean's surface as if dozens of enormous spotlights on the ocean floor had been turned on and were shooting thousand-megawatt beams into the atmosphere.

"Will, I don't know anything about ocean travel, but is that—" she pointed to the far horizon "—the way storms look out here at sea?"

"No way," he told her. "I've never seen anything like this. It's freaky."

"Do you really think we can outrun it?"

"I don't know, but I'm damn well going to try." He turned to her. "Get the life jackets. We need to put them on now, just in case. And once we do that, go below and put together some supplies—water, nonperishable food, the first-aid kit and—"

"You don't think we can outrun the storm, do you?"

Their gazes met and locked. "Pray, brown eyes. Pray like you've never prayed before."

With her head resting in Dr. Arnell's lap, Molly had lapsed into unconsciousness. Jordan noticed Dr. Arnell caressing her face, brushing stray tendrils of damp hair from her cheeks. The rest of them sat quietly. Tense, frightened and praying for help. Hoping to live. The sudden violent storm that had sunk the *Sun Dancer* died down as quickly as it had sprung to life, leaving them floating along on a calm, tranquil sea. Gradually the dark clouds surrounding them disappeared, leaving behind an azure-blue sky and shimmering sunlight.

Cheryl sat beside Jordan, her hands resting in her lap.

"I'm sorry," she said in a quiet voice.

"Huh?" Jordan glanced at her.

"I'm sorry I got hysterical and nearly capsized us."

Jordan nodded.

"Is Captain McGuire right— Are we going to die?"

"No, my dear young lady, we are not going to die," Dr. Arnell told her. "We survived, all five of us. It's only a matter of time before we come upon my island. And when we do, the natives will provide us with all that we need." He laid his withered old hand over Molly's bloody wound. "They will be able to save my Molly. You wait and see. This is just as it was fifty years ago when I lost my parents, right before I discovered the island."

"I wish you'd shut the hell up, old man," Mick said. "I'm sick to death of hearing about that island."

"You never believed in my island, did you?" The Professor looked at Mick quizzically. "I don't understand why you agreed to back this expedition, why you—"

Mick laughed gruffly. "You're a gullible old fool. All we had to do was play along with your foolish idea of a scientific exploration and we had the perfect front."

"A front for what?" Cheryl asked.

"For our drop-offs," Mick said. "In Kingston and San Juan and St. Mallon and Baccara."

"Illegal drugs." Jordan didn't know why he hadn't figured it out sooner. Because he'd had his head in the clouds, just as Dr. Arnell had.

"Yeah." Mick snorted. "You and the old man aren't so smart, are you? Book smart maybe, but dumb as dirt out in the real world."

"You said *we*." Dr. Arnell stared at Mick. "Who do you mean by *we*?"

"Who do you think I mean? Molly and me. As soon as she met up with you at the Yellow Parrot back in Puerto Nuevo, she came up with the idea of our pretending to believe in your theory about that stupid island."

"I don't believe you. Molly cares for me. I care for her. We're going to be married after I bring the miracle plant back to the world."

Mick laughed and laughed.

Cheryl reached over and patted Dr. Arnell's hand. "Don't listen to him. Whatever her original motives were, isn't it obvious that Molly does care about you? She took a bullet for you, didn't she?"

With tears streaming down his face, Dr. Arnell stroked his bony fingers through Molly's short, dark hair and cupped her head tenderly.

"Oh, my God!" Cheryl shouted.

"What is it?" Jordan's gaze followed hers. He couldn't believe his eyes.

"Land," Cheryl cried out gleefully. "I see land."

"There is no land out here," Mick said. "We're in the middle of the Triangle. There's nothing out here but ocean and more ocean."

"No, you're wrong." The Professor gazed at the horizon, a smile of pure bliss on his tired, old face. "It's my island. I knew it would come to me again. Fifty years to the day that I landed here as a young man."

"What's wrong?" Gwen asked when she realized the *Footloose* wasn't moving, that the engines were quiet.

"The engines just died," Will told her.

"What? How is that possible?"

"Hell if I know. First the radio goes out, now the engines die."

Gwen glanced over her shoulder at the approaching storm, the storm rising from the ocean's depth. "Oh... Will...Will...it's nearly on us."

"Son of a bitch!"

Within seconds, dark, menacing clouds surrounded them. High waves attacked the cruiser, tossing it about, as rain pelted them and lightning struck the starboard side of the boat.

Gwen screamed. Will grabbed her and held her.

We're going to die. Dear God, we're going to die.

Chapter 10

Gwen had no idea how much time had passed—if it had been minutes or hours—since the *Footloose* had been engulfed by a raging storm. She had clung to hope, had prayed with every breath she took, had tried to prepare herself for death. And as suddenly as the bizarre storm had descended upon them, it disappeared, as if it had been a merciless mirage, leaving behind utter calm and deadly quiet.

Will grasped her shoulders and shook her. "Gwen? Gwen, snap out of it."

"Huh? What?" From where she huddled on the double seat behind the helm, she gazed up into Will's blue eyes. Suddenly she realized that his knees straddled either side of her legs, that he hovered over her, concern in his stern expression.

He helped her into a sitting position, then rested beside her. "Are you all right?"

"Yes, I think so. What about you?"

"I'm okay."

"What happened?"

Will rose to his feet, held out his hand and, when she accepted it, dragged her up alongside him. The deck of the *Footloose* appeared undamaged, just thoroughly soaked, with water standing a couple of inches deep beneath their feet. Overhead, white fluffy clouds floated along dreamily in the clear blue sky. Beneath the cruiser, the ocean lulled softly, but within seconds she sensed something odd was happening. Will sensed it, too. With her hand in his, she felt him tense.

"We're moving," he told her.

Gwen glanced in every direction. "We're drifting due north."

"No, we're not drifting. We're being pulled."

"How is that possible? There's nothing out there to pull us."

"I don't know. It's some kind of current in the ocean and it's dragging us slowly along with it."

"Is that normal?"

He looked right at her, and what she saw in his eyes unnerved her. Not exactly fear, but apprehension. If a man like Will was concerned about their situation...

"What is it?" she asked. "Tell me."

"There was nothing normal about that freak storm we encountered. There's nothing normal about a late-model cruiser in tip-top shape having sudden engine trouble and losing radio function. Nothing works. None of the navigation instruments, compasses, our cell phones. Not a damn thing."

"Do you think what happened is because we're in the Bermuda Triangle?"

He grunted. "I don't believe in superstitious nonsense, but it's possible some type of magnetic field is wreaking havoc on the engines and the radio and other equipment. Whatever caused the storm and the cruiser's problems is what's probably creating the current that is pulling us along."

"If it continues moving us due north, it could take us closer to Bermuda."

"Or it could simply take us farther into the Atlantic and leave us stranded."

"If that happens…"

"We have water and supplies to last a few weeks, but without being able to radio for help—"

"I'm not ready for the we're-going-to-die scenario," she told him. "Not quite yet. Give me a best-case scenario."

"We're spotted by another vessel and rescued. Or better yet, the engines become operational again or maybe the radio."

"And the odds are?"

He shrugged. "I'm going to check the engines and see if I can discover anything wrong. Same for the radio."

"I wonder if my father and the others aboard the *Sun Dancer* encountered the same storm we did."

"If they took the same route we did, then the storm hit them, too, before it hit us."

"Then my father and the others could be alive and stranded just like us. Or they could be—"

Will grasped her face, cradling her chin between his thumb and forefinger. "Don't think about the alternative. Remember, no death scenarios."

Half an hour later, Will joined Gwen at the helm where she'd been sitting while he checked out the engines. Both were in perfect condition. Both should be working, but they weren't. He couldn't figure out why. Same with the radio and the ship's instruments. Although he didn't believe in the supernatural or the paranormal, he'd seen enough of the world and its mysteries to keep an open mind. Almost every strange occurrence had a basis in scientific fact, so that meant whatever had happened to the *Footloose* could eventually be explained. No voodoo-hoodoo involved.

When he approached the helm, Gwen jumped to her to feet and came to meet him. "What did you find wrong with the engines?" she asked, a hopeful note in her voice.

He shook his head. "The engines are fine. So's the radio."

Hope died instantly. "We're still gliding along, due north. I don't need a compass to tell me that."

He nodded. "Uh-huh."

"How long did that storm last?" she asked.

"What?"

"I've been trying to figure out how long the storm lasted, but for the life of me, I'm not sure if it was only a few minutes or if it was hours. Our watches don't work." She tapped her wristwatch. "Nor do the clocks. The sun is in the west now and it was in the east when the storm hit, so that must mean the storm lasted for hours, right?"

"Right." Like Gwen, when the storm had ended, he'd had no sense of time, of the actual duration of the event.

"Why can't I get a grip on time? I feel as if I've lost hours."

Will huffed. "Yeah, I know what you mean."

"You feel the same way?"

"Yeah. Everything that happened during the storm was weird, as if time stopped, as stupid as that sounds."

"No, no." Gwen grabbed his arm. "That's exactly how I felt. As if time stopped. But that's not possible, is it?"

Will shook his head. "No, it's not possible." He searched the sky, noting that the sun was deep into the western horizon, which meant it was late afternoon. "We both must have passed out for hours. That's the only explanation."

She squeezed his arm. "Do you remember passing out? I don't. I remember clinging to you, of being afraid, of thinking we were going to die. I heard the horrible noise of the wind and the waves. But from the minute lightning struck the boat until the sea calmed and the wind died away, it seemed like only minutes passed."

Will tensed. That was another thing he couldn't explain. The *Footloose* had taken a direct hit from the lightning bolt. He'd bet his life on it. But there was absolutely no sign that the cruiser had been struck by lightning.

"What is it?" Gwen's gaze bolted to his.

"Lightning didn't strike the *Footloose*."

"Yes, of course it did. We saw it hit. We felt it."

"Yeah, we thought we did." He clasped both of her arms, just above the elbow. "There's no damage to the cruiser, not even a scratch, nothing to indicate we were hit by lightning."

Gwen's big brown eyes widened. Wonder? Fear? Disbelief? He couldn't tell for sure.

"What's going on?" she asked. "I don't understand any of this and I don't like it."

"You think I do? But there has to be a logical explanation of some kind for what's going on."

"Why?"

"Why what?"

"Why does there have to be a logical explanation? After all, we are in the Bermuda Triangle, a place that's known for the unexpected, the strange, the illogical."

Hating her train of thought, he released her, his gaze narrowing as he glared at her. "The next thing I know, you'll be telling me you believe your father's mystical island is out here somewhere and we're drifting straight toward it."

Her cheeks flushed. Her eyes sparkled. She smiled.

"Damn it, Gwen, I wasn't serious. Don't you know a damn joke when you hear it?"

"You're not sure what's happened to us, and it scares you. You don't like being taken by surprise and not being able to get a handle on things."

"I'm not scared. I'm pissed. There's a big difference."

"Well, I'm scared. We're lost in the middle of the Atlantic, in the Devil's Triangle, with hours of our lives missing, a boat with inoperable motors, useless instruments and we're being pulled slowly but surely toward some unknown destination." She glowered at Will. "You're a damn fool to not be scared."

"Then I'm a damn fool." He turned his back on her and stared out at the sea surrounding them. The big wide ocean. Calm, peaceful, tranquil. Then he glanced up at the sunny, blue sky.

"Will?"

"Just leave me alone for a while, okay? I'm going below again, so stay put."

Needing to get away from her and her fanciful ideas, Will left her alone topside as he went below to the salon. He had to think, had to consider his options, few as they might be. They either stayed aboard the *Footloose* and waited to see how long the mysterious current carried them and where it carried them to, or they boarded the seven-man life raft and tried to row free of the current. Either could be a death warrant.

If he didn't report in soon, Dundee's would know he was in trouble. But since he had no idea how far off course the storm had taken them or where the current was dragging them, it could take weeks for a rescue team to find them, if ever.

Will opened the minifridge, retrieved a beer, removed the cap and took a hefty swig. After wiping his mouth with the back of his hand, he flopped down on the sofa and closed his eyes. If they stayed aboard the cruiser, they had food and water that would last for weeks, but the current could guide them into the middle of nowhere, if it hadn't already done so. If they took the life raft— No, that would be a last resort.

Damn! He hated feeling helpless. He wasn't accustomed to having no options. But then again, he'd gotten out of some deadly situations, a few that had seemed hopeless. It wasn't as if, when he'd been on assignments, he hadn't known the risks involved, that he could as easily die as live. One of the reasons he'd left government work and signed on with Dundee's was because, at almost forty, he'd wanted a little more security, to work on cases that didn't always put him one step away from the Grim Reaper's grasp.

"Will!"

Gwen's scream startled him. He dropped the beer bottle in his haste to stand, then ran up the steps and onto the deck. She came running toward him, waving her arms, gasping for breath. What the hell?

She grabbed his arm and tugged. Her eyes were bright, her lips curved into a wide smile. "Come on. Hurry. You've got to see this."

"What is it?" He allowed her to escort him to the helm.

"Look," she said, pointing straight ahead. "See for yourself."

Will looked, blinked, shook his head, closed his eyes, and then looked again. He wasn't seeing things. It was really there, wasn't it? He scoured the horizon. A greenish tint colored the sky, which in the tropics usually meant reflected sunlight from shallow lagoons or shelves of coral reefs. He checked the sky, focusing his gaze on the fixed cumulus cloud hovering over the distant land mass, while clouds all around the cruiser moved ever so slowly.

"My God, it's an island."

"Yes, it's an island," Gwen said.

Land? How was that possible? "We must have gotten blown way off course, maybe back toward the Turks and Caicos or—"

"That's not possible. We're drifting due north. All those islands are south of us."

Damn, she was right.

"It's an island out here in the Bermuda Triangle," Gwen said, a wistful expression on her face and a hopeful tone in her voice.

"It's not what you're thinking," he told her. "It's not your father's mythical island."

"We can't be sure."

"Yeah, I'm sure. And I can prove it to you, once we set foot on the island. It's probably a tiny, uninhabited landmass that's uncharted."

"We are going ashore, aren't we?"

"Yes, we're going ashore. I'll drop anchor and we'll take the raft. The raft doesn't have a keel, so we can't sail it into the wind, but we can sail downwind."

"What if the island is inhabited?" Gwen asked. "What if—"

"What if up is down and down is up? What if the

world is flat and we just sailed off the edge? What if this is your father's mystical island and you've discovered it instead of him?"

Gwen's smile vanished. "You don't have to be hateful."

"And you don't have to be stupid."

Gwen gritted her teeth.

She was right. He didn't have to be downright mean, but if she knew him better, she'd know getting angry was the way he handled frustration. Angry with himself, angry with circumstances, angry that he couldn't fix things.

He was on the verge of apologizing when he noted the stunned and hurt expression on her face had altered. She stared at him with an ambivalent look as if she were torn between hating him and needing him. What was it about Gwen Arnell that had him tied in knots, that made him act out of character? It wasn't his style to care so much about another person. But he cared that he'd hurt her. Cared so damn much that he'd been about to apologize—something he never did!

"Okay, so I'm hateful and you're stupid," he said. "Does that make us even?"

She stared at him, her nose crinkled and her eyes squinched as if she were studying him, trying to figure out what made him tick.

"Round up some water bottles and packets of nonperishable food," he told her when she didn't reply to his question. "I'll anchor the boat and get the raft in the water. Then we'll go explore the island."

"Is it safe?"

He grunted. "Safe? Probably not, but we're no safer on this boat."

* * *

Twenty minutes later Will spotted a point of land jutting out into the ocean and decided that if at all possible, that was the place to bring the raft ashore. Hopefully, safely ashore. Knowing they'd go through the surf to reach shore, Will removed the mast from the raft, then inflated Gwen's life jacket and his own. He lowered the raft's anchor over the stern, extending all the line he had. Using the paddles, he constantly adjusted the sea anchor to keep a strain on the line, knowing his actions would keep the raft pointed toward shore. Anticipating the next wave in the medium surf and feeling no offshore wind, he tried his best to keep the raft from passing over the wave too quickly and capsizing them. When the raft neared the beach, they rode it in on the crest of a large wave. Will rowed as hard as he could, bringing them as close to the beach as possible.

"Don't jump out!" he yelled to Gwen. "Wait until the raft has grounded, then get out as quickly as you can when I tell you to."

She nodded and then waited for his orders. When he told her to jump, she jumped. *Good girl.* He jumped out, grabbed the raft and pulled it ashore, securing it for their return trip to the *Footloose.*

Once ashore and drenched from the ocean waves, they lay in the sand, breathing heavily. Will came to his feet first, then offered Gwen his hand. She took it, if somewhat reluctantly. Together, they scanned every direction. A sandy beach spread out from left to right, seeming to go on endlessly. Behind them, and equally as endless, lay an island jungle, the trees and brush appearing untouched by man.

"It's so quiet," Gwen said.

"What did you expect, a party of two-hundred-year-old natives to greet us?" Damn, why had he said that? There was no way she'd think the comment was funny.

Gwen glared at him. "Are we going to just stand here or are we going to explore the island?"

Will glanced at the sun hanging low over the western horizon. "It's too late in the day to do much exploring. It'll be nightfall within a couple hours. I suggest we stay on the beach, maybe hike a mile or so down one end. Then we can sleep here on the beach and get an early start in the morning to explore inland."

"We're going to stay on the island tonight?"

"Sure. It's not a good idea to take the raft back to the cruiser tonight. Besides, if we can gather enough drift-wood, I'll build a fire."

"A fire that can be seen if a plane flies over."

"Maybe. But it could get chilly and I wouldn't want you to be too uncomfortable sleeping on the beach."

Gwen had some difficulty keeping up with Will as they trekked down the beach. She wasn't totally out of shape, but then again, she wasn't into running marathons, either. It didn't help that Will was taller, had long, slim legs and apparently had the lungs of a long-distance runner.

They had traveled at least a mile in both directions and found nothing more than pristine beach. Not a trace of humans or animals. But they did figure out after their long walk that the island was probably no tiny speck, despite apparently being an uncharted landmass in the Atlantic. At one point, they had spotted what appeared to be hills, each progressively higher as they faded into the distance, their tops shrouded in a foggy mist that hid them from view.

They returned to the raft, their arms loaded with driftwood, which they piled high away from the water's edge and near the abundant thicket behind them. She watched in fascination as Will started the fire and fanned it to life.

"Hungry?" he asked.

"Thirsty."

He'd carried the supplies in a waterproof backpack and had left the pack hidden beneath the raft. When he lifted the raft and felt underneath, Gwen held her breath, halfway expecting the pack to be gone, thinking perhaps the natives had discovered it. Will pulled out the pack, laid it on the ground, unzipped it and retrieved two bottles of water. When he tossed one to her, their gazes met.

"You look disappointed," he said. "What's wrong? Had you expected our food to be gone?"

She didn't reply. He already thought she was teetering on the edge. No need to give him more proof.

He chuckled. "You did, didn't you? You thought maybe the natives had come out of the woods and—"

"Oh, shut up! I'm in no mood to be made fun of. I'm tired, thirsty, hungry and confused."

"And touchy."

She growled. "You're acting as if this is all some sort of game. It isn't, you know. We're stranded—either on this island or on a boat that isn't going anywhere. This is a life-or-death situation and all you can do is poke fun at my foolish hope that maybe my father isn't as crazy as everyone thinks he is."

Will gave her a heavy-lidded glare. "Do you honest to God think we've landed on some mythical island?"

"Yes." She shook her head. "No." Sighing deeply, she

turned away from him. "I don't know. I told you that I'm tired and confused."

She felt the heat of his body as he approached, coming up directly behind her but not touching her. Closing her eyes, she wrapped her arms around herself in a protective hug.

"Gwen?"

She didn't reply. She couldn't. Emotion tightened her throat.

His big hands clamped down on her shoulders. She tensed. "I don't deal well with frustration. I tend to take it out on whoever happens to be around, and this time, that's you."

"Maybe it is stupid to think this is the island my father found fifty years ago."

Will drew her closer until her back rested squarely against his chest, then he engulfed her in his big strong arms. Holding her breath, needing his comfort and understanding, but afraid to expect it, she relaxed against him.

He brushed the side of her forehead with his lips and said in a soft whisper, "I think you love your father."

She did love her father, despite his having abandoned her for a hopeless dream, an obsession that had not only ruined his life, but had brought her here, to the ends of the earth, to the very brink of death.

Cheryl Kress's stomach growled. She hadn't had anything to eat since breakfast that morning on the boat and now she wished she'd eaten every bite instead of picking at her food the way she had. Standing over the driftwood fire that Jordan Elders had built, Cheryl glanced around at the others. Captain Mick McGuire sat apart from everyone else, a good hundred feet down the beach. The Professor rested against the ruptured life raft that Jordan had managed to salvage after their disastrous landing. The raft had capsized, toppling them all into the ocean. She and Jordan had managed to get The Professor and Molly ashore, neither of them concerned in the least about Mick. Her father would have said that his type was too damn mean to die.

Poor Dr. Arnell looked ninety. A tired, haggard ninety. She wondered just how long he could last if they weren't rescued soon. And Molly. She had not regained consciousness. It would be a miracle if she lasted the night.

Cheryl's gaze rested on Jordan, who sat on the other side of the fire, his back to her as he faced the dark ocean. She would never again look at him and see a nerd. From the moment the storm had hit the *Sun Dancer,* Jordan Elders had transformed from a brainy geek into a rugged hero. In one way or another, he had saved all of them, even the nefarious Mick. Odd how taking charge, issuing orders, doing what needed to be done had come so naturally to Jordan.

Walking around the fire that she hoped could be seen from the sky, Cheryl approached Jordan. Without saying a word, she sat down beside him. He neither moved nor spoke, just kept gazing at the waves as they hit the shore.

"Jordan, dear boy," Dr. Arnell's weak, almost inaudible voice called out.

"Yes, sir?" Jordan replied without turning around.

"I'm too tired to try to find help, but you must seek out the natives tonight. If you don't, I'm afraid we'll lose Molly."

Cheryl sensed the tension in Jordan and understood his situation.

"I'm sorry, but I can't go inland tonight," Jordan replied. "We lost what few supplies we had when the lifeboat capsized. I have no compass, no flashlight and I have no idea where to go. We don't have a choice but to wait until morning."

"If you won't go, then I must," The Professor said.

Jordan groaned softly. Cheryl reached over and squeezed his hand.

Their gazes met, the three-quarter moon shimmering over them as the blaze from the fire behind them added extra illumination to the black night.

She leaned closer and whispered, "Tell him we'll go now and search for the natives, then you and I can walk up the beach and out of his sight. I give him fifteen minutes, twenty at most, before he falls asleep from sheer exhaustion."

Jordan nodded, then rose to his feet and extended his hand to help her. He turned to his old professor. "Cheryl and I will see if we can find someone. You stay here with Molly. We'll be back as soon as possible."

Smiling faintly, Dr. Arnell sighed. "Thank you. Thank you, my boy."

They walked up the beach, remaining silent until they were out of earshot, then Cheryl said, "I wish this had been The Professor's island. I wish he could have his dream before he dies."

Jordan paused, looked at her and then continued walking.

"We don't know for sure that this isn't his island."

"What?" Cheryl stopped dead still.

Jordan stopped and turned to face her. "We lost our boat in a freak storm, then our lifeboat seemed to drift on a current that led us straight to this island. An uncharted island in the middle of the Devil's Triangle. Fifty years to the day that Dr. Arnell discovered his island when he was twenty."

"You can't seriously think that this is—"

"Why do you think it's not possible?"

"Well, for one thing, this island seems to be uninhabited. There are no two-hundred-year-old natives bringing us food and water and a healing plant to save Molly's life."

"They might not know that we're here."

"Okay, you're spooking me out with talk like that."

"That wasn't my intention," he told her. "And it's quite possible that this is nothing more than an uncharted, uninhabited island. But come morning, I'm going inland…in search of Dr. Arnell's Utopia."

And then she said something that she wouldn't have thought, not in a million years, that she'd ever say. "I'm going with you. And I hope we find it. The people, the plant, everything the old man believes in."

Jordan stared at her. "Either you've changed a great deal or I didn't have any idea who you really are. There's a lot more to you than just a spoiled, bratty heiress."

"Was that a compliment?" She smiled at him.

"Just an observation."

"Well, I've observed something, too," she told him.

"What?"

"That you're quite a man, Jordan Elders. And I trust you to keep me safe."

Chapter 11

Gwen sat in front of the blazing fire, her back propped against a huge piece of driftwood, her gaze focused on the dark ocean. Was there anyone out there? A ship? A plane? Someone who would come to their rescue? Or were they trapped here on this supposedly nonexistent island, doomed to die here together? Nothing seemed real. Not this island, not her journey in search of her father, not even her relationship with Will Pierce. It was as if she had stepped outside her life—her real life—and had fallen headlong into a parallel universe. Was this how her father had felt most of his life, as if he were a part of two different worlds?

"I return bearing gifts," Will said as he came back from his short visit into the wooded area directly behind them.

Gwen glanced over her shoulder. Will carried an armful of palm fronds. She watched while he arranged the huge leaves in a large rectangle atop the sand. When he finished, he bowed to her.

"My lady's bed awaits."

"Where are you going to sleep?" she asked.

He eyed the makeshift pallet. "I thought surely you'd share with me since there's plenty of room. Besides, if it gets chilly, you might need a little body heat."

"You take the bed. I don't think I can possibly sleep tonight."

Will came over and sat down beside her. "Why's that?"

"I'd think it would be obvious. We're lost in the middle of the Atlantic. No one knows exactly where we are. We have no means of escape."

"Yeah, well, there is that." He chuckled.

She glared at him. "How can you find this amusing? We could die here."

Will shrugged. "The way I look at it, given our circumstances, we're damn lucky."

"You're going to have to explain that one to me. How can you say we're lucky?"

"We have several weeks of food, water and supplies on the *Footloose*. We've landed on a tropical island. Fish will be plentiful. Plus my guess is that there are all kinds of fruit trees and more than likely a lagoon of fresh water somewhere around. We could easily live here indefinitely."

"So you think the possibility of living here indefinitely makes us lucky?"

"It sure as hell beats the alternative."

Gwen groaned. "Well, when you put it that way…"

"And there's one other plus to our being marooned together."

"That would be?"

He grinned sheepishly. "The obvious. You're a woman. I'm a man."

"Which to you equates sex, right?"

"Right."

"I think you're being awfully presumptuous."

"I'm being realistic. Even if we're stuck here for only a few weeks, we're both going to get horny. It's just a matter of time before we—"

"Speak for yourself!" How dare he assume that because of their predicament, she'd be eager to have sex with him.

"I am speaking for myself." He ran the tips of his fingers down her spine, from shoulder blades to buttocks. "I'm all for celebrating being alive. What better way to do that than to make love?"

"It would hardly be making love," she told him, wishing he'd move his hand from where he'd spread his open palm across her lower back. "It would just be sex."

"What's wrong with just sex?" He eased his palm up, then underneath the waist of her pants and slipped inside, his flesh firm and rough against her soft buttocks. She tensed.

She couldn't go all mushy female, despite the decidedly sexual sensations clutching and releasing in her nether regions. It would be a mistake to allow what she was feeling right now to override her common sense. Will didn't want her, Gwen Arnell. He wanted a woman, and she was the only one available. If he had another choice, she seriously doubted he'd choose her. She was certainly no man's fantasy, and she hated the thought of being just a warm body in the night.

"There's nothing wrong with just sex," she told him. "As long as that's what both parties want."

"And you don't want sex? You aren't the least bit interested? You can go the rest of your life without it?" He caressed the top curve of her buttocks, then moved from one hip to the other. "Don't lie to me. I can feel you trembling. You need it as badly as I do. Admit the truth."

Was she trembling?

Yes, damn it, she *was* trembling. And it was all because of Will, because he was touching her.

Maybe he was right. It had been quite some time since she'd been with a man. The problem was that she wasn't the type for meaningless affairs, and committed relationships didn't happen all that often for her. Besides, even in the few relationships she'd had since her divorce, she had never felt completely fulfilled, either physically or emotionally. Men said "I love you" as easily as they breathed if they thought it would get them what they wanted. But no matter how sincere those three little words might be, they were just words. Without the action to back them up, they were meaningless. A woman wanted to hear those words, needed to hear them, but in the long run, actions speak louder than words. And not once had any man ever proven to her by his actions that she was the most important thing in the world to him.

"You can't give me what I want." Gwen pulled away from Will and jumped to her feet.

With one swift leap, he came up beside her and cradled his hand over her shoulder. "What makes you so sure that I can't give you exactly what you want?"

She jerked away from him. "Damn it, I'm not talking about sex. I'm sure sex with you would be great. It would be mind-boggling. Unforgettable. But I'd regret it later."

"Why would you regret it? I'm not married. You're not married. We're both adults, and I can promise you that I'm disease free and I'd bet my bottom dollar you are, too. So—"

"So what about contraception? You don't happen to have a box of condoms on you, do you?"

Raking his fingers through his thick wavy hair, Will cursed under his breath. "Yeah, that could be a problem."

"As much as I'd like to be a mother someday, I'd like to be married before I have a baby."

As if some brilliant idea had suddenly popped into his head, Will grinned. "There's more than one way to have sex."

Gritting her teeth, Gwen groaned. "You just won't give up, will you?"

"Not when I really want something."

"You don't want me."

"Oh, yes, I do."

"You want sex, and I just happen to be the only available woman." Gwen glared at him. "Thanks, but no thanks."

When he reached for her, she sidestepped his grasp and turned her back to him.

"Between your father and your ex-husband, they did quite a number on your self-esteem, didn't they?" Will made no move to touch her again.

His comment hit home, hurting her as if he'd plunged a knife into her back. But only because there was an element of truth in what he'd said. "My self-esteem is just fine, thank you."

"Maybe your self-esteem as a botanist is just fine, but not your self-esteem as a desirable woman." Will's deep, soft voice wrapped around her in the darkness, its power as potent as if he'd actually caressed her. "Just because your father didn't treasure you the way a man should treasure his little girl doesn't mean you aren't worth more than all the mythical islands and youth-serum plants that might or might not exist. And just because your husband was incapable of loving and appreciating you the way a man should doesn't mean you can't inspire complete devotion from another man."

Stop talking! Don't say these things to me. I can't bear to hear you tell me what my heart longs to hear.

With emotion lodged in her throat and on the brink of tears, Gwen walked hurriedly away from Will. The farther she moved away, the faster she walked, until she broke into a slow run as she fled along the beach into the warm, shadowy night. Only the moonlight shimmering on the ocean waves and glimmering against the crystal-white sand saved her from being lost in total darkness.

Twilight had faded into night so slowly that Cheryl's sight adjusted easily to the soft moonlight that cast a golden shadow over the waves and set the sand beneath her feet sparkling like a zillion tiny diamonds. Under different circumstances, she would have found this place beautiful, a truly unspoiled tropical paradise. But knowing she was a castaway with no means of communicating with the outside world tarnished the Eden-like atmosphere. She was certainly out of her element. Being the daughter of a billionaire, she wasn't used to roughing it.

"What's the matter?" she asked Jordan when he simply stared wide-eyed at her after she'd told him that he was quite a man. "Can't you take a compliment?"

"I, er, yes, thank you. I think. But I'm afraid I don't understand why you'd say such a thing. I thought you despised me." Jordan began walking again, moving up the beach at a leisurely pace.

Cheryl followed alongside him. "I did despise you, but I despise Tori even more for getting me into this situation. I swear I couldn't understand what she saw in you, even though she tended to always go for the brainy nerds." Cheryl laughed. "Sorry. I guess being called a brainy nerd is sort of a backhanded compliment, isn't it?"

Jordan grunted. "Yeah, I guess it is."

"I think maybe she saw something in you that I see now. I guess you really can't judge a book by its cover. I'd have never thought you'd wind up being the big, strong hero."

"Me?" he asked, honestly puzzled that she'd referred to him as a hero.

"Yes, you. You do realize that without you, the rest of us would probably be dead. In one way or another, you saved all of us today."

Jordan paused and looked out at the ocean. "I just did what had to be done."

"Yes, I know. And that's what makes you a real hero."

"You've been pretty heroic yourself. Instead of falling apart on me, you've helped me with Dr. Arnell and Molly. I appreciate that."

A long, lingering silence vibrated between them. Cheryl wasn't sure what to say or do next. If she did what her instincts told her to do, she'd go up behind Jordan and wrap her arms around him. She would tell him that she wasn't heroic at all, that she was on the verge of panic, that she was scared out of her mind. If not for trying her best to follow his example, she would already have crumbled to pieces.

"Jordan?"

"Huh?"

"Is there any chance that we'll be rescued?"

"I don't know."

"If we're not…"

Jordan faced her and pulled her into his arms. "I'm scared, too. I have no idea what's going to happen to us. I'm just hoping that we can find a freshwater stream somewhere on the island and maybe fruit trees and wild berries."

Cheryl laid her head on his chest and clung to him.

"I'm pretty much useless, you know," she told him. "I've never done anything in my entire life. I've never made a bed or fixed toast or—" She burst into tears.

Jordan cupped her face in his hands and lowered his lips to hers. His kiss took her breath away.

He skimmed his hands over her shoulders, across her back and downward to cup her buttocks. She stood on tiptoe to participate fully in the kiss. Hot, hard, tongue thrusting. Wow!

They were so absorbed in the kiss that neither of them heard the odd noise; not at first. But as Jordan lifted his head and they stared dreamily into each other's eyes, Cheryl froze.

"Do you hear that?"

He clutched her shoulders. "Be still and quiet."

She did as he ordered, not moving, not speaking, barely breathing.

In her peripheral vision, she saw a dark shadow approaching.

Could it be Mick McGuire? Had the man come after them? If so, that could only mean trouble.

Oh, God, now there was another shadow approaching and another and another.

"Jordan?" she whimpered his name.

"Shh."

"What is it?"

"I don't know."

Whoever or whatever created those dark shadows, they now surrounded Jordan and her. Circled them.

Suddenly a loud, frightened scream rent the night air. *Who was screaming?* she wondered, then realized that she was.

Stopping to catch her breath, Gwen sucked in huge gulps of air to refresh her aching lungs. Doubled over and panting, she could not hold back the tears. She cried so hard that the tears streamed down her cheeks, over her nose and off her chin. Had her entire life, all thirty-three years, led to this moment, to being deserted on an uncharted island in the middle of nowhere, with a man she barely knew? Was there no chance of their being rescued, of her having the opportunity to return to her safe and secure home in Alabama? She wanted to go back to the real world, to escape from this bizarre fantasy. Had she, in the end, become her father's daughter simply by chasing after him, hoping for the impossible just as he had? When all was said and done, was there really any difference between his improbable dream and hers? He hoped to find a mythical island where a magical plant grew, while she longed for a loving, nurturing, normal relationship with her father.

Lifting her head, Gwen stared out at the dark, endless ocean. A sense of hopelessness overwhelmed her. More than likely her father and his shipmates had encountered the same freak storm that Will and she had. But if her father and those with him had survived, where were they now? An inner voice of doom whispered one word: *Dead*. Had the Devil's Triangle, that vast section of the Atlantic that had obsessed her father, finally destroyed him?

Daddy. Daddy, where are you?

She had been so absorbed in her thoughts that she hadn't heard Will approach, hadn't realized that he had followed her, until she felt his strong arms reach around her and pull her back against his chest. And it wasn't until that moment, wrapped securely in his embrace, that Gwen knew how much she needed Will. How much she wanted him.

In another place, at another time, where the world was right-side up and life had a logical order, she would not allow herself to succumb to purely physical attraction. But here, now, reality blurred with illusion, and left her vulnerable to the fear that her life had amounted to nothing, that she would die before having ever really lived.

Absorbing Will's warmth and strength, sensing that he had the power to make her feel alive in a way she so desperately needed, Gwen leaned her head back against his chest and crossed her arms over his where they held her at the waist. With her heartbeat drumming inside her head and her body pulsing with life, she sighed deeply. Will lowered his head and brushed his lips against her neck. She shivered. He nipped at her neck, then licked a moist trail up to her ear.

"Say yes," he whispered.

"Yes." That one word reverberated inside her like an echo that had no ending.

While kissing her ear, her neck, her jaw, Will eased his hands downward, over her belly, across the top of her thighs, then delved between her legs, his fingers rubbing and petting. She moaned when he cupped her mound.

When he moved his hands up to her blouse and slowly but efficiently undid each button, she simply leaned back against him and enjoyed the sexual tension steadily building inside her. He covered her breasts with the palms of his hands and lifted them just enough so that he could flick the nipples with his thumbs. Hot, shivering sensation shot through her.

He adeptly undid the front snap of her bra and freed her breasts. When his hands touched her naked breasts, her rational mind tried to interfere with the pleasure, but she shoved aside cautious thoughts and allowed what she felt to dictate her actions.

Will kneaded her breasts gently, his thumbs and fore-fingers working magic on her nipples, which tightened and extended, sending shards of excitement shooting through her whole body. While one hand remained on her right breast, he lowered the other to her slacks and worked hurriedly to unsnap and unzip the sensible tan pants.

Within seconds, he had maneuvered the garment down her hips and over her legs. When they fell to her ankles, Gwen lifted her feet out of the slacks and kicked them aside. Wasting no time, Will slipped his hand inside her white cotton panties. As his hand inched steadily lower, she held her breath, tingling with anticipation.

As his fingers slid through the curls, Will pinched one nipple and gave her neck a sucking kiss. She whimpered, the sound a plea for him to touch her more intimately, to give her what her body yearned for. He slipped between her feminine lips and inserted two fingers inside her. She closed her thighs around his hand, trapping him. Her body shivered as his rough fingertips eased out of her and then over her highly sensitive nub. With his mouth pressed against her neck and his other hand tormenting one nipple, he increased the pressure and the tempo of his caresses between her legs, bringing her to the brink, then stopping momentarily to prolong the pleasure.

"No, please, don't stop," she cried softly.

He took her to the brink hurriedly, then paused again.

"No…no…" She whimpered.

"You're so hot…so wet…so ready."

He ended her torture, taking her over the edge with several frantic strokes. She shook and shivered and moaned, her body gushing with release. Gasping air as the aftershocks of her climax spiraled through her, Gwen's knees turned to rubber. With one hand still between her thighs and the other wrapped around her waist, Will kept her on her feet.

Giving her all the time she needed, he held her, kissed her temple, and whispered softly into her ear, "I loved the way you came for me, brown eyes."

Able to stand without assistance once again, she turned in his arms. He cupped her face and brought his lips down on hers. She smelled her own musky scent on his fingers. They kissed with raw passion as Gwen ran her hands over him, ripping open his shirt and spreading her fingertips across his hard, lean chest. Oh, how she loved the feel of him.

When she undid his jeans and tugged them downward, he immediately divested himself of the jeans, taking his briefs with them. He stood there, barefoot and naked except for his gaping blue chambray shirt. Gwen kissed a trail from nipple to nipple and was rewarded with Will's deep groans. She made her way down across his belly to the thatch of brown hair surrounding his bulging sex. When she dropped to her knees in the sand, he speared his fingers through her hair and held her head, urging her to take him into her mouth.

She had never wanted to taste a man this way, to capture him with her mouth, to pleasure him so primitively. She licked him from root to tip and loved that the action made him tremble. The heady sense of power thrilled her. She licked and teased and took the tip between her lips and sucked. She repeated these movements again and again until Will captured her head and growled.

"Take all of me," he ordered, his voice a rough rumble.

She opened her mouth and enveloped him, taking him as fully as possible. The strong masculine scent of him, the feel of his tight, muscular legs, the vital energy of his pulsing sex excited her almost beyond reason. She made passionate love to him with her mouth, giving him release. As he shook and groaned, she savored the moment of complete control, knowing that she had rendered this big, strong man temporarily helpless.

After gently easing her mouth from him, she licked her lips, capturing his taste. Will dropped to his knees in front of her, yanked her to him and kissed her until they were both breathless.

Chapter 12

Will wasn't surprised by the awkwardness between Gwen and him the following morning. What did surprise him was his own reaction to what they had shared during the night. After making love that first time, they had strolled back up the beach to the bonfire and the bed of palm fronds. They had shared the makeshift bed, Gwen wrapped in his arms. And they had made love again several times, with their mouths and hands, although he had wanted to be inside her more than anything he'd ever wanted in his life. In the warm darkness, they had explored each other's bodies and had become intimately acquainted. Gwen had a lush, womanly body, with round hips and round breasts and skin as smooth as silk.

Even though love had not been involved in what they had shared, Will couldn't deny there was something more than sex involved. Just looking at her made him hard, made him want her again. He suspected even Gwen hadn't realized that beneath her cool, controlled exterior, she possessed the passion of a wild woman.

But only with me.

That thought both tormented him and pleased him. Of course he had only his instincts to guide him—and possibly his sizable ego—but he'd bet his last dime that Gwen had never let go with another man the way she had with him last night. The very fact that her actions had not possessed the expertise that came from repeated practice had excited him unbearably.

And now, this morning, watching her as she dabbled in the ocean, cleaning herself, totally unashamed of her partial nudity, a sense of possessiveness engulfed Will. On some purely primeval level, he had claimed her as his woman.

When she emerged from the ocean, she shook her head, flipping the strands of her long, dark hair around her shoulders, spraying a circle of water droplets in every direction. Her tight nipples pressed against the thin barrier of her white cotton bra, and a dark triangle was visible through her white cotton panties. One thing for sure—he'd never look at white cotton underwear in the same way, ever again.

"What's for breakfast?" she asked as she shimmied into her wrinkled slacks.

He eyed the two apples, two granola bars and two bottles of water he'd laid out atop the knapsack. "A gourmet delight," he told her.

She offered him a hesitant smile, her gaze not quite connecting with his as she picked up her blouse from their palm-frond bed and slipped into it. "I'd kill for a cup of coffee."

And I'd kill to be buried deep inside you. "If we can find a freshwater spring or maybe even a lagoon, we can have coffee later."

"I'm glad I put coffee and tea in your knapsack." As she buttoned her blouse, she came toward him.

"I didn't want to waste our few bottles of water making coffee, but if we can find fresh water on the island, then we're set."

Gwen nodded, her gaze focused on his unbuttoned shirt instead of his face. He glanced down at where the top three buttons were missing. Her cheeks flamed hot pink. He chuckled. Apparently she'd just realized that she had ripped open his shirt last night, popping off several buttons.

When he reached out to grasp her arm, she tensed. "Come on. Let's sit down and eat. After that, we'll explore the island."

Relaxing, she nodded and allowed him to help her down onto their makeshift bed. He tossed an apple and granola bar into her lap, then handed her a bottle of water before he sat beside her.

"I wonder how big this island is," Gwen said, then unwrapped the granola bar and took a bite.

"I have no idea. But it can't be all that big since no one has ever charted its existence." He unscrewed the cap on his water bottle and took a hefty swig. "Then again, it can't be all that small because the shoreline seems to go on endlessly in both directions."

"What do you think we'll find when we go into the jungle?" Gwen alternated between bites of the granola bar and bites of the apple.

"Trees."

She swatted his arm playfully. "Very funny."

"I figure we'll find fruit trees, maybe coconut at the very least. And possibly some small wild animals."

"Wild animals?"

"Small wild animals, which I can trap and we can roast and—"

"Yuck."

"I figure there's a freshwater source somewhere, which means we won't die of thirst and we can bathe in salt-free water."

They ate in relative silence, each devouring the meager fare. After Will put on his shoes and strapped the knapsack to his back, Gwen slipped into her shoes. Preparing for their trek into the wooded area, he studied her already pink face.

"You're going to blister in this hot sun," he told her. "But it can't be helped. No cap—" he tapped her bare head "—and no sunscreen." He ran his fingertips across her cheek.

She drew in a deep breath when he touched her. "I'll manage."

"Yeah, honey, I know you will." *I'll make sure you do.*

In the early morning hours, the sun low in the eastern horizon, they entered the jungle not far from the beach. Will tore away vines that clogged their path, but the underbrush grew so heavily in places that they simply waded through it, scraping their legs and arms on briars and low branches. The deeper into the jungle they went, the more certain Will became that he had underestimated the island's size. Approximately an hour into their trek, when they emerged into a clearing, Will paused, then slowly turned in a circle. When he faced due east, he did a double take. There in the distance a mountain rose high and wide into the blue sky. How was that possible? Was he hallucinating?

"I see it, too," Gwen said, as if reading his mind.

"This doesn't make any sense." Will stared at the unbelievable. "This island is much larger than I thought, which means it can't be an uncharted island."

"What if it is? What if… Oh, God, Will, what if this really is my father's island?"

"This isn't some mythical island. It can't be. There has to be another explanation." *But what?*

"I know it's difficult to believe that this might be—"

"I don't know what's going on," he admitted. "But our main concern is survival. That means finding fresh water."

Gwen stood, riveted to the spot, staring dreamily at the mist-shrouded mountain.

"Come on." He gave her a gentle shove. "Let's get going."

He chose east, directly toward the mountain, although he surmised it would take days to reach the distant foothills.

By the time the sun shone directly overhead, Will sensed that Gwen needed to rest, but suddenly and unexpectedly, before he mentioned stopping, they came upon another clearing, this one wide and vast, as if it had been cleared recently. Not a clearing created by nature but by man. A shiver of uncertainty hit him square in the gut, instinct telling him that he and Gwen were not alone on this island. In the distance, toward the east, he thought he saw a path.

"I'm tired, Will. I need to rest," Gwen told him.

"Not yet. In a minute." He grabbed her arm and all but dragged her toward the path.

She grumbled but went with him. A few minutes later they stopped dead still, at the edge of a winding stone pathway. Standing immobile, silent and unmoving, Will heard the sound of rushing water.

"I hear water," Gwen said.

He nodded.

"Will?"

"Shh."

He listened closely, halfway expecting to hear human voices. All he heard was the water.

"Follow me," he told her. "But stay behind me. And if I issue you an order, just do what I tell you to do without question. Do you understand?"

"Yes."

They followed the stone path, a path not made by Mother Nature, until they reached a thirty-foot waterfall that flowed into a small, rocky lagoon. The water was clear, the surface shimmery with golden sunlight. Thick, lush vegetation grew in abundance around the pond.

"It's beautiful," Gwen said.

"Yeah, but the main thing is that it's freshwater."

"Can we rest now?" she asked. "Is it safe?"

"We can rest. But I'm not sure how safe this place is. I'm not sure of anything right about now."

"There are—" she cleared her throat "—or there were at one time, people on this island. Human beings made that stone path."

"Yeah, you're right. That clearing and the stone path were man-made."

"Don't you think that there's a chance, even if just a slight chance, that this is the island my father discovered when he was twenty?"

Puzzled, confused and uneasy, Will didn't respond. He found a boulder near the lagoon's edge, removed the backpack, dropped it on the boulder and then sat. Gwen followed his lead and sat beside him. While they stared at the cascading waterfall, Will tried to put his thoughts in order, to make some sense of their surroundings. A land-mass large enough to hold an enormous mountain range would hardly have gone uncharted. Something this huge couldn't hide, not even in four hundred thousand miles of ocean. So that meant that either the cruiser had veered into a charted island and they simply hadn't reached civiliza-tion yet or they were on some mysterious island, perhaps even the one Emery Arnell claimed he had discovered fifty years ago.

"Did your father ever tell you any details about the island he claims to have discovered?" Will asked.

"Then you do believe it's possible—"

"Just answer my question, will you?"

"He talked about this place—this fabulous island—with a mixture of awe and excitement in his voice," Gwen said. "But I don't remember him talking about details, other than the fact that a magical youth plant grew here, one that somehow enabled the people of the island to live, free of illness for two hundred years."

"Do you remember him mentioning a mountain range?"

"No."

"Waterfalls? Rock pathways?"

Gwen shook her head. "No. His only real interest seemed to be in the plant and its effect on the people."

"What about the people? What did he tell you about them?"

"Not much, only that they lived, on average, to be two hundred, that they were never sick and…well, that's about it."

"Did he say what they looked like, if they were dark or fair or—"

"He referred to them as natives, so I assumed they were

dark-skinned, dark-eyed, but he never actually described their physical appearance."

"Didn't you think that odd, along with the fact that this island of his had no name? You'd have thought the natives would have told him where he was and the name of their country. You'd have thought he would ask. I would, wouldn't you?"

"Yes, I suppose I would. But you have to remember that my father was only twenty, he'd just lost his entire family and he'd been near death when he washed ashore here."

Will gripped her hand tightly and squeezed. "Maybe this island is where your father landed fifty years ago, but he could easily have hallucinated about the natives and their magical plant. If he ran a high fever, if he was ill."

"You're saying it's all right to believe the island exists, that we may actually be on my father's island, but that I shouldn't believe there's magic involved, because you don't believe it's possible."

He released her hand. "There's only one way to find out. We get back on the rock path and follow it to its conclusion."

"You're right." She stood. "I'm ready when you are."

Will stood, picked up the knapsack and strapped it to his back. Then, taking the lead, he returned to the stone path. Gwen kept up with him, but only because he adjusted his gait to hers.

Less than fifteen minutes later they came to a junction. The stone path formed a cross in the middle of the jungle. The north and south sections remained narrow, while the east and west sections broadened to the width of a one-lane road.

"It's a road," Gwen said.

"So it is."

"There are people on this island. You can't deny that fact."

He nodded. "There *were* people here. The stones in the path are worn deep into the earth and are smooth on top, which means the path and that road—" he pointed to the east "—have been here for a very long time, perhaps hundreds of years."

"These people could be the natives my father talked about. And don't tell me that it's not possible."

Will grunted. How could he tell her that her father's mad, rambling stories were not possible? He couldn't. Not when he stood on an ancient path, obviously man-made, on an enormous, uncharted island.

Judging from where the sun rested in the middle of the western sky, Gwen surmised that it was early afternoon, probably around two o'clock, give or take. It seemed to her that they had been following the stone road for days instead of a couple of hours. Will had stopped twice to let her take a breather and drink some water. It irritated her no end that she was worn to a frazzle, while their long trek seemed to have had no effect on him.

As they rounded a bend in the road, Will stopped abruptly and yanked her with him as he dove into the thick jungle that lined either side of the road. Dragging her behind a tree and down on her haunches, Will put his finger to his lips. Widening her eyes, she silently questioned his actions.

And then she heard what Will had apparently heard. Voices!

Although the sound came from too far away for her to understand what was being said, she recognized human voices when she heard them.

"It's—"

Will clamped his hand over her mouth and glowered at her.

Gritting her teeth, she grabbed his hand and removed it, but she remained quiet.

He motioned for her to stay put, then rose to his feet. She came up beside him. He frowned and motioned for her to get back down behind the tree. She shook her head. After grabbing her by the shoulders, he placed his mouth on her ear and whispered, "Stay here."

She shook her head.

Then he did something totally unexpected. He caressed her cheek as he mouthed the words, "Please, stay here."

How did a woman refuse a man whose motive was to protect her, even if she neither wanted nor needed his protection. *Oh, get real, Gwen, you do need his protection.*

She nodded. The corners of Will's lips lifted ever so slightly. He caressed her cheek again, then kissed her forehead. Before she could respond, he shoved her behind the tree and urged her to squat, then he disappeared into the dense brush surrounding them.

Gwen stayed put. Waiting. Wondering. And praying a little. As the minutes ticked by, she prayed a little harder, a little longer.

Reminding herself that Will hadn't been gone all that long, so there was no reason for her to panic, not yet, Gwen did her best to be patient. Her legs ached from squatting. Sweat dotted her face and trickled between her breasts.

Just when she'd given up hope of Will returning and had decided to try to find him, he came through the jungle, silent and deadly, surprising her. The moment she saw him, she leaped to her feet and rushed to him. Throwing her arms around him, she clung to him.

"It's okay, brown eyes," he told her in a soft, low voice. "I'm back."

She smothered his face in kisses, then when he grasped her upper arms, she stilled and stared right at him.

"What did you find?" she asked.

"I could tell you, but I think it's better if you see for yourself," Will said.

"All right. Show me."

When he led her back onto the stone road, she halted and stared at him questioningly.

"We can follow the road most of the way there, then veer off into the jungle."

Trusting Will, she nodded and then followed him along the road. When the voices grew louder, easily heard, he led her off into a heavily wooded area.

"What language are they speaking?" Gwen whispered.

"I have no idea," Will replied. "It's nothing I've ever heard before, and I'm familiar with a lot of languages."

He led her through the thicket, clearing the way for her, then he stopped, pulled her around in front of him and held her shoulders while he pointed her in the direction of the voices and the laughter.

Will yanked back a veil of plush vines to give Gwen an unobstructed view. She gasped, barely managing to stifle the sound.

There before her, like something from a history book or a movie screen, lay a large village of well-constructed mud huts with thatched roofs. Tall, slender, deeply tanned natives stirred about in the village square. Men, women and children. Not a white-haired person in the cluster of people. No one looked older than forty. The men wore only simple loincloths of some creamy white material, leaving their smooth, muscular legs and chests bare. The women wore short dresses, made of the same thin off-white material, their arms and legs bare. The smaller children ran around laughing and playing, all of them totally naked. Both men and women had long, black hair, the men's knotted in one long braid and the women's plaited in three separate lengths.

"They're not the same race as the natives in Central or South America," Will whispered in her ear. "Their skin is not as dark. And their features are—"

"Egyptian," Gwen said.

Chapter 13

Egyptian wasn't the first word that came to mind, at least not for Will, but he could see where Gwen might make that assumption. His first thought had been that these natives looked Middle Eastern, possibly Arabic. But he supposed Egyptian was close enough to his assessment that he and Gwen were in agreement. The fact that this island was inhabited, and by people who bore no resemblance to the natives of Central and South America, puzzled him. Although dark-skinned, neither were they descendants of the African slaves that populated so many of the Caribbean islands.

"You know what this means, don't you?" Gwen snapped around to face him, a look of astonished joy on her face.

"Don't jump to conclusions."

"It's not much of a jump to assume that this is the island my father discovered fifty years ago and these are the people who live to be two hundred years old."

"We don't know where we are or who these people are, so—"

"So there's one way to find out. We go meet them and find out if anyone speaks English."

When she turned around and took a step forward, Will grabbed her. "Not so fast. We have no idea if these people are friendly. For all we know they could be cannibals." Okay, so that notion might be a little farfetched, but his concern about their friendliness was perfectly logical.

Gwen grinned at him. "Cannibals? Look at them." She pointed toward the village. "Do they look uncivilized to you?"

"We can't just go walking into their camp," Will told her. "First we need to observe them and get some idea what's what."

"Aren't you being overly cautious?"

"It pays to be cautious. Let's get out of sight and discuss this. Okay?"

She hesitated, then replied, "Okay. I yield to your superior knowledge and experience in situations like this."

He drew her farther into the jungle, away from the village. When they were far enough away to be neither seen nor heard by anything other than the colorful birds dotting the trees, Will paused.

"No matter who these people are, we know nothing about their culture, their laws, their religious beliefs. Their culture could be radically different from anything we know. We can't walk into their camp and automatically know what is and is not acceptable to them. Do you understand?"

She nodded. "Yes, of course. It's as if we've landed on another planet, isn't it?"

"Sort of. And that's all the more reason to be cautious, to take our time making contact."

"How long should we wait?"

"At least another day. I want to observe them, get as close as possible without them noticing me. Once I determine a few things, I'll approach a single person and use sign language."

"You mean, *we* will approach—"

"No, I mean I will. Once I determine there's no danger, I'll come back for you."

She shook her head.

"For God's sake, Gwen, now is not the time to be stubborn."

"And now is not the time for you to go all macho protective on me," she told him. "If something happens to you, just how long do you suppose I could survive on my own?"

"I think you're a lot more resourceful than you think you are."

"Maybe, but it would be only a matter of time before I encountered the natives or had to go to them for help, right?"

Will knew this was a losing battle. "All right. I'll observe these people today, then we'll camp in the jungle, and tomorrow morning we'll go into the village and let the chips fall where they may."

"I have a good feeling about this. If we're friendly and courteous, I truly believe they will not see us as their enemy."

"I hope you're right." Without more knowledge of these people, Will wasn't going to assume anything. "Let's set up a campsite and get you situated, then I'll go—"

"I'm going back with you," she interrupted him again. "I'll be quiet and I'll follow your orders, but I want to observe them, too."

Will groaned. "Whatever you do, stay out of sight and don't leave my side."

By late afternoon they had been watching the village for several hours and had seen nothing suspicious, simply the daily activities of a people who apparently had no modern conveniences. They baked in huge central ovens and roasted meat over central open fire pits.

Staying on the outskirts, Gwen and Will were able to ascertain that the village was comprised of maybe thirty-five well-constructed huts, the exterior walls whitewashed. In the center of the village was what Will assumed might be a meeting house. Not far from the village, huge fields of grain grew profusely, along with several large gardens filled with a variety of vegetables. In another area, there was a grove of trees, all heavily laden with ripening fruit.

Gwen quickly studied the fields, gardens and the fruit trees, trying to identify the various plants. Without closer inspection, she could only guess, and although some appeared nothing out of the ordinary, typical tropical vegetation, others were unfamiliar, perhaps hybrids of some type.

While they watched what appeared to be a daily routine of men coming in from the fields and being met by their wives and children, a sudden disturbance caught their attention. Escorted by two guards, both carrying spears, a man whose appearance set him apart from the others walked into the village. Although obviously of the same race, he wore a tunic of deep scarlet and carried a case fashioned out of some type of leather. The man Will had picked out as the village leader met the visitor, greeted him with a hand signal that was probably the equivalent of a handshake, then led him inside one of the large huts.

Whispering, Gwen said, "Who do you suppose that is?"

"Someone important. A ruler from another village or a tax collector or a witch doctor. Your guess is as good as mine."

"I wish we understood their language."

"Yeah, that would help."

"If we knew what they were saying, it would help us to know how they might feel about us being here."

"We'll just have to hope that when the time comes, we can communicate by using some sort of sign language, and if we're stuck here indefinitely, we should be able to learn their language."

Gwen looked right at him. "In the excitement of discovering that this island is inhabited, I'd almost forgotten that we're all but marooned here."

"There's no 'all but' to it, honey, we are marooned here."

She sighed. "If this turns out to be my father's island, it won't be fair that we found it, not unless he somehow can make his way here, too. He's the one who should be rediscovering this place, not me."

Will admired her devotion to her father, even if he felt it was somehow misguided and certainly not earned. No matter what great deeds a person might perform in a lifetime, if a person failed as a father, they failed at their most important job. If he ever had a child, he'd try his damnedest to be a good parent. Better than his old man had been and for sure better than Dr. Emery Arnell had been.

"Look, someone's coming out of the house where that man went in." Gwen's attention focused on that single hut.

Will narrowed his gaze when he saw a young man—a slim, brown-haired, fair-skinned man in his late twenties, emerge from the hut. Definitely not a native. He wore tattered jeans, a dirty shirt and had heavy beard stubble.

"Look." Gwen grabbed Will's arm.

Before Will could reply, a young woman followed the man from the hut. He put his arm around the redheaded girl, who placed her head on his shoulder as she cried. Will recognized her immediately from her photograph.

"Oh, my God! That's Cheryl Kress, isn't it?" Gwen tightened her hold on Will's arm.

"Yes, I believe it is. And my guess is that the man with her is Jordan Elders."

"Then that means my father—"

As if on cue, a tall, distinguished white-haired man, his shoulders slumped and tears glistening in his eyes, emerged from the hut.

"Daddy," Gwen cried loudly.

Will cursed through clenched teeth.

Gwen released his arm and shoved aside the foliage hiding them from view. Will reached for her, but she managed to escape before he grabbed her. *Damn! Why couldn't she think with her head instead of her heart?* She was heading straight into the village.

Will rushed after her, catching up with her only after they were spotted by Gwen's father's shipmates, as well as numerous natives. Coming up behind her, Will clasped her hand. She paused and smiled at him.

"It's my father. He's alive. He's all right."

Dr. Arnell's head jerked up, his gaze scanning the area. When he saw Gwen, he did a double take, then cried out her name.

"It's my little Gwendolyn!"

He broke away from the others and hurried toward her. Despite the man's age and the weariness that etched his features, Will saw a strong resemblance between the old man and his daughter. Same dark eyes, same square jaw and prominent cheekbones, same high forehead.

Gwen broke into a run, rushing headlong into her

father's open arms. Will stood back a few feet, his gaze darting from them to The Professor's shipmates to the large group of natives collecting around them. He didn't see any weapons, other than the spears held by the two escorts who waited outside the hut where the scarlet-robed man had entered. But considering the odds, unless he had a machine gun, he wouldn't be able to take out more than a few natives before their sheer number overcame him. Maybe, just maybe, these people were friendly and not hostile. The Professor, Jordan Elders and Cheryl Kress seemed unharmed, even if they all looked tattered, worn and upset about something.

Gwen's father pushed his daughter back, clutched her shoulders and stared at her, apparently happy to see her. "It's another miracle, your being here. But it was meant to be, wasn't it? It is only fitting that you're here to share this magnificent discovery with me."

"Then this *is* your island," Gwen said. "The one you've been searching for all these years?"

"Oh, yes, this is my island. And it has a name, you know. It's Umi. It's an Egyptian word meaning *life*."

"Egyptian?"

"Yes. The village elder, Sebak, has been very kind to us. He is trying to help us. He even sent to another village for a healer for Molly."

"Molly Esteban is with you?" Gwen glanced at the guarded hut.

"She was…injured…and there seems to be nothing that can be done for her. It's too late."

"Daddy, how did you communicate with this man named Sebak?"

The Professor turned and motioned to the tall, broad-shouldered man with a dark, lean body and thick black hair braided to one side. "Please, come and meet my daughter and—" He glanced at Will.

"My friend Will," Gwen said. "He and I have been one step behind you all the way from Puerto Nuevo."

"If only I had known you would actually come to Puerto Nuevo, I would have waited," Dr. Arnell said. "But you were so adamant about not joining me."

The man called Sebak approached, his eyes alert and inquisitive as he surveyed first Gwen and then Will. "You are welcome to Oseye and to the great land of Umi." His English was excellent, spoken with only a slight accent.

Startled, Gwen said, "You speak English."

"Sebak speaks English and French and Spanish," Emery Arnell explained. "As do one or two of the other villagers. But most do not."

"The scholars of Umi are fluent in many languages," Sebak added.

"Are you one of these scholars?" Will asked as he moved protectively to Gwen's side. Although he sensed that Sebak didn't pose a threat, at least not right now, Will did pick up on something negative, some odd gut-instinct type of warning.

Sebak smiled. "No, I am simply a village elder. But my eldest son, Darius, is a scholar."

"Look, I don't mean to be rude," Will said. "But exactly where are we? Where is Umi located? I don't think I've ever seen it on any map. Why is that?"

"Please, the questions can wait until later." Dr. Arnell took Gwen's hand. "Come with me and let me introduce you to my assistant, Jordan Elders, and to—"

"No, I don't think the questions can wait." Will looked

directly at Sebak. "I've asked a simple, uncomplicated question. Where are we?"

Sebak's facial expression didn't alter, not by a twitch or a nod. He met Will's determined stare and replied, "Your question is simple, but the answer is very complicated and best left until later, until we have dealt with the woman's death." He glanced toward the guarded hut. "My people are unaccustomed to one so young dying. It will be difficult for them to understand, and I must explain to them that she and all of you who are visitors from outside Umi, are people who do not share our gift of longevity."

Gwen's gaze connected with Will's for a split second, silently communicating. He could almost hear Gwen saying, "This is my father's island and everything he has told us about it is true." And although he was pretty damn sure she was picking up on his doubts and concerns, he was certain that she thought he was overreacting, that he had no reason to distrust Sebak.

But he wasn't overreacting. Something wasn't quite right here. And it was a lot more than the weird factor, more than his when-did-we-enter-the-Twilight-Zone reaction to this entire situation.

"Sebak is right," Dr. Arnell said. "There will be time enough to ask questions, to study the island, to explore the wonders of Umi, once we've tended to my dear Molly." Tears glazed the old man's dark eyes as he squeezed Gwen's hand. "I didn't tell you about Molly because I wanted you two to meet in person and for our engagement to be a surprise for you. I haven't cared for a woman as deeply as I do Molly since your mother."

The curious natives who surrounded them began whispering in their unique language, but they quieted the moment Sebak's dark gaze circled the crowd. He spoke to them in their native language, his voice loud and authoritative, his words dispersing them, sending them back to their evening routines.

"Emery, please bring your daughter and her—" Sebak looked to Will. "Emery's daughter is your woman, is she not?"

Without giving his answer a moment's thought, Will replied, "Yes, she's my woman."

Sebak nodded. Dr. Arnell smiled faintly and sighed, as if greatly relieved that Will had given Sebak the correct answer. Another red warning flag popped up in Will's mind.

"Come along. We will prepare a place for you," Sebak said. "If you wish to stay with Emery until his woman's earthly life ends, you may do so. I will send someone with food and water." He then spoke to The Professor. "I will make preparations for your woman's farewell."

"Thank you," Dr. Arnell said.

After Sebak left them, Gwen stopped her father before he returned to the guarded hut. "What was that all about, that business of my being Will's woman?"

"Apparently, it is the custom with these people," Jordan Elders said, as he and Cheryl approached. "A woman's identity and status is based upon the man to whom she belongs."

"You're kidding?"

"No, he's not kidding," Cheryl said. "We found out pretty quickly that around here, if a woman doesn't already belong to a man, they will give her to someone. Otherwise she has no identity and quickly becomes an outcast."

"Don't go all Women's Lib on me," Dr. Arnell told

Gwen. "Please don't judge these people until we get to know them and understand them."

"I don't want to get to know them much more," Cheryl said. "They've been nice enough, but I swear, they creep me out."

"You're Cheryl Kress," Will said.

"Yes, I am. How did you know?"

"I'm Will Pierce, a private detective. Your father hired my agency to track you down and bring you home."

Cheryl's eyes widened. She smiled warmly, and fresh tears sprang into her eyes.

"You can't imagine how ready I am to go home." She glanced from Gwen to Will and back again. "How did you two hook up?"

"We met in Puerto Nuevo and quickly realized we were on the same quest," Will told her. "Once we found out that both the girl I'd been sent to find and Gwen's father were connected to Jordan Elders, we simply followed Mr. Elders's path."

"I wish you'd found us sooner," Jordan said. "I'm afraid we got ourselves hooked up with a criminal and then hit a freak storm and wound up on Dr. Arnell's island."

"I assume you came by boat," Dr. Arnell said. "Dare I hope it survived the storm?"

"It survived," Will replied. "But unfortunately the engines aren't working and neither is the radio or anything else."

Dr. Arnell waved his hand, as if brushing off any worry. "It doesn't matter. I'm sure Sebak will provide us with a boat when the time comes for us to leave."

Will noticed Cheryl rolling her eyes heavenward. Apparently, the young woman was as skeptical as he was about this island being some kind of magical paradise. On the other hand, Gwen and Jordan Elders were probably so devoted to Emery Arnell that, despite any misgivings they might have, they both wanted to share his enthusiasm over finally rediscovering his Utopia.

Utopia by any other name...

Umi. An Egyptian word meaning *life.* Isn't that what The Professor had said?

The Egyptian connection puzzled Will as much as anything else, adding to his list of questions. Questions that Sebak seemed very reluctant to answer.

Gwen had stayed with her father in the hut where an unconscious Molly Esteban had been cared for by a healer. In those quiet, somber hours before Molly died, Gwen's father had explained not only how Molly had been shot saving his life, but also about the abilities of the man he referred to as the *adom*, meaning *one* who receives help from God.

"The people of Umi are never sick, and all live to at least two hundred," her father had told her. "But they are not completely immune to accidents, to bodily injuries, and therefore they require a healer. The *adom* is somewhat like one of our doctors, only these men have a combination of medical and spiritual knowledge."

"Witch doctors," Gwen had said before thinking. "Sorry, Father."

"No, no. It's quite all right. In a way, that's what the *adom* is. But unfortunately, since Molly had never been given the Eshe plant before, giving it to her now would do little to help her. One dose doesn't heal. Only repeated doses over several years achieves the desired effect."

"The Eshe plant? Is that the youth-serum plant?"

Emery nodded. "Just as *umi* means *life* in Egyptian, so

does *eshe*. The island provides life for the people and the plant prolongs that life."

Molly Esteban died shortly after nightfall and was taken by the natives out of the hut and through the village. When Gwen questioned her father, he shook his head, requesting her silence. Then he walked away from her and went with Sebak, the two men walking slowly behind the small procession carrying Molly's body away from the village.

How at home her father seemed here, how easily and quickly he had adapted to these people and their customs. Had he, all those years ago, learned more about them than he'd ever told anyone?

A young native woman came up beside Gwen, touched her arm and motioned to her. When she spoke, Gwen did not understand a word she said, but followed the girl to a small hut on the far side of the village. When she drew closer, she saw Will, Jordan, Cheryl and another man standing outside near an open fire pit that gave off heat and light. Odd how soon after sunset the temperature had begun dropping. Not that it was cold by any means, but with each passing hour, it became chillier.

"Where's Dr. Arnell?" Jordan asked.

"Molly Esteban is dead." Gwen went straight to Will, who slipped his arm around her waist.

"Molly's dead?" the scraggly middle-aged man asked.

"Yes, and you killed her," Cheryl told him.

"He's Mick McGuire." Gwen spoke her thoughts aloud.

"And you're The Professor's little girl, huh?" Mick moved in closer to the others and gave Gwen a once-over. "You're not so little, are you? You're all grown-up and filled out pretty good."

Mick McGuire made her skin crawl. Not only did he look sleazy and dirty, his attitude gave away his white-trash background.

Will stepped between Gwen and Mick. She thought she heard Will growl, a sound deep and low in his throat.

"Don't get bent out of shape, buddy," Mick said. "I get it that she's yours. Besides, I've got my eye on one of the native girls. One of the young ones. You know, one with a firm little ass and a pair of big tits."

"Why don't you shut up, McGuire. You're disgusting," Cheryl said.

"You'll be sleeping out under the stars on a pallet again tonight," Jordan told Mick. "You're not sharing a hut with either of us." He hitched his thumb toward himself, then toward Will. "Only couples have their own huts. Single men who have been ostracized are expected to sleep outside, and since Dr. Arnell explained to Sebak that Molly's injuries were caused by McGuire here, he's persona non grata."

Mick glared at Jordan. "I'll find a corner for myself, but you just remember that when it comes time to go for the gold, I expect to get my share." Mick turned around and walked off.

"What's he talking about, what gold?" Gwen asked.

"He's talking about the Eshe plant," Jordan said. "It seems there is a special plant that grows on this island, the one The Professor told us about, and Mick wants his share of the money when we take the plant back to the rest of the world."

A tight knot of apprehension formed in Will's gut. "Does Sebak know about Dr. Arnell's plans to take the plant off the island and share it with the world?" Will asked.

Jordan shook his head. "We've been on the island about

twenty-four hours, and in that time Dr. Arnell's main concern has been saving Molly. He thought certain the Eshe plant could be used to heal her."

"What have you found out about this place, this island? And about Sebak and these people?" Will asked.

"Not a great deal." Jordan nodded to Cheryl. "As you already know, a woman has no status unless she belongs to a man. First to her father or eldest male relative and then to her mate. Every woman is placed with a man as quickly as possible. That's the reason I claimed Cheryl."

"I understand," Will told him.

"As far as I know, only Sebak and a couple of other men in the village speak English. The others speak some ancient tongue that not even The Professor is familiar with."

"Have you been able to figure out exactly where we are and why this island has never been charted, why it's not located on any map?"

"We're in the Atlantic Ocean, inside the Bermuda Triangle. This island has never been charted and isn't on any map because—" Jordan paused "—because it isn't visible to the outside world."

Will squinted as he glared at Jordan. "Run that one by me again. If it's not visible, how come Gwen and I were able to see it? Why were you—"

"I'm not sure, but I believe that Dr. Arnell's theory that the island is only visible once every so many years, maybe every fifty years, might be correct. And that means people can land on the island and depart only during a specific time frame."

"Which would be how long?" Will asked.

"When he was twenty, The Professor stayed here three weeks, then he was sent away. My guess is that the window of opportunity to arrive and depart is connected to that three-week time frame."

"If Dr. Arnell's theory is correct, that means if we don't leave this island within a specific time frame, be it three weeks or four, then we'll be trapped here for years, maybe for the rest of our lives."

Chapter 14

Gwen had wanted to speak to her father again tonight, but Sebak had forbidden it. When a loved one dies on Umi, the deceased person's mate is expected to stay with the body that night, until at midnight, when the body is cremated. Then at dawn the mate takes the ashes and distributes them over a place called the Fields of Eshe.

"Isn't Eshe the name of the plant that keeps everyone healthy and gives you a long life span?" Gwen had asked Sebak.

Sebak had nodded, but said nothing, then departed hurriedly with a group of men that Will had said he believed to be Sebak's guards. Although the natives had carried no weapons, all six of the men with Sebak had been very young, quite tall and muscular.

Since watches didn't work here on Umi, there was no way to tell the exact time. But not long after Sebak departed, natives went around and extinguished all the central outdoor fires. Two men motioned for Gwen, Will, Jordan and Cheryl to enter their huts.

"Let's do as we're told, for now," Will said. "No need to create a problem until we figure out what's what around here."

Although she and Will dreaded the thought of telling Cheryl about her friend Tori's death, they felt she had a right to know, so they invited the other couple to join them in their hut.

"Tori's dead? How…? I don't understand." Cheryl's eyes filled with tears.

"She was strangled and left on the beach in Puerto Nuevo," Will told her. "There's a good possibility that Mick McGuire murdered her."

While Jordan held a weeping Cheryl, he looked directly at Will. "What can we do? We can't let the guy get away with killing Tori and Molly Esteban, too."

"There's nothing we can do now," Will said. "But once we get off this island, we'll turn him over to the proper authorities."

Jordan took a grieving Cheryl back to their hut, leaving Will and Gwen alone to settle in for the night. For the first time since entering the hut, Gwen took a really good look. She wasn't sure what she'd been expecting, but definitely not the neat, well-maintained contents that, although certainly not modern, were not crudely constructed. There was a wooden table and four chairs in an area near a fireplace in which a roaring fire blazed. A large black kettle hung over the fire, its contents smelling of stew. A bowl of fresh fruit and a large, oval loaf of bread, surrounded by thick, fat, glowing candles, graced the center of the smooth, polished tabletop. On the other side of the room was a glossy wooden bed framed by sheer fabric that created a canopy. The bed itself boasted a thick cotton mattress and was covered with creamy white bed linens, in a cloth similar to the clothing the natives wore, and topped with a thick white quilt. The walls were a mellow cream, as if once white and now yellowed slightly by age. There was no indoor bathroom. Cheryl and Jordan had explained that the natives bathed in the nearby lagoon and that four centrally located outhouses were spread about the village.

"You're awfully quiet." Gwen placed her hand on Will's shoulder.

Sitting in front of the fireplace, his chair sideways to give him a view of the door, he glanced up at her. "There's something not right about this place."

She smiled. "You mean other than the fact that its very existence is an incredible mystery and that if the Eshe plant really can prolong life, my father will become very famous."

"And very rich."

"I don't think the money matters to him."

"Probably not," Will said. "But it will matter to others."

"You mean once we're off the island and my father takes the plant back to the world."

"Yeah, if that ever happens."

"What are you trying to tell me?"

Will's shoulders heaved, then relaxed as he took a deep breath. "There is no logical explanation for why this island even exists, yet here we are. And for all intents and purposes, we're trapped here, with no way to leave."

"Don't you think Sebak will help us leave, just as someone once helped my father leave all those years ago?"

"Possibly. We can hope they will. But something tells me that they're not going to be too keen on the idea of your father taking samples of the Eshe plant with him."

"But why would they object?" Gwen knew the answer the moment she asked the question. "Oh. They don't really want anyone else to know about the existence of Umi, do they?"

"Which doesn't make sense if your father's theory is correct that this island is visible only every fifty years." Will rose to his feet, rubbed the back of his neck and cursed under his breath. "Do you realize how crazy that sounds? An island the size of Umi going undetected just isn't possible."

"We're like *Alice Through the Looking Glass,* aren't we? We've entered another world."

"You said it, honey. That and then some." Will paced back and forth, then paused and looked right at her. "If this island is invisible, then these natives or maybe the scholars of Umi that Sebak mentioned know a way of cloaking the island or it happens naturally somehow. Then for some reason, every so often, maybe every fifty years, or twenty or whatever, it becomes visible to the outside world. If it's every five or ten years, then once this place is known to the world, and the Eshe plant is proven to provide longevity—"

"The world will come calling and the island will be overrun by outsiders."

"Exactly."

"My father won't leave here without the Eshe plant," Gwen said.

"We need to talk to Sebak tomorrow and get some things settled." Will grasped her shoulders. "You have to convince your father that our only chance of leaving this place alive may depend upon him."

Gwen glowered at Will. "How can you ask me to persuade my father to give up his lifetime dream of bringing back this miracle plant to the world?"

Will tightened his hold on her shoulders. "What's more important, your father trying to take the Eshe plant with him or our living long enough to leave this island?"

Gwen jerked away from him. "What makes you so sure that it's an either-or situation?"

"Gut instinct," he told her. "And if you'll think with your head instead of your heart, you'll know I'm right."

Dr. Emery Arnell observed the beautiful sight as dawn light shimmered pale-gold over the Fields of Eshe, a valley located four miles from the village of Oseye. Emery and Sebak had been taken from the crematorium to the fields by a rickshaw-type conveyance pulled by two strong young men from Sebak's village.

Emery stood on a knoll overlooking the endless fields where the tall, willowy Eshe plants grew in profusion. Their yellow-green leaves glistened with dewdrops in the faint illumination. The early morning air was crisp and clean.

"Come," Sebak said. "I will walk with you as you distribute your woman's ashes."

Emery held the silver urn in which Molly's ashes had been placed. He had known her for such a short time, but had come to adore her, perhaps only in a way a doddering old fool can love a beautiful, young woman. Even knowing that she had played him for a fool did not lessen his fondness for her. After all, in the end, she had given her life to save his.

As they entered the fields where the knee-high plants grew, Sebak pointed to the urn. "Turn the cap and it will open partially, enough to allow a small amount of ashes to come out, a little at a time."

Emery nodded, turned the urn's round cap and then followed Sebak as he led him along the narrow paths, up and down the rows of Eshe plants. It took no more than five minutes to empty the urn, which Sebak took from him, laid on the ground and stomped on it with his foot. The silver urn, apparently made of some porous and easily broken material, smashed into tiny shards no bigger than a child's fingernails.

Sebak then turned to Emery and said, "We will walk to the end of this row and then offer our prayers for the after-life of your woman before we return to Oseye."

Sebak's prayers were in his native tongue, one Emery suspected was unknown anywhere else on earth, perhaps a dialect spoken thousands of years ago.

They were taken to within a mile of Oseye by the rickshaw-type buggies, then were put on foot to continue their journey.

"I have many questions," Emery said.

Sebak nodded.

"I told you that I washed ashore on this island fifty years ago, when I was only twenty. I have been searching for Umi all these years without any success. Why was I never able to find this island again?"

"I recall when I was a youth of forty, a young boy from the outside world arrived on Umi, in the nearby village of Niut. I have a cousin who lives there who told me about this boy." Sebak walked slowly, keeping in step with Emery. "You were helped by the people of his village, and once you were recovered, you were sent back to your world."

"Why did your people send me away? Why wasn't I allowed to stay and—"

"You were sent away to save your life, just as you and the others must leave very soon. You cannot stay in Oseye. It is not safe for outsiders to remain on Umi."

"I'm afraid I don't understand."

Sebak was silent for several minutes, then he paused and faced Emery. "Here on Umi, we live a long, healthy life filled with peace and contentment. We have good food, sweet music, happy days of work and nights of pleasant sleep."

"You live in paradise," Emery said.

"Yes, paradise." Sebak's brow wrinkled. "There are several villages spread out over the island, all similar to Oseye, but the high priest and his scholars, along with their elite brigade and their families, live in the center of the island, atop Mount Kaphiri."

Emery's heartbeat accelerated as excitement flushed through his body. A high priest. An elite brigade. Brilliant scholars.

"I must meet with your high priest," Emery said. "I must see everything here on Umi. Meet everyone—"

"No!" Sebak clamped his hand over Emery's shoulder. "The only contact we have with the priestly tribe is when the Eshe is distributed every year to the villagers."

"I don't understand, if you grow the Eshe, why is it not available to you—"

"The Eshe does not belong to us. It belongs to our high priest. He and he alone harvests the crop each year. We are given enough Eshe for the entire village…." Sebak paused, then his gaze locked with Emery's. "We exchange the life of one villager for the Eshe. Usually the oldest person in the village volunteers to go with the elite brigade."

At first Emery was uncertain that he had understood correctly what Sebak had told him. Surely he did not mean that a villager's life was given in exchange for the Eshe. Perhaps the person simply went into some type of servitude.

"What happens to the person who is taken?"

Sebak said quietly, "This person is sacrificed by the high priest to appease the gods." Sighing heavily, Sebak released his hold on Emery's shoulder.

The truth hit Emery hard. This incredible paradise, this magical island that he had spent his life pursuing was ruled by an order of priests who demanded human sacrifice in exchange for giving the villagers long life and good health.

"Outsiders do not understand the ways of our world," Sebak told him.

"Have very many outsiders found Umi?"

Sebak nodded. "Many? Over thousands of years, quite a few have been brought to Umi. When the island is visible for one month every ten years, the sea brings visitors to our shores. In the past, long ago, the high priest ordered their deaths, fearing the world would learn of Umi. But we are not killers. We do not wish harm to anyone. We, the people of Umi's villages, send our unwanted visitors away whenever we can, before the elite guard learns of their existence and takes them to the high priest. This is what was done for you fifty years ago."

Emery grabbed Sebak's arm. "Can you help us leave Umi as soon as possible?"

"Yes, of course. The elite brigade will not make their rounds to Oseye for three weeks. We are the last village on their route."

Clutching Sebak's arm tightly, Emery asked, "And you will give me some samples of the Eshe plant to take with me, won't you?"

Sebak flung Emery's hand from his arm. "No, you cannot take any of the Eshe plants with you. It is forbidden for anyone to cut the Eshe plants except members of the elite brigade. We are allowed only to scatter the ashes of our loved ones in the fields to nourish the roots of the Eshe plants."

"But how would the elite brigade know if I took only a few plants."

"The Fields of Eshe are guarded day and night by the power of the high priest. If one plant is removed, Lord Baruti would know."

"I don't believe this. It's simply something you've been told to prevent you from harvesting the Eshe yourselves."

"The high priest does not lie to his people. It is blasphemy for you to say such a thing."

Realizing he must reassure his host, the man in whose hands his fate and the fate of his party rested, Emery said, "Then I apologize. I meant no offense. I will, of course, abide by your laws." Yes, he would apologize. He would try to make things right. He would say whatever was necessary to reassure Sebak. But in the end, no matter what, he would not leave this island without a sample of the Eshe plant.

Gwen woke warm and safe in Will's strong arms. When had he come to bed? What time was it? Why was she in his arms? Coming out of a restless sleep, she opened her eyelids, then closed them when Will's lips pressed against her neck. She shouldn't be lying here enjoying this moment. She should still be angry with Will. They had argued last night. She had been so furious with him that she had walked away from him, to end an argument neither of them could win. She had gone to bed, fully clothed, leaving him standing by the fireplace. She had lain there for hours, waiting for him to come to her, to apologize, to tell her that he understood her need to support her father, that he would stand by her, come what may.

But she had fallen asleep waiting.

Will nuzzled Gwen's ear. She shivered. All he had to do was touch her and she unraveled. She hadn't meant to fall in love with Will. After all, she knew only too well that he wasn't in love with her.

"Still mad at me, brown eyes?" he whispered as he eased his hand down over her belly and slipped it between her thighs.

Her femininity clenched and unclenched, longing for the feel of his fingertips without the restriction of her slacks and panties.

"I might still be a little upset with you," she told him.

"Tell me what I have to do to make things right." He nipped her neck as his thumb stroked her through the barrier of her clothing.

"Mmm-mmm. Please don't do that. I can't think when you touch me."

He flipped her over onto her back and straddled her hips. Gazing down at her, he smiled. "It's not necessary for you to think. Just feel."

He kissed her throat, then nudged his way to the V-neckline of her blouse. She quivered as his hot breath fanned over her skin. And when he opened his mouth and brought it down on one breast, she gasped. He suckled her through her blouse and bra, making a damp mark on the material.

She bucked up, bringing her mound against his hard sex.

"We've got on too many clothes," he told her, then lifted himself up and off and quickly removed all his clothes.

She unbuttoned her blouse and removed it, then discarded her bra, slacks and panties. When he came back to her, they were both naked and aroused. She held open her arms to him.

"Do you have any idea how much I want to be inside you?" He rubbed himself intimately against her.

She grasped his shoulders and lifted herself against him, joining him in the undulating dance. "I want that, too, but we can't."

"Yeah, I know."

When he kissed her and his big, hard body covered her, she longed for any excuse to succumb to temptation. They were trapped on an island that wasn't supposed to exist, in a world that neither of them understood. Weren't the odds against their ever escaping from Umi? If they were forced to remain here, she would continue to be Will's woman, wouldn't she?

As his hands caressed her, aroused her, and his mouth tormented first one breast and then the other, all rational thought ceased to exist for Gwen. She was ruled by her needs, by the primitive longings urging her to mate with Will.

As her hands covered his body with enticing caresses, her desire grew stronger. "Make love to me."

"That's what I'm doing," he mumbled against her breast.

She circled his erection and urged him between her thighs, opening herself for him, inviting him in.

"Are you sure?" he asked, his voice a husky groan.

"I'm sure."

He didn't wait for her to have second thoughts. He slipped his hands beneath her, cupped her buttocks and lifted her up to meet his downward lunge. He shoved into her; she expanded to take him completely. Nothing had ever felt so good, so right. She wanted to shout, "I love you." She wanted to hear him say that he loved her, too. But as soon as he began moving inside her, in and out, increasing the tempo ever so gradually, she didn't need words any more than he did. All she needed was Will. Buried inside her. Making passionate love to her. Filling her world so completely that nothing and no one else existed.

Her release came first, in a frenzy of sensation. And then, as if her climax triggered it, his came seconds later. They moaned and shivered with pleasure. And when Will collapsed on top of her, she wrapped her arms around him, capturing him, keeping them joined as the aftershocks of release rippled through them. Minutes later, he rolled over and off her, then pulled her to his side and kissed her.

Neither of them spoke for a good while afterward. They just lay together enjoying those lethargic, sated moments after sex.

Will caressed her naked hip. "Are you okay, brown eyes?"

"I'm fine," she said. "No, I'm better than fine. I'm wonderful."

Will chuckled. "We're good together. You know that, don't you?"

"Yes, I know."

"When we get off this damn island, I'm buying you some red panties and a red bra and we're going to spend a week in bed at some swanky hotel, doing nothing but making love."

"A whole week, huh?"

"Yeah, at least a week, then we'll—"

A loud banging on the hut's single wooden door interrupted Will midsentence.

"What the hell?" he grumbled.

"Will. Gwen. It's Cheryl. Jordan sent me to get you two. The Professor is back and he's talking crazy, saying all kinds of wild things about high priests and human sacrifices."

"We'll be there in a minute," Will said.

"Hurry, will you? Jordan's trying to calm The Professor, but he's not having much luck."

Will and Gwen rummaged around on the floor and the foot of the bed searching for their rumpled clothes. After gathering up their garments, they took turns hurriedly washing up, using water from a clay pitcher sitting on the hearth. They dressed and left their hut, intending to go next door to the hut Jordan and Cheryl shared. But once outside, they heard Jordan and Emery Arnell arguing, then Gwen's father came storming out of Jordan's hut.

"Daddy!" Gwen called to him.

He stopped and stared at her.

"What's wrong?" She went to him, took his hands in hers and forced a smile, hoping to reassure him. "Please, tell me what's going on."

Jordan and Cheryl emerged from the hut, but didn't approach Emery. Will glanced at Jordan who shook his head.

"Jordan refuses to believe me. He thinks I've lost my mind," Emery said.

"I'm sure that's not true." Gwen glanced at Jordan. "Please, tell my father that you don't think he's crazy."

"I didn't say he was crazy," Jordan said. "I told him that he was talking crazy." Jordan focused on Emery. "Tell them what you told me. About the high priest and the human sacrifices and—"

"It's true," Emery said, his eyes wild. "Sebak told me. There are villages all over the island, but high atop the mountain is a city where the high priest lives, along with his scholars and an elite brigade. Although the *villagers* are kind to visitors from the outside world, the high priest orders outsiders to be killed. He will not let them leave the island."

They all listened as The Professor rambled on. His tale of the sacred Eshe plant, human sacrifice, a diabolical high priest and a murderous elite brigade seeming far-fetched. But the more Will listened, the more convinced he became that Emery Arnell was telling the truth, that Sebak had shared this crucial information with him.

When Emery finished talking, he leaned against the hut, obviously exhausted. Gwen put her arm around her father and hugged him.

"I believe him." Gwen glared at the others.

"So do I," Will said.

"Have you both lost your minds?" Jordan asked.

"There's one way to find out," Will told them. "I'm going to speak to Sebak. If what Dr. Arnell has told us is true, we need to get off this island as soon as possible. Today."

"No!" The Professor cried, "I will not leave without a sample of the Eshe plant."

"Then you stay here and risk your life," Will told him. "The rest of us are leaving today. We'd be better off floating around in the Atlantic, hoping to be rescued, than waiting here on this island, knowing we were going to wind up as human sacrifices."

"I agree with Will even though I wanted to find this island so desperately," Jordan said. "But if Sebak backs up The Professor's story, then we must leave the island today."

Will looked at Gwen. "Talk to your father. Make him see reason. I'm going to find Sebak."

Before the sun rose high overhead, Will returned and gathered everyone together, including Mick McGuire, inside his and Gwen's hut. His gaze went around the room, studying each person for a brief moment.

"Dr. Arnell was telling the truth," Will said. "Sebak thinks we will be safe here for a few days, possibly another week or two, but the longer we are on the island, the greater the odds that the high priests' elite brigade will discover that we're here. If there was only one of us, it would be easier for them to hide us. But there are six of us."

"Then I say we leave the island as soon as possible." Jordan glanced at Emery.

"Leaving here sounds good to me," Mick said. "But just how do you propose we do that? Our cruiser was destroyed in the storm and you said your boat's motors aren't working."

"Sebak told me that my boat will take us to safety. He explained that when the high priest lifts the cloaking spell from around Umi, that act creates freak storms and disrupts everything within a hundred miles around the island. It's some sort of weird magnetic field. Sebak feels certain that the *Footloose*'s engines will work now. I know it sounds crazy, but it's our only hope."

"And you believe this crap?" Cheryl asked.

"I'm going to take the lifeboat that Gwen and I left on shore, row back to the *Footloose* and check the engines myself," Will told them.

"Won't that be dangerous?" Gwen looked at him with great concern.

"How do we know you won't make it to the boat, find

out the engines are working and go off and leave us?" Mick got right up in Will's face.

Will tapped Mick in the chest, warning him to move back, which Mick did. "I'd like to leave your sorry ass here on Umi and let the high priest's elite brigade take care of you, but there's no way in hell I'd leave the others." Will looked directly at Gwen. "I'd die before I'd leave you behind. You know that, don't you?"

Gwen's heart lurched, tightened by a combination of joy and sorrow. How did she tell him that she couldn't leave her father, who would not leave Umi without a sample of the Eshe plant?

"I trust you," Jordan told Will. "Is there anything I can do to help you?"

"Just look after Gwen while I'm gone."

"I can take care of myself," she said.

"In our world, you probably can," Will told her. "But not on Umi. I've told Sebak where I'm going and that I'm leaving my woman under Jordan's protection. Do you understand?"

"Yes, I understand, and I'm sorry that I let my feminist instincts surface," Gwen said. "You have enough to worry about right now. I promise that while you're gone I'll behave myself and not get in any trouble."

"I won't leave here without samples of the Eshe plant." Dr. Arnell spoke up loud and clear, reiterating his intentions.

Gwen patted his hand. "Now is not the time to discuss this, Daddy. First, Will has to make sure the *Footloose*'s motors are working. Once he does that, we can make plans to leave."

"As long as you understand—all of you—that I must have samples of the plant to take with me," Dr. Arnell said.

Picking up his backpack, Will motioned to Gwen, who

followed him outside the hut. He cupped her chin between his thumb and forefinger, then kissed her. "While I'm gone, don't take any chances. And do your best to keep your father from going off half-cocked."

He kissed her again, then strapped his knapsack to his back and headed toward the road that would take him through the jungle back to the beach. Gwen stood and watched him until he disappeared from sight.

Cheryl came up beside her. "You're in love with him, aren't you?"

"Oh, yes. I'm most definitely in love with him."

"What are you going to do?"

"About what?"

"About choosing between your father and the man you love. The Professor won't leave this island without a sample of the Eshe plant, and Will Pierce won't leave this island without you."

Chapter 15

Will returned to Oseye before nightfall and gathered everyone together inside his hut, where Gwen was waiting with the others. During Will's absence, she had tried again and again—unsuccessfully—to make her father see reason.

"I will not leave Umi without samples of the Eshe plant," he had told her repeatedly.

No matter what tactic she took, no matter what she, Jordan or Cheryl said to him, he refused to change his mind. In the end, Gwen knew what she would do, what she had to do for her father.

When Will entered the hut at twilight, Gwen ran to him, relieved that he had made the journey and returned safely. If anything had happened to him…

He lifted her off her feet and hugged her fiercely, then set her in front of him and smiled. "Good news, brown eyes. I can't explain it, but the motors on the *Footloose* are working just fine. The radio is still out, but with the cruiser operational and the instruments online, we can leave this place first thing in the morning."

"Man, am I glad to hear that." Cheryl hugged Jordan. "I am so ready to leave this damn place."

"Why not get this show on the road and leave tonight?" Mick McGuire asked. "As soon as the old man gets his Eshe plants, I say we hightail it out of here before the goon squad finds out what's happened."

Will glowered at Mick. "We're leaving at dawn tomorrow morning. It will be safer traveling through the jungle and entering the ocean waters after daylight. And we will be leaving Umi without any Eshe plants."

"No way," Mick said. "The old man's going to get those plants. They'll be worth millions, maybe billions. And he's going to share equally with all of us. Isn't that right, Professor?"

"Quite right," Dr. Arnell said.

Will looked from person to person. "Trying to steal samples of that plant will be signing a death warrant for all of us."

"This is something Mick cooked up between him and The Professor," Jordan said. "Cheryl and I agree that we should leave as soon as possible, without the Eshe plant samples."

Gwen took Will's hand. "I need to speak to you alone." She nodded toward the door. "Outside. Okay?"

"Yeah, sure." He opened the door and went with her a few feet away from the hut. She took both of his hands in hers. "Daddy refuses to leave Umi without samples of the Eshe plant, and he's convinced Mick that he can make him a wealthy man if—"

"Then I'll just knock your father on his ass and carry

him with us to the *Footloose* tomorrow. And if McGuire gives us any trouble, I'll leave him here."

"No." Gwen swallowed hard. "My father is an old man. He has spent his entire life searching for this island, dreaming of the day that he could take the magical youth-serum plant back to the world as a gift. How can I ask him to leave here without the Eshe plant? It would kill him."

"And if he stays here, he'll die."

"I know. But there is one other solution."

"I'm already not liking the sound of this."

She squeezed his hands. "You take Jordan and Cheryl with you at first light in the morning, back to the shore where you left the lifeboat. I will go with Daddy and Mick before dawn to the Fields of Eshe and help them gather a few samples. Then we'll join y'all. If we don't make it, if we're captured or—"

Will grabbed her by the shoulders and shook her. "No way. No way in hell."

"Please, Will. I have to do this."

"No, Gwen, you don't."

She pulled free of his tenacious grip, then turned and walked farther away from the hut. He came up behind her, not touching her, not saying a word.

"Daddy and I have talked this through, and we've agreed that it's the only way. No matter what happens, you and the others will be safe." She couldn't face him, couldn't look him in the eye, knowing how angry he was.

"To hell with my being safe. If you think I'll leave you here, you'd better think again."

"Please, Will."

"No. And that settles it." He grasped her shoulders and yanked her back up against his chest.

"You can't knock all three of us out and drag us with y'all through the jungle," Gwen told him. "If you do this my way—"

"I'm not leaving you. Get that through your head." He encompassed her in a possessive embrace. "If you won't leave this godforsaken island without your father, and he won't leave without that damn plant, then I'll go to the Fields of Eshe at dawn and get the samples for him."

She whirled around in his arms. "I would never ask you to take such a risk." She caressed his cheek. "If anything happened to you, I couldn't bear it."

His eyes narrowed as his gaze locked with hers. "Then you know exactly how I feel."

"But you don't understand. I love you and—"

"Do you think you're the only one who's in love?"

She didn't dare believe her own ears.

He captured her face with his open palms. "Of everyone in our group, I'm the only one with the kind of training it will require to go into those fields, steal a sample of the plant and get away without being captured."

"You can't go in alone. I'll go with you."

"No. You will take your father, Cheryl and Mick back to the beach and wait. I'll take Jordan with me and we'll meet up with y'all as soon as we have samples of the Eshe plant."

A bittersweet feeling engulfed Gwen as she realized the depth of Will's love for her and knew that she couldn't allow him to risk his life to fulfill her father's dream.

"All right," she said, lying to him. "We will do this your way."

"That's my girl."

When he kissed her, she clung to him, wanting to hold on to him forever.

* * *

Will woke with a start, but had no idea what had roused him. After making love with Gwen, he had fallen asleep almost instantly. He turned over in bed and reached for her. The other side of the bed was empty. He shot straight up and surveyed the dark room, the only illumination coming from the dying embers of the fire in the fireplace and the moonlight shining through the open window.

"Gwen?"

No response. Completely naked, he got out of bed and searched the hut. Where the hell was she and why hadn't he heard her leave?

After putting on his clothes, he went outside. She was nowhere in sight. A sick, gut-tightening sensation gripped him. He made his way to the hut next door and knocked softly, calling Jordan's name.

Within minutes Jordan opened the door. "What's wrong?"

"Have you seen Gwen?"

"No. Why? What's happened?"

"She's gone."

Cheryl came up beside Jordan. "Maybe she went to see her father, to try to talk sense to him again."

"Why would she go in the middle of the night?"

"You think something's wrong, don't you?" Jordan asked.

"I know something's wrong."

Gwen hoped Will wouldn't wake up until it was too late to try to stop her. If he figured out where she'd gone, he would come after her and risk his own life. She couldn't let him do that. Not for her. Not for her father. She was Emery Arnell's only child. It was her duty to stand by her father, to do her best to care for him, to help him.

The small child that still existed inside Gwen believed that if she did this, if she enabled her father to fulfill his lifelong dream, he would be grateful to her. He would love her.

Before her father and Mick McGuire had left her hut last night, she had told her father that she would slip away from Will in the night and come to him.

"Tell Mick to stay with you and when I can get away, I'll come get you and we'll go to the Fields of Eshe and get the samples you want."

"But I thought Will was going to—"

"No, Will isn't going." She had told her father what she wanted him to believe. "Will was lying to you, to pacify you. He has no intention of getting the plants for you. If you want the plants, we have to get them ourselves, before dawn."

She, her father and Mick had made their way by moonlight to the Fields of Eshe. The knee-high stalks glowed softly in the predawn darkness, as if they were lit from within.

"There's not a guard in sight," Mick said, keeping his voice low. "This should be a piece of cake."

"Sebak said that Lord Baruti, the high priest, has a power that oversees these fields," Emery told them. "We can't be too careful. You two must let me gather the samples."

"Go to it, old man," Mick said. "Just make sure you get enough." He gazed at the acres of flourishing plants that gleamed like yellow-green gold in the moonlight. "And I'll carry them plants for you, Professor. They'll be safe with me."

"We will each carry a sample," Emery said. "That way at least one sample should survive."

"Good idea." Mick's smirking grin made Gwen's skin crawl. He was such a sleazy bastard.

"We'll stand guard while you retrieve the samples."

Gwen kissed her father's cheek. "I'm so proud of you, Daddy. You're going to be very famous."

"And rich as Donald Trump—like a billionaire," Mick added.

Her father smiled broadly. "This is the most exciting moment of my life. Nothing can compare to the knowledge that I will be able to give the world a precious gift and prove to my colleagues that I am no fool."

Gwen's heart beat loudly in her ears as she watched her father enter the fields. He walked slowly along the rows, inspecting the plants, taking his time as if there was no rush.

"What the hell is he doing?" Mick grumbled.

"He's savoring the moment," Gwen replied.

When her father had gone approximately twenty feet down the second row, he reached into his pants pocket and removed an old switchblade knife and a tattered handkerchief. He knelt down on his knees, spread the handkerchief out on the ground and grasped the tall, willowy Eshe plant, holding it with one hand while he used the knife to carefully dig around the roots. He unearthed one plant, laid the roots on the handkerchief and repeated the procedure with two other plants.

Gwen held her breath, waiting for an alarm to go off, for hidden guards to appear, for iron bars to come up out of the earth and surround the fields. But nothing happened. The only sound she heard was her own heavy breathing.

"Sebak was lying to the old man." Mick laughed. "These people are stupid to let some high and mighty leader scare them from taking these plants for themselves."

"Shh. Be quiet," she warned him.

"Why? It's not like the plants can hear us." He laughed louder.

Emery came to them carrying the Eshe in his arms, the plants' delicate roots wrapped in the handkerchief. "I will need to water the roots and keep them damp. But they are large and healthy and should survive the journey without any problem."

Mick slapped Emery on the back. "We're in the money now, huh, Professor."

Emery frowned. "Yes, yes, we're in the money."

Gwen realized her father was simply humoring Mick because he believed he could use the man's greed to his advantage.

"There's no point hanging around here," Mick said. "I say we get these million-dollar babies—" he eyed the plants in Emery's arms "—aboard the *Footloose* as soon as we can and set sail for the nearest port."

"Aren't you forgetting something?" Gwen asked.

"If you're talking about the others, forget them," Mick said. "The Eshe plants are ours. I prefer dividing up the billions three ways instead of six. Besides, I've got no intention of letting your boyfriend turn me over to the authorities when we get back to civilization."

Before either Gwen or her father could contradict Mick, beams of blinding white lights shot up from the earth, all around the Fields of Eshe.

Gwen gasped. Emery clutched his beloved plants to his chest. Mick's eyes bugged out in shock.

"What the hell?" Mick bellowed.

"We have to make a run for it," Gwen said. "Come on, Daddy. Hurry."

Mick fled, leaving Gwen and her father, who couldn't run. With her arm through his, Gwen hurried her father along, away from the fields and toward the jungle, intending to steer clear of the stone roadway. As they scurried for safety, Gwen heard a loud, thundering noise behind her, but realized turning back to see what pursued them would simply waste valuable time.

She caught glimpses of Mick as he rushed ahead of them. Suddenly a thin white light came flying through the air and hit Mick in the back. He dropped instantly, falling out of sight. Dear God, was he dead? Had their trackers killed him?

Suddenly her father grunted, then dropped to his knees. In her effort to keep him on his feet, Gwen went down with him. She wasn't strong enough to hold him, so all she could manage was to ease him to the ground as slowly as possible. His arms fell open and the Eshe plants tumbled freely onto the grass.

"Daddy? Daddy!" Gwen patted his cheek.

With his eyes wide open but dazed, he looked either dead or unconscious. She felt for a pulse. He was alive, but just barely.

Daring a glance over her shoulder, through the plush jungle greenery, Gwen saw what appeared to be ornately carved golden chariots off in the distance, just outside the fields. But before she could ascertain whether she was hallucinating or not, a thin beam of light struck her chest and the world went black.

Sebak led Will, Jordan and Cheryl to the Fields of Eshe. They arrived moments before dawn. Will realized what had happened as soon as he discovered that not only was Gwen missing from Oseye, but so was Dr. Arnell and Mick McGuire.

"They've gone to the Eshe fields," Will had told the others.

"But why? They knew you were— Damn!" Jordan shook his head. "Gwen did this, didn't she?"

"She didn't want you to risk your life," Cheryl said.

"Yeah. And I should have known what she'd do. Damn stupid woman!" His chest ached with emotion. He'd never been so angry with anyone and at the same time had never been so certain that a woman loved him beyond all reason.

"What can we do?" Cheryl had asked.

"What else? Go after them."

So, here they were approaching the fields, with Sebak in tow as their guide. But there was no sight of Gwen, her father or McGuire. The Fields of Eshe looked serene and undisturbed.

"Fan out and search for any sign of them, anything the least bit out of the ordinary," Will ordered. His gut told him that they were too late. "Cheryl, you search around the periphery while we enter the fields." He turned to Sebak. "If they aren't here—"

"You will not find them," Sebak said. "I tried to tell you that the elite brigade captured them and took them to Mount Kaphiri to be punished by Lord Baruti."

Glowering at Sebak, Will grabbed him. "If we don't find them, you will guide us to Mount Kaphiri and tell us how to find this Lord Baruti."

"No, I cannot. I am but a lowly village leader. I am unworthy to ascend to Mount Kaphiri."

Will shook Sebak, then circled his neck in a death grip. "Worthy or unworthy, you're going to show us the way. Either that or I will wipe out your entire village, starting with you."

"You cannot think you are capable of overpowering an entire village. You and Jordan are only two men."

"Two men with weapons. Guns. Do you know what a

gun is? I just happened to have picked up a couple of them when I went back to my boat yesterday, and they're safely tucked away in my backpack."

"If your guns are weapons that render people unconscious, then I know what they are. The elite brigade have such weapons."

"Do their weapons kill?" Will asked.

"Kill? No, they do not kill. There have been no murders on Umi in a thousand years."

"No murders, huh? What do you call human sacrifice?"

While Sebak stared at Will, a perplexed expression on his face, Cheryl cried out, "I've found something!"

Will forced Sebak forward. Cheryl, who had gone approximately thirty feet into the jungle, turned to face them, a dirty handkerchief in her hand. Jordan came running up behind them.

"It's The Professor's handkerchief," Cheryl told them.

"They were here," Jordan said.

"And now they are gone." Sebak shook his head sadly.

"We're going after them." Will didn't care what it took, didn't care if he had to move heaven and earth, he was going to find Gwen. "Sebak says the elite brigade took them to Mount Kaphiri."

"It will do no good to follow them," Sebak said. "You cannot rescue them. Their lives are now in the hands of Lord Baruti."

Will gave Sebak a hard shove. "And your life and the lives of your fellow villagers are now in my hands. Do you understand?"

"Yes, I understand. I...I will show you the way to the foothills of Mount Kaphiri, but I can go no farther. I would be of no help to you. I have never been up the mountain itself, but when my son, who is a scholar, has visited me, he has told me that there is a road that leads from the foot-hills straight to the high priest's palace. But the elite brigade guard the entrance to the palace, day and night."

Gwen regained consciousness slowly, at first not re-membering what had happened, but the minute her eyes opened and she didn't recognize her surroundings, the events of their capture came back to her. When she sat straight up, her head pounded unmercifully, forcing her to lie back down on the soft pillow. Lying flat on her back while the throbbing ache in her head subsided, she glanced right and left, up and down. She lay in an intricately carved black bed. Ebony? The sheet beneath her felt like silk. The walls were decorated with murals, island scenes of water-falls and villages and the Fields of Eshe.

When she tried sitting up again, more slowly this time, she realized that she was naked. Dear God, what had hap-pened to her?

And where was her father? Where was Mick? For that matter, where was she?

She wrapped the silk sheet around her and tucked one end under the edge that crisscrossed over her breasts, then walked across the room to the gilded door. The handle was gold, en-crusted with gems—rubies, diamonds and emeralds.

She tried the handle. The door opened to reveal a long, narrow hallway with stark white walls and a black marble floor. The moment she stepped into the hallway, four women came through a door at the end of the long corridor and rushed toward her.

She stopped and waited for them to come to her. Better to get this initial meeting over now, she told herself.

When the women came near, they paused and looked at her as if waiting for her to either say or do something. The four women looked like sisters, each dark-haired, tall, slender, doe-eyed and elegantly dressed in azure blue off-the-shoulder dresses tied with silver cords directly below their breasts.

"Where am I?" Gwen asked, hoping beyond hope that one of them could speak English. "How long have I been here?"

"You were brought to the palace of Lord Baruti yesterday," one of the women replied.

Yesterday? That meant she had been asleep—unconscious—for at least twenty-four hours. She vaguely recalled seeing a white light hit Mick and then her father. She had been the last struck with the weapon. A tranquilizer of some kind? If so, it certainly was powerful, to produce such a long-lasting effect.

"Lord Baruti is the high priest, isn't he?"

"Yes," another answered.

"I was brought here with two men. Where are they?"

"The men are in another area of the palace," a third woman responded. "You will join them for an audience with Lord Baruti."

"When?" Gwen asked.

"Before the sun reaches a midpoint in the heavens," the fourth woman told her. "We have come to prepare you for the ceremony."

"The ceremony?" Gwen's stomach tightened.

All four women smiled, but only the first one spoke, as if they had to take turns. "The Ceremony of Olumfemi. Those who are sacrificed are the beloved of the gods. Even those who have done great evil find redemption in death."

Chapter 16

On the trek to Mount Kaphiri, Will had given Jordan a minicourse in combat and survival. Despite his lack of experience, the guy had picked up on the essentials quickly and agreed without question that Will was in charge. When they had reached the foothills at daybreak and stopped in a village called Bahiti, Will had made the decision to leave Cheryl behind. There was no point putting her at risk, especially since she would only slow them down, and Jordan would be distracted by her presence because his first priority would be to protect her.

Will's gut told him he could trust Sebak not to give them away. After all, if he or the other villagers had wanted to turn them over to the elite brigade, they could have done that immediately after they arrived on Umi.

"I will take care of your woman," Sebak had told Jordan. "If you do not return, I will make sure she leaves

Umi safely. If you return, I trust you to do no harm to my village."

"Your village is safe from us," Jordan assured him, then looked to Will. "Isn't that right?"

"We will repay you for your help by not harming you or your people," Will said.

Jordan had thanked Sebak for all he'd done for them, then spent a few minutes alone with Cheryl to say goodbye. Will had led Sebak aside and questioned him, knowing that any knowledge the man possessed could help them when they reached Lord Baruti's palace.

"How long do we have?" Will had asked.

"I do not know for sure," Sebak had replied. "They will not perform the Ceremony of Olumfemi before the sun is at its highest point in the sky."

"This ceremony—"

"A ceremony of sacrifice. Emery and the others will be sacrificed to the gods, and in this way, they will be redeemed for having committed a grave sin."

Sebak's knowledge of the high priest's palace was limited to what his son, the scholar who lived atop Mount Kaphiri, had shared with him. But even that information was better than nothing.

During their climb up the mountain, Will and Jordan used the roadway that wound steadily upward like a slithering snake. At any hint of danger, Will led them off the main pathway, a twenty-foot-wide rock lane similar to the ones that ran through the jungles, only this road was wider. Twice on their journey, Will spied checkpoints that were guarded by two men he assumed were members of the elite brigade. Their physical appearance was similar to the other natives, but their attire differed. They wore dark-blue loincloths, silver breastplates and heavy sandals with straps that rose to midcalf. The two men stood at either side of the road and each held a spear, but the tips were rounded instead of pointed, which made Will wonder about their purpose.

Taking no breaks, they arrived outside the walls of the palace shortly before high noon. Will ascertained from their appearance that the walls were undoubtedly more for decorative purposes than protection. Rising no higher than eight feet, with sections of silver-and-gold metal stakes carved in intricate designs, the open fencing allowed a breathtaking view of the interior. Built a good twenty feet higher at the very apex of the mountain, the palace rested like a goddess on a cloud. Will guessed the palace covered at least an acre. It was a magnificent structure of stone, with numerous enormous columns and huge statues guarding the entrance.

Richly dressed people stirred about, each one apparently rushing to the same area of the palace. Rushing to witness the Ceremony of Olumfemi?

"We can't enter through those front gates," Will said. "There are too many guards. We'd be spotted in seconds. We'll have to find another way to get in."

"All those people are hurrying in one direction." Jordan's gaze focused on the palace. "Maybe that's the way to the temple where Sebak said the ceremony will be performed."

Will looked up at the noonday sun. "We don't have any time to waste. Just remember to follow my orders. And if anything happens to me, leave me behind. Save Gwen, then get her and Cheryl off this godforsaken island."

With an expression of somber acceptance on his face, Jordan nodded.

Obviously, those who lived high above the lowly natives on the island below had few worries about uninvited guests. Will found it far too easy to breach the security of the palace grounds and even the palace itself. If their physical appearance was not so vastly different from the people of Umi, Will would have secured native clothing for Jordan and himself.

"We watch and wait," Will said. "Once the coast is clear and everyone is assembled in the temple, we'll make our move."

Jordan nodded.

Suddenly a loud trumpet sounded. Jordan's gaze met Will's.

Will ventured a guess. "It's a signal that the ceremony is about to begin."

"Yeah, that's what I thought."

"You know how to use the Ruger I gave you, how to aim, fire and how to replace the clip. When the time comes to act, don't stop and think about what you're doing, just do it. If we get out of this alive, there will be plenty of time later to think about how many people you killed."

Jordan swallowed.

"If we can save all three of them, we'll do it," Will said. "But my main objective is to rescue Gwen. Understand?"

"Understood."

The four doe-eyed maidens had dressed Gwen in a diaphanous, single-strap, cream gown, then placed golden sandals on her feet and a heavy gold choker about her neck. They had braided her long hair into three layers and painted her face with the type of makeup they wore. Although she had asked them numerous questions, they had responded to only a few, while keeping up a stream of idle chit-chat.

As they led her down the black-marble-floored corridor, one phrase the women had used often kept repeating itself in Gwen's mind. "A willing sacrifice will receive great honor in the afterlife."

A willing sacrifice? Not hardly. But until she saw her father, knew that he was alive, she planned to cooperate. Besides, what good would it do her to put up a fight? The maidens had informed her that resisting was useless, that if necessary the elite brigade could use the *sefu* of Baruti to subdue her. It had taken her several questions to get enough meaningful answers so that she could figure out that the round-tipped spears her abductors had used to shoot a powerful white light to render her, her father and Mick unconscious was what the maidens referred to as the *sefu* of Baruti.

The maidens led her along three different corridors, taking her from building to building within the palace grounds. She caught only glimpses of the exterior, slashes of palm trees in magnificent garden areas that boasted incredible greenery and an abundance of flowers. As a botanist, she could happily spend endless hours exploring the gardens.

When they reached a structure slightly apart from the main palace—a two-story, tan building decorated with bright emblems in reds, blues, yellows and greens—the maidens paused, as loud trumpets proclaimed the beginning of the ceremony. The massive silver doors swung open to reveal two long lines of the elite brigade flanking either side of the path that led to a dais where an elaborately clothed man of undeterminable age stood waiting. Gwen assumed he was the high priest, Lord Baruti.

At Lord Baruti's side stood Gwen's father. Her heart leaped with joy when she saw that he appeared to be not only alive, but well. Like she, he had been dressed in elaborate native attire.

While keeping her gaze focused directly on her father, Gwen caught flashes in her peripheral vision of people standing behind the elite brigade.

As she neared the dais, she hazarded a quick glimpse to her right, where a small group of robed men knelt, their heads bowed. She counted six men in all. Then she glanced to her left. Blazing fires flickered like freshly lit torches atop six twelve-foot pillars that lined the wall directly behind a large marble slab.

Gwen gasped.

A completely naked Mick McGuire lay atop the marble altar, his arms lifted over his head and secured with gold chains. Identical gold chains around his ankles held his legs in place.

Her survival instincts told her to run, to escape by any means necessary. Forcing down the salty bile that rose to her throat, Gwen focused once again on her father's face. Oddly enough, he appeared not only calm but serene. Had he been drugged?

When they reached the steps leading up to the altar, the maidens stopped. Her father held out his hand to her. She hesitated, then walked up the two marble steps and hurried to her father's side. He opened his arms and wrapped her in a trembling embrace.

"This is your daughter?" Lord Baruti asked. "Your only child?"

"Yes, Lord Baruti." Emery released Gwen and turned her so that she stood in front of him, facing the high priest.

"You have risked your life to aid your father," Lord Baruti said. "Such devotion and loyalty to a parent will be rewarded."

Gwen released a quivering breath, wondering if by some miracle this all-powerful ruler intended to spare their lives. After all, his attitude toward her father was far from hostile.

Nothing else was said before the high priest turned, leaving Gwen and her father on the raised podium. Drums beat rhythmically, a repetitive cadence, a musical announcement. With his sheer robes floating behind him like transparent, low-slung wings, Lord Baruti descended from the podium and walked directly to the altar. Gwen reached down and clasped her father's hand.

A member of the elite brigade, who carried a four-foot-long silver case, approached the high priest, knelt in front of Lord Baruti and lifted the case high above his head. The priest opened the case and removed a gleaming golden sword with a shimmering two-foot blade.

Gwen watched in mesmerized horror as Lord Baruti approached the altar where Mick McGuire squirmed, his voice ringing out with threat-filled obscenities. Lord Baruti stood over Mick and lifted the sword with both hands over his head. A robust shout erupted from the onlookers.

Squeezing her father's hand, Gwen stood on tiptoe and whispered, "Can't you do something to stop this?"

"The gods demand sacrifices," her father murmured. "McGuire will have a chance to redeem himself in the afterlife."

Releasing her death grip on her father's hand, Gwen stared at him, unable to believe that he could accept this inhuman act with such a cavalier attitude.

"Daddy?"

"Quiet, daughter." He hushed her. "Show this solemn moment the respect and reverence it deserves."

Oh, God! Why was her father acting this way? It wasn't possible, was it, that he had been brainwashed in less than twenty-four hours? Didn't he realize that once Mick McGuire was killed, they would probably be next?

Will and Jordan managed to sneak onto the narrow mezzanine area of the two-story central chamber inside the temple. The chamber was filled to capacity, but the upper level was vacant except for the carved stone dignitaries seated in silver pews. Will glanced at the silent, imposing figures and wondered who or what they represented. With no more time to waste musing about this strange place, Will motioned for Jordan to go left while he went right. They kept down, out of sight, and moved in absolute silence. Positioned on either side of the overhanging railing, which was fashioned out of pink marble and decked with heavy metallic ropes, Jordan and Will peered down at the ceremony taking place in the temple.

Will clenched his teeth when he saw the man he assumed was the high priest raise the glistening sword and slash open Mick McGuire, from neck to pubic area. Mick screamed in pain as the blade cut him open, effectively gutting him.

Will's gaze connected with Jordan's. Will issued him a silent warning—suck it up and sit tight. Well aware of the fact that Jordan had never been exposed to such deadly violence, Will hoped the young guy didn't fall apart on him.

While the priest's assistants caught McGuire's blood in a silver bowl, Will scanned the room and saw a pale-faced Gwen standing beside her father on a raised platform. She wore a sheer gown that revealed the ample curves of her body. A thick coating of heavy makeup had been applied to her face, and her long, dark hair had been plaited in three braids.

The soft, eerie music of flutes filled the temple, the sound unnerving and oddly out of place at a ceremony that glorified human sacrifice. The priest's underlings brought the bowl of blood to Lord Baruti, who carried it with him as he returned to the podium. He set the bowl on a marble stand, then turned to Dr. Arnell and Gwen.

"For the high crime of removing the life-giving Eshe plants from the holy fields, the first sacrifice has been made," the priest announced to his audience. A loud cheer rose from the crowd. "But the gods are not satisfied. They demand another sacrifice."

Gwen's heart caught in her throat when Lord Baruti looked directly at her father. What had he meant by another sacrifice? Had her father made a bargain of some kind with the priest, a bargain to save Gwen's life?

Lord Baruti motioned for them to come to him. Her father went without hesitation, all but dragging Gwen with him. The priest smiled.

"Emery Arnell, you came to Umi to steal the precious Eshe plant and take it back to your world. But it is forbidden for anyone other than my elite brigade, under my guidance, to harvest the Eshe plants. Do you understand the severity of your crime?"

"Yes, Lord Baruti," Emery replied.

"And do you understand that the penalty for stealing the Eshe plant is death?"

"Yes, my lord."

"But you still desire the Eshe plant, do you not? You treasure it above all else?"

Gwen's stomach knotted painfully.

"I do, Lord Baruti. I have spent my life searching for Umi, dreaming of the day I could return to my world with samples of the Eshe plant and give all people the gift of good health and long life."

"You are a benevolent seeker," the priest said. "I shall spare your life and allow you to return to your world with a sample of the Eshe plant, if you are willing to pay the ultimate price."

"I will give you anything you ask for," Emery said. "No price is too high."

Baruti's ring-adorned hand lifted. He pointed his index finger directly at Gwen. "I give you the choice—your life and a sample of the Eshe plant in exchange for your daughter's life."

Gwen held her breath.

Emery turned to her, grasped her hands and sighed heavily. "You know that I love you more dearly than anyone on earth."

"Yes, Daddy, I know."

"I wish it could be different," he said. "I wish I did not have to make such a terrible choice."

Every nerve in Gwen's body trembled with realization, every muscle constricted.

"It is with great regret that I give you my daughter as a sacrifice," Emery told Lord Baruti.

Despite hearing her father's declaration, Gwen did not fully comprehend that he had chosen his own life and the Eshe plant over saving her life. Before her brain absorbed the horrific truth, Gwen watched as the high priest motioned her father to him, then led him to the bowl filled with Mick McGuire's blood. He dipped his index finger into the blood, painted a slash across her father's forehead and across each cheekbone.

Another riotous roar rose from the assembled group. The elite brigade stomped their spears, the *sefu* of Baruti, against the marble floor.

It was at that moment, with the roar of the crowd thundering in her ears and the glazed look of madness shining in her father's eyes that Gwen realized he had finally lost his mind.

"You, Emery Arnell, are a fool to believe that anything, even the Eshe plant, has greater value than one who is blood of your blood, bone of your bone." The priest bowed his head for a moment, then shouted, "For such unforgivable foolishness, both you and your daughter will be sacrificed to the gods!"

"No, no!" Emery cried. "You can't do this. You promised me the Eshe plant. You swore to me—"

"Silence!" Lord Baruti motioned for two members of the elite brigade to come forward and take Emery.

Emery struggled against them, crying out to Gwen, who tried to go to him but was restrained by one strong, burly guard.

"Daddy!"

Lord Baruti followed the precession to the altar, where others of the elite brigade were unchaining Mick McGuire's mutilated body. The guard restraining Gwen dragged her off the podium while the drums began beating again. Loudly. Rhythmically. As if announcing the departure of one soul and the beginning of a new ritualistic sacrifice.

All eyes focused on the altar and the high priest as

Mick's body was carried away and maidens rushed forward to wash the bloody marble slab. Gwen's guard loosened his tenacious hold on her, enough so that after a few minutes, she managed to free herself without him noticing. She stayed at his side, not wanting to alert him that she was only biding her time until she could slip away from him.

While the drums pounded and the people chanted, Gwen searched the temple for any means of escape. As her gaze lifted to the mezzanine, she saw a flash of movement near the pink marble banisters. Her heart caught in her throat when she noticed a man cut through one of the metallic ropes draped across the banisters. With the crowd's attention focused on the ceremony, Will climbed down the metallic rope and dropped onto the floor, only a few feet behind a group of people absorbed in the gruesome spectacle. Gwen slowly moved away from her guard and managed to edge ever so gradually toward the back wall. By the time the guard realized she was missing, Gwen had escaped. Within minutes, she met up with Will, but not before they were spotted.

"We've got to get out of here," Will told her as several people in the crowd started moving toward them.

"But I can't leave my father."

"It's too late to save him." Will grabbed her arm.

She hesitated for half a second, then, knowing Will was right, she followed him. Before they could reach an escape route, Will stopped, shoved her behind him and pulled his pistol from the waistband of his pants. He aimed and fired repeatedly, sending half a dozen natives to the marble floor, their life's blood oozing from them.

Barely managing to escape the temple, Will would not allow Gwen to look back, to slow down for even a second.

They met up with Jordan outside the temple and the three of them fled down one exterior corridor after another, at least ten members of the elite brigade chasing them. The white light of one of the *sefu* spears grazed Jordan's shoulder. He staggered like a drunk, but somehow managed to stay on his feet. Will shoved Gwen behind a twenty-foot pillar and covered Jordan while he struggled to catch up with them, shooting several guards and halting their pursuit.

Will hurried to Jordan, circled his waist and dragged him behind the pillar with Gwen. He took the Ruger hanging in Jordan's limp hand and handed it to Gwen.

"Do you have any idea how to use this?" Will asked.

She shook her head. "Don't worry about hitting anything. Just aim and shoot. Got it?"

"Got it."

"Leave me," Jordan said, his speech slightly slurred. "You can't get away…with me holding you back."

Ignoring Jordan's pleas to leave him behind, Will and Gwen flanked him, lifted him under his arms and crept away from the pillared corridor. Will didn't understand why the elite brigade wasn't following them, but he didn't stop to check out the situation. They needed every advantage they could get. A five-minute head start might give them a fighting chance, especially if they could lose themselves in the jungle area of the mountain. How close he could take them to the village where they had left Cheryl and Sebak remained to be seen.

"Why aren't they coming after us?" Gwen asked, slightly winded, her face dotted with perspiration.

"I have no idea, unless they're trained to tend to their wounded immediately regardless of anything else," Will told her. "It's only a theory, but I don't give a rat's ass why they've stop chasing us, at least for now. We need to get moving while we have the chance."

Will led them along the fence until they reached a closed gate. When he tried to open the gate, he found it locked. Not hesitating, he aimed his gun, fired and blew off the lock. With no more than a nudge, the gate swung open, and they left the palace grounds. They emerged closer to the massive stone entrance than Will realized and were confronted by four members of the elite brigade. Shooting, he downed two guards in rapid succession. As the remaining two aimed their weapons, he shoved Gwen and Jordan to the ground, shouting for them to roll. He managed to sidestep an oncoming light ray, all the while firing his gun repeatedly. Another guard fell, but the fourth man stopped suddenly, dropped his spear and stared at his downed colleagues, a look of bewildered horror on his face.

It was in that moment, brief though it was, Will realized these men had never seen anyone killed in any other way except ritual sacrifice. They were stunned by the deadly force of Will's weapon.

Will eased over to the nearest dead guard, grabbed his spear, then stuck his gun into the waistband of his pants.

"Come on," he called to Gwen and Jordan, then helped them to their feet. "Let's get the hell out of here while we can."

"What's the matter with that guard?" Gwen asked. "He looks as if he's gone into a trance."

Will hurried her along, helping her with Jordan, who seemed to be sleepwalking. As they headed toward the stone roadway leading off the mountain, Will answered Gwen's question. "I think he was stunned to see his three comrades dead. I believe that's the reason the other soldiers stopped following us."

"Oh my God!" He saw the look of realization in Gwen's eyes. "The *sefu* only tranquilizes its victims. Here on Umi, death usually comes only to the very, very old and to the human sacrifices."

"We need to get off the road and into the jungle as soon as possible. We can't be sure that once they come out of their shock and regroup, they won't come after us."

They didn't reach the village of Bahiti until the following morning. Will could have managed to keep going all through the night, but neither Jordan nor Gwen would have made it without the half dozen brief rest stops. During every moment of their escape, Will had stayed constantly alert to any signs that they were being followed.

Despite her exhaustion, blistered feet and brush-scratched arms and legs, Gwen had not uttered one word of complaint, and thankfully, before dawn Jordan returned to normal, the effects of the tranquilizer having finally worn off.

The central fires in the village burned brightly, warming the chilly morning air. Men were already working in the fields and women were busying themselves in the village. Small, brown-skinned, naked children ran around laughing and playing. A tropical paradise, Will thought. So deceptive.

Cheryl saw them as they entered the village and came running, rushing straight into Jordan's arms. Sebak emerged from a nearby hut and waited for them to come to him.

"Did Lord Baruti allow you to leave Mount Kaphiri?" Sebak asked, his eyes wide with astonishment.

"Not exactly," Will said.

Sebak looked behind them, searching the pathway that led into the village. "Where is Dr. Arnell? And the other one?"

"They're dead," Jordan replied. "Both of them were sacrificed."

Cheryl cringed.

"It's only a matter of time before the elite brigade come after us. Not only did I save Gwen from being the third sacrifice, but we killed at least a dozen guards when we escaped," Will said. "We need to get to the beach on the other side of the island as fast as we can and leave Umi today."

"I understand. I will guide you back to Oseye," Sebak said. "From there, you must go on your own."

"What will the elite brigade do to you and the other villagers?" Gwen asked. "They'll know that you helped us, that you didn't report our presence on the island."

"Your weapons kill," Sebak said, as if that explained everything.

"We forced you and your village to help us. You did as we ordered you to do out of fear for your lives." Will knew that the elite brigade would believe Sebak's reason. Hadn't they panicked and become stunned to the point of terror when they realized that guns killed, not simply tranquilized?

Grasping Sebak's hand, Will said, "We owe you our lives, my friend."

Will, Gwen, Cheryl and Jordan reached the beach at twilight. Despite the dangers involved in taking the raft back to the *Footloose* in the dark, Will knew that other risks were far greater if they waited until the next day to leave.

While Will started the engines and manned the helm, Gwen stayed at his side. Cheryl and Jordan stood on the deck and gazed back at the mystical island of Umi. When they were several miles out to sea, Will handed Gwen the *sefu* of Baruti spear.

"You know what to do with this," he told her.

She nodded, stood, left the helm and joined Jordan and Cheryl on the starboard deck. Will knew what Gwen thought—that the spear was warm, as if alive, and as light as a feather. She lifted it over the railing and tossed it into the Atlantic.

When she rejoined Will at the helm, he slipped his arm around her waist. She rested her head on his shoulder. They remained that way for quite some time.

Finally Will broke the silence. "I'm sorry about your father."

"So am I."

"If I could have saved him—"

"No one could have saved him. He was lost long before he rediscovered Umi. His obsession destroyed him. In the end he was insane."

Will kissed her temple. As tears trickled from her eyes, Gwen clung to Will.

"I love you," he told her.

"I know," she said. "You've proven to me just how much you love me."

"More than anything or anyone on earth."

"You already know that I love you in the same way."

"When we get back to the States—"

"You're going to buy me some red silk undies."

"Yes, ma'am, I am. And you're going to wear them on our wedding night."

Gwen sighed deeply. "Was that a proposal?"

"Let's call it a trial run. Once we get home and we put our lives back together, I'm going to do it right. A diamond ring, flowers, music, me down on bended knee."

"Will we ever be able to put our lives back together?"

"Eventually. But the only way we can do that is if the four of us—" he nodded toward Cheryl and Jordan "—never reveal the truth about what happened to us, never breathe a word that your father's island and the magical youth plant exist."

"I think they'll agree, don't you?"

"Yeah, I think so. Something tells me that they want a future together, just as you and I do."

Gwen snuggled against Will as he took the *Footloose* due west, straight toward the Bahamas. In time the anger and pain and disappointment that she had experienced in the temple of the high priest's palace atop Mount Kaphiri would lessen, and perhaps someday vanish completely. Forgiving her father would not be easy, but with Will's love and support, Gwen knew that she could learn to release the past and happily face the future, knowing in her heart of hearts that she, and she alone, was Will Pierce's only obsession, just as he was hers.

Epilogue

Gwen stood over Will where he sat on an armless chair in their honeymoon hotel room, his gaze riveted to her body. She did a sexy little dance, shimmying her hips and swaying her breasts. The red bra she wore was sheer lace with underwired, pushup cups that made the very most of her B-cup breasts. The matching bikini panties were strips of silk holding the V-shaped lace that barely covered her. She had never worn anything so blatantly skimpy and alluring in her entire life. But loving Will brought out the vamp in her, and there was nothing she liked more than giving her man what he wanted.

This was the third set of matching red underwear that Will had bought for her, and each set had become progressively skimpier and sexier. The first set, which he'd bought a few weeks after their return to the United States, had been relatively tame, but she hadn't managed to keep them on long enough for him to appreciate them. One look at her in the satin bra and panties and Will had ripped them off her. The second pair had been red silk with black lace trim. He'd bought them at an exclusive lingerie shop in Atlanta before he moved to Huntsville a few months ago and opened his own P.I. agency. She had worn them for him on the night of their engagement party six weeks ago.

They had married this morning, seven months after meeting in Puerto Nuevo, in an afternoon wedding at the Huntsville Botanical Gardens. Cheryl Kress, newly engaged to Jordan Elders, had been Gwen's maid of honor, and Jordan had been Will's best man. Will's family had flown in from Texas—brothers, sisters-in-law and nephews, as well as his mother and stepfather from Louisiana—and several Dundee agents had driven over from Atlanta. Gwen's ex-husband and his partner, along with her friends and colleagues had attended the ceremony. The wedding had been perfect, and only once had Gwen allowed herself a moment of grief, giving that little girl inside her a chance to wish that her father was there to give her away. But she had walked down the aisle alone, knowing that once she became Will's wife, she would never be alone again.

Gwen slid downward slowly and seductively, then straddled Will, who was as naked as the day he was born. He reached up and unhooked the front snap of her bra, freeing her breasts.

After nuzzling each breast, he asked, "Is it my imagination or are these beauties getting bigger?"

She squirmed against his erection, eliciting a pleading groan from him.

"They may be just a tad bigger. I believe it's quite normal for a woman's breasts to enlarge throughout her pregnancy."

Will grabbed her hips to stop her from moving against him. "What did you say?"

"It's a good thing you made an honest woman out of me today," she told him. "I took a home pregnancy test this morning and I'm definitely pregnant. If my calculations are correct—"

Will let out a loud whoop, then wrapped his arms around Gwen, effectively trapping her against him as he took her mouth in a hot, hungry kiss. When they were both breathless, they broke apart and grinned at each other.

"It happened six weeks ago," he said proudly. "The night of our engagement party. Right?"

"Mmm-hmm. That would be my guess."

"You're happy about the baby, aren't you?" He caressed her shoulders.

"If I were any happier, I'm not sure I could stand it." She wrapped her arms around his neck. "What about you? Do you want to be a daddy?"

"You bet I do. I want a little girl who looks just like you, brown eyes."

"Well, I want a little boy who looks just like you."

Six months later, they both got their wishes, only in reverse order. Willard Hunter Pierce III, with his mother's brown eyes and dark hair, came howling into the world five minutes before his twin sister, Gwendolyn Jean Pierce, who was her daddy's spitting image.

* * * * *

Turn the page for a sneak preview of
IF I'D NEVER KNOWN YOUR LOVE
by
Georgia Bockoven

From the brand-new series
Harlequin Everlasting Love
Every great love has a story to tell. ™

One year, five months and four days missing

There's no way for you to know this, Evan, but I haven't written to you for a few months. Actually, it's been almost a year. I had a hard time picking up a pen once more after we paid the second ransom and then received a letter saying it wasn't enough. I was so sure you were coming home that I took the kids along to Bogotá so they could fly home with you and me, something I swore I'd never do. I've fallen in love with Colombia and the people who've opened their hearts to me. But fear is a constant companion when I'm there. I won't ever expose our children to that kind of danger again.

I'm at a loss over what to do anymore, Evan. I've begged and pleaded and thrown temper tantrums with every official I can corner both here and at home. They've been incredibly tolerant and understanding, but in the end as ineffectual as the rest of us.

I try to imagine what your life is like now, what you do every day, what you're wearing, what you eat. I want to believe that the people who have you are misguided yet kind, that they treat you well. It's how I survive day to day. To think of you being mistreated hurts too much. If I picture you locked away somewhere and suffering, a weight descends on me that makes it almost impossible to get out of bed in the morning.

Your captors surely know you by now. They have to recognize what a good man you are. I imagine you working with their children, telling them that you have children, too, showing them the pictures you carry in your wallet. Can't the men who have you understand how much your children miss you? How can it not matter to them?

How can they keep you away from us all this time? Over and over, we've done what they asked. Are they oblivious to the depth of their cruelty? What kind of people are they that they don't care?

I used to keep a calendar beside our bed next to the peach rose you picked for me before you left. Every night I marked another day, counting how many you'd been gone. I don't do that any longer. I don't want to be reminded of all the days we'll never get back.

When I can't sleep at night, I tell you about my day. I imagine you hearing me and smiling over the details that make up my life now. I never tell you how defeated I feel at moments or how hard I work to hide it from everyone for fear they will see it as a reason to stop believing you are coming home to us.

And I couldn't tell you about the lump I found in my

breast and how difficult it was going through all the tests without you here to lean on. The lump was benign— the process reaching that diagnosis utterly terrifying. I couldn't stop thinking about what would happen to Shelly and Jason if something happened to me.

We need you to come home.

I'm worn down with missing you.

I'm going to read this tomorrow and will probably tear it up or burn it in the fireplace. I don't want you to get the idea I ever doubted what I was doing to free you or thought the work a burden. I would gladly spend the rest of my life at it, even if, in the end, we only had one day together.

You are my life, Evan.

I will love you forever.

* * * * *

Don't miss this deeply moving Harlequin Everlasting Love story about a woman's struggle to bring back her kidnapped husband from Colombia and her turmoil over whether to let go, finally, and welcome another man into her life.
IF I'D NEVER KNOWN YOUR LOVE
by Georgia Bockoven
is available March 27, 2007.

And also look for
THE NIGHT WE MET
by Tara Taylor Quinn,
a story about finding love
when you least expect it.

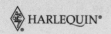

HARLEQUIN® *Romance*®

presents a brand-new trilogy by

PATRICIA THAYER

Rocky Mountain
BRIDES

Three sisters come home to wed.

In April don't miss
Raising the Rancher's Family,

followed by

The Sheriff's Pregnant Wife,

on sale May 2007,

and

A Mother for the Tycoon's Child,

on sale June 2007.

"Kate..." *his voice* *was husky*

Her lips parted, her blood thundered. Trembling, she looked up at him, gazing into his smoky blue eyes. Then, without quite knowing how it happened, she was in his arms, pressed close to him, and she knew that the past still lived in her, that he only had to touch her to set every cell in her body aflame.

He was alarming, his sexuality too potent for her to fight, no matter how hard she tried. And she wanted him now as she had wanted him then.

"Kate..." Again her name was torn from him, the harsh thread of triumph barely contained as he told her huskily, "I've always known how it could be for us."

DIANA HAMILTON creates high-tension conflict
that brings new life to traditional romance. Readers
find her a welcome addition to Harlequin and look
forward to new novels by this talented author.

Don't miss any of our special offers. Write to us at the
following address for information on our newest releases.

Harlequin Reader Service
P.O. Box 1397, Buffalo, NY 14240
Canadian address: P.O. Box 603,
Fort Erie, Ont. L2A 5X3

DIANA HAMILTON

The Devil His Due

Harlequin Books

TORONTO • NEW YORK • LONDON
AMSTERDAM • PARIS • SYDNEY • HAMBURG
STOCKHOLM • ATHENS • TOKYO • MILAN
MADRID • WARSAW • BUDAPEST • AUCKLAND

Harlequin Presents first edition November 1992
ISBN 0-373-11507-5

Original hardcover edition published in 1991
by Mills & Boon Limited

THE DEVIL HIS DUE

CHAPTER ONE

So HE was still a sucker for a pretty face! Kate Jones tossed the morning paper into the waste-bin, her clear grey eyes very grim, the familiar knot of intense dislike surging, as usual, whenever she was unguarded enough to think of him, making every last muscle in her slim body clench.

But that instinctive gesture of repudiation couldn't obliterate the image of the darkly sardonic, totally masculine face that had stared mockingly at her from the newsprint, or the few words of pure journalese:

> The City's Slickest, Seth Presteigne, pictured leaving Covent Garden Opera House with the Honourable Lucy Mortiboys. Is the lovely Lucy the hottest contender for the position of mistress of Montstowell? Sources suggest she may be well ahead of the pack.

Grinding her teeth, Kate walked to the filing cabinet. Seth Presteigne made her sick! Since she'd first sat up and taken notice there had always been a simpering lovely in his life. He had never exactly flaunted the army of nubile darlings which progressed through his life with dismaying regularity, but he hadn't been ashamed of his blatant promiscuity, either. Yet when it came to *her* morals, or what he had implied, six years ago, to be the lack

5

of them, he could be more censorious than any Victorian father!

She turned on her heels, dropping the file she'd been looking for down on her desk, and Sally, the secretary she shared with her partner, Rob Mallin, came through, the morning post in her hand.

'Hi, Kate! Nice to see you back. How did it go? Was the Baronessa bowled over?'

'All the members of the Brunelli family were delighted with the finished result,' Kate responded, smiling, affection for the other girl warming her clear grey eyes. Sally had always been round, from her auburn curls to her tiny plump feet, and advancing pregnancy added considerably to the overall picture.

'So the trip went well,' Sally commented as she put the opened mail on her employer's desk. 'Rob will be pleased. He phoned in to say he won't be in until this afternoon—he's working on the Countrywise project at home.'

'Fine,' Kate replied absently, already seated at her desk, skimming through the post. 'I'll phone him later and catch up on his progress. If Countrywise like his designs we'll land the commission to revamp all forty of their fashion stores. That would keep the wolf from the door!' It was said with a throwaway laugh, because business was booming. In two short years she'd made it, right up there among the top rankers in the world of interior design. Overnight, almost, it had become fashionable for the wealthy to use the services of the Kate-Mallin studio, but never once did she allow herself to forget the early days, when no matter how hard she'd struggled it had looked as if the studio would fold through cash flow problems.

Her voice clipped, she enquired, 'Where's Anna? Have I got any pressing appointments booked in this week? And has anything I should know about cropped up?'

Sally rolled her dark, round eyes and planted her hands on her hips, her pregnancy very pronounced. Looking down on the top of Kate's expensively cut short sable hair, on the businesslike set of the slender shoulders beneath the severely styled clerical grey suit she wore, Sally smiled. A go-getter, this one. But nice with it.

'Anna's chasing a Chinese lacquer screen she saw advertised out Pimlico way,' she began answering the staccato questions in order of receipt. 'You were looking for one for the Maybury job. And your only firm appointment is for lunch on Friday with Brian Rose from Interior Textiles.'

'Fine.' A smile curved the corners of Kate's perfect leaf-shaped mouth. Brian Rose, as company solicitor with Interior Textiles, had assumed, in her eyes, the mantle of a saviour.

Two years ago the small interior design company she had founded with nothing more than a burning need to prove herself, confidence in her own ability and a small legacy from her father, had looked like biting the dust. The few highly satisfied clients she'd serviced hadn't been enough to keep the one-designer and part-time secretary firm afloat. It had been then, precisely then, just like a miracle, that the rotund, fatherly Mr Rose had contacted her in his professional capacity.

The board of Interior Textiles, he had explained, had noted her award-winning work on the interior renovations of Hopeley Old Hall in the west country, had also noted that she had used their fabrics throughout the project, and, in short, were interested in sponsoring her as one of the most promising up-and-coming new designers.

The sponsorship had been a lifeline and she had blessed the day she had decided to try for the small but prestigious award that had brought her to Interior Textiles notice. A large cash loan, at a ridiculously low rate of interest, had enabled her to expand as well as simply keep afloat. Her fiery Arien nature demanded scope and challenge, a goal. Kate knew that without a goal her life would be meaningless.

Needing to be in three places at once, she had frankly head-hunted Rob Mallin, a brilliant young designer whose talents were, she knew, under-utilised in the large studios he had joined after gaining his degree.

The partnership, and the loan from IT, had enabled them to take more commissions, employ Sally full time and take Anna on board as runner.

'And something important did come up,' Sally was saying but, behind them, the phone rang and Sally shrugged. 'Won't be a tick and then I'll fill you in,' she said, and waddled away to her adjoining cubby-hole office.

Pulling her diary towards her, Kate began pencilling in appointments. The Honourable Nigel Stockynge for Tuesday, if it could be arranged. He wanted his Mayfair apartment redone. Black leather and chrome, dramatic lighting and white porcelain. Nigel had definite ideas of his own and Kate could do the job with her eyes shut, and she wasn't enthused. But because of the simplicity of the project it represented a substantial profit, and, within limits, profit was the name of the game.

She sighed, leaning back in her chair, feeling unsettled. And that was due, she acknowledged, to the photograph in the paper. She had been away from Montstowell for six years but the passage of time hadn't lessened her hatred of Seth Presteigne, or the way that even the thought of him had the power to pluck at her nerve ends.

Bending her glossy dark head to her diary again, she determined to put Seth out of her mind but was immediately thwarted in the attempt when Sally, plodding out of her office, said in awed tones, 'That was Seth Presteigne himself. He wants you to phone him back.' She pulled up a chair and sat down. 'Because I hadn't had time to brief you, I told him you were in a meeting——'

'What are you talking about?' Kate interrupted brusquely, trying to cover the feeling of sick rage brought on by the fact that he had, for some reason, contacted her firm. She hadn't set eyes on him in years and yet in the space of twenty minutes or so she had seen his face staring at her from the daily paper, and heard her secretary say he wanted to speak to her.

'That's what I was starting to tell you when the phone rang,' Sally explained, unbothered by the look of prickly impatience on her employer's lovely young face. Since her pregnancy nothing much bothered her. 'It was the "something important" I was going to tell you about. He phoned while you were in Rome last week supervising the final touches to the Brunelli apartment. He wants us to completely redesign the interior of Montstowell. And he particularly asked for you—Miss Kate Mallin.' She smiled. Since the partnership, and following on the specialist publicity since Kate had walked away with that award, the mistake in names had often occurred. 'Apparently,' Sally continued, clearly impressed, 'you're to have a completely free hand.'

So Lady Beatrice had to be dead, was Kate's first thought. The autocratic old matriarch would never have allowed so much as a hearthrug to be changed during her lifetime. And immediately, pushing that thought out of existence, came the second, the one she voiced impulsively.

'It's not on. Phone him back—apologise and tell him we're fully committed into the foreseeable future. Then point him at one or two of the top studios. He can afford the best, after all.' She wanted nothing to do with him. Nothing at all.

'But that's not true!' Sally yelped, her smooth brow furrowing. She would be leaving her job in a couple of months' time, settling down to wait for the baby, looking forward to being a full-time wife and mother, but that didn't mean she wasn't concerned about Kate. She had worked with her—admired her—for too long to sit by and say nothing while she carelessly, and with characteristic impulsiveness, tossed aside the chance of such a highly lucrative and prestigious piece of work.

Kate's mouth quirked wryly. It was common knowledge that on the death of his father, Brigadier Presteigne, twelve years ago, Seth had taken the handful of neglected family owned businesses and had wrestled them into shape, forcing them into the tail end of the twentieth century, and into profitability, creating a huge financial safety net for Montstowell, for his mother, Lady Bea. It would have been totally out of character for him to do anything less. His Scorpio ego was total, his vitality and the grim determination to win prodigious. Character traits that might frighten or overawe some, but not Kate, who openly admitted that tilting at windmills made life exciting. But not this windmill, not this time.

'There's nothing Seth Presteigne could possibly want that he couldn't afford,' she said drily.

Sally shook her head, telling her, 'That isn't what I meant. I meant,' she stressed with laboured patience, 'that we could easily take the job on. All it would need would be a bit of juggling. We're not so secure that we can afford to turn away that sort of work.'

Kate swivelled her chair around, her unfocused gaze on the window, not seeing anything. Sally was right, of course. The job of completely redesigning the interior of Montstowell would be a major feather in Kate-Mallin's cap, produce some serious income.

Montstowell, the family home of the Presteignes for over two hundred years, had last been renovated in the 1880s. The interior of the huge, stone-built Tudor house had worn its dreary, uninspiring Victorian mantle with little grace and, even as a child, Kate had instinctively wanted to sweep the sombre clutter away, to fill the great rooms with the furnishings its period cried out for.

Of course it would have been sheer chance that Seth had decided to use the Kate-Mallin studio. He wouldn't have known that Kate Jones, the 'unsuitable' head gardener's child, had founded the business. He hadn't known of her interest in fabrics, furnishings, lighting, colours and style. She hadn't known of it herself until the end of her foundation year at college. By which time, of course, her father had been dead, the estate cottage she'd grown up in inhabited by a new head gardener and his wife and child, all her own ties with Montstowell irrevocably cut.

'Think of the new work that would come in,' Sally persisted. 'This Seth Presteigne's a pretty formidable fish in the financial pond. He's bound to entertain. And most of our work comes in by word of mouth, personal recommendations—you know that.'

Kate did. The redesigning of a country house such as Montstowell would, in due course, result in more such work for the studio, and work, success, was what Kate craved most. Not for her the need for the emotional props of a husband and children, the daily round of caring for others that some women preferred. Sometimes, though, looking at Sally, who wore her contentment like an aura, Kate wondered. . .

'It's not like you to pass up a challenge,' Sally stated the well-known fact, adding untruthfully, 'Not that it bothers me. It's your business, after all.'

And so it was, Kate reflected wryly. It was her baby, all she had. And if Sally knew exactly why she was hesitating then she would understand. But the early years of her life, happy until the day after her eighteenth birthday, were something she had never spoken to anyone about. Her happiness with her lot, her life, had ended there. Right there, in total, utter humiliation.

'You're right, of course,' Kate conceded. Masking a sigh, she swivelled back to face her secretary, her composed features revealing nothing. 'Let me have his number; I'll phone and accept.'

The relief on Sally's open face gave the lie to her earlier statement and, as she hurried back to her office, Kate's nostrils flared as she fought to swallow the feeling of sick panic she felt at the thought of actually having to speak to Seth again.

But the studio came first. It always would. And Rob couldn't take on the Montstowell project; he was too involved in the early, all-important stages of the design work for Countrywise. Asking Anna to tackle something as important as Montstowell would be professional suicide. Anna had had no formal training, but she had flair, she was bright and quick to learn. She could finish the Maybury job—supervising the team of sub-contracted decorators would be all she actually needed to do at this stage. So that left her, Kate, and she would do the job because it would be good for the studio.

Her mouth tightening, she glanced down at the paper Sally handed her and began to dial. . .

The drive from London to Shropshire had taken three hours. But she had left the motorway now and, with the need for concentration less intense, Kate began to feel dithery. The thought of what she'd taken on when she had agreed to return to Montstowell and work for Seth Presteigne wasn't a pleasant one.

She had been too busy during the past week to have time to have the jitters and on Friday lunch with Brian Rose had been an oasis of peace. As usual, he had told her of his directors' satisfaction with the way she was progressing, scanning the audited accounts of the previous six months' figures, which he would be taking away with him, with warm approval. Only when she'd mentioned the Montstowell project had she thought she'd detected a hint of surprised reservation on his face.

But she must have been imagining that, because her sponsors would be as pleased with the commission as Rob, Sally and Anna had been. She was the only one with reservations, deep ones. But she was too professional to allow them to jeopardise something that could benefit the studio, and too self-controlled to talk of them to anyone—even to Rob, who had become the closest friend she had.

As the passing countryside became more sparsely inhabited, more thickly wooded and rolling, she began to regret the fact that she hadn't spoken to Seth when she'd phoned to accept the commission. When a male voice, introducing itself as Seth Presteigne's personal assistant, had said, 'I'm afraid Mr Presteigne was urgently called away on business, but he instructed me to say that he will expect you at Montstowell on Monday next,' she had literally sagged with relief. She had been dreading hearing that clipped, slightly mocking voice again. And when his PA had gone on to say that, naturally, she would stay at Montstowell, she had bitten back the hot, unprofessional words of denial that had instantly sprung to mind, merely allowing herself a rueful grimace at the way Kate-Mallin's immediate acceptance of the commission had been so blithely assumed. It might have been better had she broken the ice of six long years by speaking to Seth himself. Might have been.

On the brow of a hill she drew her Metro on to the verge and wiped the slickness from the palms of her hands with a tissue. From here, for as far as the eye could see, lay the great acreage of the Montstowell estate. Almost below her was the Home Farm, a cluster of rosy brick buildings drowsing in the warm April sunlight. Cows at pasture, looking like toys, someone ploughing, the tractor creeping like an insect over the meadows near the lake. And beyond the gleam of blue water, partly hidden by stands of oak, the house. Montstowell. A stone jewel softly cradled in a bed of rich English farm and woodland.

She had always thought it an enchanted place, a place where she belonged, had roots. But Seth had shown her that her childish belief in belonging had no foundation whatever, that her presence was unwelcome, her assumptions a gross impertinence.

She squared her shoulders, her clear grey eyes coolly determined. She was now a success in her own right, an assured young woman of twenty-four, whose talent and drive many would envy. She was no longer the gawky, wide-eyed gardener's daughter who had had the impertinence to make a Presteigne of Montstowell fall in love with her, who had had the gross presumption to assume that she would be welcomed into that exalted family.

Briefly, she wondered if Ralph Presteigne would be at home still. Ten years younger than Seth—her own age—he had often told her how desperately he wanted to walk away from Montstowell, make his own life as a painter. Not for him the degree course in estate management which his mother, Lady Bea, had planned for him. He was expected to eventually run the estate, he'd explained moodily, while Seth wrestled with the failing family business enterprises. Seth might have knuckled down, 'done his duty', but Ralph would be damned if he would! An attitude which hadn't exactly earned him his mother's approval, Kate remembered. And to make matters very much worse, on the night of her eighteenth birthday Ralph had announced his intention of marrying the totally unsuitable gardener's daughter!

If, before then, she hadn't been able to understand Ralph's desire to leave the place she had loved best in the world, then the events that had followed that announcement had drawn a very clear picture of why he had wanted to get as far away as possible from his autocratic mother and supercilious, devious brother!

Kate restarted the car, her mouth a tight line. Apart from the obvious advantages to the Kate-Mallin studio, the one good thing to come out of her forthcoming encounter with Seth Presteigne would be the opportunity to show him that now, at last, she was someone to be reckoned with.

Six years ago he had forbidden her the estate, thrown her out, and now—albeit unknowingly—he had invited her back, would be paying her handsomely to set foot inside the inviolate home of his precious ancestors!

For the first time the irony of it struck her as amusing and she couldn't wait to see his face when he realised exactly who he had insisted on commissioning. She just couldn't wait!

CHAPTER TWO

As THE final bend in the immaculately maintained drive afforded her a heart-stopping view of the façade of Montstowell, Kate gritted her teeth. In that first moment of seeing again the perfectly symmetrical late Elizabethan house, the golden stone warm and glowing in the sunlight, the lump that had unaccountably lodged in her throat when she'd turned off on to the private road solidified painfully, making her chest feel tight.

Angrily, she fought the sensation. There was no room in her busy life for nostalgia, no room at all. She was here to do a job, to finally prove herself in the eyes of the man who had ordered her to leave his young brother well alone, to remove her insignificant person from the estate.

At the time she had been bewildered, more by what he had done than by what he had actually said. His method of demonstrating exactly how amoral he thought her to be had been devastating.

But she wasn't a bewildered, heartbroken eighteen-year-old now. She was fully in charge of her own destiny. She knew where she was going, where she was at.

Blinking a haze of unwanted tears from her eyes, she slowed the car down to a crawl as a rider, astride a tall black horse, emerged from the cover of beech and oak that bordered the drive.

She would have known him anywhere, known the arrogant carriage of his dark head, the wide-shouldered lithe leanness of his black-clad body.

The encounter had come sooner, more informally, than she had expected, and that was why her heart had begun to knock crazily against her ribs. No other reason.

She braked, watching as he urged the skittish horse towards the car, reluctantly winding down her side-window, knowing she could do nothing else— not if she wanted to maintain her air of cool sophistication.

She looked for annoyance, anger even, for what he must see as her temerity in daring to return. Then, eventually, chagrin when he realised that he had unwittingly engineered that return!

But there was nothing so obvious there. The hard, brilliant blue eyes were fixed on her face with a strange uncharacteristic hunger, as if the sight of her, here, was a need he'd had with him for a long, long time. But she knew that was crazy. Who better?

'Kate. . .' A smile flickered briefly across his face. An arresting face, almost, but not quite, austere. 'I hadn't expected you to make such good time.' A strongly made hand gentled his restive mount, firmly muscled thighs tightening, transmitting total control. 'Parker will show you to your room and I'll see you for lunch at one. You'll remember your way to the breakfast-room? We can talk over the preliminaries while we eat.'

So he wasn't surprised, not surprised at all and, as he wheeled his mount away she sat, her slim fingers drumming against the steering wheel. He had known to expect her all along, known *exactly* who would be arriving when he'd expressly asked for 'Kate Mallin'. It enraged her. She had wanted to surprise him, wanted to show him that his opinion of her worthlessness hadn't been justified. She had *needed* to make that statement.

And it was only later, when Parker—more of a general factotum than a butler—had shown her to a huge, sombrely furnished room at the front of the house, that her annoyance subsided enough to make way for questions.

Why had that look, deep in those disturbing eyes, seemed to welcome her when six years ago he had thrown her out? Why, when there were other top studios just as capable of handling his commission, had he approached her? It didn't make any kind of sense, because the last time she'd seen him he had thrown her off his land.

He was devious, tricky, no one knew that better than she. Her relationship with Ralph had offended his family pride and, characteristically, he had retaliated with a stinging backlash—so typical of his birthsign—that had wounded her deeply.

And he was astute. The way he had turned round the financial mess his father had left, creating thriving businesses out of limping lame dogs, expanding, acquiring, creating a fortune, pointed to a man of keen intelligence and singularity of purpose. A man who left nothing, but nothing, to chance.

She had finished hanging the few garments she'd brought with her in the cavernous inlaid Victorian wardrobe and walked to one of the mullioned windows, her smooth brow creased with concentration.

He had his own reasons for using her studio, for bringing her back here. At the moment she didn't know what they were, but suspected something Machiavellian. She stared down at the paved walks at the front of the house, the stone terraces, clipped yew hedges, the distant view of the lake, glimmering blue and shot with grey where it could be seen between the trees, and made a forcible effort to unravel the knot in her gut by sheer will-power. She would see him damned if he was hoping by some devious means to discredit the Kate-Mallin studio, lose her the place she had so painstakingly carved out for herself. He had hurt and humiliated her once. It wouldn't happen again.

'You've changed.' The dark voice was throaty, almost a purr, the tone lazily inviting. Inviting what? Reminiscences? Hardly!

Lifting her neat determined chin, Kate helped herself to salad and answered disinterestedly, 'You haven't,' and left him to make what he liked of that. But he had, of course. Six years and her own knowledge of what he was like, really like, had added nuances, darker tones, to the man seated opposite her at the linen-covered table. Where, as a child, she had seen nothing but kindliness in his smile, she now saw cynicism, and his powerful good looks had become translated to brooding arrogance, the outward configuration of a self-will that stepped down for nothing and no one.

'Perhaps you'd like to clarify your brief, tell me what you have in mind for Montstowell.' She used the tone she always kept for clients. Impersonal, businesslike, overlaid with friendliness, adding up to a willingness to listen, to co-operate, without being a pushover. In her business relationships she was the one in charge, the professional, and while she made a point of considering her client's wishes she made sure they were gently yet firmly thrown out of play if they went against her knowledge of what was right for the project in hand.

A quirk of his sensual lower lip, of the strongly arched brows that, together, saved his face from total austerity, denoted his slightly amused acceptance of her change of subject.

'You have a completely free hand, limitless funds.' He poured more wine for them both. She envied him his steady hands. Hers, did he but know it, were trembling slightly, something she did her best to disguise as she transferred a morsel of the delicious game pie to her mouth. And she wanted to ask, Why me? Why Kate-Mallin? but didn't because she knew she wouldn't get the truth, not from him.

For some devious reason he wanted her here and it wasn't because she was one of the best in her field. There were others as good, and a few better, much longer established. And it wasn't for old times' sake! The last time he'd seen her he'd made it perfectly clear that he couldn't wait to see the back of her and was prepared to discredit her in any way he could.

So asking him why would be a waste of breath. He played his cards very close to his chest. So she would be very, very wary, and do the job to the best of her ability—give him absolutely no cause for complaint. It would be the sort of exercise in will-power she most enjoyed.

'I take it your mother is no longer with you?' She kept her tone carefully level, her voiced assumption completely natural, never letting him guess how much in awe she'd been of Lady Beatrice, how the sight of the stern old matriarch had reduced her to a tongue-tied rabbit on more than one occasion.

'Mother died about eighteen months ago,' Seth told her, the hard eyes veiled now, the brilliant blue muted by the sweep of amazingly thick black lashes. Kate dabbed her mouth with her napkin and resisted the impulse to snipe, Then why wait until now before having the house done over?

Such a remark would be as crass as it was uncalled-for; Seth and his mother had been close, two of a kind, both autocratic, devoted in their own ways to Montstowell, putting the house, the family name, before anything else. But where Lady Bea had been a dynastic dinosaur, Seth was of a modern breed, tough, as ruthless as they came, his dedication to Montstowell and its future viability a sharp-edged weapon which he wielded without concern for those who got in his way.

And she, briefly, for one gaudy hour, had stood in his way, offended his snobbish pride, and she had felt the icy brush of cold steel as the ruthless knife-edge of his pride had severed her from Ralph, from Montstowell, from her past.

'And Ralph? Is he still here?' Her own question surprised her, robbing her voice of its customary cool control. She had promised herself that while she was here she wouldn't fall to personal levels, that she would treat Montstowell—Seth—as just another job, another client. And suddenly those hard eyes narrowed, the brilliant blue glitter laser-like in its intensity. He pushed back his chair, getting to his feet as the small breakfast-room door opened to admit a neat middle-aged woman with a tray.

'No coffee for me, Mrs Parker.' The look he turned on Kate was compounded of exasperation and malice which meant that he still felt sore about her relationship with his brother, she thought as he grated, 'I suggest you use the afternoon to look around. We'll discuss your ideas over dinner. Oh, and Kate. . .' he was at the door now, speaking over the discreet clatter as Mrs Parker laid out the coffee impedimenta '. . . I have only one stipulation to make; that you stay here for the duration of the project. Other than that you have a completely free hand and open-ended finances.'

And before she had time to even begin to object he had gone, closing the door firmly behind him.

Mrs Parker said, 'I hear the whole house is to be done up. High time too! Not that I'd say as much to Mr Presteigne, of course.'

'Of course not.' Kate smiled easily, pouring her coffee. No one spoke their mind—unless expressly invited to and then only after careful consideration—to the master of Montstowell! 'Have you been with him long?' She added cream to the fragrant liquid in the bone china cup. When she'd left here her father, the head gardener, had still been alive and the staff at the 'big house' numerous and doddery, kept on more for the sake of their devotion to the house and family than for their efficiency. Lady Bea had liked to see forelocks tugged—metaphorically speaking. Ralph had once told her, in a tone of disgust, 'There must be, collectively, a thousand years' worth of old retainers tottering around the venerable corridors!'

'Parker and I came a few weeks after her ladyship passed away,' the housekeeper imparted, tucking the fretted silver tray comfortably under her arm. 'I believe the staff here, during her time, were all well over retiring age. I know for a fact that she remembered them all in her will. But Mr Presteigne said he could manage with just Parker and me—him being away so often and the house virtually shut up.'

'But he entertains?' Kate probed, disliking herself for prying yet feeling she had to know her enemy in the war of attrition Seth was undoubtedly plotting. It couldn't be anything else. Nothing else would be in character. And, as she wasn't thinking along the lines of business dinners, working weekends, she prodded, 'Surely the lovely Lucy Mortiboys is here quite often?'

'Oh, and isn't she just? Lovely, I mean.' Happily, the housekeeper had missed the sarcasm Kate had been unable to prevent from sharpening her voice. She sat down in the chair Seth had vacated, all set for a gossip. 'Parker and I think something might come of it. Not that she's been here often, mind

you, but you can tell, can't you? When she is here
she can't take her eyes off him.'

And neither could the others, Kate thought
sourly. The progression of lovelies that had trooped
through his life during the four years when Kate had
actually woken up to the fact that whenever Seth
descended on Montstowell so did a beautiful, well-
pedigreed young female, had been mind-boggling.
She wondered if Lucy Mortiboys would succeed in
nailing him down when all the others had failed,
then wondered why she was showing an interest, in
any case. She was most definitely not in the least
concerned over the state of Seth Presteigne's love-
life!

Having extricated herself from what had given the
appearance of turning into a mammoth gossip
session, Kate returned to her room for a notepad
and pencil. Mrs Parker was a woman who obviously
loved to talk and, just as obviously, had been starved
of female companionship during her time at
Montstowell. So it would be almost too easy to gain
knowledge of Seth's current lifestyle, should she
want it. But, she assured herself, she didn't want it.
Nothing about Seth held any interest for her now—
though there had been a time when things had been
different, when her silly young heart had leapt with
joy, almost bursting inside her whenever he had
taken any notice of her.

But she was older now, a whole lot wiser, and the
fact that he had 'noticed' her to the extent of

insisting that she, and only she, took on the job here only made her wary—sensing perfidy.

Her tour of the house was largely a gesture. She knew it well and nothing had changed from the days when she and Ralph, on wet weekends or rainy days in the school holidays, had been allowed to make free of it. No one had seemed to mind that Ralph Presteigne had befriended the gardener's daughter; it had only been later, when they were both going on seventeen, that Lady Bea had unsuccessfully tried to part them. And then, a year later, it had been Seth who had thrown her off the estate.

To Kate the interior of the old house had always seemed depressing. The furniture was solid mahogany, very worthy but totally out of character, the carpets a uniform dull red, the curtains heavy and dreary, designed to keep out the sunlight. Nothing ever wore out and Lady Bea had insisted that nothing was ever changed.

It was with relief that she returned to her room, took off her shoes and lay on the bed. But behind closed eyelids her mind was active, coolly analytical. To take the job on with his stipulation, or not?

Professionally, she would be a fool to turn it down, and personally it would give her enormous satisfaction to be the one to transform Montstowell. But could she bear to be under the same roof as Seth for as long as it would take?

After showering in the huge adjoining bathroom—all cold white tiles and drab linoleum—and dressing in a carefully chosen, devastatingly simple black crêpe dress, she had reached a decision.

She would stay on and do the job, if only to show him that she could, because—whatever his no doubt devious reasons for inviting the Kate-Mallin studio to do the work, insisting that she stay and supervise—she would demonstrate her professionalism, let him see that she was now his equal. She wasn't eighteen any more, easily intimidated, easily hurt. And while she was here she would find out exactly what he'd had in mind when he had, against all reason, invited her back!

He was waiting for her, standing in a doorway further along the hall and as he stepped forward into the pool of light shed by the overhead chandelier she saw something leap to life in those brilliant, hypnotic eyes and her breath became trapped in her lungs.

But she moved onwards, accepting the fact of his unfathomable attempt to manipulate her in some way as a challenge that had to be tackled with every last ounce of her courage, her neatly cropped sable head high, her only concession to feminine frivolity this evening the spindly, high-heeled pumps that would bring her nearer to his intimidating height.

As he reached her side, however, she discovered that her tactics, though sound, hadn't had the desired effect. She felt swamped, overwhelmed. Even in the highest heels she owned the crown of her head only reached his chin. Of average height, her willowy slenderness—saved from boyishness by small but perfectly shaped breasts and smoothly feminine hips—might give her the appearance of fragility, but she was steel inside, pure steel, and she needed to be, because fighting her way to the top had been tough.

'We'll have drinks by the fire.' His hand cupped her elbow and she stiffened. She didn't want him touching her. She remembered far too clearly the last time he had touched her. . . And then she made the mistake of looking up, saw the austere perfection of his profile, the proud prominence of his nose, the curve of his beautifully carved mouth and she shuddered, the memory of how that mouth had felt on hers betraying her, making her painfully aware that, when she'd told herself that that particular episode in her life had no significance, she'd been wrong, lying to herself.

And he, damn him, picked up her thought-waves; he must have done, because his voice was a purr, like thick dark honey as he enquired, 'Cold, Kate?' letting her know that he knew she wasn't. His fingers tightened masterfully, as if, now he was touching her, he refused to let go, as if he wanted to force her to look back into the past. And she vowed he'd never make her do that, or only fleetingly and reluctantly, never with any serious intent. But, nevertheless, as he led her in through the open doorway of the book-room, memories came flooding back.

It wasn't as grand as the library but there were plenty of books around, shelves full of remembered favourites, treasures she'd plundered when she was a child. And it was here, fourteen years ago, that she and Ralph had spent almost the entire wet Easter holiday working on the huge and tricky jigsaw puzzles Seth had presented them with. Her mother had died of leukaemia only six weeks before, leaving a huge and aching gap in Kate's young life. And it had been then that Ralph's much older brother, Seth, had first started to loom so large in her life, stepping down from the lofty pinnacle the ten years' age gap had placed him on.

It had been Seth who had encouraged her to borrow books from this room, children's classics in the main, Seth who had taken her on his knee, holding her gently as she'd sobbed out her misery for the mother she had so recently lost. And afterwards he had mopped her tears and taken her back home, back to the empty gardener's cottage.

Her father, she remembered, had been working in the walled vegetable garden and mostly, after school, Kate would join him wherever he was, working beside him, doing the simple tasks he allotted her, because since her mother's death she had clung to him. But that day she had wandered off into the woodland, edgy, not in the mood for her father's slow, gentle patience. She had wanted to scream, to rage against the fate that had taken her mother from her, and she'd been kicking at the undergrowth, her small face red and twisted with fury, when Seth had appeared. And then she had cried, great howling angry sobs that had threatened to tear her skinny frame apart. And Seth had sat on the stump of a felled tree, taking her on his knee, holding her until the storm was over before taking her home.

And the little cottage that had once been so safe

and cosy but which had become an empty, alien place since her mother's death had miraculously come to life again as he had lit the fire in the tiny sitting-room and helped her to prepare the shepherd's pie against her father's return from work, all the time talking to her, almost as if she had been his age and not a mere child, telling her about his life as a student at the LSE, about his plans for revitalising the family-owned businesses.

After that he had always seemed to be there when she needed him, like a guardian angel, though, looking back, she knew he couldn't have been. But it had been Seth who had encouraged the vague friendship that had existed between herself and his much younger brother at that time, so that the two of them had become inseparable, Seth who had appeared at weekends and holidays, taking her and Ralph fishing, on picnics, on trips to the coast.

He had only been filling in time, she acknowledged now, watching as he expertly uncorked a bottle of champagne, not spilling a drop. Weekends and holidays at Montstowell must have been monotonous for a young man just into his twenties, and, while it might have amused him to play fairy godfather to a straggly schoolgirl, he had shown his true colours when that same scrawny, pigtailed child had blossomed into something approaching beauty, becoming unsuitably and romantically entangled with his impressionable younger brother. Men like the Montstowells didn't marry out of their class.

And she was seeing him clearly now, the rose-tinted glasses had been discarded along with her naïveté, and the slender sophisticated young woman in her designer black crêpe was a world away from the dewy-eyed, trusting innocent of six years ago.

He handed her a crystal flute, the straw-coloured liquid alive with diamond-bright bubbles, and, carefully avoiding his fingers, she took it, asking brittly, 'What's the celebration?'

'To homecoming, if you like.' The amazingly blue eyes crinkled, overlaid with a velvety patina of warmth which she didn't trust.

She said, to put the record straight, 'I don't like. I prefer the truth. The Montstowell estate became no more than a titular home to me when I went away to college, and ceased being a home in any sense at all after my father died.'

Her soft mouth tightened and she looked away from him, staring into the fire. She deeply regretted refusing to return to the cottage during that first Christmas vacation. She had been too proud to come sneaking back after Seth had thrown her out. Her father, not knowing the truth of what had happened, had been hurt by her excuses and evasions. She hadn't felt she could tell him what Seth had said; after all, her father worked for the wretched man. And she hadn't known then that her father was to die of a heart attack before the next January was out, but she knew it now and the misunderstanding that had crept in between them, the lost opportunity to spend that last Christmas with him, was one more thing to hold against Seth, to hold him directly responsible for.

'Then we'll drink to renewal—to friendship?'

If that was supposed to be a question then she wasn't deigning to answer and she sat down on one of the uncomfortably upright chairs angled around the fire, her movements economical, filled with unconscious grace.

'I've decided to accept your commission,' she told him, deliberately steering the conversation away from the personal. Simply being here again, seeing him, had brought the past she'd vowed to put behind her forever uncomfortably close. Their relationship now had to function on a purely business level; anything else would be unthinkable. 'However, it will mean that the present contents of the house will have to go.'

'Everything?' The slight, lazily lifting curl of his upper lip, the casual and totally relaxed way he took the chair opposite hers and lounged back, tipping his glass to her before draining half the contents, the way he tacked on, 'If you say so, of course,' made her furious.

Putting her own untouched drink down on a side-table she admitted that, subconsciously, she had been looking for a rift here. She had expected him to forcefully object to such a sweeping statement, so giving her the leverage she needed, placing her in a position of total authority over him for once. 'Do as I say or I walk out now,' were words which would have tasted sweet on her tongue, compensating, at least in part, for the things she had had to listen to from him.

But he had spiked her guns and she guessed he

knew it because the wicked glint in his eyes hinted at a far from comforting ability to read her mind.

'There will be a great deal of interior work to be done,' she imparted briskly, fighting the illogical feeling of utter apprehension she felt at being here with him. 'The ugly Victorian marble fireplaces will have to be ripped out and the original Tudor hearths exposed. Then, of course, there's the antiquated plumbing——'

'Are you suggesting we install Tudor garderobes?'

The twitch of a muscle at the side of his mouth made her want to hit him. He was laughing at her, trying to make her look foolish, but before she could retaliate he told her levelly, 'Whatever you suggest. As I said, you have a completely free hand. And now. . .' he rose with a loose-limbed grace that set her skin quivering '. . . Shall we go through to dinner? I believe Mrs Parker has arranged something special.'

Kate got to her feet reluctantly, wishing herself a thousand miles away because, since she had arrived here, nothing had gone the way she had expected it to.

And then he touched her, just the light pressure of his hand beneath her elbow, not much, but enough to shatter her equilibrium, the poise she had prided herself on maintaining, to cause an untenable sensation to erupt in the region of her stomach. And for a timeless moment his eyes held hers, reaching her, and she felt as if she were floating out of her body, yet, conversely, totally and completely aware of herself. It had happened like this just once before, this insane feeling that she hovered on the brink of some startling revelation. And then—that time—it had been when he had. . .

Instinctively, defensively, her mind slammed the door shut on that particular memory and she met the still watchfulness of his brilliant blue gaze and managed, with a coolness she was proud of, to say, 'As I was trying to explain, if the job's done as it should be done, Montstowell will be virtually uninhabitable for a few weeks.' She walked ahead of him towards the door, her spine held so stiffly that it hurt. 'But then, if you are not in the habit of spending too much time here I don't suppose you will be too much inconvenienced.'

As a hint it wasn't too subtle but she hoped the picture she had painted of a great house in the throes of major renovation work, denuded of furnishings, would be enough to convince him that taking himself off to his London apartment would be the best course to follow.

Not so. And his voice held just a trace of humour as he told her, 'You don't get rid of me that easily. I can endure a little discomfort for the sake of staying close.'

And what the heck was that supposed to mean? Kate wondered acerbically, hectic colour staining her pale skin as she allowed him to lead her to the dining-room. Whether he meant he wanted to be around to keep an eye on work in progress, or whether he meant he wanted to stay close to her, for some utterly devious reasons of his own, she didn't know. In either event, his words gave her a very sick feeling indeed!

CHAPTER THREE

KATE was wary, like a cat, and held herself aloof, and at first Seth respected her need for solitude, giving her the use of the library as an office, keeping out of her way.

They met at mealtimes, of course, and he was unfailingly polite and friendly, and if he had been anyone other than the man he was she would have called him the perfect client. She might even have attributed the strange breathless feeling that swamped her whenever he was around to sexual attraction had he been any other man but Seth Presteigne. As it was, she knew differently. She despised him, resented him for his past cruelty, and loathing could produce such compellingly uncomfortable physical sensations, she knew it could.

The strange leap of her heart when he entered the library as she put the phone down after catching up on events back at the studio was nothing more significant than annoyance at being disturbed, she reasoned. He was casually dressed this morning in faded grey denims and an open-necked black shirt. He looked tough yet sexy, too masculine, too physically compelling. Little wonder all those nubile lovelies from suitable families clung to him like limpets, she thought disparagingly, carefully allowing only the bare hint of enquiry into her voice as she asked, 'Yes?' and turned a page of her notepad.

'Beg leave to enter, ma'am.' His smile was as good as a grin, wicked lights sparkling the depths of his eyes, and the corners of her leaf-shaped mouth twitched in unwilling response.

'That's better!' He came further into the room and she lowered her eyes quickly, feeling her heart pick up speed. He dominated her space, made her feel claustrophobic.

'What's the progress?' he wanted to know. 'Any problems?'

'None at all.' Or only *him*, and she was about to add that progress would be less impeded if he left her alone to do the job but swallowed the tart words as Mrs Parker came through with the coffee tray, and two cups.

'You and your husband may as well take the rest of the day off,' Seth told the housekeeper as he took the tray and her eyebrows shot up to her hairline.

'And what about your lunch? Dinner?' she demanded, her head on one side, for all the world like a nanny remonstrating with a feckless child.

'Leave something cold for lunch,' he responded, even white teeth showing in a smile. 'You and Parker get out and enjoy the weather—it could be the last chance you have. According to Kate we'll shortly be inundated with builders and rubble, plumbers and pipes—and I am more than capable of making dinner for two.'

'Ah.' There was a wealth of meaning in that single

sound, and there was a knowing twinkle in the housekeeper's eyes as she rested them on Kate's pale little face.

Normally white-skinned, she felt the beginnings of a blush under the erroneous impression Mrs Parker had formed. But then the housekeeper had been at Montstowell long enough to acquaint herself with her employer's womanising habits! Kate looked down quickly, ostensibly absorbed in her notepad, and when she looked up again she and Seth were alone.

He poured the coffee, putting hers near her hand, sinking down on to the chair on the opposite side of the desk, swinging his feet up on to the smooth, highly polished mahogany and leather top.

A tight band of annoyance constricted her chest. Having to work for him was bad enough without him foisting his unwanted presence on her, putting his feet on the desk.

Still, it was his desk, she admitted reluctantly, meeting his lazy azure gaze and wishing she hadn't because when he looked at her like that, his eyes warmly intimate between unfairly thick fringes of black, she went weak at the knees. And, what was worse, almost forgot what an underhand cruel snob he was.

He was idly stirring his coffee, leaning back, utterly relaxed, and she distrusted that composure, resented it deeply because she herself was tense enough to scream, throw things, and the effort of hiding that parlous state from him was quickening her pulse-rate, making every breath painful. And the unwanted memory of what had happened here in this room six years ago was too traumatic to be borne.

'Have you been through the attics?' he queried, his eyes never leaving her face.

She answered, 'No,' shortly, wishing he'd drink his coffee and take his disturbing presence away.

'Then you should.' He swung his legs to the floor and stood up, walking over to the open french windows, looking out over the sunlit lawns. 'Most of the furniture which was ousted in the last century to make room for the Victorian "improvements" was stored up there. You might find you could put it into use again. At least, looking through it might interest you and help you to loosen up.'

He had turned now and the light was behind him, making his expression impossible to read and, in silhouette, he looked dangerous, utterly forbidding, exactly as he had looked on that dreadful day, the day after her eighteenth birthday, the day he had forced her to grow up, breaking her vulnerable young heart in the process.

He moved then, coming to stand in front of her and, looking up unwillingly, her grey eyes cloudy with remembered pain, she saw something flare in the brilliant depths of his eyes, saw a muscle move at the side of his firm jaw.

'Kate. . .' He began to say something but thought better of it, and she wondered what it could have been because she'd recognised the urgency in the way he'd said her name, noticed the tension as his long fingers curled within his palms, making fists.

And then he relaxed, his smile warmly intimate. 'I'll get out of your hair now and we'll sift through the stuff in the attics after lunch.'

He would have gone then but she heard her own voice holding him back, rasping hoarsely, 'Why did you give me this commission?' and could have cursed herself for the unguarded query because when she'd decided to take the job on she had vowed never to ask him why, never to refer to the past, or give any indication of how close they once had been. But her natural honesty and directness had forced it from her.

Whether the question itself had thrown him, or the harshness of its delivery annoyed him, she didn't know. But she saw his spine go rigid before he turned back to her again, his eyes narrowed as he said tonelessly, 'Because I wanted you here?'

It had been posed as a question and she rejected it, her lips tight against her teeth as she made the denial, 'No, no way.' Six years ago he had commanded her to get off his land and if he wanted her here now then that dark need pointed down twisted tortuous paths, paths signposted 'Attrition'. And although that was what she had feared, right at the outset, she wasn't sure she could handle it and so she had to deny it.

'No?' There was a cynical twist at the corner of his mouth but then he suddenly smiled, a feral smile that gave his austere features a demonic quality. 'If you say not.' He moved to the door, holding it open. 'I saw the work you did on Hopeley Old Hall and was very impressed. Satisfied?'

And then he was gone and she hoped he had told her the truth. It was feasible, acceptable. Far more acceptable than the fear that he had invited her here with the express intention of inflicting further punishment for what he believed she had done six years ago.

The events of that morning were something she never thought about now. Her father's death had closed that chapter of her life and living in the past wasn't her style. But she was sensible enough to recognise that her reaction to seeing his photograph in the paper, to his commission, pointed to the distasteful fact that, behind the closed door of her memory, his treatment of her had been festering away in her brain.

It had all been so unnecessary, she thought, her mouth tightening. Unnecessary and cruel. Since her mother's death he had carved himself a very special place in her life, showing himself compassionate enough, caring enough, to try to make a young child feel less bewildered and deserted.

Precisely when she had ceased to love him as an older brother or youngish uncle she couldn't say although, with hindsight, she thought the other kind of love might have begun when Ralph had grumbled, 'Why is it that when Seth is home there's always some soppy girl dragging along behind him?'

And that had opened her eyes to the fact that Ralph was right—Seth always had some 'soppy girl' in tow. But, in the eyes of the gawky fourteen-year-old Kate had been at the time, they hadn't been girls at all, but impossibly beautiful, sophisticated young women.

Even so, Seth had always made time for the two young teenagers and she had begun to take special trouble with her appearance when he was at home and she could still recall how happy she'd been when, after gaining his degree, he had returned to Montstowell more often, beginning the long haul of pulling the estate and the diverse, failing, family-owned businesses together.

She and Ralph had been sixteen when Seth had offered to teach them to drive, their lessons confined to the private estate roads. And on the day he gave her her first lesson Kate had discovered that she loved him, had always loved him in one way or another.

They were to be alone together in the car, no Ralph for the first time in ages, and some instinct had prompted her to experiment with make-up, to leave her long dark hair loose instead of tied back in the usual pony-tail, to leave the top buttons of her blouse undone.

He had looked more surprised than bowled over by her altered appearance and he hadn't been his usual gently teasing self, either, and that had made her sulk. And she had been too busy wondering why he was acting like a stranger to concentrate on his instructions. Going into a corner far too quickly, forgetting to change gear, she had almost landed them in the hedge, only saved from disaster by his lightning-quick reactions as he'd grabbed the wheel, a burning expletive on his lips.

Bursting into noisy tears, she had scrambled out of the car as soon as his barked and rapid-fire commands had shocked her into applying the brakes. And he had been right beside her before she had managed to carry out her intention of legging it back home, leaving him to bring the wretched car back.

Her legs had felt very tottery, she remembered, and he had taken her by the shoulders, his hands hurting, his face tight with temper.

'If I'm going to teach you to drive you're going to have to listen to what I tell you!' He had sounded as if he loathed her and she had started crying all over again and he had groaned, 'Don't cry, Kate. For God's sake, grow up!'

And that had been worse than anything, because more than anything she had wanted him to see her as grown-up already, and when his hard hands had released their punishing grip on her shoulders and begun to pat her soothingly she had flung herself against him, her emotions too much to handle, and, after a moment of shocked stillness, he had given her a brief hug and then put her gently away, taking a clean white handkerchief from the pocket of his cords.

'Mop your face while I turn the car. Then you can drive us back—doing exactly as I say.'

And she had driven back, very, very carefully, following his terse instructions minutely, and from then on everything had changed because she'd known she loved him. And oh, how she had loved him. He had never known, of course; no one had.

For two years it had been her secret. Two years of trying to be what she imagined he wanted her to be, two years of seeing a progression of young women come and go in his life, two years of jealousy punctuated by joy because none of them had lasted. Two years of waking every morning wondering if she would see him that day, of watching for him, of contriving to be where he was if he was working around the estate, of pining if he was away from Montstowell on business, as he more frequently was. Typically, she had fallen in love with the unobtainable. Two long years.

Kate sighed, giving way to the unstoppable memories that beat against her brain, demanding recognition. What a fool she'd been, too young and naïve to realise that men like Seth Presteigne didn't fall wildly and passionately in love with dewy-eyed schoolgirls!

And how cruel he'd been. If he'd confined himself to warning her off Ralph—not that she'd really needed it—her infatuation for him would have gradually and painlessly withered away.

As it was, her infatuation—it couldn't have been anything else—had died a violent death, transmuting to a hatred as bitter as gall.

She had known, of course, that Lady Bea disapproved of her continuing friendship with Ralph. She hadn't said anything, she hadn't needed to, but the way she had pointedly ignored Kate whenever they'd happened to meet around the estate, the way she'd arranged for Ralph to spend his vacations from his public school during his final year there with friends or relatives, had spoken volumes.

It had amused Kate rather than offended her. Little did Lady Bea know! She wasn't remotely interested in Ralph, or only as a friend. It was Seth she loved, wanted.

Matters had started to come to a head a week before her eighteenth birthday. Ralph had appeared, having hitch-hiked from the home of a distant cousin with whom he'd been parked for Easter while he worked for his exams and waited to hear of his acceptance at agricultural college, conditional on his results.

'Did you think I was going to stop up in that hole?' he spluttered, emerging, unrepentant, from an apparently blistering scene with his mother and Seth. 'And they're not getting me in to any damn agricultural college, either. I'm going to paint!'

His handsome young features were contorted by a scowl and Kate hid a smile, getting on with preparing the vegetables for the evening meal she would share with her father when he came in from the gardens. She had heard such protestations before, many times, and although she had said nothing she had often wondered if he had the bottle to defy his domineering mother—not to mention Seth—to such an extent.

'In any case. . .' he came to stand behind her '. . .it's your birthday next week, and nothing could make me miss your party.'

Suddenly his arms were around her, his face in her hair as he muttered hoarsely, 'I love you, Kate.'

Then he pulled her round, stating, 'I want to marry you,' his arms squeezing so tightly that she was robbed of breath, speechless, and then, before she could do anything about it, he was kissing her clumsily, and she didn't know what to do about that, either, because she had a potato in one hand and the peeler in the other.

So she let him kiss her and afterwards, gently, because she knew what it was like to love someone who didn't love you back, she said, 'Don't rush at things. Anyway, we're both too young to marry— you know that.'

'I'm eighteen, and so will you be, this time next week. We're legally adults and nothing and no one can stop us,' he asserted, his face very red. 'And there's no one else for you, is there?' he demanded, and she shook her head, more because she didn't know how to cope than in denial. She had never accepted any of the dates from the boys in the village because she hadn't been interested. And she couldn't tell Ralph that there was Seth—there would always be Seth—because that was her secret.

'We've been closer than Siamese twins since we were ten years old,' he stated. 'You can't buck that; no one can. And I love you and I'm going to marry you, Ma and Seth can rant and rave if they want— cut me off. . .'

For a moment he looked very young, very unsure, and Kate took the opportunity to tell him, 'Leave it, hmm? For a year or so—while we finish getting educated.' Seeing his skin darken, she added quickly, 'You go off and paint—whatever. And I'm hoping to study art, too, as you know. Let's review the situation——'

'**** that!' he swore violently and she stared at him. She had never heard him swear before. And he looked very cocksure now, brimming with youthful arrogance, confident that what he wanted was right simply because he wanted it.

'You're afraid of Seth and Ma. I can understand why—they make a formidable pair. But you don't need to be. Leave everything to me.'

He strutted out then and Kate stared at the closed door for long moments, frowning, before turning back to the sink. This was awful! She should have sensed what was brewing, done something about it. She felt very guilty.

There had been plenty of signs over the past twelve months. The way he had touched her more often than he needed, not accidentally but quite deliberately, the way he sulked if she spent time with one of her girlfriends, the way he'd kissed her last Christmas at the party Seth had given for the estate workers' children, his mouth hot and hard, his hands sliding down to her bottom, the way he watched her.

So what had happened today was partly her fault. She had noted the signs, vaguely, not doing anything about it because she had been too wrapped up in her adoration of Seth to think about the implications.

When she saw him next she would have to come right out and tell him that she didn't love him, not in that way. She didn't want the responsibility of hurting him, but she would have to do it.

But she saw nothing of him during the run-up to her party. She hoped he had thought better of his blurted proposal and was keeping out of her way because he was embarrassed. She put it out of her mind, too busy organising her party, secretly ecstatic because she knew Seth would be there.

Everything had to be perfect, right down to the last decoration in the big barn Seth had said she could use for the occasion, to the dress she would wear for him. And she was at the top of a ladder, tying the last bunch of balloons to the huge central beam when a voice below her said, 'Are you trying to break your neck? Come down before you fall down.'

'Seth!' For a moment she felt dizzy and it had nothing to do with the height. She hadn't so much as glimpsed him since Ralph's return. She turned round on the top rung, feeling the ladder sway then steady as Seth took hold of it in strong hands. His eyes were so incredibly blue and she saw anxiety for her written in them, and that made her feel crazy with happiness, reckless enough to flirt.

'Come and get me,' she invited, settling her neat bottom on the top rung, her voice made husky by the way her heartbeats had picked up speed. And just for a brief flicker of time she saw something burn in his eyes, something alien and new, so frightening and yet exciting that it made her drag in her breath. Her whole body felt tingling and weak, running with heat, and she didn't know what to say to him.

And then everything was back to normal again

when he said drily, 'If you fall off that thing you won't be at your own party. And who knows? I might have been looking forward to dancing with you.'

That was all it took to get her down. Not turning, still facing him, she descended carefully, one rung at a time, not taking her big grey eyes off him. She felt faint with excitement. He had as good as told her he wanted to dance with her! And he was grinning as he put his hands on her waist and swung her down off the last few rungs, putting her gently on her feet in front of him.

'I feel giddy!' Her plea of dizziness wasn't all pretence. She clung to him, her fingers eagerly transmitting the sensational feel of the hard, heated muscles of his shoulders that burned through the thin cotton of his shirt to the recessess of her brain, storing the tactile sensations away like photographic plates to be brought out at her leisure, to be savoured time and time again.

Her emotions too strong to control, she nuzzled her face into the breadth of his chest, breathing in the heady male scent of him, hearing his sharp intake of breath above the thundering of her heart. She would soon be eighteen, an adult. Old enough for him to date! And that train of thought reminded her of Ralph. She didn't want Ralph spoiling things at her party, dogging her every move, making sheep's eyes.

'Where's Ralph these days?' she blurted, half hoping to hear that he'd been packed off again to stay with his cousin.

'Immersed in paperwork in the estate office. It's the price he's paying for his rudeness in walking out on his host.'

At her mention of his brother his hands left her waist, the smile left his eyes. Eyes like hard brilliant jewels. And Kate felt awful. She was a bitch. She had actually hoped poor Ralph had been sent away again. Disgust with herself clouded her eyes, and sadness for something forever lost made her full mouth quiver and turn down at the corners. Because whatever happened, after his heated protestations of love, the days of their innocent, happy friendship had gone for good. There could be no going back to the way they had been.

And her misery was compounded as Seth muttered an inaudible expletive then swung away, walking out of the barn. She didn't know what she had done or said to make him stalk away like that.

But the natural buoyancy of youth soon took over. She would have a serious talk to Ralph when she next saw him. She would let him down gently and his puppy love would soon die the death.

Meanwhile there was heaps to do. She and a gang of girlfriends had the catering to organise, mountains of sandwiches to cut, sausage rolls to bake, salads and trifles to concoct. . .

Along with a slim gold-plated watch that had once belonged to her mother, her new flame-coloured chiffon dress had been her father's birthday gift to her. It had taken her hours to choose it but now, all ready to go downstairs to join her father who was waiting to escort her to the barn, she wasn't so sure.

The dress made her look older, especially with her long dark hair piled on top of her head, but it was more daring than anything she had ever worn before, or dreamed of wearing. The bodice, supported by tiny shoestring straps, was slashed almost to the waist and the twin concentric swirls of gold sequins over the bust had a definitely erotic appearance which she now found distasteful. But, apart from changing into the one fairly presentable cotton dress she owned, there was nothing she could do about it.

She surveyed her reflection doubtfully, chewing on the corner of her mouth and her father's voice floated up the stairs. 'Get a move on, love. You're supposed to be there to greet your guests. At this rate we'll be arriving just as they're all getting ready to leave!'

Taking a deep breath, she turned from the mirror, feeling the soft fabric of the full skirts brush sensuously against her long legs. There was no time to change now, even if she wanted to. Besides, she had chosen the dress to impress Seth, to make him see her as a mature and sexy woman instead of a gangling tomboy. She wasn't going to chicken out simply because her mirror told her she had succeeded!

'Enjoying yourself?' Seth asked, his face set. The strobing lights played over his face, making him look alien, dangerous.

Kate nodded, knowing her voice wouldn't carry over the frenzied sound of the hired disco. Yes, she was enjoying herself now because she was dancing with him.

Half closing her eyes, she swayed to the heavy beat of the music, dancing for him, not allowing herself to dwell on the fact that, in the end, it had been she who had had to ask him to dance.

Apart from telling her, right at the outset, that his birthday gift to her wasn't something to be carried around, advising her to ask her father to explain what it was, he hadn't spoken to her at all, much less danced with her, as he'd said he would.

All evening her eyes had hardly left him, hungry eyes, yearning eyes, her heart twisting painfully inside her because as far as he was concerned she didn't exist. Not even the daring flame-coloured dress could make him see her as a desirable woman. And Ralph had glued himself to her side, his eyes eating her, and although she had wanted to tell him to make himself scarce, she hadn't. He was her friend.

She had wished she could tell him the miserable truth, that she was hopelessly in love with Seth and dying inside because, for him, she didn't exist. But she couldn't allow herself that relief, and when Ralph said, 'I've got something for you. . .' patting the pocket of his fawn trousers '. . . But you'll have to be patient for an hour or so,' she merely shrugged uncaringly, misery making her churlish.

Eventually, feeling desperate, she sent him for some of the innocuous fruit punch from the depleted buffet tables and when he was safely out of the way she walked over to where Seth was talking to her father and some of the other older estate workers, her small chin tilted at a determined angle.

'Dance with me,' she demanded, her dark grey eyes fixed on his unsmiling, inscrutable face. Her father said, 'I'm off now, love. Four hours of loud music and my head's about to drop off.'

She smiled, his words hardly impinging as she took one of Seth's hands and tugged him on to the crowded dance space.

And now he was dancing with her, but he wasn't touching her, and Kate thought that maybe the oldies had had something with their foxtrots and quicksteps. And any minute now, when the music changed, he would walk away, she just knew it!

Desperate situations called for desperate remedies. She wasn't an Arien for nothing! She knew what she wanted—Seth—and she was going to get him and if he wouldn't touch her then she would touch him! Moving closer, she placed the palms of her hands against his chest, the skin of her splayed fingers tingling, catching fire as she felt his body heat. And suddenly, her legs turned to water and she sagged against him, making a small throaty sound that seemed to come right up from the pit of her stomach.

'Hey. . .' His strong hands supported her, almost spanning her tiny waist, his eyes darkening with concern as he told her, 'Don't faint on me. Let's get out into the air. It's the heat, the noise.'

It wasn't that, of course it wasn't. It was touching

him, being so close to him. But she wasn't arguing. Let him think she needed fresh air if it meant them being alone together in the sweet soft darkness. And maybe he would kiss her. . .

Then, from the corner of her eye, she saw Ralph mount the makeshift stage, say something to the DJ, and then the music stopped, and the chatter from the guests died away and into the silence Ralph said, 'Come on up, birthday girl!'

Kate could have hit him! Ralph looked very young and cocky, very sure of himself, but he wasn't smiling as he added into the microphone, 'Give me my girl back, Seth. It's not like you to go in for cradle-robbing.'

After what seemed like forever but was probably no longer than a moment, she felt Seth's hands slide from her waist and her eyes jerked to his face and his blue eyes were glacial in the stark austerity of his features and she knew Ralph had spoiled everything. Everything!

And then some of her friends were manhandling her, pushing and jostling her towards the stage, and Ralph stretched out a hand, dragging her up beside him, laughing down into her flushed, cross face.

'I want you guys to be the first to know,' he addressed the microphone but he was looking at her, 'that Kate and I are engaged.' And then he was pushing a ring on her finger, cold and hard, and the barn errupted to cheers and whoops and cat calls and she swept dazed eyes over the sea of upturned faces, desperately searching for Seth. But Seth had gone.

Apart from grabbing the microphone and categorically denying what Ralph had said, there was nothing Kate could do. She couldn't humiliate him so publicly but she would give the ring back at the first opportunity. It would be the shortest engagement on record!

She was still feeling shaky as she pottered around the kitchen next morning, making breakfast. She hadn't had an opportunity last night to speak to Ralph privately and she could still see the grim line of Seth's mouth as Ralph had taunted him from the stage.

'I thought you'd have wanted a lie-in,' her father said, pouring tea for them both. 'What it is to have so much youthful stamina!'

But it hadn't been stamina of any kind that had brought Kate downstairs at her usual early hour. She simply hadn't been able to sleep. The party she'd looked forward to for so long had turned into a disaster. She couldn't imagine what had got into Ralph and, worse than that, Seth had been so offhand. His behaviour had left her in no doubt that he would never see her as a desirable woman, no matter what she did.

But when the phone rang ten minutes after her father had left for the greenhouses, the leaden lump that had been her heart began pattering, light as a bird.

'Kate, I'd like to see you. In the library, at ten.'

Murmuring something incoherent, she put the receiver down, her hands shaking. Seth wanted to see her! She didn't fool herself that such a formal interview would be about anything other than that crazy engagement announcement but at least she would have the opportunity to tell her side of the story. And, who knew, his brother's desire to marry her might have opened his eyes to the fact that she was woman enough, old enough, to be loved?

She ran upstairs to change, feeling as light as air. She wouldn't make the mistake of overdressing but she wouldn't wear her usual jeans and shirt, either. Dressing in a flared white cotton skirt and an emerald-green blouse and brushing her long dark hair until it shone like silk, she completed her preparations with a touch of green eyeshadow and a dash of her favourite light cologne.

Hesitating, she picked up the diamond ring Ralph had pushed on to her finger last night, more than half tempted to ask Seth to return it to Ralph. That, more than anything she could say, would convince him that the sorry farce hadn't been of her making. But it would also be cowardly, and unfair to Ralph. Whatever she was, she wasn't a coward.

Sighing, she dropped the ring back on the dressing-table where she had put it as soon as she'd returned home last night, thankful that her father had left the party before Ralph had lost his marbles and made that shock announcement.

Her heart knocking, she entered the library by the open french windows, standing stock-still while she drank in his astonishing male beauty as he paced the floor, his dark head bent, immersed in some papers he held in his hand. And then he glanced up and saw her, hovering just inside the windows, and their eyes held. Her heart skipped a few wild beats. He was looking at her as if he'd never properly seen her before.

'You want me?' she managed huskily, cringing inside for the inanity of her comment, not understanding his answering wry grimace.

'Sit down, Kate.' He indicated a chair at one side of the huge desk but she shook her head, knowing she couldn't simply sit still. She contained far too much unexplained energy, so she prowled, slowly, letting her eyes drift. Edgy, excited, she was looking for a composure she wasn't old enough or sophisticated enough to find.

The library was one of the few rooms at Montstowell she wasn't familiar with. When Brigadier Presteigne had been alive it had been his private sanctum, the fox-hole he'd chosen to hide in, out of Lady Bea's way, some had said, and for some reason—unfamiliarity or Seth's obvious disapproval—she felt unsafe, on dangerous ground.

'About last night,' he began, his voice very cool. 'You must see that an engagement between you and Ralph is totally out of the question. Both his mother and I have spoken to him but he refuses to listen. I'm hoping you will be more reasonable.'

Her heart pumping erratically, she turned to face him. He sounded so cold, so condemning, so different from her beloved Seth that he was like a stranger. If she'd seen one hint of warmth, of kindness, in those glacial blue eyes she would have found the strength to tell him everything.

But he was looking at her as if she were something

loathsome and her young heart quailed, her mouth going dry, making speech impossible.

'Are you pregnant?'

The question came out with a grating harshness that shocked her. It sickened her. How could he think that? How *could* he? She felt herself blush cruelly, and that didn't help. She knew she looked like a beetroot. He thought she was a common tramp, having sex with Ralph, using her body as bait in the oldest trap of all.

'Kate. . .' His voice tore at her screeching nerves. 'I have to know!'

The admission seemed torn from him and, hating herself for the lack of sophistication that would have enabled her to cope with the dreadful situation, she hung her head, the dark wings of her hair hiding her face as she muttered thickly, 'No! Course not!'

'I see.' He sounded relieved and after that he didn't speak for some time and she just stood there, not knowing what to do or say, her eyes fixed on the Turkey red carpet, hating him, hating herself. Nothing was going as she'd hoped.

The calm explanation of the facts that she'd planned in her head on the way over here had remained unspoken, her composure had been shattered, her whole being shocked by his harshly voiced, horrible suspicions.

'You're too young to marry,' he said at last. 'You can't possibly know what you want, either of you. Your engagement to Ralph is out of the question. I won't allow it to happen.'

The bitter harshness of his tone brought her head

up. He was standing at the windows, looking out, his hands bunched into the pockets of his trousers.

Kate flicked her tongue over her dry lips, desperately trying to summon the words that would explain her part in the stupid affair, but his next words shocked her back into silence.

'I want your word that you'll keep away from Ralph, and that means away from Montstowell. While he knows where to find you he won't settle to anything, see any sense!' He swung round, his narrowed eyes fixed on her face and she thought she had never seen him look so tired, so drawn.

'Obviously you'll have to finish your schooling, but I'll make damn sure that Ralph isn't around for the next few months, and after that you'll be gone. I understand you may have a place at a design college. So I suggest you get yourself off Montstowell land, fix yourself up with accommodation in London—in any event, stay away from here.'

She couldn't believe she was hearing this, not from her beloved Seth. Her huge eyes swam with tears. He was ordering her off the estate; he didn't care where she went as long as he didn't have to set eyes on her again!

All thoughts of defending herself went out of her head. She felt ill, as if she might faint for the first time in her life, yet angry, too; too angry to allow herself to be dismissed like a no-account nuisance.

'Let me put it another way,' he bit out harshly. 'I will not stand by and watch you try out your emerging sexuality on my brother. It may seem like harmless fun to you, but not from where I stand.

Ralph's young enough and gullible enough to take the sparkling promise in a pair of big grey eyes literally, and the invitation of a perfect pair of pouting lips too seriously.' He moved closer, sheer menace in those brooding hypnotic eyes. 'I don't want to see you here again until——'

'Hell freezes over?' she supplied on a yell, her fiery temper breaking all the restraints of common sense. 'I suppose the gardener's daughter isn't good enough for a lofty Presteigne!' she stormed, meaning Seth himself, not Ralph, only he wasn't to know that, and then horrified herself by bursting into a tempest of tears in front of him for the second time in her life. And, for the second time, he moved to comfort her, enclosing her in his arms so that she was wrapped in warmth, lapped in care, only this time it was different, very different as she melted into the hardness of his body and felt him shudder, and she wondered if he felt it, too, this wicked tension, each nerve-ending and cell coming alive in some new and indefinable way.

Kate wriggled, trying to get closer, driven by a primitive urge to absorb him into her eager body, gasping as never-before-experienced sensations invaded her, the deep pulsating heat melting her to pure feminine fluidity. . .

Blindly, her heart thundering, she turned her face up to his, her lips parted in invitation, tears quivering on her thick dark lashes, her huge eyes awash. And then, into the thickening tension, the still silence, the library clock struck the half-hour and Seth groaned.

She felt the sudden shudder that racked his lean body and then his head came down, his mouth taking hers, his hunger savage, palpable, forcing an answering need from her as she instinctively wound her arms around his neck, feeling her aching breasts crushed against his chest as she opened her mouth to him, a wild moan of wanting clogging her throat as his tongue plundered the sweetness of her mouth.

And all was fire and need and passion, his hands moulding the contours of her body with heady urgency and she whimpered with mindless pleasure, her fingers finding the bone-hardness of his skull beneath the thick soft warmth of his hair. And there was one thought in her head, one beautiful precious thought: He loves me! Seth loves me! He couldn't kiss me like this if he didn't. And that thought was so large, so overwhelming, that it filled every space in her mind, blocking out everything else until a harsh expletive, exploding somewhere outside their beautiful private world, brought Seth's head up, his face a grim mask as Ralph said from the open french windows, 'You said you wanted to see me, Seth. I can just imagine why!'

So could Kate. It took a few moments before she caught on and then everything was horribly clear. Seth wouldn't have been completely sure that she would obey his command never to set foot on Montstowell land again. And so he had set this up. Planned, coldly and cruelly, to discredit her in Ralph's eyes forever.

As the clock had struck he had started to kiss her and, as he had known he would, Ralph had appeared. 'You wanted to see me,' said it all. Seth hadn't kissed her that way because he loved her but because he had commanded his younger brother to report to the library at half-past ten!

Her legs were shaking, her stomach heaving with the destructive amalgam of humiliation and betrayal, but she forced herself to walk to the open windows, brushing past Ralph, not even seeing him.

She wasn't going to cry, not ever again, and she wasn't going to run. Such reactions were for children. And she wasn't a child any more. She had grown up, completely and painfully, during the last few minutes and she would never run from anything again. And she no longer loved Seth Presteigne. She hated him for the devious, cruel monster he was!

CHAPTER FOUR

KATE was perfectly composed as she followed Seth up to the attics after lunch. Naked light bulbs beneath the great roof timbers revealed ranks of shrouded, looming shapes, tempting now because she knew what they were.

She had only been in the Montstowell attics once before and then the bulky shapes had seemed sinister. She and Ralph would have been about twelve at the time, and she'd followed him up here, clinging on to the back of his jumper because the dimly lit, twisting stairs had made her feel uneasy—probably because they'd spent the dark winter afternoon sitting in front of the book-room fire telling each other ghost stories.

And because this morning's regression had had a cathartic effect she was able to ask, 'Where does Ralph hang out these days? What's he doing?'

'He's doing his own thing, as usual,' Seth answered brusquely, obviously unwilling to pursue the subject. Kate shrugged. It was no concern of hers, of course, but it would appear that Ralph hadn't knuckled down and taken that course in estate management.

'I'd like to see him again,' she added sweetly, not really meaning it because she'd put her childhood memories of her past out of her mind a long time ago. Seth had spoiled them for her and spoiled memories weren't pleasant to live with. But she wanted to needle Seth. Ever since he had manipulated her return he'd been so darned *nice*. Too darned nice. She wanted, perversely, to prick him into revealing the darker side of his character.

But apart from a fleeting grimness in his eyes, in the tight slashing of his mouth, he wasn't revealing anything. He said smoothly, 'Do you feel up to investigating this lot? It hasn't been touched since Father had it all unpacked and treated against woodworm; there was even talk of selling it, but it never came to anything. What my father had, he liked to hold on to.' He took a penknife from the pocket of his jeans and began to cut cords and Kate watched him, grey eyes narrowed as she desperately fought against the quickening of her senses.

He had always had this effect on her: the ability to make her pulses race. Understandable when she'd been young and gullible and had imagined herself in love with him. But why now? Why, when she disliked and distrusted him—with very good reason?

He continued working, apparently unaware of the undercurrents that were making her so uneasy, telling her, 'Then after Father died Mother wanted to auction the whole lot off. Cash was short in those days. But I preferred to make new money rather than rely on old. Like my father, I suppose, I hold on to what I value.'

He straightened up, the shroud-like ticking falling away beneath his hands. But Kate didn't see the severely beautiful lines of the long, low Tudor sideboard—she was transfixed by the compelling intensity of his eyes, unable to look away, her breath suddenly difficult to find.

He was an intense and complicated creature and she didn't need him to tell her of his single-mindedness, the sheer drive that had enabled him to make a fortune from the family's once ailing business ventures. She knew him well enough to know that he didn't believe that life owed him anything—if there was trouble he simply went out and bested it. Neither did she need reminding of the dark arrogance that had made him unable to accept that a Presteigne should forget his standing enough to make him want to marry the daughter of a humble employee! There had been no room in that exalted family tree for the gardener's daughter.

He moved on, lifting a couple of full tea chests from the top of what appeared to be—from the shape of the protective wrapping—a large refectory table and, unable to stop the excitement that was at last beginning to unfurl inside her, Kate ran her hands over the sideboard with sensuous pleasure, admiring the craftsmanship of the long-gone carpenter whose work it was.

They worked through the long afternoon and in the excitement of discovery Kate forgot who he was, what he was. His enthusiasm for the pieces they were unveiling matched her own; he became simply a partner in the adventure of exploring a long-hidden treasure house. It was Seth who called a halt.

'Seen enough?'

They had barely uncovered half the contents of

the dim and dusty attics and as disappointment dragged the corners of her mouth down his amused glance followed the direction of her eyes and he grinned. 'I know. It seems a crime to leave without unpacking the lot. But it would take a good four hours more, and it's getting late.'

Kate's lips quirked wryly. She was acting like a child who was having to be dragged away from a toy shop, and she admitted, 'You're right, of course. It's been here for well over a hundred years—it won't go away overnight.' She turned to him, relaxed and smiling because she had forgotten to hate him, to be wary. And found he was close, much too close, and met his eyes, met his lingering enigmatic look. And suddenly she was painfully aware of him as a man, stingingly conscious of that graceful, lean body clothed in narrow black demins, his white lawn shirt smeared with dust, open at the neck to reveal the strong line of his throat, the dusting of body hair crisp and dark against the olive-toned skin of his chest.

Her breath caught in her throat and heated blood began to race through her veins as her heart picked up speed. This was the man she had once loved with all the hedonistic passion of youth. And suddenly it was as if time had run backwards and she was young again, too much in love, too adoring. And something must have shown in her eyes because he reached out a hand, gently, so gently, touching her hectic cheeks. 'You've gathered some dust.'

The gesture took her back to her teens. It was so

natural, so easily intimate, and it froze her, sexual
tension making her face turn white.

'Kate. . .' His voice was husky, velvet soft, dark
with nameless drifts of passion, and her lips parted,
her blood thundering, and, trembling, she looked up
at him, gazing into the smoky blue eyes and then,
without quite knowing how it had happened, she
was in his arms, pressed close to him, and she knew
that the past still lived in her, that he only had to
touch her to set every cell in her body aflame.

He was alarming, his sexuality too potent for her
to fight, no matter how hard she tried. And she
wanted him now as she had wanted him then.

Shame forced a whimper through her lips but not
even shame was enough to give her the strength of
mind to pull away, not yet. Her head thrown back,
she clung to him as his lips moved, feather-light,
across her cheekbones down to the lobe of her ear,
sucking softly there until she felt faint with the
ecstasy of what he was doing to her, and when his
head descended, his mouth tasting the arching length
of her exposed throat, she was engulfed in a sheet-
fire sensation that took her breath away, turned her
mind to mush, her capitulation compounded when
he made her aware of the extent of his arousal as he
pulled her hips into the hard male arch of his pelvis.

'Kate. . .' Again her name was torn from him, the
harsh thread of triumph contained there sounding
alarm bells in her fuddled mind as he told her
huskily, 'I've always known how it could be for us.'

'Always known'? Since when? Since he'd staged
that cruel scene in the library, having told Ralph

precisely when to present himself. It had been a diabolical ploy to make Ralph see her as a tramp. Anyone's.

'No!' She found the strength to twist away from him, her eyes enormous in her paper-white face. He had betrayed her once; he wouldn't get the chance again.

But his hands trapped her wrists and his blue eyes were grim as he taunted, 'Why not? Don't tell me you weren't enjoying it. It's only the second time I've held you as a man holds a woman, but on each occasion your response has been little short of cataclysmic.'

'Swine!' She jerked her hands free, her eyes blazing. Did he think she needed reminding about the way she'd abandoned herself in his arms six years ago, offering herself, her heart, body and soul, little realising she'd walked into a trap?

'OK.' He held his hands up in a cruel parody of surrender and his eyes were mocking, very hard, his mouth touched with cynicism. 'Let it ride, for now. But I can recognise when a woman's sexually aroused.'

And Kate thought, I bet you can! And wondered if he could remember how many women he'd seduced to the point of capitulation and beyond. But she wasn't going to add to that forgotten number. No way! And she faced him, her pale features rigid with the effort of appearing cool and unflustered.

The truth was, he was beginning to frighten her, the strength of his personality was too much for her to cope with, and the attics were suddenly claustrophobic, the dim shadows in the far corners menacing, the man himself more menacing still.

Her nostrils pinched, she made to side-step him, to walk out of here, but he moved, only minimally, his big body effortlessly blocking her path.

'I'm sorry.' The obvious apology in his voice produced a puzzled frown between Kate's fine dark brows. Seth Presteigne apologising? It was totally out of character. He did as he pleased, this one. Always had done, expecially when it came to members of her own sex. 'I shouldn't have rushed things. It wasn't my intention.' His mouth compressed, as if suppressing something, words he deemed best left unsaid, and, with her standing so close to him, the roiling sensation deep inside her intensified, making her suck in her breath. And he said, 'We need to talk, you and I,' and took her hand, leading her down the twisting stairs. 'I'll make dinner. We'll have the whole evening to ourselves.'

That wasn't the way she wanted it at all. There was a sensuous half-smile on his mouth and he sounded very confident, very assured. Kate shuddered. There was warmth in his voice, too, and caring, and he sounded like the man she had imagined herself in love with all those years ago. The thought of an evening spent with him, in this mood, quite frankly terrified her. The effortless urbanity of his charm allied to that potent sexiness, bound with a mood of sweet reasonableness, made him lethal.

Fleeing to the fragile sanctuary of her own room on the pretext of cleaning herself up, Kate sagged back against the door she had deliberately locked behind her and waited until the dizzying sensations of panic began to subside.

Knowing Seth, she shouldn't be surprised by what had happened. If the progression of women she had witnessed herself before he'd thrown her off Montstowell land, the stories in the Press, were to have any meaning then Seth Presteigne had to have a woman in his life, no matter how fleeting and meaningless the relationship might be.

He had been far too nice to her and that, not to mention the occasional openly sexual looks she'd surprised, should have warned her that it would be only a matter of time before he made a pass. Droit de seigneur, and all that! He wouldn't be averse to a short relationship, a closet one, of course.

No, it was herself she couldn't understand. She knew exactly what a devious bastard he was, so why had she responded when he'd taken her in his arms and kissed her senseless? Why had she—if only briefly—allowed herself to be swept away in a tide of unstoppable emotion when he'd rained kisses over her face, her throat, right down to the open V of her tailored shirt?

Without conscious thought, she lifted her hand to her neckline, the tips of her fingers touching the heated skin between the edges of the crisp fabric, touching where he had touched, where his lips had travelled over the delicate upper curves of her breasts.

Then, her face flaming as she realised what she was doing, she pushed herself away from the support of the door and marched to the comfortless bathroom. The excuse that she needed to freshen up was perfectly valid. Apart from experiencing a dangerously unwary pleasure in his company as they'd uncovered exactly the type of furniture she had always wanted to see in this house, and collecting a few heady kisses, she had picked up her fair share of dust and grime.

Still thoroughly disgusted with herself, she stripped and clambered into the huge chipped bath, sinking gratefully beneath the hot water that alternatively roared or hiccupped from the tap. The fact that Seth was the only man she had ever responded to physically was no excuse at all for her lack of self-discipline.

She had been too determined to get the most out of her years at college to indulge in the casual affairs her peers had seemed to regard as part of their education, and, later, setting up her own business, she had been too busy to have time for men, to accept more than the occasional date. And even then she had discovered that a one-to-one relationship with a man left her cold, unable to respond. She had invariably called a halt before the intimacy had progressed beyond the first kiss. She simply hadn't been interested.

In her youth she had idolised Seth, believed him—even though he had seemed so unobtainable—to be her perfect mate. No other man, ever, had had the power to interest her, but all that earlier love for Seth had done was to produce an uncharacteristic bitterness. She had turned from fire to ice as completely as only an Arien could.

Rob was her only man friend, she reflected wryly as she turned off the taps and began to soap herself, the only man she felt comfortable with. And that was probably because he had a very low sex drive, and saw her simply as a partner and friend.

It was her misfortune that the only man to set her alight was a Machiavellian monster!

She couldn't stay. She should never have taken the job. She would have to find some excuse to leave before her conflicting emotions pulled her apart.

'Thank you.' She accepted the glass of very dry sherry he gave her, an aloof little smile the only expression she allowed to cross the carefully schooled frigidity of her neat features.

The clever little black dress had been brought into play again, this time the severity lightened by a Victorian pinchbeck choker and as she walked towards the fire she felt the soft crêpe move sensuously against her breast and thighs, making her more aware of her body than she had ever been before.

And, as if her body's unwanted sexuality was potent enough to transmit itself to him, she saw his veiled eyes drift downwards, the look an open caress as it rested devouringly on her small round breasts, the feminine flare of her hips, the slight enticing swell of her abdomen.

The moment she had stepped inside this room she had known that to stay on here, as he had stipulated, would be to test her control to the limit. Already she wanted to slap him, to rail at him for his disgusting treatment of her in the past. She either had to go, or give in and follow where the intimacy in his eyes told her he would lead. Forget the past, remember only that he was the only man she had ever wanted. And that she would never do.

He had chosen the book-room for what her intuition warned her would be the seduction scene. The main light doused, the soft glow from the fire, from a strategically placed standard lamp and the candles on the gate-legged table he had spread with ochre linen, embellished with silver flatware, crystal and a single long-stemmed rose, made a definite statement of intent, of intimacy. An intimacy that was already making her hackles rise in self-defence.

She ached to be able to lie to herself, to deny her chaotic feelings, but since she couldn't she said briskly, 'There's no earthly reason why I should stay on here. I've already contacted the people who will be responsible for the interior structural alterations. I've used them before and they're good—otherwise I wouldn't be using them again. I can't do anything until they are out of the way and I do have a business to run.'

A look of impatience darkened his eyes. But it was quickly smothered, replaced by the familiar teasing smile as he took both their glasses for a refill and told her, 'I shall be paying you handsomely for your time. Kate-Mallin won't lose out. I want you here.'

She stared mutinously at his broad back. Dressed in body-sculpting black trousers and a soft silk shirt that must have cost a fortune, he presented an altogether too attractive appearance, his male sexuality posing an almost insoluble problem. One look from those clear blue eyes, one smile, the slightest touch would be enough to sweep her back in time, to have her hungering for him all over again.

But she wasn't going to let that happen.

'And if I refuse to stay?' she asked, tight-lipped, looking into the heart of the fire as he walked back towards her, a glass in either hand. He had always moved beautifully, possessing an unconscious masculine grace that had moved her deeply. She couldn't bear to look at him; it made her heart ache. And she couldn't think why he wanted her here, unless it was some perverse and Byronic need for gratification.

He hadn't answered her question so she added snappishly, 'I can draw up designs for Montstowell just as well back at the studio. It would be more convenient, in fact.'

From the corner of her eye she saw him deposit the glasses on the mantelshelf, the pale liquid catching fiery lights from the gently flaming logs. And she heard the slow, infuriating sound of his laughter, heard him say, 'Your mouth looks frozen when you take it into your beautiful head to be prim. It makes me ache to kiss it back to life.' A finger tracked the perfect leaf shape of her mouth and for one shocking moment Kate fought the impulse to open her lips, take that erotically moving finger between her teeth and nip it, lap it with her tongue. Fought the impulse and won, jerking her head aside, and his eyes were as hard and blue as splintered sapphires as he told her quite calmly, yet brooking no argument whatsoever, 'Leave before the job's finished and I withdraw the commission. It's as simple as that.'

Simple and devastating. Walk away and she'd lose the studio a plum of a job, lose the respect of her colleagues. A move very typical of a Scorpio. The sting in the tail!

Her impulse was to tell him to go to hell, to give her fiery temper its head. But she had her colleagues to think of. Back in London, Rob and the girls could manage adequately and while she was waiting for the team of craftsmen to finish she could work on other jobs here. She almost groaned but stiffened her shoulders instead.

'I see.'

'I'm sure you do.'

Was it a trick of the light, or was that an unholy gleam she glimpsed deep in his eyes? Whatever, she was thoroughly unnerved, almost ready to grasp at his suggestion. 'Why don't we forget about the job, just for this evening?' He placed himself directly in front of her, making her feel smothered, drowning, out of her depth. 'Tomorrow you can go back to being the ultra-efficient, tacks-in-the-mouth interior designer, if you must. But in the meantime perhaps you'd like to explain where the Kate I knew and loved disappeared to.'

He was devilish! By a few well-chosen words, delivered in that rough silk sexy voice, he could imply so many things. And all of them wrong, she reminded herself as she turned away from him and perched primly on the edge of a rigid-backed chair as far away as she could get without looking utterly ridiculous.

'Knew and loved'—ye gods! For a time, when she had been a mere child, he had seemed to care about her welfare, she had to give the devil his due. But he'd never loved her. Never. Never remotely approached it. She doubted if he knew how to love.

He had used her obvious infatuation for him to bring his brother to his senses. And maybe, just maybe, her innocent yet wanton response had appealed to his jaded palate. And maybe, on seeing her again, he had remembered that and because, perhaps, the lovely Lucy was out of circulation or withholding the fun, holding out for marriage, Seth had decided to amuse himself with her.

She just didn't know what his motives were and decided to treat his remark with the contempt it deserved, to ignore the assuredly manufactured bleak query in his remarkable eyes. And since, apparently, the subject of work was taboo, she asked lightly, 'What are we eating, and when?' letting him know that banalities were all he had a right to expect from her. And before he could answer—if he had been willing to descend to such trivialities—the door was flung open and Ralph stood there, dishevelled, looking bone-weary and more than a little out of his depth as his glance fell on Kate and held.

'Good God! You've come back. I never thought I'd live to see the day.' And then, still holding her with eyes that were a washed-out version of his brother's, he said to Seth, 'I'm sorry if I've walked in at a wrong moment, yet again. But is there anything to eat, brother? I'm bloody well starving.'

CHAPTER FIVE

THE cottage was exactly as Kate remembered it. Despite the lump in her throat, she was happy that nothing had changed. And then, as if on cue, a girl of about ten years old appeared from the side-door, bouncing a ball along the uneven brick path. She looked very carefree, as happy as every child had a right to be.

When I was your age I was like you, Kate told the child in her head. My mother was still alive—she spent a lot of time in the kitchen baking, as yours probably does. I was loved and happy and I didn't know a thing about cruelty because that came much later.

Outwardly she smiled at the little girl then turned and walked quickly away, lost in memories until a hand on her shoulder, Ralph's pleasant voice, stopped her in her tracks.

'Taking a walk down memory lane?'

Kate just smiled as he fell in step beside her, not willing to admit to anyone how affected she was by the sight of the cottage she'd grown up in.

'I didn't think you'd ever come back,' Ralph went on broodingly. 'Not after what happened. My mother behaved like a bitch.'

Not to mention your brother! Kate thought sourly before putting the past behind her where it belonged. She smiled up at him; he had developed into a very good-looking man but he didn't have the sheer presence, the wicked charisma of Seth. He never had. But physical attractiveness meant nothing if the soul of the man was rotten, and, underneath, Ralph was a far nicer guy than his brother.

They had skirted the walled kitchen garden and as they walked beneath the arch in the clipped yew hedge that led to the rose garden she slipped her arm through his, feeling almost comfortable for the first time since returning.

'Have you forgiven me?' The scent of the narcissi, planted beneath the twiggy rose bushes which were just coming into leaf, was heady, the sun, warm for early April, warming her through the light wool shirt she had teamed with a neat grey twill skirt.

'For preferring Seth? Yes,' he answered shortly, tacking on, 'Though I'd rather the revelation had come in a less brutal form. But no hard feelings, that's for sure. We were both too young to even think of settling down.'

'We both had a lot of growing up to do,' she agreed, thankful that Ralph could see it now. She wasn't going to rake over the murky past because, for Ralph's sake, she didn't want to highlight Seth's cruel mishandling of the affair. To tell him the truth would be to open old wounds.

'Do you visit often?' Ralph asked, a wry smile indenting his mouth. 'Has that notorious brother of mine decided to stop playing the field at last? I always knew he fancied you, which was probably partly responsible for the way I insisted on making that damn fool engagement announcement. Just for once I wanted to beat him to the post,' he admitted drily, then asked, 'Has he popped the question?'

'Good lord, no!' Kate's feet were rooted to the ground with shock. Ralph had to know, better than anyone, that the lordly Seth wouldn't set his sights so low! And as for fancying her, for anything other than a fleeting affair, well, Ralph had got it all wrong. So wrong!

The formal garden faced the side of the house, the terraces, outside the library. A shiver ran through her as she noticed the open french windows. They had been open on that warm spring day six years ago.

And then a movement caught her eye. It could only be Seth watching them from the library. Watching them. . .

She knew exactly what she was going to do.

Forcing a light laugh, she said, 'What a fool you are! I'm down here to do a job, that's all. Seth has decided to have the interior of the house redone.' Then, taking his hand, she led him to a stone seat which was in full view of the library windows, very carefully not looking that way. 'Tell me what you've been doing these last six years.'

They hadn't had the opportunity to talk before. His arrival last night, so unexpectedly, had rendered the intimate meal Seth had planned more of a farce than anything else. Seth had been obviously annoyed and Ralph hadn't had much to say, explaining that he was exhausted, going to bed as soon as he'd eaten his share of the meal, his exit one Kate had promptly copied.

Seth had broken them up six years ago, in the cruellest possible way, and she knew he was watching them now and if she could make him believe that they were taking up where they had left off then that would give her immense satisfaction! Because Ralph had got something half right. Seth hadn't 'fancied' her six years ago, but he did now. She was mature enough to recognise male lust when she saw it! The prospect of deflating his overblown male ego made excitement course wickedly through her veins.

'Doing my own thing,' Ralph answered her earlier question, leaning forward, smiling at her beneath the dark, overlong fringe of hair that fell across his forehead. 'Mind you, Seth did help. When he realised I was determined to paint he overruled Mother and insisted I went to art college for a good basic training.'

He did? It seemed quite out of character. For as long as she could remember Ralph's future had been seen in managing the estate. Maybe Seth had at last given in because he had wanted the rebellious teenager out of his hair. She couldn't ascribe his motives to anything else. She was, she admitted, programmed to thinking the worst of him.

'And now?' she prompted, producing a wide encouraging smile for the watcher's benefit. Not that she wasn't truly interested, of course; she was. In her childhood Ralph had been the best friend she'd had.

'I've just finished working on the canvasses for my

first West End exhibition.' He shot her a look that held pride and excitement at the same time.

Kate said, 'Great! Let me know the dates and I'll go and make sure everyone hears me rhapsodising over every picture!'

'And getting married,' Ralph put in quietly, grinning when Kate's mouth dropped open.

She lost the slight restraint that had been between them as she told him, 'But that's marvellous! Where is she? Why didn't you bring her with you?'

'Because she's probably still somewhere over the Atlantic right now—she's a flight attendant with British Airways, and, in any case, she and I don't visit. I only came down here last night because I was bushed and didn't fancy catering for myself in a lonely flat. The last time I was down here was just before the wedding. Seth and I had a row—he didn't approve of my marrying Sonia.'

He leant against the back of the seat, his arms crossed behind his head, his eyes closed. The revealing light of the sun highlighted the lines of strain around his eyes, the shadows.

Had working for the exhibition put those marks of stress on his face? Or was it more than that? His attitude on arrival last night had been one of defiance, almost as if he had expected Seth to throw him out. On his own admission, he and his wife didn't come here, was it because Seth had warned him to stay away if he went ahead and married without his approval?

And no prizes for guessing why Seth didn't

approve. No humble working girl would be considered good enough for a Presteigne of Montstowell! Sonia would have had to have a title, or a large fortune at the very least, before she could earn that monster's approval! The man's attitudes were archaic, his arrogance and pride out of all proportion. . .

She broke off her silent castigations, furious with herself for allowing Seth to upset her. He simply wasn't worth it. But somehow, though, her defence mechanism for distancing herself from any kind of emotional reaction to Seth seemed to have gone on the blink.

'Don't let it get to you,' she advised softly, putting her hand over his as it lay on his knee. 'Seth is an unmitigated snob——'

'Snob?' Ralph opened one eye and then the other, his mouth curling tiredly. 'I think we've got a few wires crossed here—Seth is the last——'

'Kate!' The hard voice bit through the lazy air, effectively silencing Ralph, and she froze, a shudder of reaction running through her, raising goosebumps on her arms. But she managed to turn to face Seth, her carefully schooled expression one of supreme indifference. She hadn't heard him approach and her original intention to annoy him by spending time with Ralph seemed to have been misguided. Instead of enjoying his obvious fury she felt miserable because the gentle and sometimes tantalising companion he had set out to be since the beginning of her enforced stay here had disappeared. She didn't understand herself.

'I'd like a word. Several, in fact.' The lines of his face were grim, the anger in his eyes unmistakable, but beneath that, on a different level, she saw something that, had she not known better, she would have described as pain.

'Go ahead,' she invited coolly, sitting more squarely on the stone seat, her feet primly together.

He bit out, 'In the library. Now!' He ripped round on his heels, his long-legged stride carrying him over the smoothly cut grass and Kate stared after him, her face scarlet with the ferocity of her mutinous thoughts, every last ounce of her pride instructing her to ignore the brute.

'You've got him fit to bust a blood vessel,' Ralph said, tipping her a sly smile. 'And no prizes for guessing why! You'd better run along before he marches back and drags you in by your hair!'

'You've got something there,' she admitted crossly and hoisted herself to her feet. The tenor of his anger had been very personal and in his present mood he was capable of humiliating her utterly.

Angry colour was still staining her face when she eventually confronted him in the library, and she snapped resentfully, 'Do you have to bark orders at me *quite* so objectionably?' planting her hands on her hips, her small breasts heaving, pushing against the fine wool of her shirt.

'You're here to work,' he grated, the dark skin of his face pulled taut against the bones, showing the harsh austerity of his features to full and rather devastating effect. 'Not to while the time away in flirtations with old boyfriends.'

So her strategy had worked, but with more effect than she had foreseen. She had meant to prick his male ego a little and had succeeded in taking the lid off a volcano! But, she told herself staunchly, she could handle it.

'I've already explained that there's nothing useful I can do here until the structural alterations are out of the way,' she pointed out tartly. 'So if you've finished throwing your weight around I'll continue renewing my old and valued friendship with Ralph.'

'The hell you will!' His eyes were hard and brilliant, his body very tense. 'You come swanning down here, acid-tongued and Look-How-Smart-I-Am, treating me as if I were something contagious! Who the hell do you think you are, woman? I'm paying you to do a job, dammit!' He thumped the desk and she managed, just, not to flinch.

She had never seen him this angry before and it did something to her, made the adrenalin flow, and she pointed out, spitting pins, 'I didn't come "swanning down here", as you so tritely put it! I came because you specifically asked me to.'

She was holding on to her control, but only just. Any second now she could be matching his towering rage, howling out the residual pain of what he'd done to her all those years ago. She didn't want to give him the satisfaction of knowing she'd remembered, of letting him guess how hurt she'd been.

'So I did,' he conceded. He was tight-lipped but quieter now, the ebb of hot rage leaving him cold-faced, his eyes chilling. 'I had hoped. . .' But whatever he had meant to say was left unsaid. It was as if, Kate thought, a censor in his mind had cut in, stilling his tongue.

Saying nothing, Seth went to lean against the desk, half sitting, his long denim-clad legs stretched out in front of him, his brooding eyes never leaving her face.

'Well?' he asked at last, his tone icy. 'What's it to be? You either stay or you give up the commission.'

Crunch time, Kate thought as she listened to the silence, annoyed by the fact that her heart was beginning a drum beat thunk under the probing intensity of his eyes.

While the commission would represent a healthy profit, plus a bonus in the form of the lustre of prestige, the studio could survive the loss. At the moment they were climbing high; they didn't actually *need* the Montstowell job. She could walk out of here, right now. It was a perfectly viable option and she wondered why, given the circumstances, she was hesitating.

Walking away, right out of his life, shouldn't pose any problem. But, strangely, it did. And her thoughts fluttered this way and that until the word 'compromise' presented itself and she seized on it gratefully, honesty compelling her to admit that the gratitude stemmed from the fact that—stupid though it was—she wanted to keep her options open.

A week or two away from Seth would give her the time and distance she needed to decide whether she was capable of working here, staying here with him, and still keep her immunity to his deadly brand of attraction.

'If I'm staying,' she began in a voice that shamed her by its huskiness, 'I shall need more clothes. I only brought enough with me to last for a couple of days.' She caught her breath as the probing glint of his narrowed gaze intensified, then dredged up a tone of sweet reasonableness and ploughed on, 'If I drive back now I can stay at my flat overnight, pack a suitcase and look in at the studio tomorrow.'

Mentally crossing her fingers, she vowed that 'overnight' could easily stretch to a couple of weeks. If nothing needing her urgent attention turned up at the studio she could invent something. And she could take a trip to Leeds and visit her sponsors. IT were one of the most innovative producers in the country, specialising in natural fibres and the custom-dyeing of their own weaves. It she decided to handle the Montstowell job, accept Seth's conditions, then she would be using IT fabrics throughout, so he could hardly object to the trip.

Relief at having worked herself out of the corner Seth had backed her into stopped her questioning her use of delaying tactics when common sense firmly suggested that, for her peace of mind, she would be better off turning the job down flat.

'Two days,' he said quietly, levering himself away from the desk, walking very slowly towards her. Like a predator about to strike, Kate decided, her breath coming unevenly, her skin hot. It took all her guts and determination to lift her chin and meet his gaze, eye to steely eye, and he repeated, his voice thick with soft dark menace, 'Two days. A minute longer and I fetch you back.'

Her eyes went very wide. He wanted her here and it had nothing to do with the job. Nothing at all. And as if he knew that at last she understood he nodded, dipping his head just once, very briefly, and his intent—now tacitly acknowledged—was a seemingly unbreakable bond between them.

But bonds could be broken, couldn't they? Kate licked her lips nervously then wished she hadn't because his eyes fastened on her mouth and a pulse began beating strongly at the base of his throat.

'Why?' she questioned thickly, her mind screaming, Why me? Why pick on me when for as long as I've known him he's only had to look at a woman to have her falling at his feet?

He replied tightly, 'I want you here. Isn't that enough?'

'Quite frankly, no.' Even though she felt emotionally mangled she was still fighting, her small chin lifted at a determined angle.

He shot her a narrowed look and told her with a coolness that took her breath away, 'Then I'll spell it out. I want you here. I want you in every way there is. And believe me, Kate, I'm going to have you.'

She believed him. The sudden flare of burning intensity in his eyes told her he was deadly serious. She had suspected him of wanting a brief affair— something light and frothy, easily forgotten. But she knew now that it was more than that. And whatever it was, it was dark and deadly. Nothing frothy at all about the complete subjugation she intuitively knew he would demand, his need to master and enthrall. . .

And all at once she felt the past brush by her shoulder, much too close. Nothing had changed, except superficially. When it came down to basics nothing had changed at all. She was still as vulnerable to him as she'd ever been and she knew now why no other man had held her interest for more than a moment.

She still wanted Seth. She still loved him.

Loved him? Oh, surely not! Kate shuddered with the sudden racking violence of her emotions and, his gaze on her pale beautiful features, Seth stepped forward, his eyes black with desire.

'Kate. . .' His arms were around her, pulling her close, and the contact ignited a fire inside her, devouring her in its hungry flames, and he was kissing her quivering eyelids, something in the sheer emotional urgency in the way his lips moved consumingly over her skin awakening a pagan need in her that overthrew all control, laid seige to all her principles—every last one.

'We're tearing each other to shreds,' he groaned against the corner of her instinctively parted lips. 'It wasn't meant to be that way. . .'

Blindly, an incoherent sob tearing at her throat, she sought his lips, gasping as he plundered the inner moistness she offered with drugging intensity, his knowing hands shaping her fevered body with wickedly inescapable expertise. And then, as if her blood caught fire from his, her hands were mimicking his, exploring his body, suddenly—she didn't know or care how—they were beneath his shirt, moving against his heated skin, and she felt him tremble then shuddered wildly herself as his shaking hands impatiently unbuttoned her blouse, dealt with the front fastening of her bra.

And then they were flesh to quivering flesh and he had gone very still, the heat of desire burning along his austerely carved cheekbones as he looked down at her breasts, milky white, swelling with wholly feminine invitation against the darker, hair-roughened masculinity of his chest.

'Shall I show you how it could be for us?' he questioned thickly, a muscle pulsing in his throat as he bent his head to take first one and then the other flushed and swollen nipple in his mouth, sucking with such pagan hunger that she thought she might die of the ecstasy he was giving her.

Now, at last, they had gone full circle; the past and the present were indivisible. That thought impinged with a clarity that chilled her, penetrating her fevered brain, bringing the coldness of reason to oust the sweet wild chaos.

She had travelled this road before. Six years ago, in this very room, he had made her a wanton in his arms. He had used her then as he was using her now. For different reasons, but using her just the same. He would satisfy his lust—for lust was all it could be for him—then calmly walk away, back to the suitable Lucy Mortiboys, or someone of her ilk.

He would not put her through such pain and

humiliation again. He would not tame and subdue her to such an extent!

A sudden flame of fiery inner rage burned through her and, forgetting caution, options, she charged straight in, her eyes blazing as she struggled with her clothing.

'Keep your damned commission. I don't need it, and I won't pay your price!' She slammed out of the door without a backward glance.

CHAPTER SIX

'RELAX!' Kate commanded softly, smiling at Ralph across the restaurant table. 'I can't think why you dragged me away from the exhibition. Lots of people were making very flattering comments,' she stated, her eyes teasing.

'Nerves.' Ralph accepted the menu a waiter handed him. 'Every time someone commented on one of my paintings I felt as if I were on trial!'

Kate shook her neat dark head slowly, her expression wry. She never suffered from uncertainty in anything she did and couldn't understand the failing in others.

'Anyway,' Ralph went on, 'let's talk of something else. Tell me, have you really chucked the Montstowell commission? Seth was furious—and that's putting it mildly! Sure you won't change your mind?'

Something clouded Kate's clear grey eyes, but only for a moment. She shook her head decisively. Once a decision had been made she never changed her mind.

During her impulsive departure from Montstowell two days ago she had practically bumped into Ralph on the stairs and he'd raised his eyebrows when he'd seen her mutinously set features, the overnight bag in her hand.

'Going somehwere?'

'Getting the hell out of here!' she'd exploded, her cheeks burning as she reluctantly recalled how near Seth's devilishly dark magic had come to enthralling her once again. And Ralph had called softly, his amused eyes following her rapid progress down the stairs, 'You're not to renege on your promise to attend the launch night party for my exhibition in two days' time. What's your number?'

Rashly, still flouncing, she had tossed the numbers over her shoulder, not really caring if he contacted her or not because there wasn't enough room left in her mind to think of anything except Seth and how hateful he was.

But all that was over now, forgotten, she assured herself staunchly. There'd been a few sticky moments when she'd told her colleagues that the Montstowell project had been ditched, but it had been nothing she hadn't been able to handle.

Her discovery that she still loved Seth had frankly appalled her, but she could handle that, too. She knew she could. All she had to do was push it firmly out of her mind and get on with the ever-exciting challenge of building up the studio. As far as she was concerned, the sky was the limit.

In any case, she wasn't going to think about it now. She was in one of London's smartest restaurants, wearing one of her favourite dresses—a sleek and sophisticated cocktail dress in a rich dark green heavy silk—sitting opposite an undeniably attractive, talented young artist, one who would undoubtedly be lionised in the very near future. . .

She sipped her aperitif appreciatively, determined to enjoy the evening, but Ralph queried softly, 'Why did you walk out on Seth? I'd have thought a project like that would have been right up your street. Of the two of us, you always thought more of the place than I did—you and Seth both.'

Kate didn't want to talk about it and her voice was tight as she told him, 'Put it down to a clash of personalities,' and then she recalled Seth's disgusting intention to blackmail her, through the studio, to make her his closet lover, his desire to possess her—secretly and furtively—while the suitable Lucy wasn't looking, and added explosively, 'He's such a damned snob!' then clamped her mouth shut as the waiter placed her order of melon cocktail in front of her.

'I don't know how you come up with such quaint ideas.' Ralph quirked his mouth humorously as he spread rich duck pâté on hot toast. 'He's got to be about the least snobbish person I know.'

Kate almost choked on a mouthful of the cool, delicious melon. Normally direct to the point of bluntness, she couldn't tell him how Seth had manipulated them six years ago, how he had ordered her to keep away from his brother, away from Montstowell, because she hadn't been *suitable*. So she made a mental grab for the evidence Ralph himself had provided, challenging, 'He was against your marriage to Sonia!'

'True. But not for snobbish reasons, and not in principle,' Ralph told her levelly. 'He merely decided that, in his opinion, the marriage wouldn't stand a chance while I was still struggling for recognition and Sonia's job took her away so often. He offered to find her a job in one of his London-based companies, and to loan us the money to buy a place of our own.'

He looked across at Kate, his eyes dancing. 'Sonia refused both offers, point-blank. She's almost as independent as you! We would make it our own way, she said, and if we had to live in a dreary basement flat—which we do—because we couldn't afford anything better on her sole earnings, then we would, just until my paintings began to sell. In short, thanks but no, thanks. And Seth, who likes to manipulate people if he thinks it's for their own good—or his!—didn't think much of her attitude! Hence the unholy row. And if you still think his motives are always snobbish, then how do you explain why he insisted on paying for his gardener's daughter to go to college?'

'What?' Kate's mouth dropped open as her starter was whisked away, her first course of grilled sole put in front of her. 'What the hell are you talking about?'

'His eighteenth birthday gift to you—that sum of money to be doled out at regular intervals to bolster your grant. Don't tell me you've forgotten,' he grinned. 'Ungrateful wretch!'

Kate stared at the food on her plate and then at the wine in her glass. She wasn't seeing anything, but her quick mind was racing.

At her party, all those years ago, Seth had told her to ask her father about his gift to her. She hadn't, of course she hadn't. She'd been too traumatised by Ralph's announcement to think about any such thing and later she'd been too hurt and angry, too intent on getting right away to care or remember what Seth had said about his gift.

After her father's death—coming so soon after she had started college—she had been surprised at the size of his legacy. She hadn't been able to understand how her father had managed to save so much out of his earnings. But the money, hoarded frugally, had enabled her to start up in business on her own in a small way.

How could Seth have been so generous to the girl he had accused of leading his younger, gullible brother astray? Had her initial impression been wrong?

He had thrown her out, forbidden her the estate, there was no doubt about that. And, at the time, she had believed he hadn't cared a rap what became of her.

But he had cared. Even after he had as good as accused her of leading Ralph on until he became besotted enough to propose marriage, he had allowed her father to bank the money for her education.

'Talk of the devil!'

Kate looked up and saw Ralph's attractive features wreathed in a smile of genuine pleasure as he stood up, and as she turned to look in the direction he faced her heart lurched and sank down into the toes of her elegant silk pumps then leapt back up into her throat again.

Seth! A dark, impossibly magnetic presence, his arm around the shoulders of the lovely Lucy as they waited to be seated.

Tension fizzled through Kate's veins, making her teeth clench, as Ralph invited them to their table, a waiter bobbing deferentially ahead.

Momentarily, she had softened towards him, questioning her own instincts, but now she was back to hating him with all the fiery intensity she was capable of.

He was still squiring the eminently suitable Lucy Mortiboys, the hottest contender for the coveted title of mistress of Montstowell, was more than happy to be seen in public with her, while for her, Kate, he had suggested a hole-and-corner affair. It simply wasn't to be borne! She felt degraded, humiliated, but, most of all, hopping mad!

But she pinned a bright brave smile to her face, veiling her hostility to the lovely blonde behind thick dark lashes as the introductions were made. And after one look into Seth's penetrating eyes—eyes which, as always, seemed to read her deepest secrets—Kate carefully avoided looking his way again, forcing herself to concentrate on her meal.

'It looks as though you're well on the way to making a name for yourself,' Seth was congratulating his brother. 'I picked up a lot of enthusiastic vibes, but I was sorry to find you'd just left when we arrived. However, your agent told us where we'd find you and I can see. . .' his tone had turned cutting, very dry '. . .you had other things on your mind.'

Kate knew he was looking at her, she could actually feel the power of those all-seeing, hypnotic eyes. But she wasn't responding to his nasty implications, not she!

'Lots of your pictures had collected ducky little red stickers!' Lucy put in, her voice cooing. 'What a clever pair of brothers you are!'

She might as well have said, 'What a clever family I'm marrying into,' and have done with it, Kate fumed inwardly, longing to say something cutting and acid but for once biting her impulsive tongue. She wasn't allowing her temper to get the better of her, no way; she was sipping wine and forcing conversation with the chocolate-box blonde which, she admitted, mentally screaming, was tough going because Lucy Mortiboys had fluff between her ears!

And it was only when they'd all reached the coffee and brandy stage that Kate suddenly became aware of a tense, expectant silence.

She glanced up from the spoon she'd been pushing round and round her cup, briefly noticed Lucy's sulky pout and then was shatteringly aware of the searching intensity of Seth's eyes.

'I was saying,' he remarked harshly, 'that if Ralph will see Lucy safely home I'll do the same for you. We have, as I have already explained, some unfinished business to discuss.'

His heavy brows were drawn together, emphasising the austere planes and angles of his face, and Kate said, 'No. There's nothing to discuss,' elevating her chin and straightening her slim shoulders to let him see she wasn't about to be browbeaten, or pushed in any direction she didn't want to go.

But, with an almost imperceptible tightening of his mouth, he totally annihilated her opposition.

'I'm taking you home, Kate. I'd prefer it if you didn't make a scene but, I warn you, if you do, it won't make a scrap of difference.' He rose, clearly waiting for her, his powerfully proportioned male body looking almost unbelievably, elegantly sexy in his formal evening gear.

Short of making the scene he had warned her against, there was little Kate could do. And, her heart thumping with suppressed anger, she gathered herself together, making her frosty farewells to Ralph and the obviously disgruntled Lucy, with all the dignity she was capable of assembling.

Seth was the only person capable of making her back off, she knew that. He was still water, very deep. But, even so, she would see him damned before he manipulated or humiliated her ever again!

Squeezing herself as far away from him as she could get in the back of the cab, she clutched her silky shawl around her body as if it could shield her from harm.

Not that Seth was attempting to move closer to her in the darkly intimate confines of the cab; he wasn't. And apart from asking for her address to enable him to direct the driver, he hadn't said a word since they'd left the restaurant.

Nevertheless, she was stingingly aware of his tightly controlled anger, highly potent, highly dangerous. The air around her crackled with it.

The apartment she was buying was in a block in part of London's newly restored Docklands, and if it didn't exactly cost the earth it set her back a couple of sizeable continents. But never had she regretted her rash impulse to live in comfort and style less than when she faced him across the unashamedly luxurious foyer and told him icily, 'I won't ask you up, Seth. Any business we might have needed to discuss was terminated back at Montstowell when you made certain degrading stipulations.'

'You think so?' His mouth curled derisively as he walked to stand in front of the satin-sheened lift doors, his feet planted immovably in the thick pile of the deep blue carpet, looking as if nothing short of an earthquake would shift him. And his eyes swept over her consideringly as he said, 'If you prefer our discussion to take place here, in public, then so be it.'

He wasn't going to do the gentlemanly thing and leave, and she couldn't imagine why she had ever thought he might. He was a Scorpio through and through, and could no more admit defeat than fly!

Aware of another couple entering through the revolving doors, approaching one of the other lifts and casting curious glances in their direction, Kate conceded defeat, just for now, and punched her security numbers into the panel beside the lift.

All the way up to her floor and into her apartment, she avoided looking at him, and her spine was rigid with barely contained fury as she walked into the sitting-room, tossing her handbag and wrap on to one of the long, red-cord-upholstered sofas that flanked the impressive log-effect gas fire. She loathed being told what to do, being backed into a corner.

The moment she turned and saw the way his brilliant eyes drifted in openly sexual assessment over her silk-encased body, the rich deep green fabric making the soft skin of her arms, shoulders and upper breasts gleam like ivory, she wished she hadn't been so rashly unthinking.

The concealing silk shawl had been a form of armour and she should have kept it on. She wasn't afraid of him attempting to make her take his commission on board again, she admitted uneasily to herself. No one, not even Seth, could force her to do anything she didn't want to do. But she was desperately afraid that he might touch her. She knew, only too well, how easily he could make her want him.

She needed to forget him, forget her own crazy, self-destructive response to him. He wasn't making it easy.

So, doing her best to appear cool and calm and in control, despite the deplorable rush of her heart-beats, she went to ignite the fire, her body shivering even though the apartment had effective central heating. The instant curl and leap of the gas flames among the cleverly reproduced logs was very comforting somehow; it enabled her to school her voice to frigidity as she asked, 'Coffee?'

'This isn't a social call.' He moved to one of the sofas, angling himself into the corner, his long, elegantly encased legs outstretched. Watching her. Kate felt trapped and her mouth went dry.

'Then what is it?' She forced the words past her teeth, her small hands curled into fists in her effort to hold herself together. There was something about this man that drew her magnetically—nothing could change that. She could do nothing to change the way she felt about it, but she didn't have to give in to it.

'Just a warning.' There was a world of dark menace behind the soft tones and Kate knew him well enough to know that beneath the smoothly controlled exterior a terrible anger burned.

Its cause, though, had her guessing. Surely her refusal to take on his commission wasn't responsible? There were other top studios who would be anxious to do the work! And then she was past all guesswork because he said coldly, his face tight-fleshed, 'Leave Ralph alone. He's a happily married man. When you were eighteen you were capable of driving him crazy, crazy enough to make him want to rush headlong into marriage, and six years on I'd say your capability had increased a hundredfold. So keep away from him.'

Kate was speechless with fury and the calm way he lifted his cuff to look at his watch incensed her almost to the point of lunacy. And while she was still struggling to find something cutting enough to fling back at him he got to his feet, looking down on her impassively.

'What is it with you?' he enquired bitterly. 'Do you see every man as a sexual challenge? You were barely sixteen when you began giving me the blatant come-on, just eighteen when you practically ignited in my arms—even though you'd just worked Ralph up to the point of giving you the most ostentatious diamond I've ever clapped eyes on. It always rather amazed me that you gave it to your father to return to Ralph.'

'Bastard!' Kate's hand cracked out, connecting with the side of his face with a force that rocked her back on her heels and, just for a moment, he looked at her, his eyes hard.

And then his strong, inescapable hands were on her upper arms, immobilising her, his voice grating with a bitterness she couldn't understand or place. 'Six years ago you could have been forgiven. You were just emerging into womanhood and were enjoying trying out your wings—experimenting with your sexual power. You probably didn't understand the havoc you were capable of creating.' His fingers had been like talons, biting into the soft naked flesh of her arms, but now the pressure altered subtly, his hands moving slowly, fingertips touching her skin in small hypnotic movements.

Kate's eyes widened, her pulse-beats panicky because she knew just what he was doing, and couldn't move although she wanted to, had to. . .

'But now, Kate, now we have a different story.'

His voice was rough velvet, mesmeric, holding her against her will, against every shred of common sense, the emotional trauma of the last half-hour draining her of energy. And she needed energy to fight him, fight what he was doing, deny every hateful word he said.

Slowly, his fingers slid beneath the fabric of her dress where it covered her breasts, rising again, slowly, so slowly, to feather against the pulse that beat a frantic, betraying tattoo at the base of her throat, and on, over the slope of her shoulders, finding the fastener at the nape of her neck, sliding it down, exposing the upper half of her body, her small breasts swollen, thrusting shamelessly towards him.

'A very different story,' he repeated softly. 'You now know exactly what you are doing, what you want.'

His eyes held her—she couldn't look away. Even as fear pattered quickly through her pulses, need held her there, impotent. Need for him, for the only man who had ever been able to make her burn, the only man she had ever been able to love. . .

'And I, my dear Kate, also know exactly what you want.' He touched one taut nipple almost reflectively, an unreadable smile indenting his mouth, and she shuddered uncontrollably, her vocal cords paralysed, leaving her incapable of any kind of coherent response.

Her eyes closed languorously, instinct taking over as she felt his hands move sensuously over her breasts, making her flesh ache with unfulfilled wanting, and she was all sensation, common sense flying, making her brain a useless and redundant inhabitant of her skull—and how far it might have gone she hadn't the wit or the will to fathom until he said huskily, 'And I'm available; Ralph isn't.'

The sheer calculated cruelty of his words jerked

her brain into complete and appalled awareness and she jolted backwards, white with rage, her hands shaking as she pulled up her dress, hiding her body from his treacherous eyes.

Her mouth set, she walked to the door, jerking it open.

'Get out!'

'As you wish.' He dipped his dark head briefly, his brilliant eyes amused. 'However. . .' He approached her slowly, with soft-footed menace. 'I admire your fire, your independence, I always have done. Even when you were a child I found it fascinating. But don't carry it too far. Not with me.' He stepped past her, turning, facing her from the open doorway, holding her furious eyes with his enigmatic gaze. 'I'll expect you back at Montstowell some time tomorrow,' adding in response to her disbelieving gasp, 'I made it plain, or at least I thought I did, that if you weren't back in two days I'd come and fetch you.'

'Go to hell!' Kate ground out, her nostrils pinched. 'Or do you want me to explain—graphically—what you can do with your commission?'

Did he think she'd been fooling around when she'd told him previously that she wouldn't work for him? And did he think she'd agree to do anything for him after this? After he'd just made it plain he considered her to be little better than a sex-mad tramp! When he'd so adequately demonstrated, for the second time within as many days, that he only had to touch her to make her turn to flame—when she knew, heaven help her, that, against all sense or reason, she still loved the devil!

'That, of course, is entirely in your hands,' he assured her calmly. Too calmly?

A glint of something unholy in his eyes warned her that the Scorpion was about to strike. It did.

'I think you ought to know that if you refuse the commission your sponsorship from IT will be withdrawn. Immediately.'

Something tightened around Kate's heart, a cold, iron hand. Squeezing. Hurting. What did he know about Interior Textiles? About her business relationship with the company?

She looked at him warily, trying to assess his bargaining strength, and he looked back at her with apparent lack of interest. A lack of interest puzzlingly belied by the sudden frantic beating of a pulse-point at the side of his jaw.

'I own and control IT,' he told her. 'The sponsorship you enjoy is in my gift. If I choose to withdraw it, I will. I suggest you read the small print,' he added chillingly, his mouth tight. 'And make no mistake, I will withdraw it if you fail to appear at Montstowell tomorrow. I never make threats I'm not fully prepared to carry out. Remember that.'

CHAPTER SEVEN

KATE had been up for most of the night, either restlessly pacing her apartment or frantically scribbling on scraps of paper which, almost immediately, she scrunched up and hurled against the nearest wall.

Every last bolt-hole had been explored, every last avenue of escape, but there was no way out.

Kate looked at her hollow-eyed reflection in the bathroom mirror and groaned. She looked dreadful, but that was the least of her worries. The few hours of sleep she had managed had been unsatisfying, peopled with horrors.

A few minutes under the shower made her feel fresher, marginally better, but dressing was a problem; she was all uncoordinated thumbs.

There was no way out except the way Seth Presteigne had dictated she take. The studio was paying its way, making a comfortable profit, but if she had to repay the original loan from IT in full, she would face bankruptcy.

Had she only had herself to consider she would have told Seth to go ahead. He could have beaten her into the ground to satisfy his Plutonian need for revenge—revenge for something she hadn't been guilty of in the first place, she reminded herself hotly—and she would have gritted her teeth, stuck out her chin, and hauled herself back up to the top again.

But she had her colleagues to consider. Abruptly thrown out of work, they wouldn't forgive her for letting them down, for refusing to take on a perfectly legitimate, profitable and prestigious commission. And she couldn't blame them! They didn't know of Seth's Machiavellian need for retaliation, his puppet-master mentality, or her own crazy response to him.

Sighing enormously, she made coffee. Her life wasn't going the way she had planned it. She was being manipulated, moved hither and thither like a pawn on a chessboard. And, like a pawn, she was both useful and dispensable.

Her insides squirmed as his taunting words of the night before echoed in her head, reminding her forcibly of just how 'useful' she could be. 'I'm available; Ralph isn't.'

Her own emotional reaction to him was cataclysmic, on all levels, and her defences against him were pitifully puny. He could demolish them with a single touch. And he had made it plain he wanted her sexually—another method of revenge?

She gulped down a scalding mouthful of coffee and grimaced tiredly. Oh, yes, he wanted her, but about as memorably as an ache to be relieved, an itch to be scratched and then forgotten!

Two hours later she was heading out of London, the materials she needed for her work at Montstowell carefully packed in the boot of her car.

Her colleagues had been frankly delighted when she'd told them she'd changed her mind about the commission, that she was taking it, after all.

'I can't think why you threw it out in the first place,' Sally had remarked, using her schoolmarmy tone. 'But since you've come to your senses and decided to give it a whirl you'd better pack in a few early nights. You look like death.'

But Rob, more sensitive and astute, had taken her to one side. 'Would you like me to take it on, love? You could take over the Countrywise project while I get myself over to this Presteigne guy's place.'

It had been tempting—oh, had it ever! And, for a moment, Kate had wavered. Such an arrangement would be fulfilling the letter of the agreement—that the Kate-Mallin studio took on the commission. But even if Seth went along with the arrangement, which she knew he wouldn't, logistically it was important that the designer who began a particular project carried it through to the end. Rob had already achieved an excellent working relationship with Countrywise.

But, more crucially than that, Seth wouldn't agree to the switch. He had his own devious reasons for wanting her there, right under his nose, with himself pulling the strings! He was a grand master when it came to tactical warfare and he would find a way to win, or create an explosion that would rock the vulnerable studio to its foundations!

'Welcome home, Katie.'

He had been waiting for her, meeting her on the

steps, a strange softness in his compelling eyes, his voice lowered intimately.

Kate shuddered with uncontrollable reaction but her even features were set in a cool mould as she faced him, her head high. Defeated she might be, but she wasn't going to show it. Not to anyone, and especially not to him!

'Don't call me that,' she said, her teeth snapping. The softer pet name made all the fine hairs on her body rise, reminding her with aching immediacy of the days when she'd hero-worshipped him, when he'd said her name softly, 'Katie', if she'd been upset, throwing a childish tantrum, or feeling lonely and cross, full of uncomprehending grief because the mother she'd adored had gone. 'Ask Parker to bring my stuff through, would you?' She stripped off her leather driving gloves and stalked past him into the huge hall, her nose very decidedly in the air.

She was perfectly capable of bringing in her own suitcases and working materials, but had she begun to unpack her car then Seth would have undoubtedly come to help her. And she didn't want that. She wanted nothing from him.

'I'm using the room I had before, I take it?'

Cool, huge grey eyes snapped upwards, meeting a very definitely amused blue pair, and she ground her teeth together, holding on to her temper with difficulty. He was laughing at her, damn him! He was correctly reading her haughty act as the cover-up for defeat it actually was. He could see right through her.

On the long drive down she had worked out her

plan of campaign. She would do the job of redesigning the interior of Montstowell because she had no option. And she would do it with all the professionalism she was capable of, and she wouldn't let Seth get to her.

And the only way that could be accomplished would be by keeping her distance. She mustn't allow him near her, and any conversational interchanges they shared must be kept strictly away from the personal.

But keeping personalities out of their working relationship was going to be difficult, she recognised, as his softly assured voice followed her as she marched up the stairs.

'Still fighting, Kate? Don't forget, the harder you fight, the more fun I'm going to have taming you!'

He was insufferable! she fumed as she closed the door to her bedroom with a resounding crash. He couldn't resist showing he was the master and, as her Arien birthright gave her a character that refused to be dictated to, the next few weeks promised to offer a very rough ride indeed!

She didn't know how she was going to be able to keep cool enough, detached enough, to bring her work here to a successful, speedy and professional conclusion.

She prowled the room, pushing her fingers through her short, silky dark hair, making it stick up in spikes. If only she could press a convenient button to cut off her powerful emotional response to him! Already her body was tingling from their brief encounter downstairs, feeling totally, unnervingly alive. And his softly voiced threat to tame her had made her stomach lurch violently—and not, she was ashamed to admit, unpleasantly.

'Your case, miss.' A brief knock on the door heralded Parker's appearance with the cases she'd hastily packed with anything and everything she thought she might need for the next few weeks, and she forced a smile in response to his pleasant grin. 'And I've put the other things in the book-room. Mr Presteigne said you'd be working there, as before.'

'Thank you,' Kate said inadequately, feeling ashamed that she had forced the poor man to fetch and carry for her when his normal duties around a house this size would keep him at the trot. 'I'm sorry you've had to be bothered,' she told him apologetically but his grin grew wider, if anything, as he said as he closed the door behind him,

'Think nothing of it! We're all pleased as Punch that it's all systems go again.'

And half an hour later as Kate had just finished unpacking, Mrs Parker added to her husband's greeting.

'Welcome back! We were afraid we'd seen the last of you when you cleared your desk and your room. But Mr Presteigne said you'd be back. Quite definite he was about it. He even picked these for you himself.' She gently eased aside the great bowl of white narcissi that perfumed the room with the edge of the tray she was carrying and Kate's eyebrows shot up. Seth, picking flowers for her? It didn't seem in character. The man was an enigma.

But there were no mysterious motives behind what Mrs Parker imparted next.

'He's gone now, Mr Presteigne, that is. He got called away, not ten minutes ago.' She crossed her arms over her generous bosom, enjoying a chance to stop and gossip. 'Lucy Mortiboys, it was, needing to see him urgent.' She was smiling comfortably, her little eyes twinkling, and Kate felt a surge of insane, unreasoning jealousy that was in no way helped when the other woman confided, 'We are expecting to hear an engagement announcement any time now. Parker and me thought he'd gone off her a bit but we were way off the mark. After that call he was off like greased lightning—and I've never seen Mr Presteigne jump when a lady friend snapped her fingers before!'

'Really?' Kate said sniffily, turning to inspect the tray to hide the way she was really feeling, but Mrs Parker took umbrage no more readily than she took an obvious dismissal when she was in the mood for a natter.

'Yes, really. He just threw a few things in a bag and went. Maybe they'd had a tiff and she'd phoned to say sorry. But he did make time to tell me that you'd probably not bothered to get lunch on your way down and you were to have a tray in your room and take things easy this afternoon. And he asked me to tell you to expect him when you saw him, and not to bother about getting his say-so on any of the work that needs doing here—he's happy to leave everything in your hands, he said.'

Kate stared at the tray, at the delicious-looking

prawn salad and thinly cut brown bread and butter, and felt sick.

'Thank you, Mrs Parker, you've been very kind,' she uttered hollowly, filling a cup from the teapot. And this time, thankfully, the housekeeper accepted her dismissal, and Kate stared at the quietly closing door and told herself that she would not, *not* burst into tears.

And why should she? She had known the problems she would face when she'd gone against all her instincts and made the decision to come back. She didn't like being dictated to, and she didn't like her emotional response to the dictator! But she could cope with it; she had to!

Even if Seth did put her emotions into overdrive—picking flowers for her room and thoughtfully arranging for her to have a late lunch from a tray, then walking out, dropping everything to race to Lucy's side, leaving her, Kate, in no doubt at all that while he wanted to tame her, wanted her in his bed for a spell—the lovely Lucy had prior claim on his time, his attention and affections, and always would!

Work went on and Kate told herself that she should be grateful that Lucy Mortiboys was keeping Seth away for what would appear to be the duration.

But, perversely, she missed him, missed him until she ached. She wondered if she was losing her wits and didn't know why she should be so drawn to a man who was demonstrably both cruel and calculating. And she should be down on her knees with thankfulness because he hadn't stayed around to torment her, to 'tame' her—with all that implied!

The old house began to ring to the sound of hammers and saws and drills as ancient plumbing was ripped out and replaced with new, and ugly Victorian fireplaces removed to reveal beautifully carved stone inglenooks.

Kate shut herself away in the book-room, matching samples of paint to fabrics and wallpapers, making detailed and delicate water-colour sketches of how the completed rooms must look, only emerging when she was asked to clarify her minutely drawn up plans to one of the workmen or to inspect progress in various critical areas.

Each day she kept in touch by phone with the happenings at Kate-Mallin and each day she missed Seth a little more. She wished she had never come back to Montstowell, never had to see him again. She felt torn apart. Life had been so satisfying and uncomplicated when she had been able to choose her own path, with Seth and the past placed securely behind her—or so she had thought.

Ten days into what she was beginning to call her ordeal, she decided she deserved a break. She needed just a few hours to herself followed by a really early night. No one, even if they did possess the kind of energy she was blessed with, could work seven days a week, sixteen hours a day, without feeling just a little jaded.

Moving towards the kitchen quarters, picking her way carefully over decorators' planks, festoons of the old faded wallpaper which had once, criminally,

covered the lovely oak panelling, she found Mrs
Parker resignedly contemplating an electrician and
his mate who were conferring with the men who had
come to install a shiny red electric Aga.

'Why don't you and Parker visit your daughter in
Shrewsbury?' Kate suggested. 'There's absolutely
nothing you can do around here at the moment. Stay
for two or three days.'

'Do you think we should?' the older woman asked
wistfully, then winced as someone started hammering something in the room above. 'I know Jenny and
Mark said to go any time—and we would be able to
do a bit of babysitting for them. . .' The wistful look
increased and Kate remembered being told about
the adorable four-month-old grandson the housekeeper and her husband doted on. 'But what if Mr
Presteigne should come back unexpected?'

'He won't,' Kate said with a conviction that made
her feel hollow inside. He was undoubtedly enjoying
Lucy's soft white arms and beguiling presence—why
should he return to the kind of chaos that awaited
him here? But she added staunchly, 'Even if he did,
he'd understand. Neither you or Parker can function
effectively until the new wiring and plumbing is
finally fixed.'

In the end, with assurances that Kate could
adequately look after her own few needs, the
Parkers drove off in their elderly saloon and Kate
treated herself to a long, rambling and nostalgic
walk around the estate, mentally preparing herself
for the next major onslaught—the arrival,
tomorrow, of the team of professionals who would

clean and polish the panelling that had suffered the indignity of being covered with drab wallpaper and even drabber paint.

It was twilight when she eventually returned to the house. The workmen had gone now and she was pleasantly weary.

Closing her eyes to the clutter and chaos, she picked her way to the kitchen where she cut a plate of cold beef sandwiches, purloined a bottle of Seth's best claret from the cellar and carefully made her way upstairs.

Balancing the tray, she wrinkled her nose with distaste at the state of her room. It couldn't be helped, of course. The adjoining bathroom had been gutted that afternoon and there was quite a scattering of debris around. All the bedrooms, except one, were in varying states of disorder, paper stripped from walls, furniture shrouded with dust sheets.

The only room as yet untouched belonged to Seth, and that only because the workmen hadn't got around to the master bedroom yet. And as he wouldn't be needing it Kate had no hesitation in borrowing it.

But as she switched on the bedroom light and went to draw the heavy curtains over the diamond-paned mullioned windows a great lump formed in her throat and something in her stomach seemed determined to perfect a painful form of nose dive.

His presence seemed to fill the room and clog the very air she breathed. It was as if he surrounded her, his eyes watching her every movement, as if he were suddenly very close.

Then, dismissing her fanciful notions, for this was only a room, like any other room, she walked to the adjoining bathroom and turned on the shower, determinedly ignoring the evidence of his previous occupation as she stripped off. She'd given herself a few hours off, and that included a lazy evening and early night, and she wasn't going to spoil it by allowing herself to think of Seth.

Dressed in the short silk nightdress she'd fetched from her own room, she slipped between the high-piled pillows and the soft duvet, a book by one of her favourite authors in her hand, the wine and sandwiches on the bedside table.

Fixing her mind on the printed word, she ate her way through two of the sandwiches and drank her way through some of the bottle. She was relaxing and enjoying herself, wasn't she? So no way would she let thoughts of Seth creep into her mind, thoughts of the nights he had spent in this very bed, his big body warm and totally masculine. She wouldn't think of that at all. She would finish her chapter, go and clean her teeth, then fall into a blissful sleep. . .

The mattress tilted, making Kate's head roll side-ways on the soft feather pillows, dislodging the book from her hands, making it fall to the carpeted floor with a soft clunk.

Murmuring gently in her sleep, she snuggled deeper into the comfortable bed, the sudden depression drawing her towards the middle, towards something wonderfully warm and solidly reassuring.

With an unconscious purr of contentment she snuggled deeper into the source of the warmth, too muzzy with sleep and the wine she had drunk to register the deep answering grunt of male appreciation as one of her arms twined round a naked chest that she dimly acknowledged to be very much where it should be.

Everything was right, exactly as it should be, she thought dreamily. Warm, gentle arms around her, hands sliding beneath the slithery silk of her nightie, everything blissfully, wonderfully right because hadn't she always known she had been born to be exactly where she was now, all entangled, close and cosseted, with Seth?

Seth! Her fuddled mind suddenly snapped into total and shocked awareness and took hurried stock of the situation.

Somehow, he was in the bed with her. Somehow, she had wriggled closer to him than she would hitherto have dreamed possible for two people to get. Her arms were twined around him, and so was one of her legs, and as for what his hands were doing—well, that didn't bear thinking about!

With a muffled squeal of alarm she struggled to extricate herself, but he was too quick for her, too determined, his body rolling sideways, pinning her down.

'Don't fight it, Kate,' he commanded huskily, his lips moving softly against hers. 'You know you want this as much as I do.'

With his naked body pressing down on hers she could hardly pretend to be unaware of exactly how much he wanted her. But that didn't mean she had to admit to feeling the same! She was not, most definitely not, about to add to his impressive score of sexual conquests!

But his lips were parting hers now, moving slowly and erotically over her own and the hot words of protest died in her throat as he parted her legs with a hard, hair-roughened thigh, making a sheet of white-hot sensation slice through her, making her body snatch control from her mind.

She knew exactly what she was doing, she thought crazily as she pressed her yearning body closer to his, arching her pelvis in blatant, total invitation. And she knew she shouldn't be doing it. Shouldn't be opening herself so completely to his devastating embrace, shouldn't be running eager hands over his back, his flanks, exploring every available inch.

Shouldn't be, but was, because her mind might be totally aware of what was going on but had lost all control over the wanton actions of her body!

'Kate. . .' Her name on his lips was sweet wild music and, as he rolled slightly away from her, cupping her face between his hands, her desire-hazed eyes hungrily searched his beloved features, roving over each one of them, unable to understand why something haunted should appear to be watching her from those deeply brilliant eyes.

'Tell me. . .' he began with a certain hesitancy that was completely alien to him in her experience. 'The last thing I want to do is hurt you, but do you turn on for every man like this—or am I the only one?'

Kate stiffened in his arms, suddenly icy cold, as if she had been plunged into arctic waters. He'd said he hadn't wanted to hurt her, yet he'd just said the most hateful, hurtful thing possible!

But at least it had brought her to her senses before things had got completely out of hand!

Wrenching herself round, she scrambled off the bed, only to find her wrist manacled in one of his hands, pinning her to the spot.

He eased himself over the bed, the covers barely covering his lean hips, and she turned her head quickly, furious colour burning in her face as she spat, 'Let go of me!'

'You don't mean that.' Oddly, he didn't seem in the least frustrated by her sudden and violent removal. In fact, his voice held a strangely complacent, satisfied tone, a tone she didn't trust at all.

Come to that, she didn't trust anything about this man and, attacking now because that was second nature to her, she said heatedly, 'How dare you creep into my bed, unwanted and uninvited? Let me go!'

He didn't. He simply exerted a fraction more pressure on her wrist and that meant she had to be drawn closer or suffer a dislocated shoulder.

'In the first place,' he began with infuriating logic, 'you were in my bed. And while I admit I didn't get a written invitation, I took it as read. What else was I supposed to think?' His lips parted on a sensual, utterly wicked smile. 'And we both know that my attentions were not only wanted, but most eagerly returned!'

CHAPTER EIGHT

'I HATE you!'

Kate turned the full fury of her eyes on him, no longer caring that her covering was of the sheerest, shortest silk, that his fantastically beautiful male body was barely covered at all.

It was very quiet in the room; there was no wind tonight to ruffle the trees outside the open window, to moan in the great high chimneys.

Very quiet, very still, just the direct intensity of his hypnotic eyes, the bedside light making them glitter with something entirely unreadable.

His eyes, the silence, were getting to her, so she took a shaky breath and shouted, 'Let me go!'

And to her secret amazement he did just that, rolling lazily back against the pillows, his arms crossed behind his head, his slight, satisfied smile sending a fresh wave of fury through Kate.

How *dared* he look so smug, so complacent?

Rubbing her wrist where his iron-hard fingers had manacled her, she bit back a torrent of scathing comments, turned on her heels and marched from the room, banging the door behind her.

Back in her own room, picking her way over the inevitable builders' debris, her temper suddenly cooled.

Shame for what had happened back there with

Seth made her skin burn, but even that didn't last. By the time she had whisked the dust cover off her bed and crawled between the sheets she was coolly trying to work out what to do.

It was high time she tried to analyse her tricky relationship with Seth, she decided, sitting up against the pillows, the covers drawn up to her chin.

He was a typical Scorpio, a master of the clever, coolly strategic offensive, with all the patience needed to bide his time, to probe the weakness of his quarry before he struck.

For years now, he had played the watching game, keeping tabs on her, manipulating her through that original gift to help her through college, to the sponsorship when her small design studio had been in trouble. And then, at last, inviting her to work on Montstowell.

To begin with, when she had returned, he couldn't have been nicer and had only shown the darker side of his character after Ralph had put in an appearance.

The clues all fitted, she thought with a shiver, her wide eyes staring into the darkness.

Seth would never allow a wrong to go unavenged and so he had played a waiting game, keeping a watching brief.

Six years ago he had believed she'd teased and enticed Ralph into promising to marry her while, at the same time, making a heavy play for him!

He couldn't have failed to notice her youthful attempts to get him to see her as a woman, she realised, cringing with embarrassment now as she recalled how *obvious* she had been.

And when he had schemed—and she mustn't ever forget that he had schemed—to discredit her in Ralph's eyes, by taking her in his arms, she had practically exploded with the force of her feelings for him.

So, as he had acidly pointed out when he'd threatened to ruin her studio, he had once believed her to be a wanton, a destroyer, a shameless flirt only too eager to try out her sexual powers on any man.

And what was worse, he still believed that!

Only an hour ago when, muzzy with sleep and too much wine, she had been more than welcoming his male body into her arms, he had taken time out to make his degrading opinion clear—'Do you turn on for every man like this—or am I the only one?'

Oh, it was just too much!

Battening down her temper again, she forced herself to stay calm. With Mars as her ruling planet, she wasn't used to people messing her about. And Seth, clever, calculating Seth, was doing just that. And it had to stop!

Several times she had thought of trying to clear the air between them, and first thing tomorrow she must make the attempt.

Nothing could alter the fact of the cruel and calculated way he'd manipulated her six years ago, breaking her young and trusting heart in the process, but she might be able to convince him that she had been as horrified as everyone else by Ralph's totally unexpected engagement announcement, that she had never deliberately led Ralph to believe she returned his feelings.

That her admission would certainly also serve to alert him to her true feelings—then and now—was something she was going to have to live with. She was sick of evasions and half-truths, misplaced suspicions; appalled by the need for revenge that drove Seth to play with her as a cat played with a mouse.

If he realised the true strength of her feelings for him she knew he wouldn't be slow in trying to take full advantage of them. She had had ample proof of his transitory desire to have her in his bed, and he would have to be a fool not to recognise her own helpless response to him for what it was. And Seth was no fool! Once he realised that she wasn't the promiscuous tramp he had believed her to be, he would recognise her response to him for what it was. And that would embarrass and humiliate her.

So she would just have to be strong where his fatal attraction for her was concerned. Quite how she would accomplish that hitherto unknown state she couldn't really fathom. It was something she would have to think about tomorrow.

Kate was up early but Seth was in the kitchen before her, seemingly unfazed by the clutter and debris of work in progress, a steaming coffee-pot in one hand, a brimming mug in the other.

Her heart leapt stupidly at the sight of his lean, dark elegance. Even wearing much-washed trim-fitting denims and a casual black sweater he looked sensational.

'Sleep well?' His smile was lazy, very intimate. 'I know I didn't.'

There was no mistaking what he meant—sexual frustration didn't make for easy sleep. But she hadn't set her mind on what she had to do and say, and dressed accordingly in a neat dark green skirt and trim white shirt, to be sidetracked by a pair of intimately smiling eyes and her own acrobatic heart.

Taking the battle into the enemy camp, she said bluntly, just for starters,

'About last night——'

And he handed her the mug of coffee, pouring himself another, remarking with an unforgivable trace of laughter, 'It was fun, while it lasted, wasn't it?'

Immediately, she felt the build-up to an explosion of rage begin deep inside her and had to use all her will-power to hold it back. The more she saw of Seth, the more violent her reactions became!

When building up the studio she had worked so hard to control her fiery Aries temperament, successfully acquiring a veneer of cool control, channelling her dynamic energy into making her business a real success. But, with hindsight, she could see that each successive encounter with this infuriating, sexy man found her shedding yet another slice of that veneer, bringing her right back to basics, reacting to him in a way which increasingly allowed her fiery character to take over.

So, very carefully, she took a sip of the scalding coffee, refusing to give in to the impulse to throw it at his head, and went on, as if he hadn't spoken, 'As you can see, the whole house is barely habitable, and that includes my bedroom—along with all the others. Except yours, which they haven't got around to yet. So I borrowed it, not knowing you were planning to return. For all I knew, you could have been shacked up with Lucy Mortiboys for the duration.'

Despite all her good intentions she hadn't been able to keep the betraying edge of biting sarcasm out of her voice and his small knowing smile, the infinitesimal tilt of one heavy dark brow, the way he said, 'Ah!', had her clamping her teeth together.

'Added to which——' she began again with creditable control, but he sliced through her words, his voice huskily soft.

'Stop pontificating, it doesn't suit you. Besides, I guessed what had happened.'

He had, had he? Kate fumed. Then why had he said those utterly shaming things? Making her out to be the sort of woman who crawled into any man's bed at the drop of a hat!

If he'd guessed why she was in his bed, why hadn't he done the gentlemanly thing and gone quietly away to find somewhere else to sleep? Come to that, why had he climbed into bed with her? Naked. . .

Her cheeks went pink. Silly question. She knew the answer and didn't like it one little bit.

So now was the time to put him straight over his erroneous impression of her promiscuity, never mind if it did leave him in no doubt as to the strength and duration of her feelings for him.

But he was saying, 'I take it the Parkers have

decamped? When I got back last night I couldn't find a soul. It was like the Mary Celeste.'

'I suggested they took a few days off to visit their daughter and son-in-law. Under the circumstances, I thought you wouldn't mind.' She had finished her coffee.

He took the empty mug from her, telling her, 'Of course not. It doesn't make sense for them to stay around while the house is in this state.' He turned from the sink, his eyes wicked. 'And I quite like the idea of our having the place to ourselves at night.'

That was as much as Kate could take and still retain her equilibrium. She went to the book-room, trying to look as if she weren't fleeing.

She could no more help the way she still felt about him than she could stop breathing. And he didn't help. He carried around him a magnetic force-field she couldn't withstand.

She didn't see him at all that day, or only once when she noticed him engrossed in conversation with the team of specialists who had arrived to clean, restore and polish the wealth of old oak panelling that had been uncovered.

She was kept very busy herself, at the beck and call of the various workmen and checking the progress of the orders she'd placed with IT for curtains and loose covers, bed hangings and spreads.

Congratulating herself on a day well spent, everything going ahead like clockwork—though no one but an expert would guess it from the state of the interior at present—she decided to reward her industry with a pot of tea.

A celebration doubly sweet because her deep and concentrated involvement with her work had successfully kept her mind off Seth, her destructive jealousy of Lucy Mortiboys and the unpalatable knowledge that when those two eventually married a part of her would die.

Making her way to the kitchen, she met Seth coming out of it and hastily schooled her features to a mask of supreme indifference. She was doing her best to project the ultimate image of the woman least likely to leap into bed with the nearest available man, her leaf-shaped mouth compressed into a very prim line indeed.

But he only had to look at her with those deep-seeing, brilliant blue eyes to send her pulses racing into overdrive. He had the uncanny ability to see into her soul, read all her secrets. Try as she might to hide it, he knew exactly how he affected her.

'We'll eat out tonight,' he told her, allowing his eyes to slide over her trim figure, taking his time about it. 'Seven o'clock suit you?'

Kate pulled in her breath and tilted her chin. 'You go ahead, thanks all the same. I've still got masses of work to get through.' Which was a lie.

'The work can wait and you have to eat.' Instead of letting her past, he blocked her way entirely.

Finding herself backed against the wall, his sensationally attractive male body far too close for her peace of mind, she said stiffly, 'I am not in the least hungry.'

'You will be—later.'

And there was something ambiguous about that statement, about the tantalising curve of his mouth that made her breath catch in her lungs, made her lips quiver and part on a little gasp that was part fear, part excitement and wholly involuntary.

And one of his hands was on the wall, just beside her head, and she knew what was going to happen and when it did, when his lips moved over hers, feather-light, with the sensuousness of a true voluptuary, she could do nothing but stand there and let it happen, fuzzily hoping that her suddenly weakened bones would keep her upright.

Crazily, when he drew away, she felt bereft. It would always be like this for her, with him, and, even more crazily, she didn't argue when, moving the backs of his fingers across the heated skin of her cheeks, he said in a voice which was a whisper of rough velvet, 'I think it's time you and I started from scratch, and how better than over dinner tonight? So be ready at seven, and dress up.'

And then he was gone, his easy stride making him look as if he hadn't a care in the world. And, she thought hollowly, she supposed he hadn't.

Lucy Mortiboys was safely in London, no doubt in a state of purring contentment because of the time and attention he'd recently lavished on her, looking forward to the day when she would be mistress of Montstowell—when all this upheaval was over, of course; that went without saying.

And she, Kate, was here, quietly holed away, manipulated into a situation which, for once, she couldn't fight her way out of. She was a victim of her own unconquerable emotional response to him, easy pickings, ripe for him to take whenever he felt the time was right. Whenever he decided to take his revenge—the eye-for-an-eye type—for the way he believed she'd behaved six years ago!

And would that time be tonight? Kate shuddered, feeling distinctly ill as she made her way slowly up to her room, all thoughts of a soothing cup of tea forgotten.

She knew she should be jumping in her car, booking herself a room for the duration in a Shrewsbury hotel, only turning up to work at Montstowell when the place was swarming with workmen.

But what was she doing? Finding a usable bathroom, lavishly tossing her favourite essence into the hot water, mentally deciding what she would wear. *That* was what she was doing! She began to wonder if she was seriously unstable!

Thankfully, just as she was easing up the tiny back zipper of a wickedly sexy dress—short, practically backless with the deceptively simple styling that accentuated her figure, making her look like a pocket Venus—the answer came to her.

She was agreeing to have dinner with him, just this one time, because it would be the ideal opportunity to put him right on the vexed subject of her morality—or supposed lack of it.

Of course! Her impulses had been the right ones all along and it had taken her until now to realise it, she congratulated herself as she stepped into high-heeled satin courts in the same deep rich red shade as her dress. She might have known her sun sign wouldn't allow her to give in so easily!

And she had been having second thoughts about what his reaction to the truth would be, and had decided that once Seth had been made to understand that she wasn't second cousin to a nymphomaniac he would more than likely back off. He would decide that revenge was not called for.

He was far too astute to fail to realise that she wanted him, had always wanted him, but when he realised his assumptions had been wrong he would walk away, lose interest, treat her with the coolly detached polite reserve she had witnessed him use on others in the past.

A reaction such as that would be much safer from her point of view. But could she stand it? She would have to. Somehow.

Standing back from the mirror, she admitted, without a trace of vanity, that she had never looked so alluring. And before the sneaky little regret that it would all be wasted, that after she'd had her say he would give up on his plans to wreak his vengeance on her in his bed, could grow into a monumental ache because she would never, ever know the ecstasy and fulfilment of making love with the one man who had held her heart for so long, she snatched up her suede evening bag, straightened her shoulders and walked briskly out of the room.

The restaurant Seth had chosen was only a few miles away, very classy, doubtless horrendously expensive. Newly opened, it was situated on the ground floor of an impressive Georgian house that had been converted into a private hotel.

Kate was glad she'd pulled out all the stops with her appearance but had reservations on the same subject as far as Seth was concerned.

Since meeting her at the foot of the stairs back at Montstowell he hadn't been able to take his eyes off her, and his eyes had been very appreciative, very proprietorial.

And that didn't help Kate's resolve to keep him coolly and calmly at bay, to say what she had to say and then watch as detached uninterest silvered his eyes, turning them cold, listen to him make polite conversation before taking her back to Montstowell as soon as he decently could.

So, just for a little while longer, she would enjoy the exquisite sensation of being the complete focus of his very interested attention.

They had had drinks in the lounge area, a beautifully proportioned room, tastefully furnished and boasting a comforting log fire and bowls of fragrant spring flowers on every polished table-top around which groups of comfortable armchairs covered in apple-green linen were grouped, offering complete relaxation.

And now the bowls of watercress soup which they had both chosen to begin their meal with were placed in front of them, the waiter moving soundlessly away, and Seth reached in an inner pocket of the immaculately tailored dinner jacket he was wearing and produced a small plush-covered box.

'Happy birthday, Kate.'

Momentarily startled out of her dreamy, frankly sensual mood, Kate responded with a little gasp, her big grey eyes flying open.

She had actually forgotten it was her birthday, and she could thank her involved and tortuous relationship with Seth himself for that!

'Open it,' he commanded softly. 'Tell me if I made the right choice.'

The smile he gave her was more than intimate, it rocked her to her soul, and her fingers were shaking as she opened the box, her eyes widening when she saw the brilliant teardrop suspended by a fine gold chain.

'A diamond, Kate. Your birthstone—white ice with fire at its heart.' His voice was low and vibrant with something she couldn't put a name to and she ran the tip of one finger over the flawless gem, noticing that it was just a little larger than her thumbnail and, stupidly, felt her eyes fill with tears.

'It's beautiful, Seth,' she said thickly, knowing she couldn't go all demure and say 'You shouldn't have,' or push the box back across the table and tell him that she couldn't accept anything so costly.

The glittering stone immediately meant so much to her that she would treasure it all her life—and not because it was valuable, either.

'Let's see how it looks.' He left his seat and came to stand behind her, fastening the fine chain around her neck. Softly, his fingers brushed against her nape, and the pain of wanting him, of loving him, was so great that she almost cried out.

Stoically, she did no such thing. She smiled and

sparkled throughout the meal, matching the glitter of the stone that lay between her breasts on the rich bright fabric of the sexy red dress.

But over coffee she reluctantly recalled just why she had agreed to have dinner with him tonight. And she had been so much enjoying herself, she mourned inwardly. He was a wonderful companion, his dry wit impressing her, and their minds were in tune on so many subjects, and if they did find something to argue about—she heatedly and he with that incisive directness of his—then they ended up agreeing to differ, no hard feelings.

But that was when they were discussing abstracts and what she had to say to him was very personal; revenge always was, wasn't it? And she didn't want to see her beloved Seth—who was being incredibly, sexily fascinating tonight because, no doubt, it suited his nefarious purposes—turn into the indifferent character she just *knew* he would become when he realised he'd been wrong, when he no longer had any need to punish her for the havoc he had accused her of creating six years ago.

However, it had to be said and she took a sip of hot coffee, dragged in a deep breath and announced, 'I think you ought to know that when I was growing up Ralph was the dearest, closest friend I had.'

She thought she saw something remarkably like a flicker of pain darken his eyes, but didn't pause to think about it because now she had started there was no going back, and she tacked on briskly, 'We shared all our secrets—except one, each. He didn't tell me he was beginning to see me as something more than a friend, and he——'

'And what was the secret you kept from him?' Seth cut in, his eyes veiled as he leaned back in his chair, stirring his coffee idly.

'Nothing that matters now,' Kate assured him airily. If he couldn't guess at that hopeless, deeply passionate love that had grown so swiftly and strongly in the breast of her much younger self— and still lived there, dammit!—then that would be an entirely unlooked-for consolation to keep her company during the lonely years ahead.

'He sprang that engagement announcement on me at that party,' she went on. 'I was as stunned as everyone else.'

'He'd never mentioned the way he felt before that?' Seth questioned levelly, his fine eyes weighing her, delving and assessing, and she had to admit,

'Yes. Once. A few days before the party he'd told me he wanted to marry me, right out of the blue. He swore nothing would stop him.' The corners of her mouth turned up wryly, her shoulders rising in a minimal shrug. 'He didn't ask me, he told me! In any case. . .' Her fingers played with the teardrop diamond, the coolness of its faceted surface giving her the courage to admit, 'I didn't take him seriously. He'd just had a blistering row with you and his mother, I'd gathered. I knew Lady Bea had been trying to separate us for some time, ever since I'd started growing up—seeing more into our relationship than there was. I thought his declaration stemmed more from rebellion than anything else. I told him we were too young to think of getting married and prayed he'd come to his senses.'

'And that was all there was to it,' he remarked, and it wasn't a question at all, just a simple statement, and she thought she detected a note of relief there but couldn't be sure. But Kate was nothing if not totally honest and while they were clearing the air they might as well do it thoroughly, so she told him, 'I did blame myself in a way. I *had* noticed little things—the way he went into a prolonged sulk if I spent more time with my girlfriends from school than I did with him, the way he touched me sometimes when he didn't need to——'

'But you were, and are, a very touchable lady. . .' His eyes were very warm, speaking volumes and, apparently, she was totally exonerated, Kate thought, flushing from something far deeper than relief. It had all been surprisingly easy. Too easy?

And contrary to all her in-depth cogitations on his Plutonian character type, he was not losing interest, backing off. Most definitely not.

He was saying, his voice holding a depth of emotion that was new to her, 'Thank you for telling me that, Kate. And now I think it's time you and I went home.'

Home. Together. Kate mulled over those two words during the short drive back to Montstowell. She liked the feel of them, very much indeed, and she was still happily mulling when they walked over the threshold of the great house together and stepped

into a pool of moonlight which shafted down from
one of the high mullioned windows.

'Coffee, Kate?' His voice was warm, throaty. It
sent delicious shivers down her spine, made her
bones melt in warm response. He turned to her and
he was very close, the warmth of him enclosing her.

And she smiled her generous, gorgeous smile
because he was so very good to look at, the dark
formality of his tailored dinner-jacket suiting him to
stunning perfection, the silvery moonlight softening
the austere angles and planes of his near perfect
features, darkening his eyes to a soul-stirring
enigma. . .

'Don't you think you need it?' There was a thread
of amusement there and she opened her eyes very
wide, pretending to consider. Perhaps the champagne he'd given her was responsible for her state of
euphoria—having to drive, he had only taken one
glass and she had somehow finished the rest. But,
on the whole, she didn't think so.

'No,' she said decisively. 'Do you?'

And his mouth softened, a tug of humour overlaid
with something far more complicated edging into the
smile he gave her.

'No, Kate. Coffee is definitely not what I need.'
He scooped her easily up into his arms and carried
her up the long flight of stairs as if she weighed no
more than a feather.

CHAPTER NINE

KATE was in Seth's room again and this time she had been invited. Well, not invited exactly, she admitted dreamily, her arms wound tightly around his neck, her head nestling comfortably into the angle of his shoulder.

Nothing had been said, not a word. He'd simply whisked her up the stairs and carried her to his room as if the way the evening was going to end needed no discussion.

And perhaps he was right, perhaps it didn't. And, strangely, she didn't mind being taken for granted, having such an enormous decision taken out of her hands, being made for her.

Normally, she chose her own path and woe betide anyone who tried to push her down a different way. But with Seth, it was different. With Seth everything was different.

He set her on her feet, slowly, allowing her body to slither down the length of his, and excitement fizzed through her veins like champagne bubbles, making her feel giddy and quite definitely out of control.

'Kate. . .' There was a rough note of pleading in his voice and she was close enough to feel the slight tremors of tension that moved through his body the way water moved at the onset of a storm, and she felt exultant, powerful, more powerful than she'd ever felt before, but loving, too, filled with an aching tenderness, filled with the need to give and go on giving.

Wordlessly, she lifted her face to him, reaching up to bring his head down to hers, her fingers splayed in the dark crispness of his hair, her mouth trembling as he parted her lips with a smothered groan of need and passion.

And Kate knew she had come home, was where she had always belonged, as he took her with him on a wild soaring flight of sensation, letting her touch the stars, drawing from her a response that shattered her senses.

And then he began to undress her, the tremor of his hands barely noticeable, but there. First the dress, the wickedly alluring red dress, then the cobwebby film of her tights and, slowly now, very slowly, as if the moment was to be stored and savoured, his fingers like the smooth cool drift of silk against her skin, he removed the remaining scraps of outrageously feminine satin and lace.

There was moonlight, the room was filled with it, the huge mullioned windows left uncurtained, and moonlight was all they needed, Kate thought, naked and unashamed, wearing nothing but the diamond he had given her, feeling it lie heavily between her breasts.

For a long moment he didn't move, his eyes devouring her then, in a gesture that wrenched at her heart, he was on his knees in front of her, his arms holding her tightly, his dark head pressed against the satiny softness of her belly, his mouth moving feverishly against her skin.

And this was right, so right, because she loved him. And it was inevitable, too. The only feasible conclusion to what had begun, for her, here at Montstowell many years before. There had never been anyone else for her. . .

She stiffened then, suddenly frozen into rigidity, and Seth sensed her withdrawal, she knew he had, because he got to his feet and carried her to the bed, settling her gently against the pillows, cradling her.

'Kate, what is it?' He didn't sound worried, she thought, her mind suddenly icy calm, and he should do because this was where the magic ended, for both of them. And she said stiffly, 'Lucy. Lucy Mortiboys. You're going to marry her. Everyone says so.'

'Do they?' He bent over her, touching her mouth lightly with his. Somewhere along the line he had shed his jacket and the moony whiteness of his shirt made his face look very dark.

'Yes.' Her voice was wooden. She was well aware that she should make the attempt to extricate herself, get back to her own room and the privacy everyone needed when hearts broke and dreams disappeared. But the effort was beyond her and her eyes closed over the sting of incipient tears as one of his hands gently caressed the curve of her cheek.

'And don't Lucy and I have any say in the matter?'

She didn't answer that. Couldn't. He didn't seem to need an answer, either. He simply told her, 'Lucy's father is my godfather. A year ago her mother died and her father went to pieces. He's a highly respected City financier but the death of his wife sent him off the rails. He stopped working and took to the bottle, which, as we all know, is no answer to anything.'

His fingers were tracing the outline of her mouth now and Kate wrenched her head aside, not wanting to listen to him because it wouldn't make any difference. She longed to be able to dredge up the energy to get herself out of here, but how could she when both his hands were now imprisoning her head, turning it, forcing her to face him?

Stubbornly, she closed her eyes. He couldn't force her to look at him! And she kept them closed despite a sudden urge to hit him for the laughter she detected behind his words.

'Now, Lucy may be a poppet, but she isn't too strong in the brains department. She didn't know how to handle her father and asked for my help. It's been a long haul, but we finally cracked it, or so I thought until ten days or so ago Lucy called in a panic. Dear Daddy, it seemed, had taken it into his head to sell up and go and live on a desert island, and would I come at once and put a stop to it? Well, it turned out that Lucy had all her wires crossed— not too difficult for her—and the "desert island" turns out to be Bermuda, where he's going into partnership with an old public school friend, also a widower, in the luxury hotel business. Lucy is going with him. Happy now?'

This was asked with a humour Kate could no longer object to. She felt like laughing herself with sheer happiness. But she opened her eyes and enquired levelly, 'Then you're not her lover?'

'Do I have to waste even more time answering that?' he wanted to know, his voice rough, his hands sliding over her shoulders to cup her breasts.

'You do.' The injunction came out on a husky sigh of exquisite pleasure and he shook his head, his eyes glinting wickedly.

'There's only one woman I want in my bed—and no, I am not, and never have been, Lucy's lover. Neither have I any intention of marrying her—I like my women to have a few brains—and, as far as I know, Lucy Mortiboys would run a mile if she thought I had designs on her.'

'Stupid Lucy!' Kate said thickly, relaxing back against the pillows, watching with an almost unbearable feeling of anticipation as he began to remove his clothes.

The days drifted through her fingers like golden beads, each one more rounded and perfect than the last. Every hour, or so it seemed, she and Seth grew closer, more attuned, more loving.

Apart from a few hours each morning when Seth worked in the library, a computer link-up keeping him in touch with his London head office and the many companies he owned and ran, he rarely left her side, watching and listening as she gave instructions and opinions as the work on the house went forward, injecting a few comments of his own but never going against what Kate instinctively knew was right for this beautiful old house.

And every evening they dined together, usually at a restaurant to save Mrs Parker the trauma of having to produce the exquisitely cooked and prepared food that Seth, the perfectionist, demanded in conditions which were still far from manageable. And every night they made love, and each time Kate thought it couldn't possibly get better, but somehow it did.

He never said he loved her, but, she assured herself staunchly, words didn't count. Only actions counted. And he couldn't possibly look at her the way he did, take such care of her—insisting that she shouldn't work herself into the ground, that she ate a proper breakfast instead of making do with a hastily swallowed mug of coffee—if he didn't care deeply about her.

And he couldn't make love to her with such tenderness and passion if what he felt was merely lust.

'So this is where you've been skiving!' His warm voice brought her out of her reverie and she wrinkled her nose at him, smiling.

'I thought you were still in the library.'

'Finished ten minutes ago and went looking for you.'

She was in the attics, mentally sorting out the furniture for the various rooms, deciding what would go where.

She'd brought beeswax with her, delighting in the results she achieved, but for the past five minutes she'd been sitting cross-legged on a massive refectory table which would look absolutely fantastic in the huge hall, thinking about Seth, about how her love had grown and flowered since the twin spectres of Lucy Mortiboys and her own suspected promiscuity had been exorcised.

'Miss me?' He came to stand in front of her, uncrossing her jeans-clad legs and sliding her over the table-top towards him, planting his hands on the polished surface on either side of her hips, his mouth curling in the teasing smile she'd seen so much of recently.

She pretended to consider his question, her head tilted on one side. 'After only two or three minutes? Hardly!' Her grey eyes danced with mischievous lights. They had finished their breakfast at eight-thirty and had gone their separate ways—he'd been working as usual in the library—for three hours, and each hour away from him seemed like a day.

'Minx!' The sudden pressure of his hands on her hips propelled her body into his, her legs twining round him, her arms flying round his neck, and he nuzzled his face against the side of hers, breathing huskily into her ear, 'I want you. Want you. . .'

'Here? Now?' She tried to sound outraged but her words came out on a tone that was more husky invitation than anything else.

He moved his mouth, whispering against the tiny, tell-tale pulse-beat at the base of her throat, 'Here. Now. Any time, anywhere, my lovely Kate. However. . .' he raised his head, his eyes considering '. . . I've got to get over to Leicester. Some gentlemen from Japan are showing a marked interest in a knitwear company that's been in the family for decades.' He smiled wryly, rubbing a smear of dust off the end of her neat nose with the ball of his thumb. 'That particular company has been a head-ache for years, but we've invested heavily in new machinery and design staff and I'll be damned if I'll allow some other company walk in, take over and reap the benefits. Come with me, Kate?'

'Now? Today?' She was impulsive enough to go anywhere with him, at a moment's notice, and he must have known that because he qualified,

'I'll be leaving in about half an hour and I can't see myself getting back here until Friday afternoon at the earliest. Can you take two days or so out?'

She couldn't, she knew she couldn't, and her eyes clouded with regret. Shaking her head, she told him, 'The decorators move in tomorrow and I need to be here to check everything out with them before they make a start.'

She would miss him dreadfully—two whole days without seeing him would seem like a lifetime—and her eyes must have told him that because he grinned, suddenly looking infuriatingly smug, very sure of himself—and her, as he told her, ruffling her hair, 'Pity. But it can't be helped. Just be good and work hard and think of just how much we're going to enjoy the reunion!'

Men could walk away without a backward glance, without a single regret. At least, Seth could, Kate fumed, then chided herself out of the mood of pique that had unsettled her ever since he had left for Leicester with a mental admonition to herself to grow up.

He had asked if she could spare the time to go with him, and she had had to say no, she couldn't. And that was it. Nothing could be done about it so it had to be accepted. That was the way Seth would see it. Like all Scorpios he had a logical mind.

So Kate threw herself whole-heartedly into her work, mentally ticking off the hours, and by Thursday afternoon she had lightened her workload considerably and made a great many plans.

He should be back by late afternoon on Friday and she would give herself a couple of hours off. She would spend time luxuriating in a hot scented bath, wash her hair, dress in something sensational, rustle up an appetising meal for two—she had already given the Parkers the whole of Friday off, then. . .

Here her mind cut out. If she kept daydreaming of the outcome of their reunion she wouldn't get another thing done today and time was marching— half-five already, the decorators finishing for the day, and somehow she had collected a large smear of pale jasmine emulsion down the side of her jeans and her hair was full of dust from further work among the furniture that had been stored in the attics.

So she'd stand under a shower, change into fresh clothes and put in a few hours with the paperwork waiting for her in the book-room.

She said, 'See you tomorrow,' to a straggler from the team of decorators who was on his way out and Mrs Parker came along the corridor from the kitchen regions looking harassed.

'I can't believe we'll ever be straight!' Then brightened. 'Mind you, they've finished in the kitchen—I love that honeysuckle shade you chose for the walls—only they said I wasn't to cook anything this evening, because of the steam, so will cold chicken and salad be all right?'

'Perfect,' Kate assured her, walking back towards the hall. 'I'll be upstairs in my room for a while, if anyone needs me. . .' meaning if Seth phoned, as he had done last evening '. . .and I'll eat from a tray in the book-room while I catch up on some work.'

In less than twenty-four hours Seth would be home, she told herself as she ran up the stairs, taking them two at a time, and if she immersed herself in paper work this evening, as she fully intended to do, time would fly.

Life was wonderful!

Ten minutes under the shower had her feeling squeaky clean and thoroughly invigorated again and she was smiling as she wrapped a large towel round her body and a smaller one around her head. These days she couldn't stop smiling!

Kate didn't know how Seth saw their future, or even if he considered them to have a future together at all. If he had any thoughts on the matter then he was keeping them to himself. But, being an Arien, she was the eternal optimist and was quite sure things would work out for them in the long term, and, for the next couple of weeks, until the Montstowell project was completed, she intended to enjoy her love for Seth, their relationship, and not spend too much time, precious time, agonising about what the future held or did not hold.

Picking her way carefully around a pile of rolled-up rugs, she made her way to the dressing-table and sat down, rubbing her hair absently.

Yesterday, the wide oak boards in this room, as well as the others in this wing of the house, had been sanded and polished, and she would have to ask Parker to carry the rugs down and give them a thorough beating before they were laid down again on the gleaming floor.

So many things to do, to think of, she decided wryly, when all she really wanted to do was think of Seth, of how much she loved him.

Even so, she was enjoying the Montstowell project immensely—now that she was no longer angry over the way Seth had blackmailed her into taking it on. Even in its present state of upheaval the house was beginning to look as she'd always dreamed it might, with the stuffy, dreary Victorian 'improvements' stripped away.

'Kate. . . Are you still up here? Mrs Parker told me to——' The excited pitch of a masculine voice cut through Kate's abstraction, bringing her head round, her eyes widening as Ralph suddenly appeared in the open doorway. 'Oh! Sorry, Kate!'

The grin slowly slid away from his face as he took in her state of undress, his mouth falling open, making him look foolish.

'Don't look so shattered—I am decent!' Kate smiled, amused by his sheepish expression. She stood up, draping the towel she'd been using on her hair around her shoulders, tightening the larger one more securely around her body. 'What brings you here?'

'Mrs Parker said if anyone needed you, you would be in your room, so I barged straight up, not stopping to think. It was Seth I really came to see.'

Ralph was still looking uncomfortable and, to put him at his ease, Kate grinned. 'Take it easy! You've seen me in far less than this when we used to swim in the lake. And Seth won't be back until lateish tomorrow, I'm afraid.'

'I know; Mrs P told me. Anyway. . .' he came further into the room, running his hands through his overlong hair, a great grin suddenly brightening his face, all embarrassment forgotten '. . . I've got to tell someone, or bust! And as Seth isn't here it will have to be you!'

His face was flushed, his eyes shining with suppressed excitement and his grin was infectious so Kate smiled back at him and he blurted, 'My exhibition got rave reviews and, would you believe, most of the paintings sold? Plus, I've been given a couple of really fat commissions, portraits, and what that adds up to is Sonia and I will now be able to buy that cottage in the country. It's what we've always dreamed of—a cottage with enough land to build a studio for my work. And the best news of all. . .' he looked and sounded as if he were about to burst with happiness '. . . Sonia's on a two-day stopover in New York and she phoned around lunch time to tell me it's just been confirmed—she's having our baby!'

'Ralph! But that's great news—all of it!' She was too happy for him to contain herself and she threw her arms around him impulsively, giving him a bear hug because their friendship was deep-rooted and he deserved to be happy. And Ralph responded, his joy overflowing, picking her up in his arms and swinging her off her feet, twisting round, his feet dancing, because all the good things had happened to him at once.

'I just had to come straight on over; I couldn't keep the news to myself!' he crowed, twirling round faster, losing his balance when his feet struck the pile of rugs, grunting as they both landed on the bed, his body covering hers, their arms and legs and torsos in a tangled heap.

Kate grunted, too, the air leaving her lungs in a whoosh, leaving her wide-eyed and too breathless to speak as she pulled herself together and wriggled to extricate herself from beneath Ralph's weight, the bath towel parting company with her naked body in the process, although, at the time, she didn't realise that this had happened.

And then the fine hairs on her body began to rise as some sixth sense alerted her to the fact that something was dreadfully wrong. She gave a final, vigorous squirm, just as Ralph rolled away, and sat up in the middle of the bed, naked and flushed, and met the murderous bleakness in Seth's eyes.

He was standing in the open doorway, very still, his features austerely carved from cold granite. But the look in his eyes was the worst of all; the cold violence of his anger was earth shattering in its intensity.

His mouth a thin slash, he dropped the bouquet he'd been holding with understated deliberation and walked away. And all that was left was the poignantly exotic fragrance of the spilled hothouse lilies.

CHAPTER TEN

'No! Let me handle it,' Kate instructed thickly, her throat constricted with panic and dread.

She had scrambled into a clean pair of jeans and a light sweater, pulled on all anyhow, and Ralph was hovering his face averted, his face scarlet and uneasy.

'If he'd had a gun, we'd both be dead,' he said dully. 'I take it there's something between you two?'

Kate nodded; he couldn't see her because he wasn't looking her way, but she couldn't say any more for the moment. Her throat was clogged with tears.

Seth would never resort to physical violence—his anger would take a more cerebral, more devastating form. And she couldn't blame him for the disgust she'd seen in his eyes. Disgust and bleak, black rage. He would be feeling utterly betrayed.

Returning home much earlier than expected, he had discovered his lover, naked on her bed, with his own brother. How much worse could any scenario get?

Her heart ached for him. She knew exactly how she'd be feeling had the positions been reversed.

'Are you sure you don't want me to find him and explain everything?' Ralph asked as she walked past him to the open door.

Kate shook her head. This was between Seth and herself and she wasn't a coward—she would do the explaining. She would make him understand that nothing had happened that a tumble over a pile of rolled-up rugs couldn't be blamed for. Everything would be all right—it would have to be!'

She was still repeating that to herself, over and over, like a mantra—just to reinforce her natural Arien optimism—when she opened the library door.

No one other than a Scorpio could carry on as if nothing had happened! she thought frantically, watching him feed facts into the computer, his broad, dark-suited back turned towards her.

Without turning, without her saying a word, he seemed to sense her presence and his voice, as he asked 'Well?' would have frozen a lava flow.

The impulse to go to him, to curl her loving arms around his body, was very strong, but she checked it with difficulty and said huskily, 'Please listen to me, Seth. I can explain——'

'I don't need explanations, so save your breath,' he cut in stonily. 'I can face facts, no matter how unpalatable, and I flatter myself I'm bright enough to add two and two together and come up with the right answer when I see a man on a bed with a naked woman.'

'Seth—*please* listen——'

'I'd really rather not.' He cut her short again, turning at last to face her and she saw the bleak hostility in his eyes, saw a muscle working furiously at the side of his jaw. 'I prefer to form my own opinions, make my own judgements, rather than listen to the kind of garbled trash you've obviously spent the last ten minutes cooking up. But I'll tell you one thing.' He thrust his hands deep into the pockets of his trousers, rocking slightly back on his heels. 'If Ralph's marriage breaks up because of you, I'll have no hesitation in breaking you. And that's not a threat, it's a promise. I don't blame him entirely—Sonia's away more often than she's at home and such a situation carries its dangers, as I once pointed out to them both. However, they both chose to ignore what I said and we see this kind of result—the sordid scene I just walked in on.'

His hard eyes stripped her soul naked and she knew he would never listen to a word she said in her own defence and beneath his contemptuous scrutiny she felt her face begin to burn with sickening rage.

'As I pointed out,' he intoned coldly, 'I don't entirely blame Ralph for what happened. When you choose, you can be totally irresistible and, it would seem, you choose more often than not.'

Kate gritted her teeth, fiery anger making her breath come in shallow gasps. He would never give her the benefit of the doubt, never. He would never listen. His opinion had already been formed and he wasn't going to change it.

It was grossly, infuriatingly unfair!

He was standing in judgement, handing out his deadly sentence, and her Arien character would not allow her to take it meekly.

It wasn't as if he were incapable of wrongdoing! What had happened just now between herself and Ralph had been a mistake. An accident, pure and simple. But there had been nothing accidental or pure about what he had done six years ago. It had been cruel and calculating, no accident but something he had carefully and devilishly planned!

So she lashed out, her face furious, 'I'm not promiscuous, but even if I were I'd rather be that than be your sort of devious, calculating, scheming, disgusting. . .' She ran out of adjectives and ended on a snort, then gathered herself together and charged on, 'The way you handled Ralph when he thought he wanted to marry me was little short of disgusting, and I can't think why I ever even imagined I loved you!'

She snapped her teeth shut, knowing her rash words had betrayed her, hoping he hadn't noticed. But he wasn't interested in her unthinking revelation; he merely asked icily, 'And how, exactly, did I handle Ralph?'

As if he didn't know! He'd worked it all out, right down to the last sick detail, and he was coldly asking her to spell it out! Did he think she didn't know, hadn't worked it all out for herself long ago? Did he think she was that stupid!

Her whole body was shaking with wrathful tension now, her teeth clamped together, making her jaws ache, and she ground out, 'Cast your mind back! And if you've conveniently blocked it out of your memory, then allow me to refresh it!'

Her veins were now seething with the hatred that is the other side of the coin of love and she didn't care what she said.

'You called me in—here, in this very room,' she

grated. 'Said some particularly insulting things and told me to leave and never come back. Then the clock struck the half-hour—that was your cue, wasn't it?—and you started kissing me as if you meant it because you knew Ralph would walk in. And he did, didn't he? And he saw us, and you'd successfully blackened my character and given him the cruellest shock your nasty mind could think up! Showing him was far more effective than any amount of reasoning, wasn't it?'

'You'll forgive me if I don't know what you're talking about,' he said frigidly, his whole stance dismissive. And Kate gulped back scalding tears of rage and frustration as he told her grimly, 'I'd appreciate it if you could finish your work here as soon as possible. Present your bill in the usual manner.' He was piling up papers, stacking them precisely and deliberately into a briefcase. 'And don't worry about the sponsorship loan. It will continue exactly as before—unless Ralph's marriage breaks up, in which case I would immediately withdraw it. I find your work the most acceptable of your varied *talents*.'

He stressed the last word insultingly, closed the briefcase with a decisive snap and, giving her one last uninterested look, strode from the room.

It was several moments before she could haul herself together and find enough mental and physical coordination to make her way back to the book room and the work he'd told her to wind up as swiftly as possible.

He was a brute and a beast and she hated him!

She stood in the centre of the room, shaking with rage then, without thinking, picked up the nearest thing to hand, a large glass paperweight, and hurled it through the window, the shattering of glass doing very little to relieve her boiling emotions.

'That bad, was it?' Ralph had come quietly into the room, his expression wary.

Kate said, 'I hate him! If I never set eyes on him again it will be too soon!' and meant it.

'He's gone, anyway,' Ralph told her. 'I just heard his car pull away. He went down the drive like a bat out of hell. Knowing him, he won't show his face until he's cooled down.'

'If he cools any more he'll get freeze-dried,' Kate snapped, wondering whether to send the desk lamp after the paperweight, then thinking better of it.

Ralph gave a worried look at the bright stains of colour burning along her cheek bones and groaned, running his fingers through his hair as he told her, 'It's still the same old tempestuous Kate behind that veneer of sophistication—you should know by now that that brother of mine is at his most vulnerable when he assumes that icy mantle.' He stepped closer, putting a hand on her rigid shoulder. 'He means a hell of a lot to you, doesn't he? You should have let me tackle him; I could have done all the explaining.'

'Vulnerable!' She picked up the one word that had got her on the raw, laughing bitterly, no trace of humour. 'Not a word I'd choose to describe Seth— he's about as impervious as rock! And you'd have been wasting your time, friend. He refused to let me explain a single damned thing! But I told him a thing or two—he didn't get away without a counter-attack!'

She sat down behind her desk, jerking a pile of papers towards her, and Ralph mused, 'No, I don't suppose he did, not with you.'

He perched on the edge of her desk, his smile sympathetic, and she told him without being asked, 'Trading insults with Seth is like trying to make a hole in a brick wall with a feather duster! No impression whatsoever! I told him what a devious bastard he'd been—the way he treated both of us— six years ago, and he didn't turn a hair!'

'What do you mean?' Ralph asked quietly.

Kate, temper getting the better of discretion, snorted, 'You remember—the day after my eight-eenth birthday party—when he asked you to go to the library at half-past ten? And you walked in and found me in his arms. Well, that was a put-up job, staged to demonstrate to you what unsuitable wife material I was. He's devious and vile!' she splut-tered. 'Up until then I'd been crazy about him—just think of that!'

She neglected to say that, since then, she'd been crazier than ever, loving him with the depth of a maturity she hadn't possessed six years ago. She was going to have to forget all about that, starting right now, and pick up her life and carry on as if nothing had happened.

But Ralph said quietly, 'You've got the wrong end of the stick, you know. It had nothing to do with

Seth. I'd been mooching around in the grounds, recovering from the ear-bashing Ma had given me on the subject of our engagement, when I saw her come from the terraces outside the library. She looked pretty het-up and told me Seth wanted to see me, in the library, right that minute. She practically dragged me there. I put the pieces together, later, when I'd calmed down, and realised that Ma must have looked in through the french windows, seen Seth kissing you, come across me mooching around and decided to cure me of what she'd called my "infatuation". She'd been dead against our friendship from the moment we both started growing up. And Kate. . .' he stood up, holding her bewildered eyes '. . . I've told you this much to put the record straight. Seth hadn't asked to see me—he had nothing to do with what happened that day. And I'd rather you didn't mention any of it to Seth. I never told him what Ma had done. He was always closer to her than I was, and I wouldn't want her memory to be tarnished for him.'

There was no risk of her telling Seth the truth about what his mother had done all those years ago, Kate thought acidly, since she wouldn't be seeing him again. Ever.

She hadn't properly thought about the promise Ralph had extracted from her until now—she'd been too anxious to get rid of him.

She'd pointed him at the chicken salad Mrs Parker had left out, then, leaving him to eat in the kitchen, had taken a dustpan and brush to clear up the broken glass in the book-room.

She felt ashamed of herself for her wanton destruction—several of the small diamond panes were broken and others were cracked—but she knew that, given the same circumstances, she would be furious enough to do the same thing again!

Tomorrow she would organise someone to match and fit the panes. There was a good architectural salvage company on the outskirts of Shrewsbury and she would contact them first thing in the morning. The replaced panes must be contemporary with the originals; new glass would look out of place and, despite her anger at the way Seth had treated her, she wanted Montstowell to look perfect when she cleared her desk and walked away.

Now Ralph had set off on the drive back to London half an hour ago and, sitting at her desk again, she recalled the unnecessary promise he'd asked her to give.

That she would ever see Seth again, let alone find herself in conversation with him, was highly improbable, so she pushed it all out of her mind with a determination that made her mouth grim and pulled the papers towards her again.

The final stage of her fraught relationship with Seth Presteigne was over. It had run its course, leaving her older, sadder and wiser. But she wasn't going to allow herself to dwell on it, on what might have been. The first day of the rest of her life began right here.

CHAPTER ELEVEN

'DON'T you think it's time you started to look for my replacement?' Sally asked when she brought in the morning post. 'It's only another couple of weeks before I leave, so you're cutting things a bit fine.'

'No.' Kate accepted the post, her eyes already flicking through it as she walked from her drawing table to the desk. 'I've discussed it with Rob, and we won't be replacing you. He, Anna and I will share your duties between us and if we find we can't manage we'll get someone in part-time.'

'You mean you think I'm *totally* dispensable?' Sally said on an outraged squeal, planting her feet wide to balance her now vast bulk. 'You've kept me on all these years because you were *sorry* for me, or something?'

Outraged pride and hurt feelings struggled for supremacy on Sally's normally placid features and Kate smiled for the first time in weeks.

'Cut it out! You know we could never replace you. You practically hold us together and the thought of someone else stepping into your shoes and stamping around just doesn't appeal. Besides, you might like to come back part-time when the baby's older.'

Mollified, Sally agreed that yes, she just might, and Kate went through the post, her mind only partly on it as she thought of the things she hadn't told Sally.

She had to pay off the loan from Interior Textiles, not just the laughably small amount of interest, but the capital. It was the only way. She couldn't sleep nights wondering when Seth might take it into his head to call the loan in, taking them unawares and forcing them out of business.

Besides, free of the sponsorship she had once seen as a lifeline, she would be ultimately and finally free of him.

Rob had agreed, after some persuasion, that it would be safer to be fully independent—even though she hadn't felt able to tell him of her fraught and tortuous relationship with the head of their sponsor's company. That was something she couldn't tell anyone.

Repaying the capital would mean cutting back drastically for several years to come, hence the decision to make do without a full-time secretary. Also, they would have to raise their fees to increase their profit margin, but as their fees were considerably lower than those of their major competitors that didn't seem to be a problem.

And Kate, herself, was taking a drastic cut in salary, had sold the lease on her luxury apartment and was in the process of moving into something very much smaller and cheaper.

She didn't mind how many sacrifices she made. She had to cut the last of her connections with Seth Presteigne. But apart from her need to repay that loan she didn't allow herself to think of him. Thinking of him hurt too much, and she wasn't a masochist.

Summer came and went and Kate didn't notice. She was accepting more and more commissions, spending more and more time at the studio, getting through a workload that would have sent anyone less determined and energetic than she scurrying for the nearest rest home.

'I'm surprised you don't move your bed in here,' Rob had joked one evening as he'd been preparing to leave, and Kate, crouched over her drawing-table, had countered, 'I just might do that.'

The dreary two-room flat in Earl's Court held little appeal and she only went there to sleep, but Rob, his face serious now, said, 'Call it a day, Kate. Why don't we go and grab something to eat? You're taking too much on board, driving yourself too hard. We've already reduced the IT loan considerably; it isn't worth cracking up over.'

His kindly meant invitation hadn't been even vaguely tempting and she wouldn't back off until the last penny of that loan had been repaid. Only when Seth no longer had any hold over her could she dare to relax. Then, and only then, would she be able to put him and what she had felt for him, what he had once meant to her, completely behind her.

The crack-up came in the form of a dose of flu that even she couldn't ignore. Three days in bed, swallowing gallons of orange juice, dosing herself with paracetamol, got her over the worst and left her feeling drained yet restless, a nameless discontent making her mind edgy.

Outside, it was a bright, crisp October day, but the sunlight didn't penetrate the small windows of her dismal flat, and suddenly she longed for home, for the wide meadows and woodlands, the sheer space of Montstowell, the longing poignant and deep, wrenching at her heart.

Surely she didn't still think of Montstowell as home? she agonised, appalled that she should, after all that had happened, her huge grey eyes flooding with weak tears.

The wretched virus must have taken more out of her than she'd realised, she decided, mopping her eyes, reaching with relief for the phone when it rang out, a welcome distraction from her uncomfortable thoughts.

It would be Anna, or Rob, and a chat with either of them would cheer her up, chase away the uncharacteristic blues. They'd both kept a concerned eye on her during the last three days, phoning or calling to see her.

Rob had been responsible for the cartons of juice and cans of soup she had existed on, and Anna for the cheerful pot plant whose bright scarlet leaves made a welcome splash of colour in her otherwise dreary surroundings.

But it was Ralph's voice, an untimely and unwelcome reminder of the past she was trying so hard to put behind her.

'It's a girl! Seven and a half pounds and the image

of Sonia! I wanted you to be one of the first to know.'

'Wonderful! I'm so pleased for you both.' Kate sounded as enthusiastic as she could, trying to ignore the spasm of pain that flooded through her with an intensity she wouldn't have believed possible if she hadn't just experienced it. The announcement that Sonia was well and truly pregnant, six months ago, had been responsible for what had eventually turned out to be the most devastatingly dreadful day of her life.

'Are you all right? When I phoned the studio they gave me this number and said you were home with flu. I haven't dragged you off your sick bed, have I?' the voice at the other end of the wire asked and Kate chewed on her lip. She couldn't have sounded as overjoyed as she'd meant to and she excused herself hurriedly.

'I do feel a bit light-headed—but take no notice. Tell me all about it—was it an easy delivery? Are they both all right?'

'Bright as buttons, the pair of them!' Ralph crowed. 'And we want you to be godmother— you've never met Sonia, of course, but I've told her all about you, about the way we practically grew up together, and she's anxious for you to accept. The christening will be in our village church in about six weeks' time. We've only recently moved into our cottage—all oak beams and roses round the door— but you'll see it for yourself when you come down. Try and find time for a visit before the christening, will you?'

Kate's mind was racing furiously, her stomach churning, making her feel queasy. She couldn't accept. She *couldn't*! Seth would be there, that went without saying. He would probably be standing as the baby's godfather! She couldn't face him.

'I'll give it some thought,' she prevaricated thickly. 'I'm really flattered, but I've got so much on right now, and——'

'Have you heard from Seth recently?' Ralph cut through her excuses, astutely second guessing the reason behind her evasions. 'Or are you two dunderheads still fighting fate?'

'I don't know what you mean,' Kate replied on a snap. She stiffened her spine, quite ready to slam the receiver down if Ralph persisted in pursuing this unwelcome line of conversation.

'No?' He chuckled softly. 'Well, maybe not. They always say the observer sees more of the game. And I see one protagonist being uncharacteristically chary of attending the christening of one of her oldest friends' first child and the other shutting himself away in the sort of lonely seclusion no one but a hermit could possibly enjoy. Think about it, Kate.'

She did. She didn't want to, but she did. Since that first weak wave of homesickness had engulfed her Seth had once again invaded her mind. And the conversation with Ralph most definitely hadn't helped.

For months now she had refused to think about what had happened between them. The only Seth-related thought she'd allowed inside her head had been the desperate need to repay the loan and cut free of the last tie.

But there were other ties, of loving and needing, of regrets, and of something else—something she hadn't understood because, with typical Arien rashness—the need to pick herself up, dust herself down and start all over again—she had deliberately closed her mind to past pain and the reason for it.

But now, something Ralph had told her, the last time she'd seen him, ran around her mind.

Seth didn't know that Lady Bea had sneakily manoeuvred Ralph into seeing his new fiancée in his own brother's arms. Therefore—she wrinkled her brows, dropping the sandwich she'd been unenthusiastically making for her lunch—therefore, Seth had taken her into his arms, that first time, kissing her with a passion and thoroughness that had been totally new to her, not from any devious, scheming motive, but because he had wanted to!

And, whichever way she looked at it, seen from that standpoint, his motives hadn't been suspect at all!

Throughout those six years, when she'd been thinking the worst of him, he had been somewhere in the background, caring for her. Right from the initial gift to help her through college, to his sponsorship of her business when it had looked like failing, he had seen her need, and met it. Just as he had sensed her unacknowledged need to return to her roots, when he had invited her back to Montstowell in her professional capacity, to redecorate the house.

Once that viewpoint had been admitted, her natural optimism completely took over.

If Seth hadn't actually been in love with her then he had definitely been heading that way! They had been so well attuned, so close, so very, very passionate.

And if he'd refused to listen to her account of what could happen when a scenario included piles of rolled-up rugs and a bathtowel then too bad. She would simply have to give him another opportunity to hear what she had to say. In her mind, there would always be another opportunity.

One way or another, Kate was determined to convince him that what had happened six months ago had been nothing more than an unfortunate accident, convince him that she'd always loved him—even though she'd carefully hidden that fact, even from herself, for long stretches of time!

And after that, the future would be in his hands. She just wasn't going to think about the possibility of him disbelieving her. If it happened, she'd think about it then.

It took less than half an hour to throw a few overnight things into a bag, contact Anna to let her know she would be in the country for the next day or so, and lock up her flat.

She had changed into taupe cords, neatly fitting and teamed with a darker-toned cashmere sweater, the outfit topped by a vibrant red, blouson-style suede jacket.

There was nothing much she could do about the shadows beneath her eyes or the pallor that was the aftermath of flu, except take extra care with her make-up, choosing a lipstick as bright as her jacket, making a statement of brave intent.

Her car was garaged further down the street and Kate was thankful that Rob had talked her out of the first rash impulse to sell it and offset the proceeds against the debt to IT, pointing out with a logic she had had to agree with that having her own transport was a business necessity.

She could be at Montstowell in just over three hours, before darkness set in, and she concentrated on her driving, refusing to admit that she might face defeat.

She loved Seth and nothing was going to alter that, it seemed, so it was no use pretending she didn't. And if he told her he wasn't interested well—well, she'd think about that if it happened.

The sun was sinking when she reached the turn-off to the main drive, a clinging blue mist hiding the tops of the bright autumnal trees, making the distant house look hazy, withdrawn and secretive.

Just for a moment the enormity of what she was doing made her stomach lurch. She hadn't been back since Seth had brusquely told her to finish her work and get out.

Unwillingly, she recalled how quickly she'd finished up, leaving Rob, armed with copious and detailed notes supplied by herself, to oversee the final stages of the work, checking that every last item of furniture, every curtain, painting and ornament, occupied the specific place she'd allocated in her extensive plans.

But she was coming home, she reminded herself robustly. She had been born there—if not in the big house itself, then on the estate, part of an extended family. She had been brought up here, she belonged here. Belonged here, where she had learned to love Seth, where he in turn, latterly, had learned to love her.

She was sure of that. She had to be.

Parking her car unobtrusively in a courtyard at the rear of the house, she walked quickly and with a confidence she didn't care to question in through a side-door, through what had once been an old-fashioned still-room and scullery and was now a gleaming, entirely functional laundry-room, and on into the huge, heavily beamed kitchen.

The heat from the scarlet Aga kept the room warm and the delicious aroma of a simmering casserole made Kate remember the lunchtime sandwich she'd discarded in her hurry to be away, made her realise just how hungry she was. She hadn't felt really hungry for months, she realised with a little shock.

And Mrs Parker looked up from the bowl of egg whites she was beating—probably for one of her delicious chocolate soufflés, Kate guessed—and her mouth dropped open.

'You've come back!' she managed at last, her round face breaking into a delighted smile. 'And about time, too! We wondered, Parker and me, what had gone wrong.'

'Is Seth in?' Kate asked, beginning to feel distinctly nervous and hoping it didn't show too much.

The Parkers couldn't have failed to notice the close-ness she and Seth had shared during part of her time here. Apart from her using her bedroom as a dress-ing-room, it hadn't been occupied. Her bed hadn't been slept in for many, many nights!

'Oh, he's here all right.' The housekeeper laid aside the bowl of egg whites and wiped her hands on her apron. 'Six months, and he's barely set foot off the estate. Rides every morning, early, then works on the phone and at that wretched computer thing all day and half the night. Oh, he's here—at least his body is. His mind's on another planet altogether! There's no reaching him. Would you fancy a cup of tea?' she asked, switching to another tack and, disconcerted, Kate gave her a twitchy smile, shaking her head.

'No, thanks. I'll go and find Seth.'

She could have murdered for a cup of Mrs Parker's hot strong tea, but Seth was her first priority. He always would be.

Had the disintegration of their relationship really affected him so strongly? Had the proud Plutonian withdrawn to some strange and rocky height where no one could reach him?

No, of course not. She could reach him!

Bestowing her gorgeous smile on the house-keeper, Kate left the warm, companionable atmos-phere of the kitchen and made her way to the library where Mrs Parker had told her he would be.

Walking through the vast hall, she didn't take in the results of her own efforts, the complete change in the ambience of the house. Her mind was fixed on Seth, on how very much she loved him—there was no room for anything else.

Reaching the library door, she paused for a moment, her heart hammering. She mustn't let herself think about the possibility of his taking one cold, dark look at her and throwing her out! The prospect was too daunting to allow inside her head.

Kate took a deep, deep breath and began to feel calmer as she felt the atmosphere of the ancient house gather her up in quiet welcome. Everything would be all right!

But, despite her optimism, her grey eyes were very wide, her leaf-shaped mouth trembling just a little as she rapped on the door and pushed it open.

He was standing at one of the windows, looking out into the deepening dusk. He didn't turn, and Kate's eyes swept over his black-clad body, from the angular breadth of his sweatered shoulders to the lithely elegant length of his legs, and her heart twisted inside her with love and longing.

She loved him so much, so very much. The last six months when she'd refused to think of him, about her part in the break-up of their relationship, had been a criminal waste of time. Because, now she came to think about it, the blame had been partly hers. Her instinctive impulsiveness had a lot to answer for!

Had she continued to sit at her dressing-table when Ralph had burst in with his good news, had she said sensibly, 'How nice. I'm so pleased for you. But could you wait downstairs while I dress?' then nothing disastrous would have happened.

Instead, she had overridden Ralph's initial embarrassment, flung her arms around him in an impulsive bear-hug—and all hell had broken loose!

The mood of rare introspection, the new insight into her own fiery Arien character, produced an unwelcome uncertainty, so that when he said, 'Well, Parker, what is it?' still not turning, she didn't know what to say.

And suddenly her heart began to race, beating like a steam hammer, and she was sure he heard it above the somnulent ticking of the clock, the quiet whisper of the fire in the hearth, because she saw him stiffen, his bones very rigid as he finally turned to face her, the austerity of his features heightened by the unbelievable coldness of his eyes.

Uncertainly, Kate flicked the tip of her tongue over her lips, tension making her whole body ache, and blurted, coming to the point as quickly as she could because she couldn't see the sense in hanging back, 'You have to listen to me, Seth. There was nothing going on between Ralph and me that day——'

And he cut in, sounding coldly indifferent, 'I know. He came and told me about five months ago.'

'You've known for that long!' Kate couldn't believe she was hearing this. It turned her theory about him loving her on its head. He'd known the truth. For five long months he'd known! And he hadn't done a thing about it!

The truth was too dreadful to absorb at first and she stared at him, wide-eyed and hopeless, trying to come to terms with the facts.

He'd known that the scene he'd walked in on had been entirely innocent, that he owed her an apology for the foul things he'd said—at the very least. He'd known that there was no barrier to their continuing relationship, no need to cut her ruthlessly out of his life.

And yet he'd done nothing!

Despite the warmth of the room, the fire burning brightly in the hearth, she shivered. She had meant nothing to him, after all. Just a brief affair. Fun while it lasted. And when it ended—for whatever reason—it ended. No going back. Nothing.

She had been a fool to come, to attach any significance whatsoever to the fact that his passionate kisses, six years ago, had been inspired by desire rather than the devious motives she had at one time attributed to him.

Her stupid impulses had once again led her to heartbreak and humiliation. Would she never learn?

She said stiffly, not looking at him, 'I shouldn't have come. I'm sorry,' and turned, groping for a door-handle she couldn't see because hot tears were making her eyes blind. And her heart was breaking into sharp little pieces inside her.

He said, 'Stay.' His voice was very cool, very controlled, and she went quite still, unable to move. 'Come here, Kate.' And, uncharacteristically, she found herself mindlessly obeying his command, like an automaton, programmed to perform whatever was asked of it.

He had moved, was standing with his back to the fire, his hands behind him, his feet planted wide, and she stopped a yard away, not daring to go any closer because she loved him so much and he didn't love her at all. He never had done.

She expected biting scorn, a curt demand to be told exactly, and precisely just what she thought she was doing here, what she expected to gain, but he said, as if his interest were merely academic, 'Why have you come?'

'You know why.' Her stomach lurched painfully. 'To explain what really happened that day.' Her voice was thick, her throat clogged with foolish tears. 'But you already knew.'

He dipped his dark head in brief acknowledgment and said with a trace of bitterness she couldn't understand, 'What took you so long?'

Scalding words of counter-accusation hovered rashly on her tongue, but she bit them back, reminding him as levelly as she could, 'You sent me away. Refused to listen. Did you really expect me to come crawling back?'

'Quite frankly, yes. But not crawling. That isn't your style.' He rocked back slightly on his heels, his eyes shuttered as he regarded her pale features dispassionately. 'But I did expect you to appear, breathing fire, all flags flying, *demanding* to be heard. If there's one thing that stood out clearly from that final scene between us, it was your unguarded admission that you loved me. And the Kate I thought I knew, had she truly loved, would never have given up so easily.'

His appalling arrogance sparked her temper, but

a discreet knock on the door, heralding the house-keeper, gave her time to think. And, in answer to Mrs Parker's query, she said, 'Yes, I'd love to stay to dinner, thank you. And if my old room could be made ready, I'd really appreciate it. I don't fancy driving back to London tonight.' She managed a brave smile, ignoring the sharp intake of breath that came from Seth.

She had read enough into his last remark to guess he was wearing a false face, assuming a mask of icy indifference to disguise his feelings—in the manner of a true Scorpio. Beneath the mask smouldered intense emotions, and somehow she had to reach them.

Taking her courage in both hands, she removed her bright jacket and draped it over the back of a chair, one flyaway eyebrow lifting as she asked, 'Aren't you being too self-protective?'

She saw him stiffen, sensed the sudden tension in him, and went on, her voice only wobbling slightly, 'You expected me to come here, demanding a hearing, and yet you never thought of approaching me, even after Ralph had told you the truth. Was it because you'd been looking for a way of ending the affair? You can be honest—I can stand the truth.'

For a dreadful moment she thought he was going to reply in the affirmative and her heart leapt and twisted as he said rawly, 'You know I wasn't! And as far as I was concerned, it wasn't an affair. It was far more than that.'

Kate gave a huge shudder, the emotion in his voice breaking her up. Foolish unstoppable tears welled in her eyes again and he said thickly, 'Don't, Katie, don't!' and gathered her into his arms.

Her own arms flew around him, holding him as if she would never let him go, her eyelids drifting shut as he murmured roughly into her hair, 'After Ralph made me listen to what had really happened I waited for you to come back. Every day, I waited, holding on to that slip you'd made, the admission that you loved me. It was the only hope I had. I couldn't go to you, but I told myself that if you really loved me then nothing would stop you coming back—if only to put the record straight and give me a huge slice of your mind! Your own nature would force you into taking that kind of action. But weeks followed weeks, months followed months, and still you didn't come. And you were repaying that damn loan faster than I believed possible, and that, if nothing else, told me that I'd finally killed the only thing I'd ever really wanted—your love.'

'Don't!' Kate hushed, feeling his despair as if it were her own, and adding shakily, 'I'm here now, aren't I? I did come back. And it took so long because I was too hurt to let myself even think of you. So I threw myself into my work, into repaying that loan, acting as if there were no tomorrow. And all the time there weren't any tomorrows at all, not without you.'

'Kate. . .' And then he was kissing her, and, starved of him, she was responding, all fire and passion, drowning in the sweet desperation of his tumultuous need and then he was raining kisses on her throat, her eyelids. 'Don't ever leave me again,' he demanded huskily.

She promised, 'I won't. Not even if you throw me out!' Then, pushing herself away from him, the characteristic challenge back in her eyes, she demanded, 'You said you couldn't come to me. Why? Why, when you knew I'd done nothing wrong, when you knew I loved you?'

There was silence and then he slid his hands up the length of her back, rested them briefly on her shoulders before cupping her face, his expressive eyes anguished.

'Can I make you understand?' he asked rawly. 'I felt, basically, that I was too old for you, and that particular hang-up goes back a long way, to the time when you were little more than a child, times when I wanted you more than I'd ever wanted any other woman. Also, I know how independent you are, how you need to do your own thing as much as you need air to breathe. I didn't know if you were ready for a long-term commitment—if life at Montstowell and motherhood would suit. So I reluctantly left the decision to you. If you loved me, and your love was strong enough, you'd come back, no matter what. If it wasn't strong enough, or if you valued your independence more, then you'd simply forget what had happened and get on with your life.'

Kate's eyes drifted closed, her soul shuddering. How very nearly that had happened, though for different reasons than those he had outlined. But she was here now, and she rested her head against the warm breadth of his shoulders.

'You, Montstowell and motherhood will suit me perfectly. Besides. . .' she lifted her head and smiled into his eyes '. . . I can always work from here. You seem to manage it—why shouldn't I?'

His eyes softened to pools of tenderness and his voice was rough as he whispered her name and neither of them heard the door open until Mrs Parker coughed and said, 'Dinner's ready, sir. I've put it in the breakfast-room.'

And Seth muttered 'Damn!' beneath his breath, but his smile was wide and loving as he took Kate's arm, murmuring for her alone, 'Better eat up, like good children. That way we can get to play later!'

The little breakfast-room looked beautiful, just as Kate had meant it to look. The high candle-sconces threw a mellow light over the restored seventeenth-century panelling, the carved, stone-hooded hearth was merry with dancing firelight, the small refectory table shining with beeswax, set with sparkling crystal and silver.

Seth at one end of the table, Kate at the other. Facing. Too far apart to touch. And she wanted to touch him, and go on touching him, with a need that shook her.

Smoked salmon mousse to begin with, garnished with watercress, served with wafer-thin slices of brown bread and butter. Kate ate as much as she could and wondered where her appetite had gone. She'd been so hungry before. Before Seth had asked her to marry him.

He had, hadn't he? He'd talked about her living

at Montstowell, having his children. She put down her fork and asked, 'I am marrying you, aren't I?'

'You'd better!' Seth put down his fork, too, grinning at her from the other end of the table, across the candles, the flowers—bright little button crysanthemums from the gardens—and before he could elaborate Parker came in to clear the plates and pour the wine, and Mrs Parker, all smiles and twinkling, knowledgeable eyes, brought in the casserole, the dish of fresh greens.

'There's chocolate soufflé to follow, sir, and cheese.'

Kate sighed. The meal was going to be a marathon, with the Parkers waiting on, waiting to see every last crumb eaten.

As soon as the couple had gone, for the moment, Kate took a deep gulp of wine, feeling very lonely at her end of the table, and blurted, 'You've never said you love me.'

He looked up from his meal and said softly, 'I can barely remember a time when I didn't.'

Almost choking, Kate pushed her plate away. That was the most beautiful thing he could possibly have said. Planting her elbows on the table, resting her chin on her hands, she looked at him mistily. 'Tell me more.'

And he smiled at her, his voice a whisper of love as he told her, 'I'd always admired your fiery independence, Kate. Even when your mother died you didn't sit in a corner weeping, as most children of your age would have done. You went and kicked the hell out of a clump of undergrowth, raging against

fate. And from that day on you took yourself a slice
of my heart, grabbed a piece of my love for yourself.
And that love changed, some time later, from being
brotherly to something very different. And I knew
you weren't indifferent to me, either. You were
behaving like a minx in your attempts to arouse my
interest. And believe me, if you hadn't been so
darned young I'd have let you know just how well
you'd succeeded!'

'Oh, Seth!' Kate breathed shakily. If only she'd
known, all those years ago, how differently things
might have turned out. But she said challengingly,
'What about all those others? There was always
some lovely young thing in the background. A
different one every weekend!'

'Hardly!' He smiled slowly, leaning back in his
chair, giving up on his meal, too. 'A smokescreen,
that's all. And there was safety in numbers. None of
them had time to get close; I didn't want them close.
I was waiting for you to grow up—properly. And I
thought I had everything worked out.' He shrugged,
his smile self-derisive. 'I'd help you through college,
give you the space and time you needed to find
yourself. The time to grow—away from Montstowell,
away from me, too. I knew you were infatuated by
me—how could I not?—and for all I knew you could
grow out of it. It was a calculated risk, and one I
had to take.'

He lifted his wine glass and drank deeply, and his
eyes were dark.

'I'd been sorely tempted to propose to you on
your eighteenth birthday, to make sure of you. But

I did the noble thing.' His mouth tightened. 'I decided to wait—against all my more selfish instincts, to give you that chance to find yourself. So you can guess how furious I was when Ralph announced your engagement!' He twisted the stem of his glass between his fingers, holding her with his eyes. 'I tried to tell myself I was well out of it, that you'd obviously been giving me those green-light signals while, at the same time, leading young Ralph on to the point of flying in the face of common sense, defying his mother, and swearing that he intended to marry you—even before he'd finished his education. As far as I knew, at that time, you were little better than a tramp, using your highly potent sexuality to get a proposal out of one of us. It didn't matter which one!'

'I did *not*!' Kate wailed, wondering why they should be sitting in isolated splendour, discussing the dreadful things her beloved Seth had believed about her in the past.

'I know that now,' he reassured her softly, then, arching one brow, added, 'Aren't you hungry?'

'No.' Her lower lip jutted mutinously and it took all her self-control just to sit there when she wanted to hurl herself into his arms.

He was saying, 'But I didn't know it then. Even so, after the stern lecture I gave you on the folly of committing yourself while you were both so young, when you began to cry I found I couldn't hold back. I knew I had to hold you, comfort you. So I did, and against all my principles—you were only just eighteen—holding and comforting you became something else. And you responded like a dream. And I was left wondering if you would respond to any man that way, and, one way and another, I couldn't get you out of my head, or my heart, and I kept an eye on you from a distance, ready and willing to step in and help you if you ever needed it——'

'And you did, with the sponsorship,' Kate supplied, 'and then you asked me back here.'

'Because you were the best,' he gave back. 'And not only that, I had to find out if you still felt anything for me. I'd been involved with a few women over the intervening years, and with one of them it had almost become serious. But something always held me back—my feelings for you, I suppose. And I prayed you'd still feel something for me, something I could build on, but you were so cold, so——'

'Tacks-in-the-mouth?' She remembered how he'd accused her of being just that, but she couldn't tell him why she'd reacted that way. She had believed, at the time, that he had used her infatuation for him to put Ralph off her for life, when all the time it had been his mother's doing.

But she had promised Ralph she wouldn't tell the whole story and she made a small groaning sound in the back of her throat and Seth threw down his napkin and stood up.

'You're too damned far away. I need you close.' He strode over to her, scooping her up, raining kisses on her face, his breath coming raggedly.

She nipped the lobe of his ear between her small white teeth, whispering, 'What will the Parkers think?'

Soft, sensuous kisses around her mouth sent every last one of her senses skittering and he murmured, 'Damn the Parkers!' and carried her upstairs, laying her on his bed and slowly undressing her, caressing every inch of her body, reducing her to a craving bundle of wanton delight.

And later, very much later, he raised himself on one elbow, lamplight playing over the taut lines of his naked body as he gently stroked his fingers through her hair.

'My beautiful, beautiful Kate. Now I'm fully aware that the last thing a fiery Arien wants is to be told what to do. But, at the risk of an explosion, I'm informing you that we're going to be married in four weeks' time. In the estate church. Reception here, half the county, all the estate workers and all the trimmings.'

His hands had wandered downwards, the pads of his fingers caressing the sensitised skin of her throat, her breasts, and Kate smiled a dreamy smile.

It was short notice, but she'd do it. She could do anything. Seth loved her so there was nothing she couldn't achieve.

She opened her arms to him, gathering him close. And for once in her life she wasn't arguing about anything, anything at all. Whatever he said was fine by her. . . For the rest of her life. . .

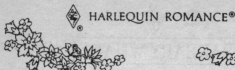

HARLEQUIN SUPERROMANCE®

A PLACE IN HER HEART...

Somewhere deep in the heart of every grown woman is the little girl she used to be....

In September, October and November 1992, the world of childhood and the world of love collide in six very special romance titles. Follow these six special heroines as they discover the sometimes heart-wrenching, always heartwarming joy of being a Big Sister.

Written by six of your favorite Superromance authors, these compelling and emotionally satisfying romantic stories will earn a place in your heart!

SEPTEMBER 1992

#514 NOTHING BUT TROUBLE—Sandra James
#515 ONE TO ONE—Marisa Carroll

OCTOBER 1992

#518 OUT ON A LIMB—Sally Bradford
#519 STAR SONG—Sandra Canfield

NOVEMBER 1992

#522 JUST BETWEEN US—Debbi Bedford
#523 MAKE-BELIEVE—Emma Merritt

AVAILABLE WHEREVER
HARLEQUIN SUPERROMANCE
BOOKS ARE SOLD

BSIS92

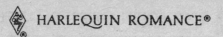

HARLEQUIN ROMANCE®

Some people have the spirit
of Christmas all year round...

People like Blake Connors
and Karin Palmer.

Meet them—and love them!—in
Eva Rutland's
ALWAYS CHRISTMAS.

Harlequin Romance #3240
Available in December wherever
Harlequin books are sold.

HRHX

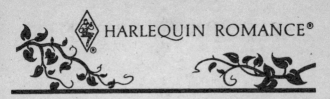

HARLEQUIN ROMANCE®

After her father's heart attack, Stephanie Bloomfield comes home to Orchard Valley, Oregon, to be with him and with her sisters.

Orchard Valley

Steffie learns that many things have changed in her absence—but not her feelings for journalist Charles Tomaselli. He was the reason she left Orchard Valley. Now, three years later, will he give her a reason to stay?

"The Orchard Valley trilogy features three delightful, spirited sisters and a trio of equally fascinating men. The stories are rich with the romance, warmth of heart and humor readers expect, and invariably receive, from Debbie Macomber."

—Linda Lael Miller

Don't miss the Orchard Valley trilogy by Debbie Macomber:

VALERIE   Harlequin Romance #3232 (November 1992)
STEPHANIE   Harlequin Romance #3239 (December 1992)
NORAH   Harlequin Romance #3244 (January 1993)

Look for the special cover flash on each book!

Available wherever Harlequin books are sold.   ORC-2

HARLEQUIN  PRESENTS®

is

- ☑ exotic
- ☑ dramatic
- ☑ sensual
- ☑ exciting
- ☑ contemporary
- ☑ a fast, involving read
- ☑ terrific!!

Harlequin Presents—
passionate romances
around the world!

HARLEQUIN PRESENTS®

A Year Down Under

Beginning in January 1993, some of Harlequin Presents's most exciting authors will join us as we celebrate the land down under by featuring one title per month set in Australia or New Zealand.

Intense, passionate romances, these stories will take you from the heart of the Australian outback to the wilds of New Zealand, from the sprawling cattle and sheep stations to the sophistication of cities like Sydney and Auckland.

Share the adventure—and the romance— of A Year Down Under!

Don't miss our first visit in **HEART OF THE OUTBACK** by Emma Darcy, Harlequin Presents #1519, available in January wherever Harlequin Books are sold.   YDU-G

HE CROSSED TIME FOR HER

Captain Richard Colter rode the high seas, brandished a sword and pillaged treasure ships. A swashbuckling privateer, he was a man with voracious appetites and a lust for living. And in the eighteenth century, any woman swooned at his feet for the favor of his wild passion. History had it that Captain Richard Colter went down with his ship, the *Black Cutter,* in a dazzling sea battle off the Florida coast in 1792.

Then what was he doing washed ashore on a Key West beach in 1992—alive?

MARGARET ST. GEORGE brings you an extraspecial love story next month, about an extraordinary man who would do anything for the woman he loved:

#462 THE PIRATE AND HIS LADY
by Margaret St. George
November 1992

When love is meant to be, nothing can stand in its way ... not even time.

Don't miss American Romance
#462 THE PIRATE AND HIS LADY.
It's a love story you'll never forget.